SONGS ABOUT A BOY

Also by Chris Russell

Songs About a Girl
Songs About Us

Chris Russell

HODDER CHILDREN'S BOOKS

First published in Great Britain in 2018 by Hodder and Stoughton

1 3 5 7 9 10 8 6 4 2

Text copyright © Chris Russell 2018

The moral right of the author has been asserted.

A CIP catalogue record for this book is available from the British Library.

ISBN 978 1 444 92920 1

Typeset in Berkeley Oldstyle by Hewer Text UK Ltd, Edinburgh
Printed and bound in Great Britain by Clays Ltd, Elcograf S.p.A.

The paper and board used in this book are made
from wood from responsible sources

MIX
Paper from
responsible sources
FSC www.fsc.org
FSC® C104740

Hodder Children's Books
An imprint of Hachette Children's Group
Part of Hodder and Stoughton
Carmelite House,
50 Victoria Embankment,
London, EC4Y 0DZ

An Hachette UK Company
www.hachette.co.uk

www.hachettechildrens.co.uk

To George, John, Tony, Danny & Jack.
My band of brothers.

1

My skin was crawling, my heart twitching in my chest, but I couldn't tear my gaze away from the letter.

Katherine's gone. She was the only real friend I've ever had, and now she's never coming back . . .

The words swam and flickered in front of me, and I rubbed my eyes with a shaking hand. It came away wet.

Before I knew what I was doing, my fingers were on the door handle.

'Charlie.'

Gabe's voice. Deep and ragged.

'Charlie?'

I shook my head, staring into the dark mahogany panelling, too terrified to turn around. A nasty heat spread across the back of my neck as I imagined him reaching out for me.

'Say something.'

Each time he spoke, I felt nausea licking at the inside of my stomach. And as I stood there, my fingers twisting around the brass handle, knuckles turning white, a single thought shivered inside my mind.

I can't even look at you.

Pulling the door open, I ducked out into the corridor and started to run.

Snatches of the building flew past me as I moved: a vase of flowers, diamond-patterned wallpaper, the housekeeper's trolley. I had a vague sense that Gabriel was calling after me from the end of the corridor, but I wasn't stopping. Not until I was far, far away from that room.

I flew out through the hotel entrance and picked a direction almost at random. I ran straight across a main road, around an empty bus stop and through a restaurant car park, weaving between vehicles. My legs just kept turning and turning, until I felt exhaustion overwhelming me.

Leaning back against the outer wall of the restaurant, I realised I was still carrying Harry's suicide note, crumpled in my hand. Against my better judgement, I opened it again.

> *I never meant to kill her ... I never meant for her to die.*

A sudden, hard sob shot out of me and I felt a pressure releasing, like the breaking of a dam. Tears poured down my face, soaking my skin; tears for my mum, my dad, for myself. And somewhere in there, tears for Gabriel.

Because maybe I shouldn't have left him like that.

Maybe this was worse for him than it was for me.

Trembling, I pulled my phone from my bag and opened my recent call list. I hit the top number and it connected almost instantly.

'Hey, CB! Calling so soon? What happened? Did you kiss? I BET YOU KISSED.'

I wanted to speak, but there was no air in my lungs.

'Charlie?' repeated Melissa, confused. I tried to force the words out between sobs.

'M . . . Mel, I . . .'

Melissa's tone changed, in an instant.

'Where are you? Are you hurt?'

'N-no, I'm not . . . hurt.'

'Right.' I could hear the sound of her bedroom door opening and her feet thudding down the stairs. 'I'm coming to wherever you are.'

'I don't . . . I'm not sure . . .' I looked around, squinting in the early evening sun. I knew this area, vaguely, but my mind was a mess. A grubby-looking shop across the road caught my eye. 'Craft Carpets. I'm opposite . . . Craft Carpets.'

Melissa's voice went a little strained, like she was bending over, lacing up shoes.

3

'That's near the Shanti Café, on Copeland Road. Remember, we went there once for Becky's weird birthday?'

'I guess,' I said, my voice hollow. I could hear Melissa clicking open the front door and stepping outside on to the gravel.

'Go there,' she said, striding across the driveway. 'Order a chai tea latte with LOTS of caramel syrup, and don't move. I'm coming to find you.'

2

As I pushed open the door of the Shanti Café, I met my reflection in the glass: tangled hair, red eyes and sticky, tear-streaked skin. There were only a scattering of people in the café, but I could already feel my cheeks burning.

Glancing around, I located the toilet door and headed straight for it. I thought I heard one of the staff saying, 'Hi there!' from behind the counter, but I didn't look back.

Once inside the white-tiled room, I made for a nearby sink. I turned on the tap, hard, and a disappointing stream spluttered out, spitting at the sides. Gathering as much water as I could in both hands, I bent down and splashed my face several times, before straightening up again.

I came eye to eye with myself in the mirror, watching the water droplets snake down my face and settle in my clothes. The cold was making me shudder, but I didn't care.

So these were the facts. When I was a baby, my mother was in a band with Gabriel's father, Harry West. The band was called Little Boy Blue. When their album began to create a buzz in America, the record label sent them over there for a tour; a tour which, in her letter, Mum described as their 'big break'. But it didn't work out that way. Harry, a part-time drug dealer, owed money to his suppliers in London, and ended up walking offstage in the middle of a show, quitting the band. Mum and the others tried to carry on as a three-piece, but Harry was the lead singer, and without him, things soon fell apart.

What happened next was unclear. All I knew was that my mother died out there, and a day later, Harry committed suicide . . . because, in his own words, he had killed her. He had killed the woman he described as his only friend.

I stared deep into the mirror, a sickness gathering in my throat. There was a second mirror behind me, and it was firing off infinite reflections, never-ending versions of me, shrinking into oblivion.

This wasn't real. This couldn't be real.

'You all right, love?'

I spun round, sniffing, to find a small, curly-haired woman standing in the doorway. I ran a forearm across my face and blinked a few times, as if that would magically transform me into a normal human being again, and tried to force a smile.

The woman smiled back sympathetically.

'Everything OK?'

OK? I couldn't imagine anything ever being OK again.

'Mm-hmm, yep,' I said, straightening my clothes. The woman pointed at the sink behind me.

'The water, it's . . .'

The cold tap was still running, spitting chalky water down the plughole. I twisted it hard, until it squeaked, then hurried back into the café, avoiding her gaze. Scanning the room, I spotted a comfy-looking booth in the far corner, scattered with colourful cushions and half-obscured by Moroccan-style drapes. I could curl up in there and forget the world.

'What can I get you?'

I looked up. I'd been sitting in the booth for over ten minutes, which meant Melissa would be arriving any second. A girl of about my age was standing above me, holding a notepad, her eyes wide.

'You go to Caversham High, don't you?' she said excitedly. 'Charlie Bloom, right?'

My jaw tightened. So much for forgetting the world.

'Yeah. Yep. Charlie.'

She bunched up her shoulders and leaned forward.

'This is kind of weird, but I heard you had, like, a *thing* with Gabriel West last year?' She glanced over her shoulder. 'Is that true?'

Just the sound of that name, *West*, cut through me like a knife.

'Sort of, uh-huh.'

There was no point in denying it. Everyone had seen the pictures.

7

'Oh my god,' said the girl, clutching her notepad to her chest. 'That is *unreal*.'

I stared at the floor, trying to control my breathing. For a few moments, neither of us spoke. Then I remembered Melissa's advice.

'Chai tea latte,' I said, sitting up. 'With lots of caramel syrup.'

The girl paused, as if she'd forgotten she was at work, then lifted a little yellow pencil to her notepad.

'Oh . . . sure. OK. One caramel chai tea latte, coming up.'

I thanked her with the tiniest nod, but she didn't move. She lowered the notepad again.

'That photo, in the papers,' she said in an almost-whisper, 'where Gabriel was beating up that guy. I mean, god . . . weren't you ever scared he'd hit you too?'

Without warning, the events of that night began to play inside my mind. The journalist, Paul Morgan, stalking me in the arena car park. Gabriel pulling Paul away from me, then being goaded into violence by him, a photographer lingering in the shadows.

The whole thing had been a set-up.

'He's not like that,' I said, firmer than I'd planned, and the girl swallowed uncomfortably.

'Right. Sorry.'

The room went quiet. I shifted among my cushions.

'I just need my drink, if that's all right?'

The girl nodded, head down, and gripped her notepad tightly.

'Yep, sure.' She mumbled my order to herself. 'Great choice.'

I attempted a smile, and the girl turned and made her way back to the counter. I let out a sigh. I couldn't blame her for asking about Gabe. Why *wouldn't* she want to know about someone from her hometown having a fling with one of the world's most famous popstars?

Ding. The small bell above the front entrance bounced side to side, and my best friend walked in.

'Charlie . . . !' exclaimed Melissa, spotting me behind the drapes, her face pale with concern. The second our eyes met, fresh tears rushed up through me.

'Oh my gosh, Charlie.'

She ran to me and sat down, grabbing both my hands, and I drew in a huge, shaky gulp of air. She tucked a damp strand of hair behind my ear.

'What on earth happened?'

In a low voice, I told Melissa the whole story, one piece at a time. How I'd arrived at Gabriel's hotel, unsure of why he'd invited me. How I'd struggled to get any sense out of him, and how he'd barely spoken, a sunken, hungry look in his eyes. Then, just as Gabriel had done to me, I handed Melissa the suicide note.

She read it, teeth tugging at her bottom lip, the blood slowly draining from her face.

'Oh . . . god. Oh my god.' She looked right at me, her eyes glistening. I wrung my hands.

'I don't know what to do. I'm supposed to see Dad tonight, and Gran, but how can I just sit there and . . . and . . .' I stared into the speckled pattern of the tabletop. 'Maybe I should just tell Dad the whole story.'

Before I'd left the house that morning, before everything had changed, I'd made plans with my father. We'd agreed to meet Gran for dinner, in Basingstoke, and the two of them would tell me the whole story. Mum's story. I could ask them anything I liked, he'd said: about her life, about the things she loved. Anything I liked.

Melissa was shaking her head, her gaze still glassy.

'You can't, Charlie. You know you can't.'

'Why not?' I said, even though I knew the answer.

'I hate to state the obvious, but your dad doesn't know you spent most of April hanging out with a world-famous boy band. If he finds out, it's game over.'

My mind wandered to the article Melissa had showed me earlier that day, on the MusicNews24 site. *Olly Samson has left the group . . . an announcement that has shocked the world . . . fans are asking: is this the end for Fire&Lights?*

'But it *is* all over, isn't it?' I said, trying not to think of my final moments with Olly, the night before, in that backstage corridor. The way he seemed to look right through me. 'Olly's gone, everything's broken, the band are splitting up—'

'We don't know that,' said Melissa, one palm on the table. 'We don't know what's going to happen. But if you come clean to your dad tonight, it won't matter, because he'd shut everything down. You know he would. You'd never see them again.'

A terrible thought hovered on the edge of my brain, daring me to let it out. *Maybe that wouldn't be such a bad thing.*

'But I can't . . . I mean, Gabriel . . . I couldn't bear to see him. I couldn't bear to be around him—'

'One caramel chai tea latte!'

Our heads snapped up. The waitress was holding my drink – a glass jar topped with a quivering mound of whipped cream, cross-hatched with syrup – and beaming perkily. She looked from me to Melissa, taking in our dismal expressions, and her smile faltered.

'Thanks,' I said, taking the drink. Melissa pointed at it.

'Another one of those, please,' she said, rummaging in her bag for her purse. She peered towards the counter. 'And we need two gargantuan blueberry muffins, stat.'

The waitress furrowed her brow.

'Gar . . . gantuan?'

'Gargantuan,' confirmed Melissa, with a nod. 'If at all possible, they should be larger than my head.'

The ghost of a smile tugged at my lips. Even at the worst of times, Melissa could still lift my spirits.

11

The waitress frowned, and scribbled something on her notepad.

'Right . . . I'll . . . see what I can do.'

After she'd gone, Melissa turned back to me.

'I know this is horrible, but think about it: we don't really know what this letter means yet. We only know bits and pieces of the story. You have to keep everything secret from your dad, at least for now.'

'But the letter,' I said, feeling my voice rise, powerless to stop it. 'The things Harry says—'

'*I know*,' said Melissa, clasping my hand and glancing around. 'I know, and I can't even imagine how that must make you feel. But we need to be patient. Just go tonight and listen to what your dad has to say. Maybe he'll . . . explain everything.'

I felt my shoulders drop. My father had been a closed book for most of my life, and it had taken him sixteen years to tell me more than a few basic details about Mum. So what were the chances of him casually bringing up a revelation like this over dinner? He'd seemed happy earlier; he'd even told me he was proud of me. That wasn't a man gearing up to tell his daughter . . . *this*.

'And you know I'm here for you, don't you?' said Melissa, squeezing my hand.

'Mm-hmm.'

'Seriously, CB. I am here for you, every second of every day, until the ends of the earth. Until the nuclear

12

Brussels sprouts they serve in the school canteen have finally started to biodegrade, and we're just two little old ladies, wearing tartan slippers and napping in front of YouTube.'

I laughed croakily. The sound felt wrong, somehow, spilling from my mouth. Melissa's face turned serious.

'You do know that, don't you?'

Her features shimmered as I smiled at her through my tears. Just hours earlier, Melissa had saved my skin. She had stayed up all night and driven herself half-mad to fix a mess which, otherwise, would have turned me into a hate target for millions of Fire&Lights fans across the world. She was amazing. She was *everything*.

'I know,' I said, picking up my latte and inhaling the sweet, aromatic scent. Melissa twisted round in her chair and squinted towards the kitchen.

'Now where are those blueberry muffins . . . ?'

I curled my hands around my drink, feeling the warmth sink into my skin, and tried to imagine sitting around a dinner table with my father and grandmother in less than two hours' time. My heart began to thump in my chest. Never, in all my life, had I been so nervous about seeing my own family.

3

The train pulled into the station with a screech that I felt in my bones. I stood up and, as the automatic announcement rang out across the carriage, I tried to push my way past a group of fake-tanned twenty-something boys who were blocking the doors.

'*The next station is Basingstoke . . .*'

They were drinking cans of lager and sniggering at each other. I reached through the tangle of orange, gym-pumped arms to press the door activation button.

'All right, sweet cheeks.'

One of the boys was talking to me from behind his beer can. His brow was lowered as he scanned me up and down.

'My mate Fogs can bench-press a hundred-and-fifty kilos.'

I ignored him, and the muffled laughter of his friends, and reached again for the button.

'Are you eighteen yet?' said another, prompting a scattered chorus of whoops and grunts. I managed to connect with the button, and the doors hissed open. 'You should come out with us tonight, see what a real man tastes like.'

On a different day, I might have said something. I might have turned round before leaving the train and called them out for the disgusting creeps they were. But today, with nerves curdling in the pit of my stomach, I just stepped down on to the platform, ears burning, and headed for the stairs. Hot, frustrated tears gathered in the corners of my eyes.

I missed my mum all of a sudden. More than anything in the world.

How you getting on, kiddo? Gran and I at restaurant, have found table ☺

As I made my way through the town, I wrote a reply to Dad's text. I knew it had confused him that I'd decided to take the train to Basingstoke, rather than catching a lift with him, but I couldn't stand the idea of being stuck in a confined space, making small talk and pretending everything was OK. Two hours in a restaurant was going to be hard enough.

Walking up to the big glass entrance to Pizza Express, I dug my fingernails into my palms, bracing myself for the lies I was about to tell. Or, more accurately, for the truths I *wasn't* going to tell.

15

'Hey . . . Charlie!'

Dad was waving from the far corner of the restaurant, while Gran sat opposite him, sipping a glass of white wine. Nodding back, I started to weave through the chairs and tables, my heart beating in my throat.

'Hello, love,' said Gran, as I arrived. I leaned over and kissed her on the cheek, before sitting down in the one remaining chair.

'Journey all right?' asked Dad. I thought of the perma-tanned boys on the train, their cans of cheap lager and the way their lips curled when they looked at me.

'Mm-hmm.'

'And your shopping trip with Melissa?'

I fingered the edge of the menu.

'It was OK.'

Dad paused, then took a slow sip from his bottle of Peroni. I could tell he was thrown by how sullen I was being, but I couldn't help it. I had to play my cards close to my chest.

He opened his menu.

'What do you think you'll have, everyone? I'm always a fan of the Sloppy Giuseppe. Mary, have you been here before?'

'Oh, no,' said Gran, setting down her wine. She traced a finger down the menu, reading carefully and making small noises to herself. Dad took another slug of beer.

'Charlie, would you like a drink?'

'Just a Coke, please.'

Dad caught the attention of a passing waiter and asked for a glass of Coke. After several minutes, it arrived, and we ordered our pizzas. Soon, we were sitting in a little silent triangle, no menus to shield us from the awkwardness. Dad shifted in his chair.

'So . . . Charlie.'

I looked up at him properly, for the first time. His forehead was set in the faintest of frowns, as if he was trying to suss me out.

'I'm sure this is all quite overwhelming for you, but, look . . . we can talk about as much or as little as you like tonight. No pressure. Your grandmother . . .' He glanced at Gran, and she shared a little smile. 'Your grandmother says she passed a letter on to you, from your mum. Which means, I suppose, that you already know more than I've told you.'

I gave a silent nod. Dad breathed in, very slowly, and ran a hand around the back of his neck.

'Right . . . right.' He cleared his throat. 'Maybe I should've done all this sooner, but the truth is, things weren't always easy between your mother and me. And the way she died . . . I suppose I just wanted to protect you from it, for as long as I could. Does that make sense?'

I stared into my drink, watching the tiny air bubbles pop and fizzle on the surface.

'I guess.'

'Anyway . . . you know by now that she was a musician. She learned when she was little – you've seen the piano, at Gran's house – and she always loved it. Didn't she, Mary?'

'Always,' agreed Gran. 'It was in her blood.'

'The very first time we met,' continued Dad, 'she told me she wanted to be a professional musician. It had been her dream since she was a teenager. She was playing piano in this little cocktail bar in Angel at the time, and I used to go down there and listen to her singing Aretha Franklin tunes.' He smiled. 'It was pretty magical, actually.'

I gripped the edge of my chair. Aretha Franklin? Why did that ring a bell?

'Eventually, she made friends with a group of musicians who were starting a band: Little Boy Blue, they were called. They needed a pianist, and they saw Katherine and just fell for her. Like everyone did.'

Aretha Franklin tunes. There was something familiar about that idea, somewhere in my recent memory.

And then it came to me.

> *I met a girl in winter*
> *She played piano in a local bar*
> *She sang Aretha over whisky and soda . . .*

The opening track on the Little Boy Blue album, the one that Gabriel had lent me. I scanned through the

18

lyrics in my head. Was that song written *about* my mother? Did it tell the story of how the band had got together?

'So, anyway,' said Dad, jolting me from my thoughts, 'she joined the band, and it took a few years, but things really started to happen for them. They played at the Troubadour a lot – like I said, weird coincidence – and eventually, they got a record deal, and the label wanted to send them to America.

'By then, of course, we had you.' His eyes went misty. 'You were this perfect little thing. Honestly, I . . . I remember looking at you, and just knowing that everything had changed. That I wanted to protect you. And Katherine, she loved you more than anything in the world, but this tour, it just came along at the wrong time. She had to leave for the States before you even turned three.'

As if from nowhere, I found my voice again.

'That's where she died.'

Dad sat back in his chair, palm on his chest.

'Uh, yeah. That's right. It was . . . very sudden.'

I folded my arms.

'How did it happen?'

'When it came to it, the tour was a bit of a disaster. The singer was in a bad way, booze and all sorts, and he ended up quitting the band. He abandoned them and ran off, and then . . .'

I waited for Dad to carry on, holding my breath. *The singer*. This had to be where he told me the truth about Harry.

'The band pushed on without him, but they had a pretty rough time of it. Then one night, driving home from a gig, Katherine had an accident. Her car came off the road, and she died at the scene.'

I tried to process what he was telling me, to square it with the scraps of information I already had. When I was little, and I'd asked Dad about the crash, he'd always made it sound like there was another car involved. 'A stranger,' he had said, 'who was driving too fast.'

'What about the stranger?' I said, my voice strained. 'The one you told me about? You said he was speeding—'

'I did,' admitted Dad, pressing his palms into the table. 'I did say that. But . . . OK. For a long time after it happened, I was desperate for someone to blame. There *was* another driver involved, but he didn't cause the crash.' He smoothed out a wrinkle in the tablecloth. 'In the end, I just had to accept it. It was an accident, nothing more.'

'But . . .' My mouth was hanging open. I had started the sentence, though I didn't know how I was going to finish it.

'Go on,' urged Dad.

I hesitated. He hadn't even said Harry's name. It was as if he was editing him out of the story, and it was on the tip of my tongue to challenge him on it, there and then.

20

I know the truth, Dad. I know Harry did something to her.

'Charlie?'

My brain was going into overdrive, thoughts firing in every direction. Harry quit the band and left the tour, but did he leave America? Because if he wasn't even in the same country as Mum when she died, how could it've been his fault? I thought about the 'other driver' that Dad had spent so many years blaming. What if he wasn't a stranger, after all? What if that actually *was* Harry?

'Sweetheart . . . ?'

My grandmother was looking at me, her mouth a thin line of concern.

'No, it's . . . nothing,' I said, scratching a fingernail on the tabletop. 'I just . . . I wish I'd had a chance to know her, that's all.'

Gran leaned forward and laid a warm hand on my forearm.

'You two would've been inseparable,' she said, her eyes a little sad. 'You're the very picture of her these days.'

Dad worried at the cuff of his shirt. 'Your grandfather took it very badly. When he found out, he drove right over to the house, and he just . . . he *ripped* into me. He told me I should never have let her go, that I should have made her stay. He said I was the man of the house, the head of the family, and she had no business flying off around the world. He said . . .' Dad took a careful breath. 'He said it was my fault she died.'

21

Gran reached across the table and took hold of Dad's hand.

'He didn't mean it, Ralph. It was his grief talking. I'm so sorry you ever had to shoulder that.' She squeezed his fingers. 'After you'd lost Katherine, it must have been too much to bear.'

Dad laid his free hand on top of Gran's.

'It's OK, I understand. If Arthur missed his daughter anywhere near as much as I did, it must have torn him apart. But he didn't understand what music meant to her. To him, the woman's place was in the home, not flying off around the world, chasing a dream.'

I thought of Mum's letter, the one that had sat for years, untouched, in her box of memories. She'd written that Gran was a talented artist in her youth, studying fashion in Paris, and her tutors believed she had it in her to become a top designer. But she was forced to give it up because, as a woman, that was just what you did in those days.

Dad and Gran parted hands, and he picked up his drink again.

'It was Katherine's dream to be out on the road, with a band.' He stared into his beer bottle, rotating it slowly in his palm. 'It had always been her dream, and I wanted to support that.' His fingers closed around the glass. 'Maybe that *was* a mistake, and I should never have let her go, but—'

'You're a good man, Ralph,' said Gran, the slightest quiver on her chin. 'And you did the right thing. Truly, you did.'

Dad set down his drink and pressed a hand to his mouth. His eyes had gone red in the corners.

Then, as if he'd just remembered I was there, he turned to me, his palms held up in apology.

'Sorry, Charlie. This was all supposed to be for you, and here I am getting all . . .' He tried to meet my gaze. 'You can ask us anything, you know.'

I gritted my teeth. *But I can't, can I?* I knew too much, and not enough, all at the same time. I couldn't just come out and ask Dad why he wasn't telling me the real story, because I wasn't supposed to *know* the real story. The fact that Harry West, father to the biggest popstar on the planet, was responsible for Mum's death. I wasn't even supposed to be aware of his existence.

'I'm fine, Dad.'

He sat back in his chair.

'Really? You seem very quiet.'

'I think I'm just tired after last night,' I said, pulling my napkin off the table and on to my lap. 'You don't need to worry.'

Though my head was down, I could tell Dad and Gran were looking at each other across the table, confused. My behaviour was baffling to them, and I knew it. But one thing was becoming painfully clear to me.

23

Even now, after all this time, my father was still keeping secrets.

'Are you sure you're all right, Charlie?'

As we pulled into the driveway, I was grateful for the cover of darkness inside the car. I'd barely spoken on the way home, and Dad knew something was up. It was written all over my face.

'I just need sleep,' I said, as the car engine died away.

'Is it your exams?'

My eyes dropped.

'Uh . . . yeah.' This wasn't a difficult line to spin, since I *was* worried about my exams. How was I supposed to concentrate at school after everything that had happened?

'I know you must feel under a lot of pressure right now,' continued Dad, sliding the key from the ignition, 'but your mock results were great, most of them, and your last report was very encouragi—'

'I should get to bed,' I said flatly, reaching for the door. Dad was about to reply when I clicked it open and stepped outside, the air still warm from a long day of sunshine. Fumbling in my pocket for my keys, I headed straight for the house, unlocked the front door, and was upstairs before my father had stepped on to the mat.

It was a waste of time. I still don't have any answers.

24

Lying on my bed, I stared at my phone, the beginnings of a headache lurking behind my eyes. Melissa's speech bubble was pulsating on the screen.

But . . . I don't understand, she replied. He must've told you how she died??

Car accident. That's all he said.

A pause. I peered out of the window, towards Melissa's bedroom. It was bathed in darkness, but as she lay in bed, glued to her phone, her face shone whitish-blue in the gloom.

What did he tell you about Gabe's dad?

He barely mentioned Harry. Not by name.

I could hear Dad pottering about in the kitchen. The soft *schwm* of the fridge door opening; the occasional clink of plates.

We'll figure this out, CB.

How?

My phone went quiet, and I glanced out of the window again. A dog barked in the distance. The amount of time it was taking Melissa to reply confirmed my worst fears: we'd hit checkmate. Either I confessed everything to Dad, or I had to live without knowing the full story. And both those options twisted my insides.

My phone buzzed.

Dammit, Bloom, you got me.

I swung my legs off the bed and slid my phone on to the desk. As if in protest, it pinged at me.

Hey, how's about a gif of a tiny turtle eating a cheeseburger?

Despite the heavy weight in my chest, I smiled. My fingers were hovering above the screen as a new text arrived.

YOU KNOW YOU WANT IT.

Shaking my head, I tapped back a reply.

OK, fine. But that turtle better be really tiny.

Ah, man, you got no idea. He is one dinky little dude.

While Melissa searched through her enormous collection of GIFs, I walked out into the hallway, heading for the bathroom. As I crossed the landing, I paused at the top of the stairs. Downstairs, Dad was sitting in his study, reading through some papers.

He was lit only by his angle-poise desk lamp, and his face was entirely in shadow.

4

I was gazing into my cereal, nudging Rice Krispies around the bowl, when an unexpected email hit my phone.

Dad looked up from the kitchen counter, where he was leaning against the sink, drinking coffee. His tie was hanging, unknotted, around his neck.

'Sounds like you've got a message,' he said, nodding at my phone. He'd been trying to engage me in conversation – any kind of conversation – since Saturday evening, and mostly failing. He drained his coffee and discarded it by the sink. 'Melissa, I imagine?'

I read the subject line and almost choked on my cereal. Dropping my spoon in the bowl, I reached for my apple juice and took a big gulp.

'You OK?' said Dad, stepping forward. I waved him away hastily, wiping my mouth on the back of my hand.

'Fine, yep. Rice Krispies just went down the wrong way.'

The message was from Tara Qureshi, personal assistant to Fire&Lights. We'd had the occasional conversation while I was working with the boys, but rarely more than a few words, so why was she emailing me? I could only see the beginning of the subject line on my lock screen – *Invitation to . . .* – but I didn't want to risk opening it with my father in the room, so I polished off my cereal, tossed the bowl and spoon into the dishwasher and headed for the stairs. I could feel Dad watching me the entire time.

Upstairs, I stood in the bathroom, brushing my teeth, and clicked open the email.

Hi, Charlie!

How are things? Dramatic night on Friday, huh??

So, listen . . . we were wondering if you're free this Saturday from 2 p.m.? We'd like you to come for a meeting at Kingdom Records, if you can. Needs to remain 100% confidential at this stage, obviously. The press are crawling all over us right now!

On a personal note, hope you're doing OK after the split. I know life with F&L can be pretty intense, especially for someone so close to them. But for what it's worth, in case you didn't already know . . . the boys think the absolute world of you :)

Hopefully see you Saturday.

TQ x

P.S. Bring your camera

'Charlie?'

29

I jumped, toothbrush sticking out from between my teeth, and dropped my phone. In the mirror, I could see Dad standing in the bathroom doorway, sliding both arms into a suit jacket. I swivelled round and we both looked at my phone, lying on the bathmat.

Dad tightened his tie, and nodded down the stairs.

'I'm off to work. Don't forget to lock up when you leave.'

'Uh, OK,' I replied, pulling the toothbrush from my mouth. 'See you later.'

Once I'd heard the front door close, I picked up my phone and re-read Tara's final paragraph. A meeting, at Kingdom Records? Was this coming from Barry? If so, why did he want me there? And what did Tara mean by 'after the split'? Was she talking about the band . . . or me and Olly?

I spat, rinsed my toothbrush and dropped it back in the holder, leaning my palms on the edge of the sink. If I went, it would mean seeing Gabriel for the first time since he'd showed me the suicide note. Neither of us had dared to make contact over the weekend, so I didn't know what state he was in, or whether he wanted to see me.

All I knew was that, if he was feeling even one per cent of what I was feeling right now, it was almost certainly a bad idea.

Five minutes later, gripping tightly to the straps of my rucksack, I stepped out on to Tower Close, my gut churning with emotions. As ever, Harry's letter was dominating my thoughts, but now there were new feelings competing for attention. Confusion over Tara's message. Anxiety at the thought of seeing Gabriel. Fear at—

'Is anyone home?'

I jumped at the sound of a voice in my ear, and clutched a hand to my chest. Melissa was staring back at me, looking worried. She curled an arm round my shoulder.

'Sorry, I didn't mean to scare you. You just . . . you were miles away.'

I shook my head.

'No, it's fine. I'm just a bit on edge at the moment.'

Melissa caught my eye, dragging my gaze upwards. Her face was crimped with concern.

'You sure you're OK going to school? We could stay home if you want.'

I raised a single eyebrow.

'My best friend, Melissa Morris, is suggesting we skip school? A *week* before exams start?'

As always, just talking to Melissa was already making me feel a little better.

'Hey!' she said, giving me a playful shove. 'I could be a rebel if I wanted.'

'No, you couldn't.'

'No, I couldn't.' She waved a finger in the air. 'But it's the thought that counts, right?'

As we walked towards the main road, the steady hum of traffic began to fill the air. Soon, dark thoughts were rushing back into my mind.

'I tried revising last night, but I couldn't concentrate. I just kept thinking about the suicide note.' My brow creased. 'What if I wreck all my exams?'

Melissa nudged her shoulder against mine.

'You won't. You're going to ace them.'

I scoffed.

'How, exactly?'

'Dude, I *know* you. You have a highly developed brain.'

We reached the pedestrian crossing and slowed to a stop. I scuffed my toe on the concrete.

'I need answers, but I don't know where to find them. I feel like I'm losing my mind trying to figure this out.'

Melissa jabbed the traffic light button and we waited in silence for the little green man. Cars passed in the street, drivers staring straight ahead, cocooned in their private worlds.

'Maybe you should meet up with Gabriel?'

I glanced at Melissa. She was probably right, but I didn't how to talk to him any more, let alone be around him.

'Actually . . .' I thought of Tara's email, sitting in my inbox. 'I've been invited to Kingdom Records, this weekend.'

'Oh my gosh, really? What's happened? Are they splitting up? Is Aiden OK? I'm asking too many questions.'

The lights changed and we stepped out on to the road.

'All I know is that Tara wants me at the label for two o'clock on Saturday, with my camera.'

'You are going, aren't you?' Melissa's tone stiffened. 'Charlie?'

'I'm not sure . . . I don't know if I can face him yet.'

'I know it's hard, but sooner or later, you ha—'

Melissa's phone dinged in her hand. She ignored it.

'You can check that if you like,' I said, as we reached the pavement. She rolled her eyes.

'No point. It'll only be Becky, asking for the eighty-bajillionth time if I've still got my geography notes on glacial erosion. I'm, like, "Becky, always with the questions, YOU ARE GLACIALLY ERODING MY SANITY."'

Her phone dinged again, and I reached for it.

'Seriously, Mel, reply to her or I'll do it for you.'

'OK . . . OK.' She unlocked the screen and read the notification. Her mouth formed into a circle.

'Heavens to Betsy.'

'What is it?'

She pointed the screen at me.

**POP GOSSIP UPDATE: Desperate to know
what's going on with Fire&Lights??! So
are we!! Check out this new video!!!!**

I felt my forehead crumple.

'I'll watch it later,' said Melissa, unzipping her rucksack as if to stow her phone. My throat tightened, but I held out a hand, stopping her.

'No . . . it's fine. Honestly. Let's watch it now.'

Melissa flashed me a guilty look, but I had to admit: even I was curious. She pulled out her earphones and offered me a bud, and soon the sound of traffic was replaced by the cheering of a stadium crowd . . .

<><><> **www.POPGOSSIP.co.uk** <><><>
☺ *where the gossip never stops* ☺

A stadium concert. Gabriel and Olly are standing shoulder to shoulder onstage: Olly's blue eyes gleaming, Gabriel staring out into the crowd from behind cascading strands of dark hair. The camera pans around them, in slow motion, while in the distance, tens of thousands of fans scream their names.

The crowd noise swells, and the action pauses. A title appears on the screen.

'The music world was thrown into chaos on the twenty-sixth of April,' begins a female narrator, over shots of Olly pushing through a jostling scrum of photographers, 'when it was announced that Olly Samson, one quarter of world-conquering British boy band Fire&Lights, was quitting the group.'

An exterior photograph of the Troubadour club fades into view . . .

My skin tingled. The framing of the photograph exactly mirrored the picture that Gabriel and I had found online of Little Boy Blue, bunched together underneath the club sign. Posted years ago on a random music forum, the shot had featured the whole band, complete with instruments, lined up on the street with a group of fans. My mum was wearing her blue beanie and beaming, while in the far corner of the shot, holding a guitar, was Harry West.

'. . . The announcement was made the morning after a catastrophic private show at the Troubadour club in West London, during which – according to reports – star member Gabriel West started a fight with Samson which led to a stage invasion, a riot and the evacuation of the building. What happened after the fans had gone home remains a mystery, but by eight o'clock the following morning, Olly Samson was no longer a member of Fire&Lights.'

A strange mixture of guilt and sadness crept over me. They were blaming Gabriel, again. Just like they always did.

'So as millions of fans across the world unite in sadness, we take a look back at the history of this fierce pop rivalry, and ask the question: did Olly Samson really choose to leave the biggest boy band on the planet . . . or did Gabriel West push him out?'

'This is total crap,' I said, pulling out the ear bud. 'They have no idea what they're talking about.'

Melissa rescued the bud, which was dangling between us.

'We really don't have to watch it,' she said, wrapping up the earphones. 'That website *is* kind of awful.'

I looked up at the road ahead, my arms crossed. We wouldn't be at school for at least another five minutes, and as much as I hated *Pop Gossip*, there was still a part of me that wanted to hear what they had to say.

'N-no,' I said, letting my arms fall by my side. 'I think we should finish it.'

'Positive?'

'Positive.'

Melissa passed back the ear bud, and pressed play.

'Fire&Lights were formed on the wildly popular TV talent show Make Or Break, by industry mogul Barry King. But, back in the beginning, Gabriel West wasn't even part of the equation . . .'

Four teenage boys are mucking about onstage in a TV studio, trying and failing to learn a dance. One of them trips over and falls into his bandmates, causing them to topple like skittles. They scramble across each other on the floor, laughing their heads off.

'At boot camp that year, Barry King took four promising young male artists – Jake Woodrow, Olly Samson, Yuki Harrison and Aiden Roberts – and formed a clean-cut, crowd-pleasing boy band. Connecting their initials, the boys called themselves JOYA and were soon making waves in the live show, consistently winning the public vote.'

A montage of JOYA's live performances begins to play. There are shots of Yuki and Aiden singing to each other onstage, and Jake touching the hands of fans in the front row.

'Viewers were particularly captivated by the friendship between Olly and Jake, who had become incredibly close in a very short space of time.'

The camera cuts to footage of Olly and Jake, standing together onstage, awaiting the announcement of the public vote. Jake has his arm around Olly, and when their inevitable triumph is announced, he pulls Olly into a hug, his hand clamped tight to Olly's back.

'But the reign of JOYA was cut short when, in an unprecedented turn of events, Barry King reshuffled the line-up halfway through the competition. Claiming that the band was missing "star quality", he sent Jake home and replaced him with the mysterious half-Brazilian singer Gabriel West, who until that point had been dominating the solo category . . .'

Slow-motion footage of Gabriel fades on to the screen. He is holding a microphone, his jaw set in determination. He pushes his hand through his hair, which tumbles around his fingers, and a handsome smile blooms on his face.

Then, one after another, photographs of Fire&Lights pummel the screen: the boys being mobbed in shopping centres, climbing out of limos, posing for the paparazzi and signing autographs backstage.

'Renamed Fire&Lights – by Gabriel himself – the band went from strength to strength, winning the overall competition and, via social media, building a global fanbase faster than any band in history. But the press soon noticed tensions between Olly and Gabriel, and in certain corners of the fandom, an angry battle was raging. The hashtags #teamolly and #teamgabriel were permanently trending online, and when Gabriel mumbled, "I'm the fire, he's the light," during a television interview, some claimed he was talking, in code, about Olly. In public, the bandmates kept up appearances, but many wondered what was going on behind the scenes. Was their intense rivalry destined to tear the band apart?'

The camera cuts to Yuki, Aiden and Gabriel, sitting on a couch, being interviewed.

'So, guys,' says a voice off-camera, 'before Olly gets here, tell me . . . what do you really think of him?'

I closed my eyes, trying to ignore the aching behind my ribs. It made me feel weirdly ashamed, spending all this worry on Gabriel and his father, when Olly and I had broken up only three days earlier. And the truth was, I missed him. I missed how safe he made me feel when we were together. How he seemed to understand me in a way nobody else did.

Would I see him again? Could we ever be friends after the way things had ended?

'What do I really think of Olly?' repeats Yuki, looking left and right at his bandmates. Then he leans forward and says in a whisper: 'I once caught him eating a banana and ketchup sandwich, bro. No fear. AND he doesn't floss. And he leaves the toilet seat up. He's a liability.'

Aiden starts to giggle, and Yuki elbows him in the stomach. Gabriel presses a closed fist to his mouth.

When the laughter subsides, Yuki's gaze turns solemn.

'Nah, but seriously.' He looks the interviewer right in the eye. 'Olly's our rock, man. He holds us together. Without that guy . . . this band would probably fall apart.'

'Oh my god, Charlie . . . d'you hear that?'

I jerked my head up. Melissa was craning her neck to look at something in the distance.

'Hear what?' I'd been so engrossed in the video that I hadn't realised we were about to walk through the gates to Caversham High.

And there were screams coming from the car park.

5

'Take that back, you little bitch!'

Melissa and I snaked through the crowds of students, eventually arriving at the edge of a circle that had formed around two young girls, probably Year Eights. They were facing off against each other, and one of them, the smaller of the two, had scratch marks on her right cheek. They were glinting with fresh blood.

'I won't, I won't!' she screamed. She was trying not to cry.

The taller girl, broad-shouldered and athletic, closed the gap between them. Her face was set in a furious grimace.

'You don't know anything *about* Fire&Lights,' she said, wiping her mouth with the back of her hand. 'You don't know *anything* about Olly.'

My stomach flipped at the sound of Olly's name. I should've guessed it would be about this.

'Shut up, I do!' said the smaller girl, a quiver on her lips. Her long, blonde hair fell into her face, and she pushed it out of the way. 'Yasmin's brother used to be in the Scouts with him, you *idiot*.'

The tall girl snorted, and wiggled her head.

'Oh, right, so he's your best friend, then?' She narrowed the space between them, and shoved the other girl, hard, in the chest. The girl stumbled backwards, her face turning pale with fear. 'Gabriel pushed Olly out of the band because he's jealous of him, and now he's going to ruin *everything*.'

The blonde girl clenched her fists.

'No, he's . . . he's not. Olly started the fight, Layla. He's the jealous one.'

'Olly didn't start the fight, you dick! Sasha was actually there, and she said it was Gabriel's fault, so you can shut your ugly face.'

Sasha: little sister to Thumper, the drummer from Diamond Storm, who had supported Fire&Lights at the Troubadour. Layla was right, Sasha *had* been at the gig, and it was no surprise that she would be defending Olly. She and her friends had started singing his song, 'She Is The Fire', from the crowd, and that was what had started everything.

'I don't care what Sasha says!' The blonde girl was losing her cool. Tears were collecting in her eyes. 'I *love* Gabriel, more than you love Olly! I love him *so much*!'

As chanting began to rise up in the crowd, Layla grabbed a fistful of the smaller girl's hair and dragged her forward. She screamed again, tears now dripping from her cheeks, and the onlookers bayed and hollered in

42

delight. Clumsily, Layla shoved her to the ground and started punching her in the side of the head.

'Shouldn't we do something?' I said, turning to Melissa. But she shook her head, pointing over my shoulder. I swivelled round to find our headmaster, Mr Bennett, striding towards the action, his face red with fury.

As students around us began to notice him, the crowd rippled and dispersed, leaving the two girls exposed. Melissa tugged at my arm and I walked backwards, a sickness rising inside me, unable to tear my eyes away from Layla's fists as she hammered blow after blow into the blonde girl's neck.

Apparently, since Friday night, it wasn't good enough just to be a fan any more. If you really, truly cared about Fire&Lights, you had to pick a side.

'One week, Year Eleven. One week until you're lined up in that exam hall, quills in hand, wielding the power to change your young lives forever . . .'

I was sitting at my desk, running my finger up and down a narrow groove in the wood. I couldn't get the car park fight out of my mind. The anger in their voices, the hate in their eyes, the fresh blood beading against pale skin. Across the world, the Fire&Lights fandom was dividing, and I couldn't shake it from my mind: I was part of it. In some way, on some level, was this entire thing my fault?

'Uh, girls?'

Mr Crouch had paused his GCSE pep talk and was pointing to the far corner of the room, where two of my classmates were having a private discussion. Their conversation soon dried up, and they feigned a sudden interest in their pencil cases.

'Something you'd like to share with the rest of us, perhaps?' suggested Mr Crouch, slowly folding his arms.

'Um, not really,' said one of the girls, turning red. Mr Crouch leaned back against his desk.

'Is it, by some freak coincidence, this boy band everyone seems to be losing their minds over this morning?'

The girls bolted their eyes to their textbooks, embarrassed smiles straining at their mouths.

'I thought so,' said Mr Crouch, with a sigh. 'Don't you think you're a bit old to be obsessing over teenyboppers?'

Two desks over, Jamie Wheeler coughed into his fist.

'Fire&Lights are *weak*, man. You should listen to grime.'

Mr Crouch's shoulders dropped.

'Mr Wheeler, please keep your opinions to yourself.'

'Just saying, sir,' replied Jamie, rolling a pencil between his fingers. 'She should get into grime.'

Removing his glasses, Mr Crouch straightened a little, rubbing his eyes with forefinger and thumb.

'And what, pray tell, is "grime"?' He slid his glasses back on. 'Other than something that collects under the rim of a toilet seat, I mean.'

'Hip hop mixed with garage, sir.' Jamie planted his tongue in his cheek, hiding a smirk. 'D'you like garage, sir?'

Mr Crouch's forehead crumpled into a frown.

'I *have* a garage, if that's what you're asking.'

'Nah, mate,' said Jamie, sniggering. On the next desk along, his partner-in-crime, Sam Croft, fell about laughing.

'Well, whatever it is,' replied Mr Crouch, 'I fear we've drifted off-topic somewhat. Let me just say this, before we return to the eminently more important matter of your GCSEs.' He scanned the room, taking in every student. 'I think it would be good for you, as the most senior students in the school, to be reminding the younger ones that these pop acts, these TV talent shows, they don't actually matter in the real world. They'll be gone by next month, and you'll all be getting your trousers in a twist over something else.'

Mr Crouch was right, of course, for most people in that classroom. But my real world *included* Fire&Lights. We were tangled up together, and I knew things that no one else at school could ever know. That Year Eight girl in the school car park, Layla, had judged Gabriel without knowing all the facts; she had blamed him for something that wasn't his fault. Something that was far, far bigger than him.

I felt the tickle of guilt in my throat. In a way, wasn't I doing exactly the same thing? Whatever Harry West had done to my family, all those years ago, it had nothing to do with his son, and yet, by running out of that hotel room without looking back, I'd treated Gabriel like he'd written that horrible letter himself.

I had to do it. I had to go back to Kingdom Records and face Gabe – talk to him, try and figure all this out together – because if nothing else, I had three weeks of exams to get through, and I needed my sanity back. I couldn't function with my nerves shredded to pieces.

'So, as your form tutor and teacher, I would suggest you all focus your not inconsiderable brain-power on studying for the rest of the week.' Mr Crouch glanced around the room, his eyebrows raised expectantly. 'Unless, of course, I've misjudged the situation, and some of you actually do expect to spend this weekend "chilling out" with a famous boy band?'

He was met with silence.

'I thought so. Now, could you all turn to page eighty-three in your textbooks, please, and we'll pick up from where we left off . . .'

I glanced at the clock on the wall, and felt my breath quivering in my chest.

Five days, two hours and six minutes until I saw Gabriel West again.

6

I stood on the broad concrete steps outside the building, staring up at its gleaming entrance sign. WELCOME TO KINGDOM RECORDS. The last time I'd stood in this exact spot, I'd been excited. Dated, but excited.

Today, my clothes felt uncomfortable against my skin, and the back of my neck bristled with nerves. Was it too late to turn around and walk away?

'Charlie!'

Tara appeared through the revolving glass doors, her corkscrew curls bouncing as she skipped down the steps towards me. She wore her trademark headset and was carrying two large coffee cups on a cardboard tray.

She hugged me, for a fraction of a second longer than I'd expected.

'How you doing?' she asked, pulling backwards, her free hand resting on my shoulder. I nodded, chewing on my bottom lip.

'Not too bad.'

'Latte?' she replied, offering me one of the cups. I took it gratefully, and she led me through the doors into the

47

Kingdom Records foyer. After signing me in and handing me a lanyard, she hit the call button for the lift, and we stepped inside.

Since the last time I'd been in this lift, they had installed a plasma screen, and it was playing the music video for 'Wild Inside', the lead single from the *Songs About Us* EP. Olly was standing alone on a deserted street, lit by the orange glow of streetlights, singing directly to camera.

Maybe I'll see you
After my show
And maybe you will smile, or maybe you will never know . . .

'Hey, listen: full disclosure.'

I pulled my gaze from the screen. Tara was watching me over the lip of her coffee cup. She lowered it.

'I know about your thing with Olly.' My whole body tensed, but she smiled sympathetically. 'I know it ended last week. At the Troubadour.'

My eyes dropped to the floor. This wasn't a conversation I especially wanted to have in a two-metres-square space.

'Oh. Right.' I sniffed. 'Does everyone know?'

'Not everyone. Just the boys, and Barry, and one or two of us in management.'

I stared through the tiny hole in the lid of my drink, blood rushing to my cheeks.

'This isn't really any of my business,' continued Tara, 'but I wanted to make sure you're not blaming yourself for any of this . . . chaos.'

I glanced up at the monitor, fingers tightening around my coffee cup. We were three floors from our destination.

Tara stowed a stray curl behind her ear.

'Between you and me, when I was a bit older than you, I had my own fling with a singer. It was my first job in the business, I was basically just a runner, and we bumped into each other backstage once . . . and things kind of got out of hand.'

I took a cautious sip of coffee.

'So he was . . . pretty famous, then?'

Tara bobbed her head from side to side.

'That was the thing. It was a she.' I nodded slowly. 'Yeah. She wasn't out, not publicly, and it all got pretty messy. Her career took this massive nose-dive, and I blamed myself for years.'

We were about to hit our floor. Guilt was churning inside me.

'You know none of this is your fault, Charlie? Right?'

Tara was looking straight at me, her dark eyes fixed on mine. I opened my mouth, but no words came out.

Ding.

The doors opened, and a bustling hallway stretched out in front of us, full of people walking this way and that. A man in an open-collared shirt nodded at Tara,

49

and she gave him a quick wave. Our private cocoon had opened up again, and the conversation vanished into thin air, as if it had never happened. But just as we left the lift, she reached over and gave my hand a squeeze.

Minutes later, we arrived outside an unmarked door on a quiet corridor. Tara pointed at it with her thumb.

'There are a couple of people in there who want to see you.' She leaned closer, a smile on her lips. 'They put in a direct request.'

She clicked open the door and, like puppies who'd been shut inside for too long, Yuki and Aiden leapt up from a sofa at the back of the room and rushed towards us.

'I'll be back in five minutes,' said Tara, laughing to herself. 'Stay out of trouble, Harrison.'

Tara walked off down the corridor, talking into her headset, and Yuki and Aiden beckoned me into the room. I wandered through the doorway, holding my camera case tight to my side. Yuki held up his hand for a fist-bump.

'Charlie, *man*.' He was smiling, but there was a look behind his eyes that I couldn't quite read.

'How are you doing?' asked Aiden, as I returned Yuki's fist-bump.

'OK, I guess,' I said, scanning the small room from wall to wall. It had a sink, some cupboards, a purple two-seater sofa and a red swivel chair designed to look like giant lips, but almost nothing else. It seemed like quite an odd place for two popstars to be hanging out.

'What are you . . . doing in here?' I asked. Yuki dropped down on to the sofa.

'I was drawing on the walls again, so Barry shut me away to think about what I've done.'

I eyed him sideways, and a short laugh burst out of me.

'I see. And Aiden?'

Yuki glanced at his bandmate, then hung his head in mock-sadness.

'He was my accomplice.'

Aiden shook his head, smiling, and slumped down next to Yuki. I took a seat gingerly on the giant-lips swivel chair, and lowered my camera case on to the carpet.

'Seriously, though . . . nobody's told me why I'm here. What's going on?'

Aiden shrugged.

'We're not sure. Barry's in some important meeting or other, and he said to wait here until he's ready for us.'

I slid my phone from my pocket and checked the time. How long would we be in here for? And where was Gabriel?

'We were worried about you, after last weekend,' said Aiden suddenly. I glanced up from my phone. They were both looking at me.

51

'Uh . . . yeah.' In a flash, I was back there, in that backstage corridor at the Troubadour. Grabbing Olly's T-shirt, trying to pull him towards me, watching as he pushed my hand away. 'I guess that wasn't a great time for any of us.'

Yuki cleared his throat sheepishly.

'Speaking of which,' he said, 'I owe you an apology.'

'What for?'

'For what happened in the cocktail bar.' He rubbed his neck, wincing. 'The way that douchebag from Scorched Earth spoke to you. That was *not* cool.'

I waved it off. 'Nah, don't sweat it. He wasn't the first douchebag, and he won't be the last.'

Yuki smiled to himself. 'You got that right. And, hey, if it makes you feel any better, their new single tanked.'

'D'you know what? It actually does.'

We shared a moment of eye contact, and I thought back to Yuki's confession in the bar. His parents were getting divorced, and his mother had taken his little brother, Shinichi, back to Japan. His family was falling apart, and Yuki had been drinking to mask the pain, while keeping the truth from everyone, including his best friend. Had that changed? Had he patched things up with Aiden?

'I see you brought your camera,' said Aiden, dragging me from my thoughts. 'So . . . I don't know, you must be here to take photos of something, right?'

52

'Maybe. But photos of what?'

The boys looked at each other, as if unsure of what they were allowed to tell me. Yuki took a deep breath.

'We've spent the entire week auditioning for Olly's replacement.'

I sat forward.

'You're replacing him *already*?'

'Barry says we have to fix this soon, or people will write us off. Fortunately, if anyone can get hundreds of wannabe popstars in a room with a moment's notice, it's Mr King.'

I could see Yuki's point. Through the *Make Or Break* selection process, Barry must have auditioned near enough every teenager in the Northern hemisphere.

I felt a heat on my neck.

'So does that mean . . . you've found someone?'

Yuki scoffed.

'Oh, yeah, we've *found* people. Hundreds of them. People who have about as much business being in Fire&Lights as I have being in the Royal Moscow Ballet.'

I pulled a face.

'That bad?'

Yuki threw a glance at his bandmate, then started to count on his fingers.

'Let me see. First, there was the really old dude. Like, he was *thirty-seven*. Thirty-seven! That's older than the Great Wall of China. Then we had Mr Shouty, who I *think* punctured my left eardrum, Pot-Belly Craig David, at least three weepers, a bunch of guys who thought they were the male Whitney Houston and, um, the kid who brought a tortoise to his audition. A TORTOISE.' He leaned forward on the sofa. 'My personal favourite, though, was the white-boy rapper wearing a wife-beater. Kanye Vest, we called him.' He dropped back again. 'It's been a horror show.'

I gazed into the carpet, lost in thought.

'I guess Olly's a tough act to follow.'

'Yeah, he is.' I looked up again, and saw that Yuki's face had turned serious. He pushed his fist into the arm of the sofa. 'I miss him, man.'

Me too, I thought. But I didn't say it.

'There's something else,' said Aiden, shuffling in his seat.

I folded my arms, hugging them to my body. 'What's that?'

'Well, you know as well as anyone that we've all got . . . stuff going on right now.' Aiden's cheeks went a little pink. It had only been a few weeks since his fledgling relationship with pop starlet Kaitlyn Jones had ended, publicly and abruptly, and I was one of the only people in the world who knew why. 'But with Gabriel . . . it's different.'

I drew in a loaded breath. It had only ever been a matter of time before his name came up.

'Don't get us wrong, Charlie B,' said Yuki, holding up an open hand, 'we all know that Gabe rocks this whole "brooding outlaw" vibe, but this is different. He's barely said a word since last weekend. He looks . . .' Yuki shook his head. 'I don't know any other way of saying it. He looks ruined.'

I felt my heart straining, pushing against my ribcage, as if trying to escape from my chest. Then, with a loud click, the door opened, and we all turned in unison.

'Barry's ready for you,' said Tara, with a nod.

In silence, we followed Tara down the hallway towards a large, airy room with its double doors propped open. Inside, it looked like some kind of rehearsal studio, with polished parquet floors, mirrored walls and a grand piano in the corner. Barry was standing in the centre, waiting for us.

'Bloom,' he said, with a clap of his hands, as we passed through the doorway. 'Glad you could make it.'

He patted me on the shoulder and I gave him a small smile, hitching my camera case up my shoulder. Behind me, leaning against the wall, I could sense a tall, dark shape, and it was making the hairs on the back of my neck stand up.

'Here we are, then, lads,' said Barry, glancing around. 'Crunch time.'

I didn't know which way to look. Should I turn round and catch his eye? Say hello? I was terrified that seeing him again would only remind me of Harry, and the awful things he'd written about my mum, but we couldn't go on like this forever.

'So how's everyone feeling?' asked Barry. Yuki shoved his hands into his back pockets.

'Peachy.'

Barry sighed loudly, and clamped his hands on Yuki's shoulders.

'I get it,' he said, looking right into Yuki's eyes. 'Really, I do. If I were in your shoes, I'd be feeling exactly the same way.' He let go and began pacing the room. 'I appreciate we're up against it. The press think we're finished, the fans are tearing each other apart, the internet is melting, blah blah blah. It's a scary time . . .'

I closed my eyes, wondering if Gabriel was looking at me, or if he was waiting for me to turn round. Part of me wanted to dash over and hold him, to lay my head on his shoulder, listen to his voice and feel his fingers curl around mine. But another part of me wanted to run out of the room, without looking back.

'. . . Meanwhile,' continued Barry, running a big hand around his jaw, 'the auditions. Let's be honest, they've not been going well.'

Yuki let out a hollow laugh.

'Yeah,' agreed Barry grimly. 'You took the words right out of my mouth. But the press coverage, the fan frenzy, the conveyor belt of muppets we've been auditioning this week, it's all got me thinking. The three of you, you're tight. You're a unit. You can't just stick some random fourth wheel in there and pray it works out. So I've come to a decision.'

Barry nodded at Tara, who turned and walked briskly towards a second set of doors on the far side of the studio. I glanced at Yuki and Aiden, standing together, their faces wrought with confusion. Was Barry suggesting they carry on as a three-piece?

Then, across the room, Tara pulled the door open.

'Boys,' said Barry, gesturing to the doorway, 'say hello to your new fourth member.'

6

We all stared at the open doorway in silent shock.

'Jake,' said Yuki, pushing his hair back off his face. 'I'll be damned.'

Jake Woodrow. Standing in the doorway, a guitar strapped to his back.

It couldn't be.

'Hey,' he said, stepping forward, one hand hooked around the strap of his guitar case. He was wearing a brown wool fedora with a paisley print headband peeking out underneath it, and around his neck, a silver pendant gleamed against his dark skin. I remembered from the *Pop Gossip* video that, back when he was in the band, he'd had his hair in cornrows, but it looked as if he'd grown it out a little, as one or two black strands were just about visible beneath his hat. He wore a white T-shirt with a low collar, a black jacket and a silk scarf slung around his neck.

Like the others, Jake had really grown into himself since the *Make Or Break* auditions. He had a strong, quiet presence to him. You could sense it, even from the other side of the room.

'Jake, my boy, come and join us.'

Barry walked over to greet him, laying an arm round his shoulders and guiding him towards his new bandmates. As Yuki and Aiden moved across the space to greet him, I decided I couldn't wait a second longer. I looked over my shoulder, and locked eyes with Gabriel.

His hair was messy, his clothes ruffled. His eyes were dark and sunken, and he looked drained, exhausted, like he hadn't slept in days. A sharp ache rose up through my body, curling around my lungs.

It felt like someone was strangling my heart.

'I'll be honest with you, Woody,' said Yuki, behind us, 'I did *not* see this one coming.'

Jake laughed – a gentle, husky laugh – and I heard the sound of him high-fiving Yuki, then Aiden.

'Me neither, Yuks. Me neither.'

'Welcome back,' said Aiden. 'It's grand to see you.'

Gabriel and I were still locked in eye contact, my pulse racing in my ears. We stayed in that checkmate, motionless, until Jake's voice broke the silence.

'Gabe. Hey.'

I felt the weight of every pair of eyes in the room swerving towards us, waiting for Gabriel's reply. But Jake didn't get one. Instead, Gabriel turned his head in Barry's direction. His voice was hoarse, razor-edged.

'Don't take this the wrong way, Barry, but . . .' His eyes darkened. 'Are you out of your mind?'

Jake's eyes dropped to the ground, and Barry pointed a chunky finger at his protégé.

'Let me remind you, Gabe,' he said, his jaw beginning to grind, 'that this is my band. And what I say goes. Do I make myself clear?'

At first, nobody spoke. The room prickled with tension.

'Do you mind if I say something?' Jake's voice again.

Barry gave him the smallest of nods.

'I don't want to come between you guys,' continued Jake, sliding his guitar off his back. He leaned it against a chair. 'We have an uncomfortable history, we're all aware of that. But I admire you. All of you.' He looked at Gabriel when he said this, his eyes shining bright. 'I'm not here to replace Olly. No one ever could.'

An image flashed up in my mind: Olly and Jake being interviewed for one of those *Behind The Band* videos, sitting together on a rocky outcrop in the Seychelles, grinning at each other. Now that I was meeting Jake face to face, I could see why they'd been so close. The way they spoke, it was strangely similar.

'But I honestly believe,' he continued, 'that we can create something amazing together. You just need to give me a chance.'

Gabriel held his breath and ran a hand through his hair. Barry waved a palm at him.

'Look, listen to me,' he said, addressing everyone. 'The press think they have the story of the century with Olly walking out, and maybe they do. But when you've been doing this as long as I have, you learn that there's only one way to bury a story.' He patted Jake firmly on the shoulder. 'Create a bigger one.'

Barry had a point: the media would lose their *minds* over this, and the fans would too. I couldn't wait to tell Melissa. She would flip.

'And so . . . what?' said Gabriel, pushing away from the wall. His amber eyes were ablaze. 'We're just going to pretend that you didn't *throw Jake out of the band for me*, is that it?'

Barry pushed air through his nose, like a bull.

'No, Gabe, we're not. We are going to own this. We are going to go out there and tell the world that Jake Woodrow is getting the ultimate second chance. This story is pure tabloid gold, trust me.'

Gabe cocked his head.

'To be honest, Barry, I don't care about your story. I care about the *band*.' He gestured towards Yuki and Aiden. 'The band is the only thing that matters.'

Aiden looked at the floor, shifting his weight from one foot to the other. Barry gritted his teeth.

'Unless we make a power move now, there will *be* no band. You understand me?'

Gabriel chewed this over for a moment, and then, as if admitting defeat, dropped back against the wall. Barry managed a weak smile, and turned to me.

'Now, Bloom.' He rubbed his hands together. 'You may have been wondering what in the name of Moses you're doing here, and I'll tell you. You're here to document this moment. I've got my studio guys coming down later for the posed shots, but you, kid, you know how to get behind the curtain with these lads. I want something candid. I want something the fans can *relate* to.'

I crossed my arms, confused. How was I supposed to get any usable pictures in here? The tension in the room was thicker than oil.

'You mean . . . right now?' I said, looking around.

Barry nodded.

'Where do you want us, Charlie B?' Yuki asked chirpily, trying to puncture the awkwardness. 'You want me to dance a jig? I like to jig.'

Barry gave him a playful slap on the back of the head. 'No, you twit.' He pointed at the guitar. 'Jake's going to play you a song.'

Quietly, Jake pulled up a chair and began to unzip his guitar from its case. Behind him, Tara gathered three other chairs, and sat them in a semi-circle.

'I'm not an idiot,' said Barry, rolling up his sleeves. 'You haven't seen Jake in years and, obviously, I knew this would be a shock for you lot. So I asked him to bring his guitar along and, uh, remind you all what I saw in him in the first place. Take a seat, lads.'

As Jake tuned his strings, Yuki, Aiden and, finally, Gabriel, joined him on the circle of chairs. He cleared his throat and pulled a plectrum from his pocket.

'I thought I'd play some Michael Jackson,' he said, with a smile. 'Something from *Off The Wall*. "She's Out Of My Life".'

'Vintage,' said Yuki, impressed.

As Jake began to pick at the strings, Barry caught my eye and indicated my camera, which was still zipped up inside its case. I rushed over to it, pulled it out and powered it up, and soon I was circling the boys, watching them through the lens. I waited for Jake to start singing, fiddling nervously with the focus ring, my finger poised on the shutter button. The boys weren't looking at each other, and the atmosphere was frosty.

Then, as Jake sang the opening lines, something magical started to happen. In that quiet, empty space, his voice sounded so beautiful – so soulful and melancholy – that, slowly but surely, the ice began to melt. Yuki and Aiden looked on, enthralled, and with every new lyric, Gabriel's shoulders seemed to relax, his face softening. He was mesmerised by Jake's voice. Edging around the group, I took picture after picture, capturing Jake's fingers curled around the guitar neck, the glint in his eyes as he sang, and the tanned line of Yuki's arm slung around Aiden's neck.

I'd never heard the track before, but as I listened to the lyrics, they started to get under my skin. They told of a boy who had let the love of his life slip from his hands, and now he was a wreck, a shadow, a ruin of sorrow and regret. It was too much, hearing those words while standing so close to Gabriel, and as I hovered behind him, aiming my lens at the soft contour of his neck, I wondered if he was feeling it too.

I lowered my camera, my face burning, and turned away just as Jake was singing the final few notes. Fortunately, the applause from Barry and the band was enough to distract any attention from me.

'Beautiful,' said Barry, still clapping. 'You got something in there we can use, Bloom?'

I twisted round, my camera cradled in my hands.

'Uh, yeah. I think I do.'

He made a circle between forefinger and thumb.

'That's my girl. Now . . .' He turned to the boys. 'I'd say it's time for my big news.'

While clipping on my lens cap, I stole a look at Gabe. His skin was flushed, his eyes fixed on the wall. Was he thinking about me? Or Jake?

'Jake wasn't your big news?' replied Yuki, incredulous. Barry wagged a finger in the air.

'Master Woodrow was simply the *hors d'oeuvre*,' he said, although he pronounced it *haws dervra*. He was looking tremendously pleased with himself. 'Come with me.'

We all followed Barry into the adjacent room: a long, richly furnished meeting space with floor-to-ceiling windows that looked out across the city. As I took in the sights – the crisp spring sunlight sparkling on the Thames, the London Eye standing high and proud in the distance – it dawned on me that I wouldn't be talking to Gabriel any time soon. Not here, not now. Today was business only.

'Take a seat,' said Barry, gesturing to the cherry-wood conference table that stretched almost the entire length of the room. Positioned in the centre of the table was a mystery object, around thirty centimetres high, obscured beneath a black silk cloth, and as we sat down – Jake, Aiden and I on one side, Yuki and Gabe on the other – all eyes were rooted to it.

'When we re-launch Fire&Lights to the world on Monday,' began Barry, 'people need to know we mean business. They need to know we're not dying – quite the opposite, in fact. That we're alive and kicking. And this, my boys, is how we're going to do it.'

Like a magician at a live show, Barry reached across the table, pinched the top of the black cloth and whipped it off. We all stared, rapt, at what was underneath: a small model of a jet plane, angled on a plinth so that it looked like it was flying through the air. At first, I was confused, and then I saw the name emblazoned across the fuselage.

FIRE&LIGHTS.

Yuki's mouth opened so wide, I thought his head might fall off.

'Smack my ass with a tennis racquet,' he said breathlessly. An involuntary laugh burst out of Aiden.

'Oh my god . . .' He threw a smile at Jake, whose eyebrows were climbing his forehead. Even Gabriel couldn't hide his amazement.

'On Monday,' said Barry, circling the table, 'we will announce that, far from being finished, this band is about to enter its most exciting chapter yet. Superstar-in-the-making Jake Woodrow will be joining as our new fourth member, and the scheduled summer tour dates in America will be going ahead as planned. We'll be dropping a new single while we're out there' – he pointed at Gabriel – 'something peppy, Gabe, upbeat, 'cos they like that, the Yanks . . . and what's more, when we travel to the USA, we'll be doing it in style – in this baby. The brand-spanking-new, Boeing 757, Rolls Royce turbo-fan-engined . . . Fire&Lights private jet.'

Laugher and whooping, peppered with applause, erupted from the boys. But as it faded away, I noticed Yuki looking anxious. Barry spotted it too.

'Y'all right, Harrison?'

Yuki leaned back in his chair, his forehead creased.

'This looks amazing, Barry, but . . . there's a problem.'

Yuki looked very serious for a moment, and the mood began to darken. Barry ran his tongue round his teeth.

'Go on.'

Yuki pointed at the plane.

'That thing is REALLY small,' he said, trying to hide the smile from his face. 'I mean, *maybe* you'd fit Aiden in there, but that's about it.'

Laughing, Barry slipped an arm around Yuki's shoulder and pretended to throttle him, mussing up his hair with his free hand. Aiden threw a box of tissues at them and it bounced off Yuki's shoulder, on to the floor. Lightning quick, I hammered my finger against the camera shutter, capturing all the action.

Then, as the chaos died down, Barry turned to me, a huge grin lighting up his face, and pointed right into the lens.

'New York City better roll out the red carpet, Charlie Bloom . . . because Fire&Lights are back in business!'

The Caversham High sports hall was huge and draughty, and lit by flickering, yellow-white strip lights. The walls were lined with climbing bars and folded-up cricket nets, and the whole room smelled of sweat and old rope.

A few rows behind me, I could hear muffled whispering.

'Did you guys read it, though? All the way through?'

That morning, just hours before my first exam had begun, Barry King had issued a global press release. It included the official photographs of the new line-up, a focus on Jake Woodrow, details of the band's upcoming

American tour dates and a series of eye-popping photographs taken inside the new F&L private jet.

'Yeah, I did. *Stronger Than Ever*? That is so lame.'

That was what Barry had called the summer tour: *Stronger Than Ever.* Turns out, not everyone was buying it.

'I was mainly into them for Olly,' whispered the first girl again, whose voice I recognised as Gemma Hockley's. 'I'm not bothered now he's gone.'

A pause.

'Gabriel's still fit, though.'

'Yeah, but I reckon he's got low standards, if you know what I mean.'

I heard the scrape of a chair leg, and sensed their eyes on me.

'Some guys will sleep with *anyone* . . .'

Both the girls sniggered, and I busied myself with my pencil case, biting my tongue. I was used to this sort of thing by now, and normally I'd rise above it, but my skin felt thinner than usual.

'Excuse me, at the back there?'

At the front of the hall, Mr Crouch had looked up from the pile of papers cradled in his arms. The sniggering stopped.

'Need I remind you this is an *examination*, Miss Hockley?'

'No, sir,' said Gemma, on the edge of laughter. 'History, yeah?'

Mr Crouch shook his head wearily and went back to distributing papers. Lining up biros on my desk, I tried to clear my mind of Gabriel West and concentrate on the Treaty of Versailles. Right now, for the next hour and a half, I had to block him from my thoughts. I *had* to focus.

The problem was, every time I closed my eyes . . . he was there.

That evening, I sat alone in front of the TV, a mess of French revision notes lying all around me. Onscreen, two blonde girls were sitting in a café, trying to decide whether some guy named Barclay was ready to commit to a serious relationship.

'I was, like, Barclay, you know I saw you in Yo Sushi with Poppy last week, so don't even start with your BS.'

'That guy is so rogue.'

'Bea told me he got with four different girls at the Spring Ball, which is rude as, because I was literally there the whole time . . .'

I glanced at my phone, checking for messages from Dad. He didn't like me having the TV on when I was revising, but while he was out at the shops, I figured I deserved a break.

'Oh my god, have you seen Bea's new poncho-kaftan thing that she wears all the time?'

'She looks like a duck. Like, literally. An actual duck.'

The doorbell rang, and on instinct, I switched off the television. Dad must have forgotten his keys.

As I padded into the hallway, my gaze brushed over his trainers in the shoe rack, and nerves fluttered inside me. We had barely spoken since that evening in Pizza Express, and there was an invisible pressure building between us, filling the house. He knew something was up, and there was only so long I could keep blaming it all on exam stress.

The bell rang again, and then a third time, more insistently.

'OK, OK, I'm coming . . .'

An umbrella had tumbled on to the mat, and I nudged it out of the way with my foot. Then I clicked open the door, and gasped out loud.

Gabriel was standing on the doorstep.

7

For a second, I just stared at him in disbelief.

'Gabe . . . what the . . .' Words were failing me. I glanced over his shoulder into the darkness. 'What the hell are you doing here?'

He was wearing a grey sweater, the hood pulled up over his head, shadowing his face. Our outdoor light cast a slanted orange glow across his eyes, revealing an exhausted gaze.

'We need to talk,' he said, not moving. I checked the road for signs of my father.

'You can't just . . . turn up here. Jesus, Gabe, you can't—'

'Please,' he said, taking a step forward. 'I only need a few minutes.'

I pressed my fingertips into my eyes, my pulse beating double-time. Letting Gabriel inside the house seemed crazy, but if I made him leave, my father might bump into him on his way home. And besides, he was right: we did have to talk.

Stepping backwards, I gestured for him to walk through, then shut the door behind us.

'Have you any idea how risky it was coming here?'

'I know,' said Gabriel, holding up his hands, 'but I was careful, and I waited for your dad to leave. I don't need long.'

I glanced out across the drive.

'If he takes one look at you, it's all over. You realise that? What were you thi—'

'Come to America with me.'

His words hung in the air between us, and I searched his face in disbelief. He seemed deadly serious.

'What?'

'Come to America.'

A sudden heat flowed through me, from my feet to my fingertips. I could never go to America with him, clearly, but at least he still wanted to see me, to be near me. In a way, wasn't that everything I wanted to hear?

'I . . . I don't . . . how?'

Gabriel pulled his hood down, and two dark strands of hair tumbled in front of his face.

'The tour. I want you to come.'

I shook my head, almost laughing.

'I can't come on tour with you, Gabe. Come on.'

'We've both seen that letter,' he said, stepping towards me, 'and we need to know what it means. Right?'

Harry's letter flashed up in my mind: the faded handwriting, the paper fraying at the edges. It was still in my bedroom, at the back of a drawer, hidden inside a textbook.

'I talked to my father,' I said, my eyes flicking towards his study. 'About what happened in America.'

Gabriel straightened. 'What did he say?'

'He told me a bit about Little Boy Blue, but nothing we don't already know. He said Mum died in a car accident, and it was nobody's fault. He didn't even mention Harry's name.'

Gabe sucked air through his teeth. I pulled my sleeves down over my wrists.

'I've been going through it all in my head, from every angle, but none of it really makes sense. Like . . . maybe Harry was in the car with Mum, or even driving it himself? Dad said he had an alcohol problem, so he could have been drunk at the wheel. Except, as far as we know, he left the tour and never came back, so . . .' I exhaled, defeated. 'I don't know what to think any more.'

Gabriel reached out, almost touching my arm. We both looked down, and his hand fell away.

'See, Charlie, this is *exactly* why you need to come with me. We're so close to the truth, but we won't find it here. My foster home don't have the answers, and it's obvious your dad won't give them to us . . . but we *can* find them out there. Where it all happened.'

I stared back at him, a hundred thoughts battling inside my head.

73

'I can't go to America,' I said hopelessly. He flexed his fingers.

'Why not?'

'Why not? Because I'm *at school*, Gabe. I'm in the middle of my exams. And even if I wasn't, I can't afford a plane ticket, and if my dad ever found out who you were, I don't know, he'd probably call the police.' I frowned at him. 'You seem to forget that I'm not like you . . . I'm not a popstar. I'm just some average kid.'

Gabe hung his head, his lips moving slightly. He paused, as if counting, then lifted his chin and looked me right in the eye.

'What's happening between us right now, it's killing me. Do you understand? It's tearing me apart. You tense up when you're around me, you go pale when I walk in the room, and I can't take it any more. We need the truth.' He ran a hand through his hair. 'Don't we?'

I avoided his gaze, staring at the floor. Counting the lines in the wood.

'I've been sitting in my room for days,' he continued, the faintest quiver in his voice, 'trying to write this "hit single" Barry wants from me. Peppy, he said, upbeat. And I can't write a single thing. I've got nothing.'

I looked up again, a sharp, heavy sadness building inside me. Of course I wanted the truth. Of course I wanted to fly to the States with Gabriel, and fix our broken pieces, and lay all this to rest.

But something was haunting me.

'It's just . . .' I pictured his father, standing on the street outside the Troubadour club, and hot tears brimmed in my eyes. 'Every time I look at you . . . I see him.'

It was a horrible thing to say, and I could see it on Gabriel's face. Like I'd driven a machete into his chest.

He swallowed back emotion.

'Listen to me, Charlie. I know what it's like.'

I drew the back of my hand across my face, smearing tears.

'What do you mean?'

His voice softened.

'To miss your mum. To ache for her. When you go to bed and all you want to hear is her voice . . . *I know what that feels like.*' He sucked in a jagged breath, and I felt my heart cracking. 'I miss Mama every day, every single second, and there's nothing I can do about it. But you, all those secrets, those things you want to know about Katherine . . . they're out there, somewhere. We just have to find them.'

My head snapped up. I could hear my father's shoes crunching down the driveway, and his keys jingling as he pulled them from his pocket.

'Oh my god . . . *Dad.*'

Gabriel stepped backwards, looking left and right. He *might* have had time to escape out of the back door, but—

The sound of Dad's key in the lock.

This was bad. This was *really bad*.

'In there,' I said, in a harsh whisper, pushing Gabriel towards the open door of the study. I just had to pray, with everything I had, that Dad went to the kitchen first.

The front door opened, and I was left hovering in the hallway, hastily drying my tears.

'Charlie, are you——?' Dad had his head down, wiping his feet on the mat. He thought I was still in the living room.

'Hi, Dad.'

He gave me a startled look.

'Oh. You're there. Everything all right?'

I froze, tongue-tied. The thought of Gabriel, hiding in the dark only metres away from us, had locked my jaw closed. I shook my head, and shrugged.

'Kiddo?'

'I was . . . looking for something.'

I allowed myself a cautious glance into the study. Gabriel's eyes glinted in the darkness as he pressed himself against the wall, disturbing the shiny leaves of a pot plant sitting on the desk. Letting out a small, puzzled laugh, Dad dropped his keys into the bowl by the phone and started towards his study. He reached for the light switch on the outer wall, and I found myself shouting.

'Don't go in there!'

Dad stopped, milliseconds before hitting the switch, and turned back around. He had a wonky smile on his face.

'Are you sure you're OK?'

I fumbled with my fingers, trying desperately to control the blood rushing to my cheeks.

'Y-yeah, I'm fine. I just . . . I wanted to see what you bought.'

Dad's eyebrows climbed his forehead.

'You wanted to see what I bought?'

I nodded, tight-mouthed. Without taking his eyes off me, Dad reached into the plastic bag he was holding and pulled out a tin can.

'Butter beans,' he said, confused. 'For the soup?'

'Yes. Of course. I'd forgotten.' I tugged some hair behind my ears, trying to disguise my shaking hands. 'Sorry, I think all the revision has fried my brain.'

Dad let out a sigh.

'I'm not surprised.' His eyes wandered towards the kitchen. 'D'you want a cup of tea?'

'Yes!' I said, a little too emphatically, and he gave me another quizzical smile. I busied him towards the kitchen, catching Gabriel's eye as I went and jerking my head towards the front door.

Moments later, the kettle was boiling in the corner, and Dad had his back turned, dropping teabags into two mugs. Standing in the kitchen doorway, I sent Gabriel a hurried text.

Leave. Now.

'I hope you don't feel alone in all this,' Dad was saying as he reached for the kettle. Gabriel's speech bubble throbbed: he was replying.

I'm going to make this happen, Charlie.

Go.

To the sound of Dad's spoon clinking against the mugs, Gabriel appeared in the hall, his hood back up again. Amazingly, he was still texting.

'I try not to be oblivious to what's going on in your life,' said Dad, unscrewing the top of the milk, 'but it's not always easy. Sometimes I think teenagers live in their own secret worlds . . .'

Another message appeared on my phone.

I'll think of something. I promise.

As Gabriel reached for the door, he caught my eye from beneath the shadow of his hood.

He clenched his jaw, then slipped out soundlessly into the night.

After Gabriel's visit, the days began to blur into one. Exams in the morning, exams in the afternoon. Revision and mock papers in the evenings; sometimes with

Melissa, sometimes alone. Endless cups of tea and hot cocoa. Sharpened pencils, geometry equipment, lining up outside the sports hall. Stilted conversations with my father as we passed in the hallway.

I had semi-sleepless nights, tossing and turning on my bed, the warm air closing in around me. Flashes of my mother's hands, playing the piano, and of Harry West's eyes, merging with Gabriel's, found their way into my dreams.

Some days, I would wake up and my mind would be buzzing with questions. How on earth would I sell an overseas trip to my father? Could Gabriel and I ever be 'normal' around each other again? And what even were we, now? Friends, exes? Something else?

Sitting up in bed, I would shake my head, trying to push it all to the back of my mind so I could focus on the intricacies of the data protection act, the effects of globalisation and the defining qualities of an equilateral triangle.

But then, one morning, with just a few days left before our exam timetable was over, everything changed.

'Is it just me, or was Isaac Newton kind of hot?'

Melissa and I were sitting cross-legged on her bed, cramming for our physics exam. The mid-May sun was streaming through her bedroom window, bathing everything in golden light.

I squinted at the portrait on her computer screen.

'Um, it's definitely just you.' I turned a page in my textbook. 'You know he was an egotistical maniac, don't you?'

Melissa stuck out her bottom lip.

'Well, yeah, but . . . look at his nose. So noble. And regard his voluminous hair!'

I glanced at the picture again.

'He looks like a spaniel.'

'Spaniel was a legitimate look in seventeenth-century Britain.'

I covered my ears, trying to concentrate on my textbook. No matter how many times I read about kinetic particle theory, I couldn't get my head round it.

'Hey,' said Melissa, poking my shoulder. 'I feel like you're not taking my crush very seriously.'

I nudged her away.

'I know you've got a thing for science geeks, but Isaac Newton was definitely not a hottie.'

'This doesn't sound like revision to me.'

We both looked up. Rosie was standing in the doorway, smiling. Melissa threw up her hands.

'It *is* revision, Ma! I'm revising whether or not I could've bagged a date with Sir Isaac Newton.'

'He was a total fruitloop, wasn't he?' replied Rosie, and I folded my arms in triumph.

'I knew you two wouldn't understand,' said Melissa, tutting. She pressed her arm against her forehead and fell back against her pillows. 'And so I must remain forever a spinster, admiring my beloved only from afar, weaving endless mittens for the orphan children of the village and, very likely, dying from the pox.'

Rosie suppressed a smile. 'Peculiar child.'

I felt a lightness inside me, lifting my shoulders. Pretend-working with my best friend, bantering with her mum, it was almost making me feel normal again.

'Anyway,' continued Rosie, 'enough larking about, ladies. It's very nearly exam time.'

'Roger that,' said Melissa, saluting her

'Oh, and this just came for you.' Rosie handed Melissa an envelope and turned to leave. 'See you downstairs in ten minutes!'

The door clicked shut. Melissa turned the envelope over in her hands.

'Ooh . . . I'll bet this is Great Uncle Ed's money,' she said, slipping a finger down the seam. 'Inheritance ahoy. We could go on a shopping spree! Anything you fancy?'

'It's your money, Mel.'

'No, come on,' she said, pulling out a letter. 'I'm quids in now, and you're my bestie. So how's about . . . a camera lens that works underwater? Or . . . a tripod that fires lasers into space? Or—'

Melissa trailed off as she read the opening lines. Her eyes bulged from their sockets.

81

'What?' I said, closing my textbook. Melissa's gaze was still glued to the page.

'It can't be, Charlie,' she said, breathless. 'Seriously . . . *this cannot be happening.*'

8

I glared at Melissa, waiting for an explanation, but she'd been awed into silence.

'Hey, Mel.' I waved at her. 'What does it say?'

Very slowly, Melissa sat back down on the bed and passed me the letter. I straightened it out and began to read.

Dear Melissa,

Here at Fire&Lights HQ, we really care about our fans. And that's how we know that your sixteenth birthday is coming up in a few days. You must be excited!!

Every month, we enter our fan club members into a birthday lottery, and this month, we're thrilled to tell you that YOU'VE WON THE GRAND PRIZE! ☺☺☺

This is no ordinary time for Fire&Lights. As you know, we've just announced a new line-up and an American tour, and the rest of the summer is going to be E-P-I-C. So here's the really brilliant part . . .

*****We would like to invite you, your parents and one friend to JOIN US ON OUR AMERICAN TOUR!!*****

It'll be an all-expenses-paid trip for you and your guests: we'll fly you out on our private jet, put you up in five-star hotels and keep Mum and Dad happy with spa treatments and sightseeing visits while you get to hang out with the band.

The F&L jet will fly from Heathrow to New York on 14th July, returning on 8th August. We really hope you can join us!

Give us a shout at
fanclub@fireandlights.co.uk
to let us know.

Lots of love,
Yuki, Aiden, Gabriel & Jake
FIRE&LIGHTS

I clutched a hand to my stomach. This was *insane*.

Melissa's face was passing through a carousel of emotions.

'I just . . . wh . . . America . . . Charlie . . .'

I looked down at the letter again, my chest thudding, mouth dry.

'I mean,' continued Melissa, 'what are the chances of *me* winning the Fire&Lights birthday lottery?!'

I shook my head. 'Mel, this wasn't a lottery.'

She frowned at me.

'Um . . . duh? Did you read the letter?'

'Think about it. What did Gabriel say to me last week?'

Melissa's eyes grew wide with realisation.

I'll think of something. I promise.

'Well, pickle my Wotsits . . . he actually did it.' She stared out of the window. 'He's an evil genius.'

I followed her gaze through the glass, across the driveway, and into my own bedroom. Would my father ever agree to this? A trip to America?

'And, really,' reflected Melissa, nodding to herself, 'that does make way more sense. Because the odds of me winning that lottery, if you factor in the tiering of different prizes, the size of the fan club and the random winner allocation, are about –' she tapped a finger against her chin – 'fifty-nine thousand to one.'

'You are a freak of nature, Morris.'

She grinned at me.

'Thanks.'

'But . . . I just . . .' I let out an exasperated sigh. 'We can't do this. Can we?'

Melissa took the letter off me and waved it around.

'Of course we can! Look.' She pointed at the page. 'The fourteenth of July: that's *way* after our exams finish. We'll be free as birds. My mum normally takes a few weeks off over the summer anyway, and Dad will be, like,

"Free holiday? Sign me up!" It's the *perfect* cover, CB. We'll be hiding in plain sight.'

I wrung my hands together, trying to think it through in my head. It was risky. It was *unbelievably* risky, and crazy, and yet at the same time, it was just about the most exciting thing I had ever heard in my life.

'Girls, come on!' Rosie's voice, from the bottom of the stairs. 'Time to leave.'

'Coming!'

Melissa folded up the letter and stowed it in the front pocket of her rucksack.

'We'll have to wait until later to ask them,' she said, throwing the bag on her back, 'but that's actually not such a bad thing. Mum is way more impressionable in the afternoons.'

I felt a twist in my gut, imagining what my father would say. On the one hand, if Melissa's parents gave their blessing, there was no particular reason for him to object. It would all appear perfectly above board, as far as they were concerned. But however he felt about it, one thing was undeniable.

It would bring him yet another step closer to my web of lies.

As Melissa and I turned the corner on to Tower Close, we each privately rehearsed how we were going to break the news to our parents. We'd gone out for Frappuccinos after our exam finished, then hung around Waterstones for a while, and by now, our dads would both be home from the office and Rosie would've finished writing for the day.

If we didn't ask them now, we never would.

'Is this ridiculous?' I said to Melissa, as we stopped on the welcome mat outside her house. Through the frosted glass in the front door, I could see a shape moving around in the kitchen. 'Are we out of our minds for even bringing it up?'

Melissa shook her head.

'No way.' She lowered her voice to a whisper. 'Remember, to our parents, this is just a random holiday with a boy band. They don't know who Gabe is, or how he's connected to your family. They don't know anything.'

She was right, in a way. But that could change. 'What if my dad starts Googling Fire&Lights?' I said, gnawing on a thumbnail. 'If he works out who Gabriel is, then—'

'I've met your dad,' said Melissa matter-of-factly, 'and he does not strike me as the kind of person to sit around Googling boy bands.'

I thought about this for a moment. She had a point.

'Yeah . . . I guess you're right.'

'Come on,' said Melissa, sliding her key into the lock. 'Let's do this.'

After taking off our rucksacks and shoes, we passed through to the kitchen, where Rosie was folding up tea towels. She gave us a slightly worried look.

'What's up with you two?' She winced. 'Was the exam horrible?'

Melissa glanced at me, then back at her mother.

'We have something to ask you.'

Rosie nudged the kitchen drawer closed and leaned back against the counter.

'You both look rather serious about it, I must say,' she replied, with a confused smile. 'But on you go.'

Silently, Melissa slid the invitation letter from her pocket and passed it to her mum. Rosie read it, intrigued, her eyes widening with every line.

'Oh, my.' She scanned it again, from top to bottom. 'Oh, my.' She looked up and called into the living room. 'Brian! Brian.'

'Yip?' Melissa's dad's voice sailed across the hallway.

'I think we need you in here, love.'

A short pause. We all listened as Brian muted the television, rose off the creaky sofa and wandered through to the kitchen.

'Hello, Charlie,' he said chirpily, when he saw me. 'Exams going well?'

'Not bad,' I said, with a shrug.

'Read, please,' said Rosie, holding out the Fire&Lights letter at arm's length. Brian took it off her.

'Heavens to Betsy,' he said, when he'd finished reading, and I couldn't help but smile. Melissa and her parents were so alike; it was one of my favourite things about them.

'What do you think?' asked Rosie tentatively. Brian was shaking his head in disbelief, and I suddenly felt a strangle of worry in my throat. Was he about to shut the trip down?

'It sounds fantastic!' he said, laughing. 'A private jet?! I can't believe what I'm reading.'

'Me neither,' said Rosie. Her husband leaned on the back of a chair.

'So are we saying yes, then? It would certainly save us money on a summer holiday.' He glanced at Melissa. 'I'm assuming you're up for it, squirt?'

Melissa nodded so hard, I worried she might faint.

'Well,' said Rosie thoughtfully, 'I don't know if I'd *choose* the USA, if it were up to me. Some of their food is a total ab—'

'Abomination,' interrupted Melissa, beaming. 'We know.'

Rosie smiled at her warmly.

'But I have to agree, this is a once-in-a-lifetime opportunity, and it'd be an amazing post-exam treat for you girls. Even if it does mean putting up with Dunkin' Donuts and Burger King for the best part of a month.'

'We can always take a holiday to Afghanistan *next* year, Ma,' said Melissa, wobbling her head, and Rosie stuck out her tongue.

'In that case,' concluded Brian happily, 'I'd say if Ralph agrees to it, we're good to go. And there I was, thinking the highlight of my summer would be the new series of *Bake Off . . .'*

Twenty minutes later, Melissa and I were sitting at the kitchen table, drinking cups of tea and having hushed conversations about how cool New York was going to be, when my dad walked into the room.

'Hello, everyone,' he said, glancing around. I studied him warily. His smile looked a little forced, and he was wearing casual clothes, which was unusual. He normally didn't bother changing out of his work suit until bedtime.

'Thanks for coming round, Ralph,' said Rosie. 'Cuppa?'

'Oh, no, I'm fine, thanks,' replied Dad, throwing me a quick look. The grown-ups all joined us at the table, and Dad drummed his fingers on a placemat expectantly.

'We'll cut to the chase, I think,' said Brian, nursing a coffee. He leaned forward, towards my dad. 'In a nutshell, buddy, we were hoping you'd agree to your daughter flying out to America with us next month, to hang out with a famous pop band.'

He grinned, but the corners of his mouth faltered slightly when he saw my father's reaction: face colouring, eyes rigid. There was no way Brian could appreciate why what he'd just suggested would have dropped through my father like a stone.

'America?' said Dad weakly. 'With a band?'

Brian sat back and cleared his throat. Rosie pushed the letter across the table.

'Fire&Lights, they're called. I gather you saw them play at the Troubadour a few weeks back, when Charlie was photographing Diamond Storm?'

At this, Dad actually brightened.

'Oh, yes . . . of course. Yes. I thought they were rather good.' He picked up the letter and started to read. When he'd finished, he sat back in his chair, blowing air out through his lips. 'Well, girls, I have to say . . . that's quite amazing. What an incredible opportunity.'

Melissa jiggled her legs under the table.

'So can Charlie come, Mr Bloom? Pleeeeease.'

Dad laughed, and ran a finger across the letter.

'I . . . don't see why not,' he said, gesturing at Melissa's parents. 'Provided that's really OK with you guys?'

Rosie and Brian nodded back at him, all smiles.

'To be honest,' continued Dad, 'I couldn't think of better people to be looking out for you, kiddo, so as long as Rosie and Brian are happy . . . I'm happy.' He thought for a moment, pointing at me. 'Didn't you take some photos for these Fires&Lights boys at the concert, Charlie? This could be a fantastic opportunity for you to get your photography career off the ground.'

I shrugged, trying not to give myself away.

'Yeah, maybe.'

'Hey,' said Brian, suddenly sitting up. 'Why don't you come too, Ralph? Make a holiday of it. I mean, these five-star hotels might be a bit on the pricey side, but you could always shack up in the nearest Travelodge instead?'

I gripped the edge of my chair. I hadn't even considered that Brian might suggest this, but if Dad came with us, I'd be finished. He couldn't be allowed to meet Gabriel, or—

'No, no,' said Dad, shaking his head. 'I'd love to, but I'm . . . snowed under at work.' He laughed nervously. 'You know what it's like.'

I felt a surge of relief, but couldn't help but notice: there was something off about Dad. Something that I couldn't quite put my finger on. Maybe it was just the thought of his daughter heading off to America with a band – and the fear of history repeating itself – but there was an expression on his face that I'd never seen before.

'Would you like to stay for dinner, Ralph?' asked Brian, standing up from the table. 'I'm making Brian's Brilliant Three-Bean Burritos . . . and, yes, that is their official name. They'll knock your socks off.'

'Sure,' said Dad, his smile still strained. 'That would be nice.'

Shaking off Dad's weird mood, I turned to face Melissa and we gazed at each other, unblinking, our smiles growing in unison. This was actually happening. We were going to America, on an international tour, with the biggest boy band on the planet. It would mean nearly a month away from home, with Gabriel. My heart was racing just thinking about it.

But I had to get through my exams first.

That night, I lay in bed, in the dark, staring at Gabe's name on my phone. My thumbs were poised on the screen, but my mind was clouded.

I wasn't really sure how to phrase this.

We got the letter, I began to type hesitantly. Thank you so much. Our parents are cool with it, so it looks like we'll be o

Ping. A new message hit my screen, cutting me off. It was from Melissa.

Have you seen this?? xxxxx

There was a link embedded in the message, and the summary read: *POPTUBE EXCLUSIVE: Olly Samson's first interview since quitting Fire&Lights!!* I stared at the thumbnail, my toes curling beneath the duvet. Olly was sitting on a stool, his skin glowing, blue eyes twinkling. Just seeing his face again made my heart hurt.

I sat up against my pillow, finger hovering over the hyperlink. Part of me wondered whether it was a good idea to watch it, but I knew I wouldn't sleep until I had.

Pulling the covers up to my chest, I took a deep breath

and hit 'Play'.

'Listen up, PopTubers,' said a voice off-screen, 'because we have one totally epic exclusive for you today!'

The camera was trained on Olly, who was sitting against an exposed brick-wall background, wearing a white T-shirt. He was holding a pink PopTube microphone.

'Olly Samson, welcome back to PopTube.'

Olly smiled.

'It's good to be back.'

'So, the question is . . . where do we begin? SO much drama to catch up on.'

Olly let out a small laugh.

'I can't argue with that.'

'Let's cut right to the chase: you just quit the world's hottest boy band. Where do you go from here?'

'I've already started making plans,' replied Olly brightly. 'It's exciting. I'll admit, leaving Fire&Lights really shook me, but I did it for a reason. I've been writing songs for quite a while now, and I didn't really have a chance to follow that path when I was in the band.'

'So, hang on. Does this mean that *Olly Samson: Solo Artist* is on the horizon?'

Olly nodded again.

'It sure does. We've just booked a tour of the States over the summer, and my debut single is dropping on the first of August.'

'Wow!' replied the interviewer. 'Big, big news. I'm

stoked. And hey, first of August . . . isn't that the same day as the next Fire&Lights single?'

Olly's face shifted. This was clearly news to him.

'I . . . didn't realise that.' He looked a little uncomfortable. I'd have bet money on Barry King having something to do with this. 'But that's the music industry, I guess. These things happen.'

The interviewer paused.

'And how are you feeling? About leaving the band, I mean?'

Olly drew in a breath.

'Honestly? Pretty gutted. I'd be lying if I didn't admit that. Those guys, they're my best friends in the world.'

'Sure,' said the interviewer doubtfully. 'Like, we all know how close you were with Yuki and Aiden, but you and Gabriel . . . you were more like enemies, weren't you?'

'No . . . we're . . .' Olly pressed his fingers into his forehead. 'Look, it's complicated. It's hard to explain.'

'It's no secret that you guys have had issues since the start, and the night you left the band, the two of you had a fairly public fight, right in the middle of a show. What exactly happened there?'

Olly ran a hand around the back of his neck.

'It's all a bit of a blur, to be honest. Things got crazy, and out of control, and . . .' His eyes dropped to the floor. 'Truth is, a lot of things happened that night that I regret.'

A lump formed in my throat. Was it possible that he was talking about . . . me?

'If I could go back and do it all differently, I would, but—'

I hit pause on the video, my finger shaking. I couldn't watch any more. It hurt too much.

CB??

Melissa again.

Just watched the first few mins. I really think he misses you.

I sighed.

I dunno . . . I can't think about any of that right now. It's too sad.

A pause. I concentrated hard, trying to will away the memories that were rushing through my brain; memories that, until now, I'd managed to keep locked away. My date with Olly in the art gallery, the time he sang to me on that windswept beach. The first time we ever spoke, in the corridor at Caversham High.

So he would be in the States too. America was a big

place, but the music industry was small. What would happen if we ran into each other out there?

If you need me, replied Melissa, I'm here, any time of night. You could throw pebbles at my window.

I smiled at my phone.

Or I could just text like a normal human being.

Ummmm, no   pebbles, please.

Night, doofus xxxx

Night xxxx

Slipping down beneath the covers again, I navigated back to my half-finished message to Gabriel.

We got the letter. Thank you so much. Our parents are cool with it, so it looks like we'll be coming.

He replied within a minute.

Don't mention it.

The trip sounds amazing. I can't believe you made it

happen.

Actually, it was easy.

I frowned, confused. It seemed unlikely that Barry would be mad keen on bringing some random family on tour.

Really?

Absolutely. We owed Melissa for tipping us off about that fan club girl . . . woulda been a real mess if that video had got out. She's worth her weight in gold, Barry says.

Of course: Melissa, PR wizard to the stars.

I'll pass that on – she'll be made up.

My smile faded, and I gritted my teeth. I had to say this now. I couldn't put it off any longer.

I think it's best if we don't talk for a while.

No reply. The message had delivered, but he wasn't typing. I tried again.

It's just with my exams, I really have to focus.

Thirty seconds went by, and I felt my face burning up. He'd taken it the wrong way. I should have called him. I should have explained all this on the phone, so that he didn't think—

I get it.

I breathed a sigh of relief. Clutching at my duvet, I sank into my pillow, still holding my phone. Another message hit my screen.

I'm sorry I brought all this on you.

It's not your fault, I replied, and for several long minutes, nothing happened. No typing, no new messages. Then, just as I was about to turn my phone to silent and go to sleep, he messaged again.

See you at the airport, Charlie Brown xx

See you there xx

TWO MONTHS LATER

9

An extravagant car horn sounded outside my window, and I looked up from my open suitcase. My phone pinged with two messages.

This is it, CB!!!!!!!!!!

I'm so excited I think my face might fall off.

I grinned to myself, then touched my palms to my stomach. I hadn't realised that it was possible to feel so excited and so terrified at the same time.

'Charlie! The car's here.'

Dad was calling me from downstairs.

'Yep, coming!'

I zipped up my suitcase and glanced around my bedroom. After our exams had finished, I'd tidied away all my textbooks and notepads, my revision folders and set texts, and replaced them with novels I'd been meaning to read for ages. I'd taken down my study timetables too, and hung up a bunch of selfies of me goofing around in the sunshine with Melissa. In a way, it felt like a new start.

My exams hadn't gone too badly, all things considered. As time went on, I'd managed to enter a kind of permanent study trance, banishing thoughts of Gabriel and our shared past, numbing myself to everything but stratified coastline sampling and standard deviation. But now I was actually travelling to America, *with* Gabriel, to put our ghosts to rest, and it was as if I'd unlocked the box where I'd been storing those memories and they were all about to come spilling out.

Pushing the thought to the back of my mind, I dragged my suitcase off the bed and dropped it on the floor. My phone buzzed again, and I glanced out of the window, suddenly curious as to what car Barry King had sent to take us to the airport.

My jaw dropped. That wasn't just some random car. That was a limousine.

Ummmmm, what on earth is going down in CharlieTown??? Sebastian WHO BY THE WAY IS OUR LIMO DRIVER would like to know when you'll be gracing us with your lovely face.

I laughed to myself and sent back a reply.

Hang on, just finished packing. I can see you from the
window.

Well then, sista, get your butt down here before I'm
forced to open up a can of whoop-ass on it.

Pocketing my phone, I took one last look around,
plucked my hat – Mum's hat – off the corner of my chair,
slid it into the front pocket of my suitcase, and made my
way downstairs.

When I reached the hallway, Dad was waiting for me.

'Got everything?' he said, moving forward to help me
with my case.

'Uh-huh.'

'Sun cream? Cash? Passport?'

I gave him a look.

'Stop worrying,' I said, reaching for my jacket on the
hook. 'I've double-checked everything.'

Dad tried to smile, though he looked a bit forlorn,
somewhere behind the eyes. He'd been this way for
weeks.

I couldn't help it. I couldn't stop myself saying it.

'Dad, I know . . .' I looked down. 'I know you're sad
because Mum went to America and never came back, but
look' – I pointed out of the window – 'I've got Melissa
and Rosie and Brian looking after me, and a whole team
of assistants and security guards. I'll be OK.'

He took a shaky breath, and nodded.

'I know. It's just . . . a little strange, that's all.'

'I'll message you when we land.'

I leaned over and gave him a hug. Then I walked to the door, clicked it open and pulled my case outside.

'This is an amazing opportunity for you, kiddo,' he said, from the doorstep. 'Grab it with both hands.'

My fingers tightened around the handle of my suitcase. 'I will.'

I left him standing there, still trying and failing to smile, and made my way up the garden path. The back window of the limousine slid down and Melissa stuck her head out.

'You rollin' with me, dog?' she said, from behind a pair of glittery pink sunglasses.

'I'm sorry,' I replied, 'but I was expecting my best friend. You appear to be Nicki Minaj.'

Melissa grinned. Behind her, the limo driver opened up the boot.

'Actually, no, because Minaj can't calculate pi to thirty-seven decimal places, as you very well know.'

I smiled, she beamed back, and a sudden burst of excitement filled my body. The door flew open and she leapt out, hugging me so hard I had to let go of my suitcase.

She stepped backwards, her hands on my shoulders.

'Charlie, I am freaking my tiny noggin here. I've been up since five a.m.!' She lifted her sunglasses. Her eyes looked like they were actually buzzing in their sockets. 'I've had quite a lot of coffee.'

'Uh, yeah,' I said, peeling her hands from my shoulders. 'I think we can all agree that the last thing *you* need is caffeine.'

She let out a slightly manic laugh.

'Tell me about it.'

'I mean, you came into this world pre-caffeinated.'

'Miss Bloom, your suitcase is packed.'

I peered past Melissa to find the limo driver standing beside the closed boot. He was wearing an immaculate suit, white gloves and a peaked hat. My suitcase was gone.

'This is Sebastian,' said Melissa, gesturing towards him. 'Sebastian can speak five languages and has a labradoodle named Wigbert.'

Sebastian cleared his throat. 'Digbert.'

'Digbert,' repeated Melissa, still grinning.

'Right, then, ladies,' said Sebastian, walking round to the pavement and pausing at the open car door. 'Let's get this show on the road.'

We slipped inside the car, and Sebastian closed it behind us and drifted round to the driver's seat. Rosie and Brian were sitting opposite us on the luxurious leather seating, holding sparkling glasses of champagne.

'This is a bit of all right, isn't it, Charlie?' said Brian, lifting his glass. Rosie winked at me, but there was a hint of concern in her eyes. 'You OK?' she mouthed, and I nodded.

'Ooh, I almost forgot.' Melissa passed a glass of fizz to me. 'We've got some too.'

I cocked my head, and Melissa waved a hand.

'Don't worry, it's just elderflower something-or-other.' I took the glass from her. 'I'd offer you a White Russian, but, y'know . . .' She covered her mouth, pointed ostentatiously at her parents and whispered: 'OLDIES.'

'Do you even know what's in a White Russian?' asked Rosie, amused.

Melissa scoffed. 'Yeah, obviously I do.' She counted ingredients on her fingers. 'Vanilla ice cream, two black olives, Tia Maria, a quail's egg and, um . . . banana Nesquik.'

The driver pulled away from the kerb, and I watched my dad at the front door, waving us off. It was the wrong way round, maybe, but I couldn't help feeling worried about leaving him on his own.

'Isn't this just about the coolest car you've ever seen in your entire life?' said Melissa, stroking the red-and-black upholstery. I took a sip of my elderflower fizz. I didn't have the heart to remind her that the last limousine I'd travelled in had its own hot tub.

'It's definitely up there,' I agreed, clinking her glass. As we slowed for a set of traffic lights, the driver intercom buzzed on, and Sebastian glanced at us in the rear-view mirror.

'Oh, you think this is cool?' he said, one gloved hand resting on the wheel. The hint of a smile was just about visible on his face. 'You wait until you see the private jet.'

We pulled up outside the terminal at Heathrow airport, and through the tinted windows of the limousine I watched the crowds of people wheeling suitcases through the revolving doors. My stomach flipped. For the first time, it actually felt real.

We were flying to the USA.

'Miss Bloom?'

I looked up. Sebastian had opened the door and was gesturing for me to leave the car.

'Oh, thanks,' I said, stepping out on to the tarmac, followed by Melissa, Rosie and Brian. Our bags had already been removed from the boot, and we reached for them instinctively, but Sebastian held up a hand.

'We'll handle your bags. You folks just relax.'

'I see,' said Rosie, giving me and Melissa an impressed nod. She pointed towards the main doors. 'So we just . . . go inside?'

'Oh, no,' replied Sebastian gently. 'You'll be passing through the VIP channels today.'

Melissa turned to me, agog, and mouthed, 'O . . . M . . . G.'

Sebastian noticed, and clasped his hands in front of his belt.

'Keeps you away from the crowds,' he said. 'Tara here will take you.'

'Hey, guys.'

Tara had appeared next to Sebastian, holding a clipboard. She gave me a discreet smile, then reached over to shake hands with the Morris family, one by one.

'I'm Tara,' she said brightly. 'I'm a personal assistant to the Fire&Lights boys, so I'll be looking after you during the trip. Anything you need, just shout. Charlie, good to see you again.'

I felt a sudden squeeze around my lungs, worried she'd given the game away to Rosie and Brian. But then I remembered: it wasn't a secret that I'd taken photos for Fire&Lights before, at the Troubadour gig, so as far as the Morrises were concerned, I had already met the management team. They just didn't know how many times.

Tara clapped her hands together.

'Are you ready to embrace your new VIP status?'

It turned out that checking into an airport with a world-famous boy band was *very* different to flying Ryanair. Our bags were tagged and transported to the plane entirely independent of us. The exclusive security barriers were empty and quiet, and we were through in minutes. Tara then led us through a door marked 'PRIVATE', down a series of softly lit hallways and finally outside again, on to the tarmac, where a gleaming Bentley was waiting.

'Arnold here will drive you round to the jet,' she said, opening the back door for us. 'I have a couple of errands to run, so I'll see you onboard.'

Melissa and I exchanged looks. In a way, a second luxury car felt like overkill for a journey that had to be no more than a kilometre, but we were VIPs now, and so we piled inside and were soon gliding effortlessly towards the loading bays. Minutes later, filing out of the Bentley, we all stood on the runway, staring in silent awe at the magnificent machine parked in front of us. The brand-new, publicity-ready Fire&Lights private jet.

It gleamed in the warm July sun, the band name written in burning red and yellow against the polished white metal. *FIRE&LIGHTS: Stronger Than Ever.* The band logo – a large F and a smaller backwards L, written as if by a sparkler against the night's sky – was emblazoned on the tail. I could hardly believe my eyes.

Melissa tugged at my sleeve.

'Charlie, I feel emotional.'

I drew in a deep breath.

'Tell me about it.'

'It's the most beautiful thing I've ever seen,' she said, swallowing hard. 'And I've seen *Ice Age 3*. Six times.'

'Come on, girls,' said Brian, taking the lead. 'Let's get in there before the popstars steal all the best seats . . .'

As we neared the plane, Yuki appeared at the top of the steps and gave us an enthusiastic salute. He was wearing one of those pilot's hats with the golden wings sewn on the front.

Once we were within earshot, he pointed at us and cupped one hand to his ear.

'Erm, wait up. Did somebody say PRIVATE JET?'

Melissa squealed with excitement, and we began walking up the steps, our shoes clanging against the metal. When we reached the top, Yuki sucked in a mouthful of air, and grinned.

'So how are we all feeling on this fine summer morn?'

Melissa gulped.

'There's a pretty high chance I'm going to chunder.'

'*That's* the spirit,' said Yuki, slapping his thigh. 'You must be Mel?'

'Yep, that's me.'

'And you are . . .' Yuki pressed his palms together and pointed them at Melissa's parents. 'Rosie and Brian, right?' They smiled, impressed and, no doubt, a little starstruck. 'And you, of course, are Charlie. I remember you. Photographer extraordinaire.'

Like Tara, Yuki was acting as if he'd never met Melissa before, and only knew me from that night at the Troubadour. It was a very convincing charade. Gabriel must have briefed everyone on our situation.

'Allow me to introduce myself,' continued Yuki, nudging his hat up his forehead. 'Wing Commander Harrison, at your service, and' – he patted the fuselage of the plane – 'I'll be flying this bad-boy for y'all today. Sixty thousand kilos of sheer rock 'n' roll horsepower.'

I raised an eyebrow at him. In truth, I wouldn't entirely have put it past Yuki to hold his own pilot's license.

'Oh, hey, guys!' Aiden appeared behind his bandmate, beaming at us. 'You're just in time. We're about to meet the pilot.'

Yuki rolled his eyes.

'Embarrassing,' he said, pointing a backwards thumb at Aiden. '*I'm* the pilot.'

Aiden rested a hand on Yuki's shoulder.

'So Yuki told you he's flying the plane, then?'

'He may have done,' said Brian, with a chortle.

'Erm, *Aid*.' Yuki pointed to his hat. 'They don't just give these hats out to any old loser, y'know.'

Aiden frowned.

'You got that free in a raffle.'

'Move along, maggots!' Barry's voice, from inside the jet. 'We're taking off in fifteen minutes.'

With much chatting and squeaking (mainly from Melissa), we all followed Yuki and Aiden inside the plane, and as we passed from the entrance vestibule into the main cabin, I actually gasped. It was like stepping into a futuristic private members' club.

'Ruddy bloody heck,' said Melissa, her eyes like saucers. 'I am dead. I have died. Please forward my mail to the afterlife . . .'

The whole space was decked out in midnight blue and silver, with twinkling stars spread across the ceiling. There were huge, curvy leather chairs for reclining in, plasma screens everywhere, arcade machines and neon-lit fridges, and a cluster of fancy snack-making gadgets in the corner: coffee makers, juice dispensers and a popcorn machine.

Nearby, Barry was sitting in a lazy-boy chair, one leg crossed over the other, typing on his phone. From the back, Jake spotted us, smiled and started to walk over.

There was no sign of Gabriel.

'Oh, and if you get bored of playing Pac-Man,' Yuki whispered to Melissa, next to me, 'there's a cinema in the back.'

'*Get out of town.*'

Peering past the arcade machines, I noticed a narrow, dimly lit corridor leading away towards the back of the plane, dotted with closed doors. Private chambers, perhaps? Was that where Gabe was hiding?

'Hi, everyone!'

We turned round. A tall, keen-eyed woman was standing behind us wearing navy blue trousers, a crisp white shirt with golden epaulets and a black tie. Her blonde hair was pulled up into a bun on top of her head.

'Nice to meet you all. I'm Kirsty, your pilot.'

Yuki and Aiden exchanged a surprised look. The corner of Kirsty's mouth curled up into a smile.

'You were expecting a man, weren't you?'

'No!' said Yuki abruptly, holding up his hands. 'No, sir. I mean, madam. I mean, er . . .' He arched an eyebrow. 'Brigadier?'

'Just Kirsty will be fine, Mr Harrison,' she replied, with a laugh. 'So I gather this is your first time on a private jet? Well, we're delighted to have you. I've never flown a boy band before, so this is a first for everyone.'

'Yeeeah,' said Yuki, leaning against a nearby chair. 'It *is* our first time, but we're pretty, y'know, chill about the whole thing.'

'That's good to hear. And speaking of chilling out . . .' She held up two fingers. 'I have only two rules: be safe, and have fun. Oh, and at some point, I expect you guys to sing me a song. Sound fair?'

'You've got a deal,' replied Aiden.

'Good.' Kirsty brushed her hands together. 'With all that sorted, I'd say it's time for me to actually fly this thing. I'll see you guys on the other side.' She turned to open the cockpit door, then stopped, and threw a look over her shoulder at Yuki.

'Nice hat, by the way.'

Yuki's cheeks turned red, and she disappeared.

'Seatbelts on, everyone,' said Barry, rising from his chair. As he looked around, counting heads, he noticed Melissa's parents and walked over to greet them. I smiled to myself. Never in a million years had I imagined I'd see Brian Morris shaking hands with Barry King. 'Good to have you both onboard,' he said genially. 'I'm in charge of this rabble of idiots, if you can believe that.'

He leaned forward and jerked his head towards the back of the plane.

'If you want my advice, head to the back room there. We've got olives, bubbly and earplugs. If you ride up front in The Animal House, you'll have to listen to this horrible lot talking about GIFs and twerking and god knows what else for the next eight hours.'

'Works for me,' replied Brian, grinning. Barry extended an arm.

'In that case, just follow the sound of popping champagne corks. *Mi casa es su casa* . . .'

While Rosie and Brian headed to the back room with Barry, Melissa and I took our seats next to the boys. Instead of rows, the seats were grouped together in haphazard semi-circles, and as the plane took off, we hung out in a group, laughing and chatting, watching through the windows as London shrunk away beneath us. But it all felt wrong, somehow, doing it without Gabriel. And I was pretty sure he was lying low because of me.

116

'Good afternoon, Team Fire&Lights,' came Kirsty's voice, over the intercom, once we were cruising above the clouds. 'Take-off went without a hitch, so it's time for you all to sit back, relax and enjoy the flight. Who wants snacks?'

Cheers erupted from our little group, and soon enough, a steward arrived with soft drinks, coffees and bowls of nuts, and we all tucked in. Jake and Yuki started rapping a nonsense song about peanut M&M's, and Aiden beatboxed along.

'Hey, whizz-kids. Explain something to me.'

The rap tailed off as we all looked up from our refreshments. Barry, who had reappeared from the back room, was frowning at his iPad. 'I *cannot* get my head round this . . .'

'I've *told* you, Bazzer,' said Yuki, setting down his can of Sprite. 'When a mummy and daddy love each other very much, they have a special grown-up kissing party and that's how babies are made.'

Barry poked at the screen.

'Hilarious, mate. But no. This thing . . . Yuken. What is Yuken?'

My eyes darted upwards and met Melissa's. She had told me about this on the way to the airport, and I had a feeling it was about to make things awkward.

'I'm being told hashtag "Yuken" is trending on Twitter,' continued Barry, his brow furrowed, 'and it's got something to do with you lot?'

117

Silence. The boys seemed reluctant to share.

'Go on,' insisted Barry. 'Spit it out.'

Yuki cleared his throat.

'It's a portmanteau.'

'A portman-what?'

'A mash-up of my name . . . and Aiden's. *Yuken.*'

Barry made a face. 'And that means what, exactly?'

Yuki cleared his throat again, shifting in his seat. He patted his hands together thoughtfully.

'It means . . . well, it means that there are one or two fans out there who think that me and Aiden are . . . a couple.'

Barry snorted. 'You what?'

'They think that me and Aiden are together.' He waggled a finger between himself and his bandmate. 'Y'know, boyfriend and . . . boyfriend.'

Barry's eyes went wide.

'Oh.' He looked at Aiden, who seemed to shrink in his seat. 'Oh.'

'Yeah,' replied Yuki, forcing a laugh. 'It's crazy, really, 'cos Aid is *way* out of my league. Neeever gonna happen. And believe me, I've tried. I ran him a bubble bath, I put *Love, Actually* on the DVD player. Didn't even get to hold his hand.'

Yuki aimed a secret, sympathetic smile at his bandmate. Aiden tried to smile back, but his eyes said otherwise.

'Oh, wait. Here we go.' Barry began to read from his iPad. '"*Since popstar Aiden Roberts' mysterious break-up from celebrity squeeze Kaitlyn Jones, rumours have been flying around the fan community that he is secretly gay and engaged in a romantic relationship with Fire&Lights bandmate Yuki Harrison.*"' He looked up again. 'Just when I think I've seen it all.'

I thought about the conversation I had had with Aiden, backstage at the London Complex, earlier in the year. About how he'd never had romantic feelings towards another person, not even Kaitlyn, and was afraid to tell anyone. I was the first person he'd confided in, but judging from the way Yuki was taking the lead on the 'Yuken' debacle, he'd been the second.

'Anyway, we don't need to talk about all that, Barry,' said Yuki, waving it away. 'It's just fans having a laugh. I mean, do you remember the rumour that I was allergic to fresh air, and any time the fans saw me outside, it was actually a body double?! That was crazy! Where would you find another me, for a start?'

I couldn't help glancing over at Aiden again. He'd been trying to laugh it off, but his cheeks were flushed, his fingers knotted together. Whatever he was going through, clearly it wasn't over.

10

We'd been flying for about an hour when I noticed Aiden sitting alone, staring out of the window. Melissa was busy discussing her favourite *Make Or Break* finalists with Jake, so I drifted over and leaned on the back of the seat next to Aiden's. Outside the window, the sun was casting a stunning orange glow across a blanket of clouds.

'We're a long way from Galway, eh, Dorothy?'

Aiden started, and turned round. He smiled.

'Oh, hey, Charlie.'

'Fancy some company?'

He indicated the empty chair.

'Be my guest.'

We sat quietly for a moment, squinting at the sun as it refracted through the plane window. I took a sip from my Dr Pepper.

'How did you know I'm from Galway?' asked Aiden.

'Well, for a start, you told me.'

He shifted round to face me.

'When?'

'Last November, on the tour bus. Also, I live next door to Melissa Morris, unofficial chairperson of the Aiden Roberts Fan Club.' Aiden glanced over at Melissa, who was gesticulating enthusiastically at Jake, and smiled. 'Oh, and you're pretty much the most famous Irishman on the planet, so that helps.'

Aiden wrinkled his nose at me, unsure. Even after all this time, he still seemed a little uncomfortable with fame.

'What do you think of Gertrude?' he said. I drew my head back.

'Who's Gertrude?'

'Who's Gertrude, Yuks?' called Aiden, across the cabin.

'You're inside her, people!' replied Yuki, who was playing *Street Fighter* in the corner. He slammed a button on the arcade machine and it released a short victory tune. 'Yeah, taste my fury, you big green freak.'

Aiden leaned across to me.

'He named the plane Gertrude.'

'You can't name a plane Gertrude.'

'That's what I said!'

We both watched as Yuki loaded up another street-fighting bout.

'So you two are cool again, right?' I asked Aiden, lowering my voice a little. He nodded.

'We sure are. Thank you for that.'

'What? I barely did anything.'

'Whatever you say, Charlie,' he said, side-eyeing me. 'Whatever you say.'

Yuki's computer game blipped and twinkled, and he yanked enthusiastically at the joystick. I looked beyond him, down the corridor, towards the private suites. Gabriel still hadn't emerged.

'Gabe's keeping pretty quiet,' I said, flicking at the ring-pull on my soda can. 'Is he OK?'

Aiden lifted one shoulder.

'He's been quiet all summer. He doesn't admit it, like, but I think the gossip's starting to get to him. They're trying to pin everything on him, and it's not fair.'

I sighed.

'Gossip sucks.'

'Yeah. It does.' He made a pained expression. 'It's like this "hashtag Yuken" thing. I know it shouldn't bother me, and people don't mean it in a nasty way, but . . .'

'It makes you feel like public property.'

'Exactly.' He glanced out of the window again. 'You know, I've been thinking lots about what you said to me at the Pop4Progress concert.'

'Yeah?'

'I've tried so hard to come to terms with it, but—'

'Whatcha talkin' about?'

Melissa was leaning her elbows on the back of the seat in front of us, grinning. Aiden and I exchanged looks.

'Oh, nothing,' I said hastily, searching my brain for a change of subject. 'Just . . . photography.'

Melissa rolled her eyes. 'God, same old, same old.'

I poked my tongue out at her.

'Is she boring you, Aid?'

'Never,' said Aiden, with a laugh.

'Actually,' I said, thinking on my feet, 'I was about to tell Aiden how I'm hoping to meet up with Carrie while we're in New York.'

The day after the EP launch at the Troubadour, I'd received an email from Carrie Shakes, the world-famous music photographer. She said that she'd be in New York all summer and, if I found myself in the States, I should give her a call. Of course, at the time, I'd assumed it would never happen. But things had changed.

'That's a great idea,' said Aiden brightly. 'Carrie's my fave. Her Fire&Lights photos are something else.'

'She pretty much inspired me to start taking pictures of bands in the first place,' I said, thinking of her iconic images of Coldplay, The xx, Mumford & Sons. 'But the idea of actually meeting her, it's . . .'

That morning, I had fired off a message to Carrie, asking if I could meet her for coffee while we were in the city. Hanging out with famous people was becoming almost a habit for me now, but with Carrie, it was different. She was everything I wanted to be. She was my idol.

'You should just go for it,' said Aiden, lifting up his legs to sit cross-legged. 'Everyone knows you've got what it takes. And Olly told me that Carrie *loves* your stuff.'

At the mention of Olly's name, all three of us went quiet. The silence was soon filled by Yuki, at his arcade machine, waggling the joystick and delivering sarcastic one-liners to his street-fighting opponent. Jake wandered over to him, munching on an apple, and without taking his eyes off the game, Yuki raised his hand for a high-five. Jake obliged.

'So I've been chatting with Jake,' said Melissa, trying to lighten the mood. 'He's dead excited about the tour.'

'He's learned everything real quick,' agreed Aiden, picking up a bottle of water from the table. 'And his voice, it really adds something to the sound, y'know?'

Melissa nodded. 'Totally. But . . .' She rested her chin on the seat back. 'I'm still super sad Olly's gone.'

Aiden rolled his head so that he was gazing out of the plane window, and the sun fell across his face, turning his pale skin golden.

'Yeah,' he said, with a sigh. 'So am I.'

The plane's engines roared as its wheels made contact with the runway, and a scattering of celebratory whoops rang out around the cabin. Barry rapped a knuckle on the window.

'That, my boys and girls, is what I like to call the U . . . S . . . of mother-loving A.'

'Land of opportunity,' said Aiden, yawning.

'And liberty,' added Jake.

Yuki punched both his fists in the air.

'And PHILADELPHIA CHEESE-STEAKS.'

'We need to nail this tour, lads,' concluded Barry, as the plane slowed, noisily, to a halt. 'Absolutely nail it.' Then he added, under his breath, "Cos if we don't, we're finished . . .'

Something stirred in the corner of my vision, and I glanced up. Standing in the far doorway, barefoot and pressing a palm into his eye, was Gabriel. His hair was tangled, his shirt open. He blinked in the light.

'Are we there yet?'

'It lives!' proclaimed Yuki, running over to Gabriel and wrapping his arms around him. Gabriel tried to prise him off, but was unsuccessful. He let out a reluctant laugh.

'The prodigal son,' commented Barry, standing up and sliding his hands into his pockets. 'Did you sleep?'

'Uh . . .' Nudging Yuki away, Gabriel parked a hand in his bedraggled hair. He looked dazed and disoriented. 'Yeah, kind of.'

'Good. You needed it.'

Still blinking off sleep, Gabe glanced around the cabin, doing up the buttons on his shirt. Before I could turn away, his eyes met mine, and we both froze. I could feel nerves firing beneath my skin.

A hand touched my shoulder.

'Come on, ladies,' said Tara, behind our heads. 'Let's get you through security.'

Twenty minutes later, Tara led us out of the revolving doors at John F Kennedy airport, and a sticky heat slammed into me, like a wave. Brian dabbed at his forehead with a handkerchief.

'Woo, lordy. You feel *that* one in your armpits, that's for sure.'

'Ew, Dad,' protested Melissa, tugging at her T-shirt collar. 'Gross.'

Tara chuckled to herself and checked her watch. It was early evening in New York, but the middle of the night for us. Jetlag was about to hit us like a freight train.

'So,' said Tara, tucking a curl behind her ear, 'one of our cars is on its way, and should be with us in abou—'

'Tara . . . ?'

Melissa was toying thoughtfully with the luggage tag on her suitcase.

'Uh-huh?'

'Would it be OK if we took a cab?'

Tara looked surprised.

'A cab?'

'Yeah. You know, a yellow cab,' said Melissa. 'I've just always wanted to ride in a proper New York taxi.'

A smile spread across Tara's face.

'I think that can be arranged.'

Soon, we were cruising towards Manhattan in a yellow-and-black taxi, surrounded by white city buses and gigantic, gleaming trucks. Brian was in the front, chatting to the driver, and I was sitting in the back, flanked by Melissa and her mum. Melissa was giving us a running commentary as we travelled.

'Oh my gosh, look at that billboard! . . . Wow, a Taco Bell! . . . Hey, Charlie! A fire hydrant!'

'So listen,' said the cab driver, over his shoulder, 'it's quicker if I take you through the midtown tunnel, but I figured you might get a kick outta the Brooklyn Bridge instead? You can see the Statue from there.'

'You, sir,' replied Melissa, 'are my new favourite person. Drive on!'

Eventually, we joined the mighty metal structure of the Brooklyn Bridge, and as we passed over the East River, downtown Manhattan spread out before us in the coppery evening sun. Reddish-brown apartment blocks, distant blue skyscrapers, and in the centre of it all, the Empire State Building, reaching for the clouds with its distinctive silver spike.

'There she is,' said the driver, gesturing to the left, out of his window. 'The Statue of Liberty.'

Melissa peered out through the metal girders.

'It's very small, isn't it?'

Rosie batted her on the leg. 'Darling, it's quite far away, you know.'

'Thanks, Mother dear, but I do understand perspective.' She shrugged. 'It's just smaller than I expected.'

As I stared at the iconic landmark, small but striking in the distance, an unsettling realisation passed over me. This was the last country my mother ever visited. Maybe she'd crossed this bridge when she arrived too, full of hope and excitement, a red-hot fire in her belly. Her band, Little Boy Blue, were on the verge of their big break, and they'd just landed in the spiritual home of rock 'n' roll.

Little did she know that she would never come home again.

'This is Manhattan,' said the driver, once we'd left the bridge and joined the central island. 'Looks just like the movies, right? Up in front, that's City Hall . . . you got the NYPD behind us on the right . . . and across there, that's Broadway. Y'know, from the song.'

'You don't charge extra for the sightseeing, do you?' joked Brian, from the passenger seat. The driver laughed a rugged laugh.

'Not for the British, pal . . .'

We joined Sixth Avenue and drove north, past banks and coffee houses, diners and pizza parlours. There were American flags everywhere, and men in grubby aprons were selling hot dogs on street corners, plumes of steam

128

rising from their metal carts. After about fifteen minutes, the driver pulled up outside a smart-looking building with black awnings above its windows, beautifully manicured plants on the street outside and one of those classic New York entrances with the canopy stretching out across the sidewalk. He pointed through the windshield.

'Here you go. Home sweet home.'

'That's our hotel?' said Melissa, pressing her nose up against the window. 'You have GOT to be kidding.'

The lobby of the Eagle 519 Hotel was like nothing I'd ever seen before. With its high, ornate ceilings, velvet furniture and blue neon strip-lighting, it looked like a cross between a stately home and a luxury nightclub. Ahead of us, a row of twin marble pillars led away towards an enormous roaring fire, where groups of bearded hipsters sat around low tables, sipping cocktails and chatting over chillwave beats. To our left, a grand, sweeping staircase curled upwards into the building, while to our right, three sharply dressed clerks – all of whom looked like they could be models – stood behind a shining black reception desk.

One of them gave us a playful smile.

'Is this your first time at Eagle 519?' she asked. Melissa looked around, then leaned on the counter.

'Mate, this is my first time outside a Holiday Inn. You have NO IDEA how happy I am right now . . .'

After we'd checked in and our luggage was spirited away, Melissa and I parted company with Rosie and Brian and headed to our room on the fourteenth floor. We were drowsy after the flight, but Tara had recommended we order in room service and try to stay up for a few hours if we could, so the jetlag didn't wake us up at a crazy hour in the morning.

All of which was how I ended up slumped in a wingback armchair, watching Melissa bounce up and down on her bed, dressed in an Eagle 519 bathrobe, reading the hotel menu at me.

'Oooh . . . Korean beef tacos . . . caviar! What even is caviar? Fish eyes, right? . . . Uhm, lemongrass jiaozi? Sounds rancid . . . Wait, maybe there's a kid's menu . . . here we go! PB&J double-decker sandwich. Hello, sailor.'

I was distracted. I didn't know how Gabe was feeling about me, or his father, or being here in the States, and I had no clue when I was going to find out. I felt guilty for not being all giddy like Melissa – this was, after all, the most incredible thing that had ever happened to either of us – but the excitement I'd felt that morning, before I'd left the house, had soured on the flight over. Was Gabriel deliberately ignoring me? How long would it be before we had a chance to talk?

'Wait!'

Melissa had stopped bouncing and was pointing at our giant plasma screen television. I'd been flicking through Apple TV, scrolling aimlessly through her YouTube feed.

'Look. There's a story about F&L landing in New York.'

I wrinkled my brow.

'Do we really need to watch that? I mean, we were literally there.'

Melissa dropped down on to the end of the bed and puffed her cheeks out.

'I know, but Tara did say we have to stay up, *for our own good*, so . . . you know.'

A cheeky little smile crept on to her face, and I found myself smiling back. Picking up a scatter cushion from a nearby chair, I tossed it at her and clicked 'Play' on the video. Soon, a harsh New York accent was wafting out through the speakers.

'Whaddup, YouTube.'

The video had been shot in a very pink, very brightly lit studio. The neon sign on the back wall read *Miss Cheef > At Your Service*, and in the foreground, a girl in dark glasses and a pink suit jacket was sitting on a throne.

'Miss Cheef, at yo' service.' A short, brassy fanfare played, and she clapped her hands together. 'Now . . . who's in town tonight, kids? I'll tell ya: FIRE. AND. LIGHTS.'

A Union Jack materialised in one corner of the screen, and a photograph of Fire&Lights in the other.

'These British boys are my one true love, *for realz*, but this whole beef between Ols and Gabe is freaking me out, y'know? I mean, they're fighting each other, they're fighting other people, my gorgeous Gabe gets paparazzied beating the crap outta some random dude in a parking lot . . .' She leaned forward, raising her shades. 'I love the guy but, uh . . . turns out you really don't want to rub him up the wrong way.' She winked, and dropped her glasses again. 'Not like that, you filthy animals.'

I chewed the inside of my cheek, anger rising inside me. I hated the way everyone was painting Gabriel as some kind of violent bully.

'Anyways, y'all know I have tickets for the show at Madison Square Garden, and I am made up like it's Christmas freakin' DAY . . . but here's the thing. With Olly gone, will my boys still have the magic?' A slideshow of old Fire&Lights pictures began to play onscreen: Olly and Gabe singing into the same microphone; Aiden holding his guitar aloft; Yuki pointing at the fans and grinning. 'There are some *crazy* divides in the fandom right now, and with Olly's single dropping on the same day as the new F&L record, things gon' get ugly, *trust* me.' The photographs faded away and, back in the studio, Miss Cheef was on the edge of her seat. 'So whose side are you on, people? Team Olly, or Team Gabe? Hit me uuuuuup in the comments, I wanna hear from ya. And *theories, please*, about hashtag Yuken: I say those two would be cute as PIGLETS together. Ooh, and finally –' she wagged a finger at the camera – 'don't forget to tune into *Good Day USA* in the morning for the band's *first-ever* live appearance without man of my dreams, Olly Samson. It . . . is . . . crunch time.' She blew a kiss and settled back into her throne. 'Later, haters.'

Staring at the screen, I turned her words over and over in my mind. *With Olly gone, will my boys still have the magic?*

I dropped my head back in the chair, pulled my knees up to my chest and closed my eyes. Either way, in less than twelve hours, we'd all find out.

I was jolted from sleep by a knock at the door.

'Room service.'

I shook my head, my brain heavy with jetlag. Across the room, Melissa groaned and rolled over.

'What time is it?' she said, her voice muffled, most of her head still hidden beneath the covers.

'It's . . . um . . .' I tried to focus on my phone. 'I think it's breakfast time?'

'Ugh.' Melissa sat up, rubbing her eyes. Her hair was sticking out at seven angles. 'I feel like a cow slept on my face. Jetlag sucks.'

Another polite knock at the door.

'Room service!'

'One sec,' I mumbled, dragging my sluggish body out of bed and padding to the door. When I opened it, a waiter was standing there behind a gleaming metal trolley.

'Morning,' he said perkily. 'Can I come in?'

I moved out of the way.

'Um, yep. Sure . . .'

He pushed the trolley inside the room. Four large, domed lids were sitting on top.

'Breakfast for you, ladies.'

I folded my arms across my chest, and yawned.

'But . . . we didn't order breakfast.'

'Good point,' said the waiter, with a smile. 'This is a gift.' He pulled a receipt from his pocket and checked the details. 'From a Mr Harrison and a Mr Roberts.'

Melissa sat straight up in bed.

'Holy guacamole!'

The waiter lifted off the lids, two at a time, to reveal tall glasses of fruit juice, several piles of sumptuous-looking food and two heart attack-inducing milkshakes.

'No avocado, I'm afraid.' He smirked at his joke. 'But you do have just about everything else: fresh mango juice, chai-spiced granola, pancakes with melted marshmallows, chocolate croissants, Belgian cinnamon waffles and . . . wait for it . . . two vanilla mousse, caramel, popcorn and chocolate fudge Nutella freakshakes.' He winked at us. 'Enjoy!'

With that, he tucked one hand behind his back and walked out of the room, closing the door softly behind him. For a moment, Melissa and I just stared, stunned, at our breakfast bounty. Then she leapt off her bed and scurried over to it.

'There's a note!' she said, unfolding a small piece of paper. ' *"This is just a little pick-me-up to kick jetlag's ass.*

New York breakfast, Fire&Lights-style. See you in a bit!! Yuki & Aid".' She pointed at the piece of paper, her mouth agape. 'And they put *seven kisses* at the end!'

Melissa picked up a croissant and took a gigantic bite, sending a puff of icing sugar into the air.

'I can't believe this is my life,' she said, grinning, a smudge of chocolate smeared across her chin.

Good Day USA was the biggest breakfast show in America. According to Barry, it was watched by over four-and-a-half million people, and it had the power to make or break the entire tour. Which made waiting for the interview to begin all the more painful.

Melissa and I were standing just off-set, watching as final preparations were made for the live stream. The *Good Day USA* studio was mostly glass and chrome, and looked out over the flickering billboards of Times Square, which twinkled and throbbed in the background. The boys were sitting on high stools, with the presenter – a tall, blonde lady in a bright red pencil skirt – standing next to them, having her hair touched up by a make-up artist.

'OK, everyone. Positions, please. We're on in thirty seconds.'

Technicians rushed to their places, cameras swooped down from above and, as if by magic, the presenter turned on a winning smile.

'Good Day, USA!' she announced cheerily, as the credit music faded away. 'I'm Tiffany Childs, and, boy, do we have a treat for you this morning. The amazing, the always charming, UK boy-band sensation, Fire&Lights!'

The camera swept across the four bandmates, while a thumping blast of 'Dance With You' played in the background. The boys were actually looking pretty sharp, which was impressive since they must have been as jetlagged as we were. I couldn't help but notice, though, that Gabriel and Jake had been positioned at opposite ends of the line.

'So, Aiden, tell me,' began Tiffany, moving to his side, 'what's it like to be back in America?'

Aiden beamed.

'Ah, man, we love it here. Best country in the world.' He inclined his head. 'Apart from Ireland, obviously.'

Tiffany laughed, but it turned into a frown.

'You're not quite the same band you were the last time you hit American shores, though. How does that feel?'

'It's a bit strange, like,' said Aiden, with a shrug, 'but you have to move on. And we're dead excited to be here. We just can't wait to get onstage and see the fans.'

'Speaking of the fans,' said Tiffany, with a wry smile, 'there's been all kinds of web chatter these past few days about this "Yuken" hashtag.' A faint panic flashed across Aiden's face. 'Let me see if I understand this correctly: the term is "shipping", right? And there's a whole bunch of fans out there who claim that you and Yuki are—'

'He's very shy,' interrupted Yuki, waving a splayed hand in the air. 'We have been on *one* date, yes – he took me out for grilled chicken – and I ate way too much peri peri sauce and disgraced myself. And, well . . . let's just say I am no longer allowed within twenty-five metres of Hammersmith Nando's.'

There was a smattering of sniggers from behind the cameras, and even Aiden allowed himself a little smile.

'There you have it,' replied Tiffany, amused. 'Straight from the horse's mouth.' She turned her attention to Jake. 'Now, Jake. You're the new kid on the block, if you'll pardon the boy-band pun.' ('Nice,' said Yuki, under his breath.) 'What's it like stepping into the shoes of Olly Samson?'

'Not easy, to be honest,' replied Jake, rubbing his neck. 'You know, Olly and I were really close during *Make Or Break*, and I respect him so much as an artist, but I don't see it as my role to replace him. You can't replace talent like that. All I can do is try my best for the fans, and see how it goes.'

'And what about you, Gabe?' Tiffany was standing at Gabriel's side now. I held my breath, hoping she wouldn't ask him anything too probing. 'You've had a tough time recently, with the press on your back. What's that been like?'

Gabe gave her his most dashing smile.

'It's been a lot of fun.'

'You guys and your British humour,' she replied, pointing at him. 'But in all honesty, doesn't it get to you?'

Gabriel shrugged it off.

'That stuff on the gossip sites, none of it matters. All that matters is the fans. We wouldn't be here without them.'

'Well, you certainly have a ton of fans here in the States, and I'll bet most of them are tuning in right now.' (Scattered whoops from off-camera.) 'Do you have a message for them?'

Yuki looked left and right, then lifted a finger.

'Yeah, I do.' On the monitor, the camera zoomed in on his face. 'You people have this thing out here called "Cheez Whiz", and it's yellow and gooey, and I do not understand what it is but, darn-tooting, I LIKE IT.'

Tiffany fought a grin.

'That's cute, Yuki, but I was thinking more along the lines of, y'know, rumours have been flying since Olly left, and I know the fans are anxious to hear you're not going anywhere . . . so what do you say to those people who claim it's all over for Fire&Lights?'

There was a pause. Aiden glanced down the line at Gabriel, whose mouth was tightly closed, and I dug my nails into my palms, willing one of them to speak. Silence wouldn't be a good look right now.

Then, just as it seemed like no one was going to answer, Yuki spoke up.

'Can I ask you a question, Tiff? Can I call you Tiff?'

She smiled at him, all teeth.

'Sure.'

'That window behind you . . . does it open?'

'The window?'

Yuki nodded. 'Uh-huh.'

'I believe it does.'

'Could we open it up?' asked Yuki, adjusting the collar of his shirt. 'I feel like some fresh air.'

A floor tech appeared in the background and set about unscrewing the fastening. I watched Yuki, who was waiting patiently on his stool, and my forehead sunk into a frown. Where was he going with this?

Tiffany addressed the camera.

'You know, I think this might be a first on *Good Da*—'

She trailed off as the floor tech swung open the window and the most almighty roar I had ever heard spilled upwards from the streets outside. The fans were screaming, shouting, hollering at the tops of their voices, and it felt as if Times Square might come apart at its foundations, as if New York itself might split in half.

With a smile, and a glint in his eye, Yuki turned back to Tiffany and said: 'Does that sound over to you?'

When the interview was finished, the programme went to a commercial break and the stage crew readied the band for their performance. They stood in a line, each holding a microphone, quietly warming up their voices. Just like in the interview, Gabriel and Jake had been positioned at opposite ends.

'So how are we feeling, lads?'

Barry was striding along the line, his arms spread wide. He clapped his hands.

'Have you got this?'

They all nodded silently. Barry leaned forward.

'I said . . . have you got this?'

'We've got it,' confirmed Aiden, giving him a thumbs-up.

Barry glanced over his shoulder, and lowered his voice.

'I mean, that interview could've easily gone south, but you totally smashed it out the park. The window trick, Yuki? Solid play, kid. Solid play.'

'Thanks, boss. Do I get a special treat?'

'You're not a dog, Harrison.'

'Are you guys good to go?' asked one of the technicians, appearing next to Barry. The boys all nodded again, and the tech turned round and made a gesture at the cameraman.

'Jake.' Barry clamped a hand on Jake's shoulder. 'This is where it all starts for you. You ready?'

Jake shifted his jaw from side to side, determination in his eyes.

'As I'll ever be.'

'OK, people. Sixty seconds until we're live. Mr King, can we have you back behind the cameras, please?'

Barry walked backwards off the set, pointing at the boys with both hands. Gabriel ran a hand through his hair. Aiden drew in a deep breath.

I looked at Melissa, who was standing next to me, chewing on her sleeve. I was suddenly aware of the blood pumping furiously through my veins.

If they screwed this up, the entire country would see it happen.

12

'Now, in a world exclusive – the first time ever with their new line-up, singing their upcoming single "This American Girl" – the extraordinary Fire . . . and . . . Lights!'

The studio went dark for a few beats, and then fading slowly up, as if approaching from the distance, came an insistent, club-style beat. Red lights began to sweep across the stage, pulsing and throbbing, and then – *boom* – an explosion of white light, and a lively, sweeping synth riff bounced around from floor to ceiling, lasers firing. It was catchy, instantly infectious, and straight away, you were transported to a nightclub dance floor.

Stepping forward, Jake sang the opening lines.

> *She told me, "Welcome to New York,*
> *Hey, baby, welcome to New York City,"*

Spinning his microphone deftly, Yuki picked up the thread.

"You won't get tired of this town
We never sleep and the lights are so pretty"

As Aiden took his turn on lead vocals, I began to wonder about the 'American Girl' from the title. Who was she? When had Gabriel met her? I knew that he'd written the song in the last couple of months, so was she a new friend, or . . . something more?

Midnight strikes and we cruise on the avenue
2 a.m., yeah, we'll dance in the dark
NYC, baby, you're gonna make me a star

It was possible, I supposed, that Gabriel had made her up, but that wasn't really his style. His songs were normally *about* something. Something real.

At that moment, I was pulled from my thoughts by the sight of Gabriel himself, arriving at Jake's side, microphone at the ready. The song crashed into the chorus, and they sang it together.

We'll hit the city tonight, like we're dynamite
We're young and free and we've got money to burn
You'll see her name up in bright lights, she's rocking my
    world
This American girl

144

I watched them, transfixed, combing over the lyrics in my mind. *She's rocking my world.* Had Gabriel been seeing someone all this time? Was he meeting up with her out here?

Could that be the real reason he'd been avoiding me?

> *She said, "Now, tell me what you want*
> *Yeah, baby, everything you desire*
> *You're gonna find it in New York*
> *Give me a kiss and we'll light that fire"*

While Yuki and Aiden sang the second verse, I stepped backwards and leaned against the wall, taking long, slow breaths. I had to nip this in the bud. I'd spent so much of the past year fretting over what Gabriel's songs really meant, and it had never ended well.

> *Midnight strikes and we cruise on the avenue*
> *2 a.m., yeah, we'll dance in the dark*
> *NYC, baby, you're gonna make me a star*

As the song exploded into the chorus again, I tried to empty my mind and focus on the action in front of me. Jake and Gabriel were back at the front of the stage, singing in harmony. Their necks were straining as they hit the high notes, and their eyes were locked, like two wild animals in a stand-off. It almost reminded me of the way Olly and Gabriel used to look at each other onstage, and I suddenly wondered whether this had been Barry's plan all along. He needed some heat in the band, some friction, and where better to get that than between someone who was once thrown out of the band, and the star who had taken his place?

As the track barrelled on, the strobes shimmered and the bass drum thundered, I took a step backwards and watched the action unfold through a nearby camera. It all looked amazing on the small screen, and, no doubt, in the homes of a million Americans, it seemed like Fire&Lights were back with a vengeance. But standing there on the sidelines, I felt weirdly hollow. It just wasn't the same as before. Maybe the boys were tired, or maybe this was how performances in sterile television studios always felt, but as the song drew to a close, I couldn't ignore the feeling in my gut. It had left me cold.

'Wow! Fire&Lights, ladies and gentlemen . . .' As the music faded out, Tiffany strutted back on-set, applauding the boys. 'I feel like I'm going to have that tune stuck in my head for days!'

She turned to the camera.

'As for you guys at home, "This American Girl" will be released on Friday the first of August, the very same day that ex-F&L superstar Olly Samson drops his debut single. So stay tuned for that, America. I sense a battle for number one coming on!' She clasped her hands together.

'We'll see you back here in ten minutes, right after the news and weather.'

Within seconds, the bustle of the studio had started up again. Furniture was repositioned, lights were rotated, technicians stepped over cables and spoke into walkie-talkies. Remembering that Barry had asked me to take some backstage pictures of the band before they headed across town for more interviews, I pulled my camera from its case.

'They smashed it, CB!' exclaimed Melissa, watching the boys file off the set. 'And that song is catchy as hell.'

She hummed the riff to 'This American Girl' while I fiddled with the settings on my camera. I lifted it up and peered through the lens.

'Didn't you think there was, I don't know ... something a bit "off" about it?'

After 'Wild Inside', and the other tracks on *Songs About Us*, the lyrics in the new single felt quite throwaway to me. But that wasn't the real reason they were bugging me.

'Are you speaking ill of Fire&Lights?' said Melissa, stepping in front of me so her face filled the viewfinder. I laughed, and lowered the camera.

'No, I'm not. I just mean, the lyrics. They seemed kind of ...'

She raised an eyebrow.

'Charlie, you are seriously harshing my mellow here.'

'Look, you know their music better than anyone, and the lyrics on the last EP, they had real depth. Right? But this song, it's like . . . it's . . .'

It was no use. Even if I *was* prepared to admit what was really bothering me, Melissa wouldn't have the answer. She didn't know, any better than I did, who the American girl in the song was. Or why Gabriel was falling for her.

'Hey, aren't you Charlie Bloom?'

I turned to find a tall, skinny Puerto-Rican boy standing next to me. He was maybe seventeen or eighteen years old, with glowing skin and lively black hair that stood up off his forehead in a fifties-style quiff. He had a Fire&Lights laminate around his neck.

'Uh, yeah. I am.' I lifted my camera off my shoulders. 'Hi.'

'I'm Leo,' he said, unleashing a smile that would have tamed lions. His eyes sparkled. 'I was hoping I'd get to meet you.'

He seemed very young to be on the F&L management team. I pointed at his laminate.

'You work for the band?'

'Well, kinda. Work *experience*. I run to Starbucks and pick up people's dry cleaning.' He shrugged it off. 'But, listen, I wanted to say that your photos are incredible. Like, it's *crazy* you're only sixteen and you're already photographing a famous boy band. You're basically one of my heroes.'

I turned off my camera.

'Wow. Thanks.'

'Hi,' said Melissa, in a smaller-than-normal voice. 'I'm Melissa.'

'Do you take photos too?' asked Leo. She went pink.

'Um, n-no ... I'm just ... well, I'm not really anything.'

Leo looked a little stumped by this. There was an awkward pause, and Melissa winced at herself.

'Anyway,' said Leo, turning back to me, 'I have to go pick up brunch for everyone now, so I shouldn't stop, but ... I just wanted to say hi.'

'Well, hi,' I said, nodding. 'Nice to meet you.'

'Catch you guys later.' He smiled again, rubbed the back of his head and walked off across the studio. I turned my camera back on and looped the strap over my neck.

'He seemed nice.'

Melissa didn't reply. I nudged her foot with mine.

'Are you all right?' I asked. She was watching Leo walk away, her eyes unblinking.

'His skin,' she said, transfixed. 'It was like ... poetry.'

'Um, say what?'

She gulped. 'I think I'm in love.'

Smiling to myself, I clicked through to the gallery on my Canon and deleted a couple of old photographs.

'Maybe you should ask him out, then.'

'Are you out of your freaking tree?'

I looked up. Melissa was glaring at me.

'Huh?'

She pointed back over her shoulder.

'Charlie, he couldn't take his eyes off you.'

'What are you talking about?'

She dropped to a whisper.

'Seriously, he may as well have opened his mouth and let a giant tongue roll out across the floor.'

'I think you're exaggerating a bit there.'

She folded her arms.

'Nuh-uh. I was watching him the whole time. Plus, you heard what he said: you're one of his "heroes". As far as he's concerned, I'm just the sidekick. Period.'

I laughed again, but Melissa's cheeks had gone blotchy.

'Come on, Mel. It's not like that.'

'It's just . . .' She jabbed her toe into the ground. 'It's not fair. You've got, like, a bajillion popstars in love with you. You're fully booked. But me, I have a vacancy. A Leo-shaped vacancy.' She swallowed. 'And he barely even noticed I exist.'

I felt an ache behind my ribs, and reached over to squeeze her hand. In the distance, I noticed Leo staring at me from across the room. He smiled, and I quickly broke eye contact.

'Word up, my wicked peeps!'

Yuki was approaching from across the studio, carrying two cans of Coke. 'I thought you might fancy a beverage.'

'Thanks, Yuk,' I said, as he handed the drinks over. 'How're the guys doing? Up for some photos?'

'Should be. Although it's *possible* Aiden's taking a nap . . .'

Melissa popped her can open and took a sip.

'Great show, by the way.'

'Ah, thanks, Mellotron. Bazza reckons it'll be a hit on the club scene, which is good because I've always wanted to be one of those guys who wears a fur coat and hangs out in nightclubs drinking champagne out of crystal skulls.' He clicked his fingers. 'Hey, have you kids heard what we're doing tomorrow?'

I thought back to the schedule that Tara had given me on the flight over.

'Filming a music video, right?'

Yuki nodded, a grin spreading across his face.

'Yeah, but have you heard *where* we're filming it?'

I stuck out my bottom lip, and shook my head.

'Ah, man, buckle up!' He slung an arm around each of our necks. 'This is going to be the best . . . day . . . *ever.*'

13

The sign above our heads was green and yellow, surrounded by flashing bulbs and blinking television screens, and at least five metres wide. Cartoon-style speakers blasted out a soundtrack of manic, thrashy rock music, artfully mixed with the sound of people whooping and screaming, and underneath, standing in a row on the pink asphalt, Melissa, Rosie, Brian and I gazed upwards in astonishment, the red-hot sun prickling our pale English faces.

WELCOME TO THUNDERLAND
The biggest, baddest theme park on the East Coast!

'I'm not sure I'm cut out for this,' said Rosie, as we passed through the park barriers.

'Come on, Ma,' said Melissa, dragging her mum by the arm. 'All you've done since we've arrived is eat fancy food and lie around with hot rocks on your back.'

'It was nice while it lasted,' replied Rosie, rolling her eyes. 'Uh . . . is that a praying mantis?'

To our right, in front of a hot-dog stand, a park employee dressed in a praying mantis costume was dancing a jig. Melissa waved, and it waved back, its limbs wiggling.

'Thing is, Mum, you said yourself that we should be taking lots of day trips to experience local culture, and *this*' – Melissa gestured around at the blinking, twinkling, blaring fibreglass paradise spreading out before us – 'is local culture.'

'Well, really I meant the Guggenheim or the Museum of Modern Art, not . . .' Rosie squinted at the entrance to a nearby ride. '"Rickshaw Rick's Chinatown Death Race".'

Brian's eyes expanded.

'That looks terrifying.'

'Morning, Morrises.' Barry King was strolling towards us, designer shades glinting in the sun. 'Glad you could join us. Roller coaster fans?'

'Not . . . entirely,' replied Rosie diplomatically.

'Christ, me neither. Absolute death traps. But the kids love it, for some reason . . .'

Over Barry's shoulder, something caught my eye. It was Leo, the boy from yesterday, walking through the park behind a group of management types, holding a cardboard tray of steaming coffee cups. He lifted his free hand to wave at me, and I gave him a small wave back. Thankfully, Melissa didn't notice, but I still felt my muscles tighten. I'd played it down in front of her, but secretly I was really hoping she was wrong about him. A random crush was the last thing I needed right now.

'. . . About half the rides are open,' Barry was saying, as I tuned back in, 'so the girls are welcome to have a crack if that floats their boat. Fans'll be rocking up in about an hour, and then we'll get filming—'

'Avast, ye hornswaggling blaggards!'

We all turned to find Yuki sauntering across the park, wearing a leather jerkin, an eye patch and a gigantic hat with ginger ringlets dangling from it. He waved a plastic scimitar at us.

'Hands off me booty, Jolly Rogers! To the poop deck!'

Barry looked him up and down.

'Harrison, you prize turnip.'

'Actually, it's "Captain Merrywhiskers, Terror of the Northern Seas" to you landlubbers.'

Barry eyed him suspiciously.

'Where'd you get that costume?'

'The giant squid over there lent it to me,' said Yuki, pointing over his shoulder at a park employee wearing an octopus costume. 'Nice bloke. Lovely tentacles.'

Rosie scratched her head.

'What exactly is the theme of this theme park?' she asked. Yuki adjusted the angle of his hat with the tip of his sword.

'No one knows for sure, but if I were to take a guess, it would be: "some dude got high and built a theme park".'

'Whatever it is,' said Barry, tapping his expensive-looking watch, 'I need you looking like a normal person again by eleven-thirty.' He frowned. 'Well, as close to normal as you can muster. And, Rosie, Brian? If you need a break from these imbeciles, there's a café about a hundred metres that way. Turn right at the singing cheeseburgers, and you can't miss it.'

With that, Barry strode away, heading in the direction of a nearby camera crew. On the way, he passed Aiden and Jake, who were walking towards us with sticks of candy floss in one hand and huge, luminous slushies in the other. As they arrived behind Yuki, Jake jabbed an elbow in his ribs.

'I think Jack Sparrow might need his wedding outfit back,' Jake said, taking a slurp of his drink. He smiled around the straw, and Yuki fake-scowled at him.

'Hey, hey. HEY. Woodrow. Jealousy doth not become you.'

'So who's coming to the Satanic Realm?' asked Aiden, turning to us. 'Apparently, Beelzebub is the world's fastest zero-gravity roller coaster.'

'It's true,' confirmed Jake. 'Be very afraid.'

'Me!' said Melissa, her hand shooting up in the air. 'But Charlie has to come too, because I'm scared.'

'I think your father and I might take a wander,' said Rosie, opening up her Thunderland map. 'I'm not entirely sure I fancy a roller coaster named after Satan. Stay safe, everyone!'

After Rosie had led Brian away, bound for the singing cheeseburgers, the rest of us headed for the Satanic Realm on the opposite side of the park. With the three bandmates taking the lead, I hung back and snapped some photographs, catching them walking in a row. It was a stunning day, the sun hanging high and bright above the park, and the sky was as blue as I'd ever seen it.

As I reviewed the shots on my camera screen, though, I couldn't help but think of the first time I had met the band, when I'd taken pictures of them getting their make-up done at Reading Arena. How there'd been an empty chair where Gabriel should have been, and how I'd discovered, much later, that he suffered from stage fright, and needed to be alone before a performance. Was that why he was lying low today? Was he nervous about the video shoot? Or was he simply avoiding everyone else because, like me, no matter where he went or what he did, he couldn't escape the memory of his father's suicide note?

We didn't see him at all that morning. We rode the zero-gravity roller coaster, and a runaway train, and shot lasers at robots in a futuristic haunted house, and laughed until our faces ached. But through it all, Gabriel never left my thoughts. During my exams, I'd told him that I needed space, and I did. But the time for us to try and work through this on our own was over. I had to break the silence, before it broke us.

As the morning drew to a close, we were all called to the park's signature ride, Thunder Five Thousand, where the video for 'This American Girl' was being filmed. The boys were sent into a nearby cabin for hair and make-up, and Melissa and I joined the large crowd of fans – competition winners, Tara explained – who had gathered to be part of the video. Some would get the chance to ride with the band on the roller coaster, while the rest of us would stand underneath, waving and dancing as they passed.

There were cameras dotted all around the area, technicians taping cables and lighting operators adjusting their lamps. Barry had hired a compere to warm up the crowd, and he was onstage, vamping, while the band got ready to emerge.

'Are you ready . . . for the biggest boy band . . . on planet earth??'

He threw his arms in the air, and the fans cheered. He shook his head.

'Ooh, I don't know, guys. I don't see the boys coming out unless you *really* mean it, y'know what I'm saying?' More whoops and hollering. 'I said . . . are you READYYYYY . . . for FIRE AND LIGHTS?'

Total pandemonium followed, and to the opening strains of 'This American Girl', Aiden, Yuki, Gabriel and Jake filed out on to the stage, holding microphones and waving. Melissa and I had been given prime positions in the front row, and as I stood there, looking up at the stage, a thrill rippled through me. This was how it felt to be a fan at a Fire&Lights show.

'Hey, guys, how're you all doing?' called Aiden, grinning. 'Man, we are super excited to be here!'

Another wave of cheering surged through the crowd, and shouts of, 'We love you, Aid!' and, 'Marry me, Aiden!' filled the air. I could feel warm bodies pressing up against my back.

Jake lifted his mic.

'Hey, I'm Jake! I know I'm new to some of you, but I couldn't be more thrilled to be here in the States. Are you guys ready to shoot a music video, or what . . . ?!'

I looked around, getting jostled from every side, noise crackling in my ears. The fans were taking photos on their phones, waving posters and banners and jumping up and down. They held on to each other, laughing and screaming, some of them sobbing, reaching out for the boys whenever they came close.

All of them, that is, but one.

'Yo, FireLighters!' Yuki had taken the spotlight. 'How are we enjoying Thunderland? Make some noise for the giant squid, y'all!'

One particular girl stuck out among the frenzied crowds. She was standing a few metres away from me, by the metal barriers, and had long, perfectly straight, white hair. Shocking white, almost as if it had been dyed. She seemed a little older than the average Fire&Lights fan – possibly in her mid-twenties – and was being ignored by the people around her. In fact, the longer I watched, the more it became obvious that she was entirely on her own.

And she was staring right at Gabriel.

'What's your name?' On the far corner of the stage, Yuki had knelt down and was addressing a fan in the front row. 'What's that? Your name's London? Dude, stop it, you're making me homesick . . .'

It wasn't unusual for fans to be staring at Gabriel, but this was different. She didn't seem excitable, or starstruck, or overcome with emotion. She was just staring at him, totally silent and standing stock-still, as if in a trance.

'So, apparently . . .' Gabriel was talking now, and as he spoke, the girl mumbled under her breath, like she was trying to match his words. 'Apparently, according to the guy talking in my ear, it's time for us to hit Thunder Five Thousand.' The crowd clapped and whistled. 'Are you ready to roll, America?'

The cheering reached fever pitch, and the boys were guided off the stage and led towards the roller coaster entrance. With the help of a team of security guards, Tara split the fans into groups, sending some to ride the coaster and others, like us, to line the perimeter fences. Soon, Thunder Five Thousand was rushing around the track – 'This American Girl' blasting out all around – with Yuki, Aiden, Gabriel and Jake sitting in the front row, miming the lyrics and laughing their heads off. Even Gabriel, for as long as he was rushing through the air, seemed to forget his demons.

In total, the boys went round four times. By the time they were finished, Aiden looked a bit green, but judging by the crew conversations happening around us, the director was pleased with what they'd got.

Once we were all back by the stage, penned in by the metal barriers, the compere stepped up to the mic.

'OK, folks! That's the main roll shot now, but the crew are keen to grab some bonus footage of you guys all going crazy in the park, so if you make your way in *this* direction . . .'

The security team moved aside one of the barriers and began herding the fans away from Thunder Five Thousand, while Tara, who was standing by the catering table, beckoned us over. As Melissa and I moved against the flow of people, I spotted the white-haired girl again, still alone, floating along with the crowd. She wasn't responding to anyone around her, or scrolling on her phone, or even looking at the rides: she was just drifting. I wasn't quite sure why, but something about her put me on edge.

Ahead of us, on their way back from the coaster, the boys reappeared, their hair tangled and messed up from the ride. They were handed water and towels, and were making their way towards the make-up cabin to freshen up when shouting could be heard from the middle of the crowd.

It got louder, and louder, and louder, and I felt a stirring in the pit of my stomach. Something bad was about to happen.

14

At first, the shouting was indecipherable, and might have been mistaken as general crowd noise. But as the fans began to realise what was happening, their chatter faded away, and one lone voice was left bellowing into the hot, humid air.

My throat went dry.

'We hate you, Gabriel! We *hate* you!'

My first instinct was to locate the white-haired girl, but she'd disappeared, swallowed by the herd. In any case, the sounds that were vaulting through the sky seemed too angry, too vicious, for such a timid-looking person.

'It's all your fault, Gabe. We wish *you'd* quit the band!'

Security guards were searching the heads of the crowd, trying to locate the culprit, pointing at each other and talking into their collars. Then, when a group of fans emerged together from the melee, joined at the hands, it became obvious that the shouter wasn't alone.

'Team Olly!' called one boy.

'You pushed him out!' yelled a girl next to him, rage warping her features. All around, security guards were starting to close in, and I felt a hand on my shoulder. It was Tara. With a jerk of the head, she guided me and Melissa out of harm's way.

'We want Olly back!' shouted the original girl, as she dragged her comrades towards Gabriel. Lightning quick, the band's head bouncer blocked them with his body and signalled to a colleague, who threw an arm around Gabriel and hastily led him away.

'Hey, kid, just calm down,' said the head bouncer, squaring up to the girl. 'You don't want to do this.'

'I do!' she shrieked, tears building in her eyes. 'I hate you, Gabe. I *hate* you!'

The tears cascaded down her face, and as he was hauled away to safety, all Gabe could do was watch, the blood draining from his cheeks.

'You're *selfish*, you only care about yourself!' screamed the girl, her sticky face glowing red with anger. 'You only care abou— Let me go!'

His clothes tangled, hair tousled, Gabriel looked on in horror, the bouncer's meaty arm clamped around his chest. Then, just as he was being bundled back inside the cabin, she unleashed one final, killer blow.

'Why don't you just go back to England and *die?*'

The hotel lift rose smoothly through the building, dreamy electronica drifting out through speakers in the ceiling. Its walls doubled as screens, playing rolling images of constellations, shooting stars and luminous gas clouds. It felt like we were floating through outer space.

'So today was a little intense, huh?'

Tara puffed a ringlet out of her eyes, and Rosie and Brian *mm-hmm*ed in agreement. Melissa and I shared concerned looks.

'Still,' continued Tara, pulling a set of keys from her pocket and jingling them in the air, 'nothing like a good after-party to relieve the tension.'

As the lift sighed to a halt, Tara aimed her keys at the bank of numbers on the wall. We'd stopped at Eagle 519's tenth floor, which, unlike every other floor in the hotel, had a circular lock instead of an illuminated button.

She slid one of the keys into the lock and twisted it. The doors hissed open.

'*Whoa*,' said Melissa, holding both her hands up. 'That is some James Bond business, right there.'

Tara smiled.

'This is a private floor,' she said, gesturing through the open doors. 'And tonight, it's all ours.'

We stepped out into the corridor and were immediately met by a thumping, pulsing club track, mixed with the sound of raised voices and boozy laughter. There were groups of people dotted all the way down the hallway, glugging drinks and knocking back shots; some were from management, some were from the Fire&Lights backing band, but most I didn't recognise. Industry types, maybe, or hangers-on? There were rows of open doors on both sides of us, revealing ever more extraordinary sights as we walked: a gloomy, purple-lit pool room, a long banquet table piled high with exotic fruits and colourful desserts, a raised set of decks with a shades-wearing DJ bopping behind them. Finally, at the end of the hallway, in the largest room, we found a circle of tipsy-looking girls filling up saucer-shaped glasses from a champagne fountain.

'Wow!' exclaimed Rosie, looking back up the hallway, towards the lift. 'What shall we do first?'

Melissa tilted her head.

'We?'

'Oh, your dad and I thought we'd chill with you girls all night, didn't we, Brian?'

Melissa's mouth fell open, but her mum let out a small snicker.

'Gotcha!' said Brian, raising his hand for a high-five. Rosie pushed a palm towards him, but half-missed. 'No, you girls zip off and do your thing . . . but *no mischief, please.*' He pointed at the champagne fountain. 'And stay away from the hard stuff.'

Melissa watched her parents disappear into the room with all the fruit and ice cream, and relaxed her shoulders. Then she sniffed the air, like a small animal.

'I smell hot dogs.' She peered up ahead, where a large set of glass-fronted double-doors led out on to a wide, crowded terrace. In a far corner, a plume of smoke was twisting up into the sky, and a juicy sizzle could be heard above the chatter. 'This way!'

I trailed Melissa outside, surveying the sea of faces. We'd been to Fire&Lights after-parties before, but this one felt different. There were so many people, and I barely recognised any of them. Most of them were older, so they must have been music critics, or from the record label.

Where were the VIP fans?

'Chocks away!'

At the sound of Yuki's voice, we both spun around to find him curled up in a ball and vaulting through the air, plummeting towards the undisturbed surface of a circular swimming pool. He landed with an almighty splash, sending an undulating wave spilling out in all directions.

While he was submerged, I followed the sound of delighted giggling and clinking glasses towards a group of mini-skirted girls standing nearby. The VIP fans.

'Hey, it's Charlie and Mel!' spluttered Yuki, after he'd broken the surface again. He swam to the edge and heaved himself, dripping, on to the poolside. He was wearing sodden jeans and nothing else. 'Fancy a dip? This thing has a *glass bottom.*'

Yuki pointed through the water and we both edged hesitantly towards it. He was right. The bottom of the pool was entirely transparent, and as the water swished, bobbed and eventually calmed, a dizzying view of the Manhattan streets was revealed in front of our eyes.

'Ugh,' said Melissa, almost gagging. 'I can't even look at that. It's giving me the willies.'

She covered her eyes and held her stomach, and I slid an arm around her shoulders.

'I think we'll just grab a hot dog for now,' I said, guiding her away. 'Maybe raincheck the swim?'

'Suit yourself!' said Yuki, flicking a hand through his soaking wet hair. He twisted around. 'Anyone joining me for round two?'

Yuki stood up and fell comically backwards into the pool, and as Melissa and I made our way towards the sizzling barbecue, I could hear several of the fans jumping in after him.

Ten minutes later, Melissa and I were sitting on stools around a silver table, hot dogs and fries steaming in front of us. The food was delicious, but I couldn't finish mine. I just didn't feel that hungry.

'Do you think he's OK?'

Melissa was waving a hand in my face.

'Huh?' I said, distracted.

'Gabriel.' She tossed a fry into her mouth. 'You've been staring at him ever since we got here.'

Melissa was right: I'd barely said a word to her since we'd sat down to eat. Gabriel was sitting on a bench table on the opposite side of the pool, staring into his beer bottle, surrounded by people. They were trying to talk to him, but he wasn't taking it in. He had a hollow look in his eyes.

'Sorry,' I said, picking at my hot-dog bun. 'I'm just really worried. What happened at the park earlier, it was so horrible. And if it keeps on happening—'

'Is this seat taken?'

We both looked up. Jake was standing by our table, holding a bright blue cocktail.

'You want to sit with *us*?' said Melissa. 'That is so cool.'

Jake slid on to the stool next to her.

'Seems to me you guys are an important part of this whole operation, and we've barely had a chance to talk yet. You having fun?'

'Well,' mused Melissa, waving a fry in the air, 'let me see. It's the summer holidays, I'm living in a five-star hotel in New York with my best friend, I get to hang out with Fire&ActualLights every single day and I just spent the last six hours riding roller coasters. So, things have definitely been worse. Chip?'

'Don't mind if I do,' said Jake, taking one.

'But, really, it's Charlie who's the important part of the operation. I just, uh . . . what do I do, exactly?'

Jake glanced over at Rosie and Brian, who were standing a few metres away, leaning on the railings, admiring the view. He lowered his voice.

'I heard you did something pretty epic, which we can't really talk about, but it basically saved the band.' Melissa blushed, and nibbled on a fry. 'So how are you guys finding America?'

'The food is *stupidly* good,' said Melissa, chewing.

'Isn't it?' agreed Jake. 'Yesterday I ate a pastrami sandwich that was bigger than my face.'

I laughed, and Jake took a sip of his cocktail. Then his eyes went wide and he reached into his back pocket.

'Oh my god, I have to show you guys something.' He set down his drink and pulled two tickets from his jeans. 'These are all-access passes for the New York Knicks. *Courtside seats.*'

'Shut up!' said Melissa, her eyes bulging. 'I mean, I don't know much about baseball—'

'Basketball,' corrected Jake, with a laugh.

'Basketball, but still . . . that sounds pretty sweet.'

Jake nodded, looking around.

'I don't want to be uncool or anything, but being in this band is seriously blowing my mind. All the free stuff, the fans, the after-parties . . . there are actual movie stars here, you know.'

'Really?' said Melissa, sitting up. 'Who?'

'Tammie Austin. I saw her by the champagne fountain.'

Tammie Austin. The girl I had met at the Rochester Hotel, while looking like a drowned rat, and falsely accused Gabriel of sleeping with. I took a careful glance over my shoulder, feeling my neck turn red.

'Do you mind if I ask you a question, Jake?' said Melissa, aiming the tiniest glance at me, as if she knew I'd be grateful for a change of subject.

'Go for it.'

She leaned in closer.

'What was it like having to leave Fire&Lights? If that's not, like, the rudest question of all time.'

Jake smiled.

'Hey, not at all. I'd be curious myself. But . . . yeah. It was pretty grim.'

'I always liked you, you know.' Melissa's expression turned stern. 'It was *not cool* when they chucked you out of the band.'

'Ah, thanks,' said Jake, sliding the basketball tickets back into his pocket. 'I appreciate that. And, sure, I know it's just a TV show, and it was nothing personal, but it really hurt. To get so close to your dream, and then have it torn away.'

Melissa flicked at the ring pull on her can of Pepsi. 'That must've sucked.'

'It really did, but' – Jake gestured left and right at the people drinking, dancing and laughing all around us – 'here I am now, on this amazing tour, in the greatest city in the world, and I've been given a second chance. That sort of thing doesn't happen very often.' He took in a lungful of air, then exhaled happily. 'And, who knows, maybe one day, I'll have my own solo career, like Olly.'

Jake's eyes sparkled when he mentioned Olly's name, and for just a second, I really, really missed him. The soft edges of his voice, the curve of his shoulders. Somewhere, in another corner of this gigantic country, he'd be at a party just like this, or onstage at a show, or working on lyrics in his hotel room. Was he lonely, without the boys? Did he miss them at all?

Did he miss me?

'Oh my god.' Melissa was sitting dead straight on her seat, her eyes flicking sideways. 'Don't look now, CB, but he's checking you out again.'

Jake peered past Melissa's shoulder.

'Who is?'

Melissa let out a sigh.

'This guy, Leo, he's one of the runners. He's a super-mega-turbo dreamboat, but he's totally in love with Charlie and, *oh my god, he's coming over*.'

I braved a glance across the terrace and, sure enough, Leo was heading our way. I felt my toes curl inside my shoes.

'Hey, guys!' he said, giving us a wave.

'Hey,' replied Melissa, a little sadly.

'How's it going, Jake?' said Leo, as he arrived at our table. 'We haven't actually met yet, but I'm—'

'The famous Leo,' said Jake, a smile playing on his lips. Leo frowned, confused.

'Thunderland was fun, right?' said Melissa hastily, before things could get weird. 'Did you see all the octopuses? I was, like, dude, talk about your . . . y'know . . . eight-legged creatures.' Her nostrils flared, and I could tell she was panicking. 'Octopuses also have eight brains.'

'I did not know that,' said Leo, flashing her a smile. She virtually melted in her seat.

'So, Charlie.' He turned to me, suddenly looking serious. 'Can we talk a second?'

'Uh, sure,' I said, glancing at Melissa. She had turned beetroot.

Leo nodded towards the hallway. 'In private?'

Moments later, I was standing in the corner of the champagne room with Leo, keeping half an eye on Melissa, through the window. She was sitting at our table, opposite Jake, picking listlessly at her fries.

'The thing is, Charlie . . . ah, man.' Leo ran a hand through his hair, and looked at the floor. 'This is kind of awkward. I think you're really cool. Too cool. In fact, to be honest, I'm kind of intimidated by you, which makes this a whole lot harder to say—'

'I think you might have got the wrong end of the stick, Leo.'

His face dropped.

'Oh. Really?' He rubbed the back of his neck. 'But . . .'

'Things are just *crazy* complicated right now, and—'

'Does Melissa have a boyfriend?'

I stared back at him, my mouth open.

'What?'

'Does she have a boyfriend?' he repeated. When I failed to reply, his face dropped. 'Oh, god. I shouldn't have said that. I am such a *schmuck*.'

A smile broke on to my face.

'No,' I said, shaking my head. 'I'm the schmuck.'

'Huh?'

I waved it away.

'Never mind.' A grin spread across my face. 'So you like Melissa, then? Of course you do. She's insanely lovable.'

'Is she with anyone? Back home, I mean?'

I glanced through the window again. Melissa was teaching Jake how to fold a paper napkin into a swan.

'No, not currently.'

'See, truth is,' continued Leo, 'I've wanted to ask her out since the second we all met the other day, but I'm just too nervous. I can barely say a single word to her. I know it's super lame, but I thought I'd ask you.'

I narrowed my eyes at him.

'What are you, twelve?'

'Yeah, OK, point taken.'

'She doesn't bite, you know.'

'I know, but *look* at her.' Leo gestured through the window. 'She's gorgeous. And she seems real smart too.'

I tucked my hair behind my ears.

173

'Yeah. She is.'

He lifted his shoulders in a slow shrug.

'I really don't want her to think I'm just this dumb American.'

I smiled again.

'I doubt she thinks that.'

'So what do you think I should do?'

'Well, I'm no expert on these things, but how about you go back out there, offer to bring her a second helping of fries, and then . . . just . . . talk to her.'

Leo thought about this.

'Talk to her,' he said, almost to himself. 'Right.'

'I hope you know your linear equations from your algebraic fractions, though.'

His eyes went suddenly wide.

'What?'

'I'm kidding,' I said, and he let out a breath, relieved. 'Now get back in there before some other cute American steals her first.'

Leo clenched his fists, determined.

'Thanks, Charlie. You're the best.'

'Don't mention it.'

He took one final look at Melissa, through the window, and made for the hallway.

'Oh, Leo?' I said, stopping him in his tracks. 'One thing.'

'What's that?'

174

'Melissa is my favourite human being in the entire universe, so if you break her heart, I will be forced to destroy you.'

He smiled, and gave me a nod.

'Understood.'

I watched as Leo walked back out on to the terrace and over to our table. By now, Melissa was alone, slumped among the plates of food, chin on her arms, flicking bits of tissue paper against a ketchup bottle. When Leo appeared and said something to her, she sat up straight away, surprise flashing across her face. Then he sat down opposite her awkwardly, and they started to talk. After a couple of minutes, Leo said something with his head down, and Melissa's eyes shone as bright as headlights.

She nodded enthusiastically, and I felt my chest swell with pride.

For the next hour, the two of them sat across from one another, chatting endlessly and drinking strawberry milkshakes through stripy straws. People buzzed and milled around them, but they barely took their eyes off each other for a second. Melissa's face was stuck in a perma-smile, her cheeks glowing. I wasn't sure if I'd ever seen her so happy.

I passed the time with Yuki and Aiden, listening to Yuki's extensive plans about the underwater theme park he was going to build once he'd made his first billion.

Gabriel, meanwhile, had already gone back to his room, and from the sounds of it, he hadn't opened up to anyone about what had happened at Thunderland.

I unlocked my phone, staring at his name in my message inbox. He needed a friend right now – that much was obvious – so I started several messages, asking how he was, but deleted them all. I just couldn't shake the feeling that I'd waited too long. That now he had his mystery 'American girl', he didn't need me any more.

That maybe he was slipping away from me.

Central Park Lake, New York City. I was sitting in a rowing boat with the Morris family, in the blazing sun, as Melissa tried her hardest not to steer us round and round in circles. It wasn't going especially well.

'I think there's something wrong with the oars, Ma,' she said, wrinkling her nose at them. 'They won't row straight.'

'Funny that, eh?' said Rosie, winking at me. Melissa tutted.

'We should definitely ask for a refund.'

Melissa was sitting in the middle of the boat, with me at one end, finishing off an ice cream, and her parents at the other. Rosie was leaning back against Brian, who was gently stroking her hair, a contented smile on his lips. It was making me wonder what my parents would have been like at their age, if Mum hadn't died so young.

'So what do you girls think of Central Park?' asked Rosie, closing her eyes in the sunshine. 'I realise it might not be quite as exciting as Madcap Larry's Corkscrew Massacre, but still . . . not a bad way to spend an afternoon.'

'It's amazing,' said Melissa, to the sky. 'Everything's amazing. THE WORLD IS AMAZING.'

Unsurprisingly, Melissa was still on a high from her unexpected first date with Leo. Rosie was watching her with fascination.

'You're in an exceedingly good mood today, my love. Any particular reason for that?'

'Um . . . maybe.'

Rosie sat up a little.

'Spill the beans, then.'

Melissa thought for a while, then stopped rowing and put on a solemn face.

'The truth is, Mum and Dad: I have a boyfriend now. I am a girlfriend, and I am in possession of a boyfriend.'

Rosie and Brian buried their smiles.

'His name is Leo,' continued Melissa, very seriously, 'and I want you to know that he's a gentleman. He's tall and lovely and clever and sweet and harbours no nefarious intentions.'

'That's good to hear,' said Rosie, still biting back her smile. 'So what's he like, Charlie? Good enough for our little girl?'

'He'll do,' I said breezily.

'Are you happy, squirt?' asked Brian, with a sniff. 'Because that's all that really matters.'

'Happy?' Melissa dropped the oars, with a clank. 'I'm happier than a sackful of puppies on a trampoline.'

'Well, then,' said Brian, smiling at her. 'Case closed.'

We floated aimlessly around the lake for a while, gazing out at the lush green trees and the opulent buildings of the Upper West Side. It was amazing to me that such a peaceful place could be hidden away at the heart of one of the busiest cities on earth.

Suddenly, Melissa sat bolt upright, rocking the boat.

'Careful,' said Rosie, touching a hand to the side.

'Oops, soz. But look, over there! A pretzel man.' She pointed towards a nearby bridge, where a stubbly man was selling pretzels from a silver cart. 'Can we get some, Dad?'

Brian checked his watch.

'It's nearly dinner time, isn't it?'

'Yeah, exactly,' said Melissa, nodding her head. 'Pretzels will be the perfect palette cleanser for Wendy's.'

Rosie raised a flat hand to shield her eyes from the sun.

'What's Wendy's?'

'It's a traditional American burger joint, Ma. They don't have them anywhere in the UK. It's *local culture*.'

Her mum arched an eyebrow.

'Is it now?'

'Uh-huh. Have you seen the adverts, CB? The burgers are SQUARE.'

I narrowed my eyes at her.

'I really don't think meat should have corners, Mel.'

'Either way,' she said, rowing towards the bridge, 'it don't get more American than pretzels and cheeseburgers, so I say we get our asses to shore . . .'

Eventually, after some hefty wrangling, Melissa made it to the edge of the lake, and she and Brian clambered on to the path and headed for the pretzel cart. Rosie and I stayed in the boat, which was bobbing gently on the surface of the water.

'You OK, chuck?' she said, after a while.

I didn't know what to say. Sometimes, as much as I loved hanging out with the Morrises, it only reminded me of all the things I would never have.

'Mm-hmm.'

'You've been a bit quiet ever since we arrived in the States.' Rosie shifted closer to me, glancing towards the pretzel cart. 'I mean, *everyone's* quiet compared to Melissa, but you know what I mean.'

I attempted a smile, but all I could think about was my mother, and those haunting words in Harry's suicide note.

. . . I never meant to kill her. I never
meant for her to die . . .

'You know you can talk to me about anything, don't you?' said Rosie, and she was right. She had always been there for me, and I really could talk to her about anything.

Except this.

'Change of plans!' Melissa was running back towards us, phone in one hand, bag of pretzels in the other. 'Have you seen the message from Tara?'

I slid my phone from my pocket. There was a text on my lock screen.

Hey, girls! So Barry's flown in the boys' families to hang out with them backstage at MSG. Fancy joining?? Tx

'I've always wanted to meet the Roberts family!' Melissa was saying, as she reached the lake's edge. 'Can we go, Mum?'

'Of course,' said Rosie, standing up cautiously. 'I think we'll leave you to it, though. Give us a chance to have a wander round Greenwich Village . . .'

As Brian held out a hand and helped Rosie and me back on to shore, I tried to ignore the throbbing in my chest. It was all very well that Barry was flying in the boys' families, but he seemed have ignored one important fact. Not all of them had families to fly in.

15

'Oh. Oh dear. That is not good.'

Melissa was scrolling frantically on her phone as we followed Tara through the back entrance of Madison Square Garden. I glanced around at the vast, echoey space, taking in the exposed grey piping, the forklift trucks and the massive fluorescent floodlights. It always amazed me how unglamorous the back entrances to concert venues were: like aircraft hangars, all concrete walls and industrial debris

'Charlie, you need to see this.' Melissa looked up from her phone. Her face was tight with concern.

'What is it?'

She passed it to me and, as I read the headline on the screen, my stomach dropped.

ANGRY FANS HURL ABUSE AT GABRIEL WEST
Is the boy-band superstar about to
lose his teen idol crown?

My eyebrows scrunched together. That story shouldn't have got out. Barry had even said afterwards, at the party, how relieved he was that there hadn't been any paparazzi presence at Thunderland. But it appeared that someone had been watching, and as I thumbed down the page, it became clear who it was.

Story by P. Morgan

Paul Morgan: the tabloid reporter who had been trailing Gabriel for months. The man who had followed us to the cliffside in Devon and papped us from his car. Who had manoeuvred Gabriel into a fist-fight outside the StarBright Arena, then 'exposed' him in the media as a violent thug. He was closing in on us, just as he had warned us he would. *I know things. I'm working things out. I see you,* he'd said. Was he in America now? Was he tracking Gabriel's every move?

Yesterday afternoon, while recording the music video for their upcoming single 'This American Girl' at New Jersey's Thunderland theme park, UK sensations Fire&Lights ran into hot water with a group of crazed fans, upset over the recent departure of founding member, Olly Samson. The fans yelled vicious abuse at West, claiming he was responsible for Samson leaving Fire&Lights – an opinion shared by many in the fan community. One even shouted at the controversial popstar: "Why don't you just go back to England and die?" The offending fans were held back by security and ejected

182

from the premises, but with several weeks of the band's American tour still to go, one thing remains clear. The once untouchable Gabriel West is turning into one of the most hated figures in pop music—

I locked Melissa's phone, anger seething in my bones. Paul Morgan was distorting the story, just like he always did. He was writing his own version of reality. Gabriel wasn't 'one of the most hated figures in pop music', but it was obvious what Paul was doing. If he wrote it down enough times, it might just become the truth.

'Poor Gabe,' said Melissa, as I handed her phone back. 'Do you think he's seen it yet?'

I looked up ahead, watching Tara push through a large door signposted 'BACKSTAGE'. Maybe Gabriel had seen the article, maybe he hadn't. Either way, we were about to find out.

'Listen up, lads.' Barry was giving the band a pep talk as we approached. 'By now, you've all seen the blowback from the Thunderland debacle. And, yeah, I *know*, it seems bad, but we can stop this. We can fight back.'

Yuki, Aiden and Jake were standing together, in a row, hands in pockets. Gabriel was sitting just behind them, elbow on his knee, fist to his mouth.

It would seem that we had an answer to our question.

'We just need to show the fine folk of America that you're still the cuddly British scamps they fell in love with, back in the day. Launch a counter-attack. And with that in mind . . . I've got a surprise for you all.'

On cue, an assistant opened a nearby set of double-doors to reveal a group of people assembled in the entranceway, smiling. Some adults, some children. Aiden hurried towards them.

'Dad! Oh my god, Mum! Erin. I thought we weren't seeing you guys until South Carolina?'

Aiden's little sister ran up to him and clamped around his waist.

'I shipped them in early for you, kid,' explained Barry, with a smile. 'You can't say I'm not good to you, eh?'

Behind Aiden's family stood a tall, gentle-looking man, who I assumed to be Jake's father, and a slim, well-dressed Japanese lady: Yuki's mum. Yuki's kid brother, Itchy, was hiding behind her leg, holding a toy lightsaber.

'Hello, everyone,' said Barry, strolling towards the group. 'Grand to see you again. Now . . .' He turned slightly to address the whole room. 'There's a camera crew just parking up outside, and they're gonna be talking to you all, finding out what it's like to see your pride and joy again, asking if you miss your dear old mums and dads, and whatnot. Enjoy yourselves, turn on the cheese, and don't be afraid to gush. We're on damage limitation here, people.'

'Hey, is that . . . is that my favourite little dude in the whole wide *universe*?'

Yuki was kneeling down and pointing towards his brother, who was still hiding behind his mum's legs. When he heard Yuki's voice, Itchy dashed out and flew towards him, jumping into his arms. Yuki hoisted him effortlessly on to his back, and Itchy clung on like a monkey.

'Charlie, Mel.' Yuki gestured at us. 'Come on over here and meet my bro.'

We headed over to join the brothers, and Yuki touched a hand to my shoulder.

'Itch, this is Charlie Bloom, the greatest music photographer on God's green earth. And this is her friend Melissa, who could tell you things about computers that would *blow your mind*.'

'Hi, Itchy,' Melissa and I said simultaneously. Itchy pouted shyly, and hid his face in his brother's hair. Yuki glanced over his shoulder.

'He's kinda bashful. Aren't you going to say hi, little dude?'

'Girls are scary,' said Itchy, his voice muffled by hair.

'Well, that is true, sometimes, but not these ones. They're the best ones. Do they get a high-five?'

Rotating his head so that one eye was visible, and just the corner of a smile, Itchy extended his hand, and Melissa and I high-fived it in turn.

'That's my little dude,' said Yuki, laughing. 'So what do you think of Madison Square Garden?'

Itchy thought for a moment.

'It smells bad.'

Yuki shrugged.

'Can't argue with that.' He dropped his shoulder and carefully lowered Itchy to the ground. 'What do you want to do first? Get some pizza? See the drum kit?'

Itchy's face went serious. He blinked at his brother.

'I haven't seen Daddy in a long time.'

Yuki drew in a breath and looked past Itchy, towards their mother. She made a move to join them, but Yuki held up a palm, then lowered himself down and laid his hands on his brother's shoulders.

'I know, buddy. Me neither.'

I looked at Melissa, very aware that we were intruding on a private moment, and began to back away. Yuki caught my eye, though, and mouthed, 'It's fine.'

Itchy clutched his brother's T-shirt sleeve.

'When is he coming home?'

My throat lurched as I remembered what it was like to be so young, and to find out something huge about the world, something too huge for your heart to handle. *Why is Mummy still in America?* I used to ask Dad, before I was old enough to understand that she was never coming back. *Why doesn't she want to see me?*

'Here's the thing, Itch.' Yuki pursed his lips. 'I don't think Daddy will be coming home to live with you again. I'm sorry.'

Itchy's lip trembled. He shook his head.

'I don't believe you.'

Yuki took his brother's hand, and it disappeared into his own. He hushed his voice.

'Listen to me, Itch, all right? It's going to be OK. I promise.'

Itchy's shoulders went right up, then back down again, his lightsaber scraping against the concrete floor. He was trying not to cry, but two big, fat tears had gathered in his eyes.

'Why don't Mummy and Daddy love each other any more?'

He blinked again, and the tears broke free. Yuki rubbed them away with his thumbs.

'I know it's tough, little dude. It's hard for me too.' He looked right into his brother's eyes. 'But even if Mum and Dad don't love each other, they'll never stop loving *you*, and neither will I. I'll always be here for you, understand?'

Itchy nodded, slowly, then dragged his free hand across his face, sniffing through his tears. Yuki tapped his finger against his lips.

'Hey, tell you what . . .' He leaned in closer. 'I know what'll cheer you up.'

He cupped his hand around Itchy's ear and whispered a few words. Itchy's eyes lit up, and he waved his lightsaber in excitement.

'Yeah, that's what I thought,' said Yuki, grinning. He straightened up, still holding Itchy's hand. 'Come on, little fella, I'll show you the stage. Say goodbye to the girls.'

'Goodbye to the girls,' said Itchy, with a teary smile. We all waved at each other, and then the Harrison brothers walked away, hand in hand, towards the empty arena.

'Aiden, can you shift over just a . . . yep, that's perfect.' The assistant lifted his eyebrows at the camera operator, who returned a thumbs-up. 'OK. I think we're ready to go.'

Aiden and his family were gathered together in front of a stack of aluminium flight cases, bathed in bright white light from the camera crew's lamps. Aiden's sister, Erin, was singing 'Dance With You' to herself.

'Man, I am in *love* with the Roberts family,' whispered Melissa, as we watched from the sidelines. 'They're so cute, I wanna put them in my pocket.'

I shushed her, pointing at the interviewer, who looked like she was ready to begin. She glanced up from her clipboard, and her mouth extended into a placid smile.

'So tell us, Aiden, what's it like to have your family fly all the way from Ireland to see you at the world-famous Madison Square Garden?'

Aiden beamed at her.

'Ah, man, it's the best.' He looked around at his mother, father and little sister. '*The best.*'

'It must be difficult being apart from them for so long, though?'

Aiden's mouth pinched. Behind him, his mum pulled in a breath.

'It's the hardest thing, you know? Like, you're living at home, and you're going to school, and you have your whole family around you. But then all this happens, and in a second, they're gone. You're out on the road, and your boys . . .' Aiden glanced off camera to where Gabriel was sitting. He swallowed. 'Your boys *become* your family, see?'

Gabriel nodded slowly. Then his eyes dropped to the ground.

'But that's not the same as having your real family around you, is it?'

Aiden drew his sister gently to his side, and she peered up at him. She had blonde hair, just like her big brother, and these incredibly inquisitive green eyes.

'It's not, no,' he agreed. 'And I miss them, so I do. Every day.'

The interviewer turned to Aiden's father. Like Aiden, he was quite small, and constantly looked deep in thought.

'What about you, Conor? It can't be easy for you, either?'

Conor nudged his glasses up his face with a single finger.

'You want to have your boy around you, know what I mean?' His accent was lilting, and soft around the edges. 'You want to take him down the pub for his first pint and a game o' darts, like, but he's out, flying around the world, doing things you could never even dream of, and . . .' He glanced at his son. 'Well, now he's *had* his first pint, and I wasn't there.'

A pause.

'That sounds hard.'

'It is. But it's . . .' Conor nudged his glasses again, and cleared his throat. I found myself smiling at how much he reminded me of Aiden, just twenty-five years down the line. 'Look, I'm an ordinary fella from a small town. I was born in Galway, and I've been there my entire life. I grew up in a two-up, two-down, and my da', he grew up in a two-up, two-down, and my grandfather, and his grandfather before him: all the same. And then, Aiden . . . he . . .' Conor paused for a moment. 'He buys us this house, with his money from the band. It's got a garage, and this fancy new shower, and a big old garden for his baby sister.' He took his glasses off and brushed a tear away. 'I'm just so proud of my boy, y'know? I'm so proud of him.'

He slid his glasses back on, and the corner of Aiden's mouth lifted into a smile.

'My da' taught me everything,' he said, burying his hands in his pockets. 'He gave me everything. I'm the luckiest kid in the world.'

The interviewer let the moment hang, and my gaze drifted towards Gabriel in the corner of the room. His eyes were glued on Conor Roberts, and his jaw looked solid.

'That's great, guys. Well done. Perfect. Can somebody track down Randall and Jake, for me? Thanks . . .'

I watched as Gabriel stood up, pushed through a windowless door and walked away down the corridor.

'Will you keep hold of my camera for a moment?' I whispered to Melissa, passing her the case. 'There's something I have to do.'

Slipping away from the group, I followed Gabriel through the door and spotted him at the far end of the corridor, disappearing into an unmarked room. The door swung shut behind him, and I paused, listening to the waspish buzz of the strip lighting above my head. He probably didn't want company right now. In fact, I might just be the last person he wanted to see.

But it was time for our silence to end.

Click.

The latch in the door made a sharp metallic noise as I opened it, but Gabriel didn't notice. He was standing in the far corner, facing the wall, his chest heaving. He was wiping his eyes with the heel of his palm.

'Gabe.'

Startled, he turned round. His eyes were red, his hair wild.

'Charlie?'

'Are you OK?' I said. He wrapped his arms around his body.

'Uh . . . yeah. Yeah, I'm fine.'

I closed the door behind me.

'Are you avoiding me?'

Gabriel's arms tightened around his torso.

'I thought that's what you wanted.'

'No, I . . . I don't.' I shook my head, searching for the right words. 'Not any more.'

'You said . . .' He dropped his arms to his side. 'You said that when you looked at me, you saw him.'

'I shouldn't have said that,' I replied, stepping towards him. 'I didn't mean it. It was a mistake.'

Gabriel didn't move.

'But you were right.'

'No, Gabe, I wasn't. Don't say that.'

'You are,' he insisted. 'He's half of who I am. I can't change that.'

I thought back to Aiden's interview, and the things he'd said about his father. *My da' taught me everything . . .*

'I'm sorry you had to hear Aiden saying those things about his dad. That must have been hard.'

Gabriel shrugged, almost smiling.

'Conor's a really good guy . . . Aiden's a really good guy. You do the maths.'

The room fell silent. I tried to think of something to say, but my mind was tangled.

'It's not going to work, you know,' said Gabriel, after a while.

I frowned at him. 'What isn't?'

'Barry's PR drive. Trying to fix everything by posting videos of Aiden and his family, and Yuki playing *Star Wars* with his kid brother.' He looked right at me, for the first time, and pressed a splayed hand to his chest. '*I'm* the problem, Charlie, and we all know it. Barry says he'll tell the press that my parents couldn't make it because of a "family emergency", but it won't help. Everyone out there says I'm destroying the band, and . . . I don't know. Maybe they're right.'

My hands balled into fists.

'Don't say that. Don't ever say that.'

'Why not? It's true, isn't it?'

'But . . . they *need* you, Gabe.'

'What for?'

'They need your lyrics, for a start. There'd be no single without you.'

Gabriel let out a small, hollow laugh.

'The single.' His eyes flicked up at me. 'What do you think of it?'

I felt a blush on my cheeks. I knew what I wanted to ask him, but I didn't have the courage. *Who is the American girl, and why haven't you told me about her?*

'Well . . .' I began hesitantly, 'I suppose it's—'

'Honestly.'

His gaze was unwavering.

'It's catchy,' I said.

'But?'

I tugged at the hem of my T-shirt.

'It's just . . . normally your songs are a bit more—'

'I didn't write it.'

Gabriel pushed a hand through his hair. I cocked my head.

'I don't understand.'

'I had nothing to do with it.'

I pointed back towards the door.

'But at the meeting, Barry said—'

'Yeah . . . Barry *wanted* me to write it. He shut me off in a rehearsal studio with a laptop and a piano and told me to come out with something "upbeat and cheerful". But apparently I can't do either of those things any more, so he sent it back to the Speedway Collective.'

The Speedway Collective were the group of professional songwriters who wrote the music and beats for Fire&Lights tracks. Normally, Gabriel added the lyrics on top.

'So what happened?'

'Speedway finished it off. *They* wrote the lyrics. They're professionals, and they write to order, like a factory. Don't get me wrong, they're brilliant at what they do, but they just churn it all out.' He stared into the floor, his cheeks reddening. 'I can't do that. I need to feel something, or I can't write about it. And since the suicide no—' He paused, and took a breath. 'Since the letter, the things I'm feeling, they terrify me. And I can't write them down.'

I closed the gap between us, perching on the arm of a sofa.

'You shouldn't be afraid of your feelings, Gabe. You can't just turn them off.'

He went quiet, staring into space. Then he caught my eye, and his neck tensed.

'I hate him, Charlie. I wish he'd never met your family.'

'I know, but, please . . . don't stop writing songs *because* of him. All these things you're feeling, this is why we have music in the first place, isn't it?'

Gabriel began to pace across the room, muttering under his breath. He stopped at the wall and leaned against it, pressing his palms into the breezeblocks.

'Gabe?'

'So I got back in touch with that Sabbath guy.'

I rubbed my eyes, disoriented by the change of subject.

'Oh . . . right.'

He was talking about SabbathRules, the music fan we'd found online who had a vague connection to one of Little Boy Blue's old roadies. Gabriel had contacted him under the pseudonym 'Adam', claiming to be researching forgotten indie bands, and that's how we'd found out about Harry leaving the tour. About him being a 'real messed-up guy', who dealt drugs and owed money to his suppliers back in London. About how he walked offstage, in the middle of a gig, and never came back.

'I told him I was in the States,' said Gabriel, talking to me through his back. 'I asked him if that roadie, Jogger, knew of anyone out here who might have more information.' He tapped a fist against the wall. 'He must know someone. He *has* to.'

I stood up from the sofa.

'Maybe we should talk to Barry.'

Gabriel turned around, his eyes narrowed.

'About what?'

'We know he has some kind of connection to the Troubadour. Olly said . . .' Gabriel tensed, and I broke eye contact. 'We know Barry used to spend time on the Old Brompton Road, and it was his idea to hold the EP launch at the Troubadour. That must mean something.'

'I can't bring Barry into this,' said Gabriel, one palm in the air. 'I'm on thin ice right now, and if he finds out I'm looking into all this stuff, he'll shut it down. He'll be watching me like a hawk.'

I folded my arms. Maybe he was right, but I couldn't help thinking that Barry *must* have had information that could help us. I just had no idea how I would ever get it out of him.

'I have to go warm up my voice.' Gabriel was reading a clock across the room. He pushed away from the wall.

'Oh . . . OK.'

He drifted towards the door, and as he passed me, I felt the air around his body move the air around mine. He stopped next to me, and our eyes locked.

I wanted to hold him so badly it hurt.

'I'll see you after the show,' he said, and walked out of the door.

16

'May I say, Aiden, that your family are impossibly charming.'

Melissa was reclining on a big, plump beanbag in the corner of Aiden's dressing room, while I flicked through the menus on my camera screen. Aiden was sitting on the counter, his feet resting on a chair.

'You may.'

Switching to shooting mode, I lifted the camera and shifted to the side, trying to frame Aiden's face against the bright white lights bordering the mirror.

'If you could collect families,' mused Melissa, 'y'know, like Sylvanian Families or something, I would totally collect yours.'

'That's very sweet,' said Aiden, his mouth curling up at the corner. 'And not at all terrifying.'

He grinned at her, and I could sense her grinning back.

'Hey, Mel.' I peeked out from behind my camera. 'Could you nip over and move those empty Fanta cans out of frame? They're messing up my shot.'

Melissa heaved herself out of the beanbag, tutting.

'Charlie thinks I'm just some gormless assistant,' she said to Aiden, in a low voice, 'but one day I will rise up against my oppressor. This is slave labour.'

'Less chatting, more action,' I said, clicking my fingers.

Melissa picked up the cans and took them to the bin, dragging her feet and groaning as if they were unimaginably heavy. Aiden chuckled, setting off Melissa, and as I listened to them laughing, I began to feel like the odd one out. Shooting Aiden had taken my mind off my encounter with Gabriel, but he never strayed far from my thoughts. This whole mess with our parents was coming between us, and I didn't know how to stop it.

'Miss Bloom, your studio is Fanta-free. Proceed!'

After Melissa had dropped back down on to her beanbag, I trained my viewfinder on Aiden again, found the perfect framing and adjusted the focus. *Click.* He ran a hand through his hair. *Click.* His phone beeped, and he reached into his pocket. *Click.*

I paused. Aiden was looking troubled.

'You OK?' I asked.

'Just one of my old mates, from Ireland.' He frowned at his phone. 'Asking me about this Yuken thing.'

I lowered the camera. Aiden locked his phone and shoved it back into his pocket.

'He's only kidding about, but . . .' He slid both hands into his hair. 'Why won't it go away?'

I bit my bottom lip, unsure of how to reply. Melissa didn't know that Aiden had opened up to me about his sexuality – I normally shared everything with her, but this was Aiden's secret, not mine – and I didn't imagine he'd be very keen on discussing it now.

'It will go away,' I said, feeling a bit useless. 'Eventually.'

Aiden exhaled.

'It's just . . . sometimes I feel like . . .' He gestured towards the door. 'People out there, they don't understand who I am. Not the real me.'

Melissa stood up from her beanbag and leaned against the wall.

'Who cares about people? You be you, that's all that matters.'

Aiden looked at her, very thoughtfully. He flicked at one of his fingernails.

'Can I ask you something?' he said. Melissa made her hand into the shape of a little gun and aimed it at him.

'Shoot.'

'If you found out that, like . . . one of your friends, they didn't . . .' He looked down, his hands fidgeting in his lap. 'What I mean is, if you found out that one of your friends didn't really *fancy* people, they just had these really intense friendships, and they didn't . . . they weren't into . . . um. Would you think that was weird?'

Melissa screwed her face up.

'Not at all. Asexuality is entirely normal.'

I held my breath. She had said the actual *word*.

To my surprise, though, Aiden's face brightened.

'Really?'

'Dude, one per cent of all human beings are asexual. That's over seventy million people.'

Aiden scratched his head.

'How do you know that?'

'She's freaky smart,' I said, lifting the camera strap off my neck. Melissa shrugged.

'I do have some smarts, it's true.' She tugged at one of her plaits. 'But, seriously, one per cent of humans, and a bunch of animal species too. Hammerhead sharks, Komodo dragons. I forget the others.'

'I guess . . .' Aiden scratched his ear. 'I guess I just always thought it was weird. Freakish, like.'

Melissa leaned forward and spoke in a whisper.

'This isn't really about a friend, is it?' she said gently. Aiden's face coloured.

'Right, then, Aiden Conor Roberts. You listen to me.' She pointed at him. 'I may have a boyfriend now, but that doesn't change the fact that I've wanted to marry you since the first second I saw you on my telly-box.'

Aiden opened his mouth, but no sounds came.

'Seriously, I'm not kidding: I've planned our entire wedding. The canapés were going to be FIRST CLASS.' She thought for a moment. 'You like tiny sausages on sticks, right?'

'Uh . . .' Aiden threw an alarmed glance at me. 'I guess so?'

'I knew it,' replied Melissa, waving a finger in the air. 'But my point is, I have loved you *long time*, so I wouldn't be saying any of this if it weren't true. Because this whole situation does very little for the prospect of our nuptials.'

Aiden narrowed his eyes.

'No, I . . . suppose it doesn't.'

Melissa continued, undeterred.

'All this stuff you're feeling – if indeed we are talking about you, which, hey, we might not be, but if we are – it's *totally* normal. And the only reason you don't already think that is because people hardly ever talk about it.'

Aiden went quiet for a few seconds, and his shoulders began to relax. His green eyes sparkled.

'Thanks, Melissa.'

'Any time.'

A contented silence settled in the room. Fractured sounds drifted through the walls from distant parts of the building: footsteps in a nearby corridor; the slamming of a door. The insistent *dm-dmm* of the bass drum soundcheck.

'Bees!' shouted Melissa suddenly, and Aiden almost slipped off the counter in shock.

'What?' he said, baffled.

'That was the other asexual animal I was thinking of. Certain species of bee.'

Aiden looked at me, his mouth hanging open, and I felt a smile creeping on to my face. After a pause, we both burst out laughing.

'What?' said Melissa, looking from me to Aiden and back again, blinking. This only made us laugh harder. 'Hey, guys, come on. What's so funny about bees?'

Through the soles of my feet, I could feel the building shake. Madison Square Garden was full to capacity, and the air was crackling with excitement.

'New York City . . . how are we doing toNIGHT?!'

Fire&Lights were three songs into the opening show of their tour, and the venue was buzzing. Spotlights flashed and dived, giant balloons floated and bounced above the heads of fans, and all across the sold-out auditorium, a galaxy of phone lights twinkled in the darkness.

Jake was standing at the front of the stage, drinking it all in.

'This, America, is my dream come true.' Twenty thousand voices cheered and whooped, and Jake shook his head in happy disbelief. 'Seriously, I could never have imagined it would feel *this* good to stand up here. Thank you all, so much, for coming.'

More applause, and the distant chanting of Jake's name. Watching from the wings, I could almost feel his elation, rushing through my veins. To be up on that stage, finally, after losing out the first time round, must have been incredible.

Aiden strolled over, stopping next to him, and lifted an arm in the air.

'Are you guys ready for a special guest?'

A roar from the crowd. Aiden smiled.

'I can't hear you!'

The roar doubled in volume, and Aiden pointed across the stage towards Yuki, who appeared on the big screen. He spun his microphone in his palm.

'Right, then, New York. Listen up. We have an exclusive guest for you tonight, someone I guarantee you are gonna LOVE.' He gestured to the wings. 'Here, in his first-ever live performance in the United States, put your hands together for . . . my baby brother, Shinichi!'

The musicians played a resounding crescendo of rolling drums and wailing guitars, and out ran Yuki's little brother, his eyes wide and glinting beneath the lights. The crowd went wild, cheering and whistling, and a huge 'aww' rippled from front to back. Itchy ran straight to his brother and hugged him round the waist, prompting another adoring sigh from the fans, and a wave of laughter. Embarrassed, Itchy wriggled in between Yuki's legs.

'You coming out from there, little dude?' said Yuki, between laughs. Itchy shook his head, but he was grinning. 'Are you sure? Because I reckon these good people out here would like to see you dance.'

The crowd hollered in appreciation, and the big screen zoomed in on Itchy, peering out from between his brother's knees. The band struck up a song – the introduction to 'Have You Seen My Girl' – and Yuki crouched down on the stage, whispering into Itchy's ear. Itchy laughed, and Yuki held the microphone under his chin. Itchy grabbed it with both hands.

'Mek sum noyse, Noo Yok!' he said, and the most almighty cheer rose upwards from the crowd. The band thundered into the first verse of the song, and as Aiden sang the opening lines, Yuki led his brother on to a raised platform, and started to dance. It was an awkward, dorky dance, and it drew screams of delight from fans in the front row. Then, slowly but surely, Itchy began to mirror his brother. Yuki waved his arms and wiggled his bottom, and Itchy copied. He marched on the spot, his elbows sticking out, and Itchy mimicked the action. Soon, the Garden was juddering with applause. The brothers were stealing the show.

Across the stage, Gabriel, Jake and Aiden carried the song, while the Harrison brothers hopped and jigged around each other in almost perfect synchronicity. When the song reached its final, triumphant chorus, Yuki lifted Itchy on to his shoulders and he clapped his little hands to the beat, pure joy written across his face.

'Ladies and gentlemen, you saw him here first,' said Yuki, lowering his brother to the floor, as the track drew to a close. 'My kid brother, Itchy Harrison!'

While the crowd showed their appreciation, Yuki knelt down and hugged Itchy close to his chest, not letting go for several seconds. They broke apart and Yuki looked him right in the eyes, saying something inaudible. Itchy nodded, gave a wave to the audience, and then turned and ran back off the stage into the arms of his waiting mother.

Applause still ringing all around him, Yuki watched his mum and brother holding each other tight in the wings. He was facing away from the auditorium, so his expression was hidden from the fans, but standing backstage, I saw it. His eyes were shiny, his jaw locked. He blinked slowly, then, steeling himself, raised a smile and turned back around. When his face reappeared on the big screen, the fans roared, the drummer laid down a fresh beat and the boys launched into their next song.

I felt my heart straining against my ribs. Yuki just wanted to look out for his younger brother, but he couldn't protect him forever. He couldn't change what his father had done, and he couldn't stop his parents from separating. Sometimes, families just came apart.

There was a sudden flash of light, a loud bang, and two gigantic plumes of glitter shot into the air. Shifting my gaze from Yuki, I looked out across the heads of the fans, watching the twirling squares of glitter as they fell like metallic snow, and something odd struck me. Almost everyone was jumping up and down, grabbing at the glitter and laughing as it settled in their hair – but in the midst of all the chaos, one person in the front row wasn't moving at all.

I squinted in the low light, barely able to believe my eyes.

It couldn't be . . . could it?

17

Standing there, unmoving, face framed by her long white hair, was the girl from the theme park.

All around her, glitter was eddying and whirling through the air, and fans were yelling and screaming, delirious with excitement. But she was standing entirely still, just like she had been at Thunderland, her eyes locked on the stage.

On Gabriel.

She moved only when he did, turning her head on her pale, swan-like neck to follow him around the stage. She seemed entirely unaware of the world around her, of the glitter storm, the shouting and the screeching, and the tumultuous pounding of drums.

I wasn't sure why, but I was hit by a sudden urge. An urge to photograph her.

I wasn't supposed to take pictures during the show, but I figured that, if I edged behind the thick black curtain hanging beside me, I'd be near enough invisible. Taking a side-step, I carefully removed my Canon from its case and turned it on. My fingers trembled a little as I located the girl in my viewfinder, and I was suddenly aware of a guilty pulsing in my throat. Was this how the paparazzi felt when they photographed people against their will? Was that what I had become?

Willing the thought away, I zoomed in on the girl, framing her head and shoulders. Her eyes came into focus, and I frowned against my camera. They were a pale, speckled grey, the colour of granite. I'd never seen eyes that shade before.

Holding my breath, I bided my time, waiting for the swooping spotlights to pass across her face, and then – *snap* – I caught her. A perfect shot. My chest thumping, I looked down at the screen and felt my insides curdle. In the picture, she was no longer looking at Gabriel. She was looking at me.

I didn't think about what I did next. I just glanced up instinctively, and our eyes met in real life. But, somehow, it was as if I was still looking at the photograph. She hadn't moved, and she wasn't blinking. Just watching me.

My heart thudding in my ears, I pulled away from the wings and backed against a wall, camera clutched to my body, sweat breaking out across my brow.

Three days passed. I found myself coming back to the photograph every few hours, fascinated by the girl with the granite eyes. Her porcelain skin and pale eyebrows, the elegant curve of her neck. The way she was staring straight into the lens, unwavering. What did she want? Was she just another fan with a Gabriel West obsession, or was there more to it than that?

Something else was bothering me too. As far as Barry was concerned, the opening show of the tour had been a huge success. Sold-out crowd, spectacular light show, solid performance from the boys. #bringbackitchy was even trending online, with thousands of photos being shared of the Harrison brothers' dance-off, and Itchy memes dominating Tumblr. But, like the band's performance on *Good Day USA*, in a way that I couldn't quite explain, the concert had left me feeling empty. Jake was incredibly talented, and he more than held his own, but the magic I had felt the very first time I'd seen the band perform at Reading Arena . . . that was missing. It was as if it had disappeared with Olly.

Meet me on the rooftop.

Late one morning, two days before the band's next run of concerts, I received a message from Gabriel. I hadn't seen him since our backstage conversation at the Garden.

What – now?

Yep.

I stared at my phone. The night before, the Fire&Lights management team had thrown an industry meet-and-greet party on the rooftop at Eagle 519. Besides the three-sixty view of Manhattan, there'd been an infinity pool, a pan-Asian buffet and an international gin bar.

> I try not to drink gin before lunchtime. Ruins the afternoon.

No reply. The seconds passed, and I began to regret making a joke. Maybe it was too soon for that. Maybe we weren't ready—

> Cute. But not that rooftop, the other one.

> There's another one?

> Take the lift to the top floor and turn right, there's an unmarked blue door opposite the ice machine. Code's 4738. See you there in 2mins.

As I made my way to the top floor of the hotel, I felt like an intruder. Secret hotel rooftops weren't meant for people like me; they were meant for popstars, supermodels and secret agents. But after punching the code into the blue door and emerging into the fresh air, I forgot all my hang-ups. It was a stunning sight: an intimate Japanese garden, hidden away from the city, complete with water features, hanging plants and exotic-looking fish, floating lazily in gilt-edged ponds. It was deserted, apart from Gabriel, who was sitting under a nearby pagoda.

I followed a row of circular paving stones across a babbling stream, weaved between two trees heavy with powder-pink blossom, and sat down beside him.

'Hey,' I said.

'Hey.'

I braved a glance at him.

'So this place is pretty amazing.'

Gabriel shrugged.

'I'm just trying to impress you.'

The hint of a smile crept on to my face, then his. Our eyes danced around each other.

'I'm sorry about the other day,' he said, his forehead creasing. 'It's just . . . how are we supposed to deal with all this?'

'Search me.' I pushed my hair off my face. 'But I figure we're better off not dealing with it together, right?'

'Right.' He cleared his throat. 'In fact, that's kind of the reason I wanted to talk to you.'

'Oh?'

'I heard back from SabbathRules.'

I straightened, the hairs on my arms rising up.

'What did he say?'

'He called up that roadie he knows, and the guy told him about a place in New Jersey. It's an old gig venue – just a bar, really – but they've been hosting bands there since the eighties. According to Jogger, it was the last place Little Boy Blue ever played.'

I looked out across the garden, my eyes settling on a cluster of skyscrapers in the distance. This was a real lead.

'Anyway, Jogger says the man who ran the place, guy called Nate, he's still there . . . and he can remember just about every band they ever booked.' I felt Gabe looking at me, and my gaze drifted back to his. 'I think we should go.'

I frowned.

'But . . . how?'

'We could take a road trip. Have a few days off, head some place where nobody knows us. Visit the venue on the way.'

Pinpricks dashed up my spine. A road trip, just the two of us? It was an exciting idea, but there were so many obstacles. Would Barry ever agree to something like this? And how would I swing it with Rosie and Brian?

'I don't know, Gabe. I'm here with Melissa's parents, and they're supposed to be looking after me. We can't just . . . run off.'

Gabriel's face tightened, and he sat back in his seat. Over his shoulder, I noticed a hotel employee watching us from behind the cocktail bar. He was talking on the phone, but his eyes were glued on us.

'This could be our best chance to find out what happened,' continued Gabriel, unaware we were being watched. 'That's why you're here in the first place, right?'

'I know, but it's not that easy. Rosie and Bri—'

I trailed off as I noticed the hotel employee walking towards us. He had a curious expression on his face.

'Sorry to interrupt, Mr West,' he said calmly, as he arrived, 'but Mr King would like to meet you for lunch at The Vader Club. In fifteen minutes.'

Gabriel exhaled.

'Really?' The man nodded slowly. 'Well . . . OK, fine. Sorry about this, Charlie, I—'

'Both of you,' interrupted the man. 'He asked to see both of you.'

We looked at each other. Why would Barry want to have lunch with *both* of us?

'There's a car waiting for you at the front entrance. I'll take you down.'

The Vader Club was dark, luxurious and exclusive. The guests were dressed in expensive-looking pin-striped suits, their shirts crisply ironed, metal cufflinks winking at us beneath the ceiling spotlights. Mostly men, they sat around large, circular tables, fingering whisky glasses and speaking in hushed tones, as if afraid of being overheard.

One or two of them gave us wary glances as we followed our concierge through the restaurant.

Barry was sitting at the back of the room, alone, in a green leather booth. He raised a glass to us as we arrived.

'Well, if it isn't Sonny and Cher.'

We sat down tentatively opposite him, and behind us, the concierge melted away into the darkness. Serious-sounding jazz played above our heads.

'I've ordered you Cokes,' said Barry, rotating his whisky tumbler in the palm of his hand. The golden liquid glinted in the low light. 'Apparently not even a rockstar can have a drink in this country if he's under twenty-one. Philistines.' He set the drink down and clapped his hands together. 'Anyway, before we go any further . . . Gabe, will you take a look at these for me?'

He reached beneath the table, produced a stack of papers and dumped them in front of us.

'What's all this?' asked Gabriel.

'Fan-mail,' said Barry, leaning back in his seat. 'Tara passed it on.'

Gabriel furrowed his brow.

'But we just did signings last week.'

'Yeah, I know,' said Barry, plucking an olive out of a nearby bowl, 'but Tara flagged this stuff because it's, uhm . . . *different.*'

'Different?'

Barry tossed the olive into his mouth.

215

'Yep, but when I say "different", what I really mean is – ' he chewed for a bit, pulled out the olive pit and dropped it on a side plate – 'totally effing crazy. Tara was kind of freaked by it, she said you might be able to shed some light.'

'How on earth would I know anything?' said Gabriel, as our Cokes appeared beside us. Barry scratched his ear.

'Well, from the looks of it, this girl has managed to get pretty, erm, *close* to you in the past. Look.'

We both studied the top sheet of paper. It was a print-out of an email, featuring a grainy, close-up photograph of Gabriel, onstage at Madison Square Garden. Underneath, the message read: *gabriel, i see you in my sleep.* His eyes widening, Gabe sifted through the pile, and each email was the same. A close-up picture of him at a signing, or a concert, or at the theme park, accompanied by an unsettling message.

let's run away and never come back

i nearly touched you today

one day soon, we'll be together – for always

'Ah, man,' said Gabe, ploughing a hand through his hair. 'Why are you showing me this stuff?'

Barry sighed, fiddling with one of his gold rings.

'We wouldn't normally bug you with crazy fan-mail,

as you know, but it looks like this gal has a way of getting up close and personal with you. So we figured you might've seen someone, I don't know, in the front row at concerts, acting a bit shifty? All the emails are signed "Delfina".'

Gabriel pushed the papers away and reached for his drink.

'There are thousands of people at our concerts, Barry. How am I supposed to—'

'I think I might know who this is.'

They both turned to me, surprised. I hunched my shoulders.

'I could be wrong, I don't know. I just keep spotting this same girl at concerts and promo events and things, and she seems kind of . . . different.'

Barry leaned forward, resting his elbows on the spotless white tablecloth.

'Go on.'

'She stands right at the front,' I explained, the photograph I'd taken at the Garden flashing up in my mind, 'and she stares at Gabriel. She doesn't really move or talk or anything, and I'm pretty sure she's always on her own. She just . . . *watches* him.' I felt Gabriel shift in his seat. 'Anyway, I guess she's twenty-three, twenty-four, maybe, and she has this long, totally white hair, so you can't miss her.'

Barry nodded, impressed.

'Well spotted, Bloom. Who knew photographers were so observant?' He chortled at his joke, then raised a palm. 'Anyway, Gabe, she's almost certainly harmless, so I don't want you to worry. I've seen the type before. Either way, I'll tell security to keep an eye out for her.' He winked at me. 'And at least she stands out, eh? I mean, how hard can it be to spot a twenty-three-year-old girl with Gandalf's haircut?'

He laughed again, a husky laugh, then drained his whisky and smacked his lips.

'Right, then. You two. Talk to me.'

Gabriel glanced at me, then back at Barry.

'About . . . what?'

'Don't muck around, kid,' said Barry, nudging his glass away. 'There's something going on between the pair of you.'

I felt my breath catch in my throat. How much did he know?

'Barry,' said Gabriel, his voice almost a whisper, 'Charlie and I aren't togeth—'

'I don't mean *that*,' said Barry, batting a hand at us. 'I'm not interested in that. What you do behind closed doors, etcetera. But, look, I might be old, but I'm not blind. There's something' – he searched for the right word – '*weird* between the pair of you. You look at each other funny. Half the time you don't speak, the other half you're off having secret conversations.'

I kept my eyes down, heat gathering under my skin. Had Barry been watching us this whole time?

'There's something *wrong*,' he continued. 'It's obvious. And after everything that's happened this past year, I need it fixed. Gabe, I need you focused. Bloom, you're a damn good photographer, and I don't want your standards slipping. So go on, spit. What the hell's going on?'

He waited patiently for a reply, but Gabriel said nothing. I could feel the truth nagging at me. I'd wondered all this time whether Barry had information that could help us, and I might never get a better opportunity than this one.

The words were coming out of my mouth before I could stop them.

'The Troubadour,' I said suddenly. Gabriel tightened his grip around his Coke glass.

'Charlie, not n—'

'The Troubadour,' I said again, meeting Barry's eye. 'Why did you hold the EP launch there?'

Barry's face crumpled.

'What does that have to do with the price of corned beef?' he said, looking a little shifty.

'It's relevant, I promise. We just need you to tell us. So we can tell you.'

Barry sucked in a low, slow breath. Then he glanced behind us and raised a single finger at the waiter. Seconds later, a fresh whisky arrived, and he took a sip. He ran his tongue around his mouth thoughtfully, then leaned in towards us.

'Fine. I'll tell you. But before I do . . .' He looked from me, to Gabriel, and back again. 'This stays between us, you understand?'

We both nodded.

Barry ran his hands down his face, and began to speak.

18

'Back in the nineties, I was just starting out in the music business. I'd jacked in law, too boring, and I was hanging around all these clubs, watching bands, trying to figure out what the kids were into.'

As Barry spoke, my stomach turned with a heavy mixture of anticipation and fear. My skin felt too tight, my pulse skipping.

'I found this hip little venue, the Troubadour, on the Old Brompton Road. They had music nearly every night of the week, and it attracted a whole bunch of arty types – musicians, painters, activists and that – who used to near enough live in the place. It was kind of a Mecca for bohemians, and I used to go there loads, scouting for talent. Half the acts they put on were pretty forgettable, but every now and again, you'd find a diamond in the rough. And I'm there, one rainy Thursday, hoping to stumble on the next big thing, and sure enough, I find it.' He glanced at Gabriel, and paused, just for a millisecond. 'His name was Harry West.'

Gabriel drew his head back, his breath suddenly short. Barry had known for years that Gabriel's parents were dead – he was, in fact, virtually the only person apart from me who *did* know – but he'd never mentioned this.

He carried on.

'Yeah. He was in an indie band called, uh . . . oh, something from a nursery rhyme . . . Blue Boy . . .' He scratched his forehead. 'Little Boy Blue, that's it. They were pretty big at the Troubadour in those days, mainly thanks to Harry. He was the lead singer, and, trust me . . . he was phenomenal. You watched him, and you knew – you just *knew* – he had the makings of a superstar.

'So I courted them for a bit, bought them drinks, talked about managing them, maybe even starting a label so I could sign 'em up. Problem is, they signed with some other bunch of chumps, went off on tour to America and bloody split up. Harry West, he . . .'

Barry blew air out through his lips.

'It's OK,' said Gabe, his eyes on the table. 'Charlie knows.'

Barry took another slug of whisky.

'Well, with Harry gone, it was all over. To be fair, by that point I'd realised there was no money in indie anyway, and the future was pop. But I never forgot him. Blew my mind.

'Anyway, years later, I'm running auditions for *Make Or Break*, and this kid walks through the door. He comes onstage, and he starts singing "Cat's in the Cradle", just like Harry's band used to. They played it at almost every gig. And I'm listening to him, and it hits me. He's a dead ringer for Harry West. And he's singing the same song.

'I get talking to him afterwards, and he tells me that he lost his parents when he was little, but he doesn't want anyone to know. I start putting two and two together, and I realise . . .' He looked up at Gabriel. 'It's his son. This kid, it's only Harry West's bloody son.

'Anyway, I find this out, and I think . . . it's fate. I was *meant* to find Gabe here, so I could turn him into the superstar Harry never was. And, Gabe, luckily, you were pretty amazing as a solo artist, but as the show went on, and I worked out that something was missing from the boys' line-up . . . I realised it was you. You needed a band, just like your dad. And that's why I got rid of Jake, and brought you in.'

Gabriel stared into the tablecloth, and I thought back to something Olly had told me earlier in the year, at Kingdom Records. About how Barry King, despite his no-nonsense demeanour, was surprisingly superstitious.

'But . . . I don't understand,' said Gabriel. 'Why did you never tell me any of this?'

Barry half-shrugged.

'You were pretty fragile at the time, and in business, I work on a need-to-know basis. If you don't need to know, I ain't telling you. And you didn't need to know that. I thought it might freak you out, so I listened, agreed to keep your secret . . . and that was that. I thought it would be the end of it.'

There was a brief silence. Gabriel lifted his drink, took a sip and set it back down.

'It isn't the end.'

Barry jiggled the ice in his whisky glass. 'What do you mean?'

'Do you remember the piano player in Little Boy Blue?' asked Gabriel. Barry made a face.

'Not especially.'

Gabriel glanced at me. 'Her name was Katherine Bloom.'

Barry's face remained blank at first, but after a few seconds, his gaze drifted over to me, and his eyebrows crept up his forehead.

'Christ on a bike. Not . . .'

'Mum,' I said, the tiniest catch in my voice. Barry wiped his brow.

'So *this* is why you two have been acting so screwy?'

I looked at Gabriel, wondering how much more he was going to reveal. Would he keep the suicide note to himself?

'Yep. That's it.'

'Fate,' said Barry, under his breath. 'Blow me down.'

'It's not fate,' I interrupted firmly. 'There's no such thing.'

Barry folded his arms across his chest.

'How else do you explain it all? Coincidence?'

'I don't know,' I said, flustered. 'There just . . . there must be connections we haven't found yet.'

Barry slapped his hands against his thighs.

'Well, Charlie, whatever it is, I can tell you this. I'm glad you found your way on to our team. You've got one helluva talent.'

I allowed myself a small smile. Gabriel drained his Coke and set the glass aside.

'Barry, we need to ask a favour.'

'What's that?' asked Barry, rubbing his jaw.

'We want to get away. Just for a few days, after this next run of concerts.'

'What do you mean, "away"?'

'Away from here.' Gabriel gestured around the restaurant. 'From New York. Away from the press, and the fans. I need some headspace. I'm going stir-crazy.'

Barry laughed. 'I'm not letting you two gallivant off like bloody Thelma and Louise. I think we all remember what happened last time.'

He was right, of course. When we'd gone AWOL in Devon, we'd been tailed by Paul Morgan, the journalist from *The Record*, and ended up getting papped.

'But this would be different,' protested Gabriel. 'That's why I'm asking your permission first. You could send security with us – Amos and Marty, those guys are excellent – and they'd be on us the whole time.

Plus, we'd go somewhere where nobody knows who I am—'

'Some place where no one knows who you are?' Barry scoffed. 'And where might that be? The fifth moon of Jupiter?'

'Think about it; this is America. There are whole states out here where people listen to nothing but country music. We must be able to find *some*where where they don't know, or care, who Fire&Lights are.'

Barry scratched the back of his neck.

'Well . . . I guess you may have a point there, but—'

'But what? I *need* this, Barry. We both do.'

I gazed into my half-empty glass. Gabe was just trying to sound persuasive, but he was right. We *did* need this. We'd been so awkward around each other since we'd arrived in America, and spending some time alone might actually fix that.

Either that, or it would break us apart forever.

'If I'm going to find my songwriting mojo again,' he continued, 'I need some space. The others can take up the slack on the promo front for me for a few days, right? All I'm doing right now is making things worse anyway.'

Barry mulled this over, tugging at his shirt collar. I wasn't sure whether Gabriel meant what he said about songwriting, but it was a very smart move. From where Barry was sitting, this would mean there was something in it for him.

'Fine,' said Barry eventually. He smoothed both hands across the tablecloth, and raised a finger. 'But, Charlie, I need permission from the Morrises – in fact, I need permission from your parents too.' He stopped, his eyes narrowed. 'Come to think of it, what does your mum think of all this?'

Blood rushed to my face.

'She . . . she died.'

Barry sighed, and rubbed his eyes.

'Ah, nuts. I'm sorry, kid.'

'It's OK. It was a long time ago.' I tucked my hair behind my ears. 'Anyway, that's fine, about the permission. I can get that. I'll just . . . I'll tell them it's a photography project, or something.'

Barry patted his hands together lightly, and leaned back into the leather seating.

'All right, we have a deal. But you listen to me.' He pointed a chubby finger at us. 'You toddle off, you get some headspace, you keep yourselves to yourselves, you write some songs and you come back to the city. Got it?'

We both nodded.

Barry let out an audible sigh. 'The things I let you lot talk me into . . .'

The following week passed in a blur. The band's concert schedule began to pick up, and they played every night in a different venue on the East Coast. We travelled with them each time, and after a while, the sight of a new dressing room, catering table or empty stage became as common to us as the school gates were back home.

Melissa was spending her days with Leo, and I couldn't blame her. They were totally smitten with each other. The boys, meanwhile, were run off their feet with promotion, and although we did sometimes hang out before gigs, taking photographs, I ended up spending much of my time alone.

It was during those hours, when I was on my own, that my mind turned to my mother. Gabriel and I were drawing ever nearer to the truth behind Harry's suicide note, and there was still a part of me that didn't want to hear it. Maybe the venue owner in New Jersey wouldn't know anything, of course, and we'd be back to square one. But if he did, we risked digging up secrets that would haunt us forever.

I had to keep my brain busy. It was the only way to avoid a never-ending spiral of anxiety about my mother, and Harry West, and what really happened all those years ago. It would have been the perfect time to meet up with Carrie, but I still hadn't heard back from her and was starting to wonder whether her first email had just been a polite way of fobbing me off. So, instead, I began a project. A project where I would archive every single photograph I'd taken of the boys, from that first day at Reading Arena, right up to the American tour.

There were so many amazing memories inside my camera. Gabriel falling off a skateboard at the Reading after-party. Yuki juggling bananas. Aiden and Olly walking side by side down the backstage corridors of a television studio, Olly's hand on his bandmate's shoulder. If I was lucky, some of these pictures might end up being picked for Fire&Lights photobooks in the future, as my first batch had been. But, somehow, that didn't feel like it was enough.

So much had changed since that first day, and we weren't the same people any more. Before I met the band, I'd lived in this tiny, predictable universe – school and home, Melissa and my father – but being with Fire&Lights had brought the rest of the world rushing in. It had amazed me, and frightened me; it had opened my eyes and broken my heart, and I wasn't alone. The boys had been changed too: Aiden searching for an identity, Yuki's family splitting up, Gabriel tortured by his past. And Olly, forced from the band, leaving his best friends behind and striking out on his own.

As I sorted through the pictures, a story began to emerge in front of my eyes. The story of four teenage boys, trying to grow into adults while the entire world watched them. The story of four friends with an incredible talent, which first brought them together, and then tore them apart.

It was a story that needed to be told.

A gleaming black Mercedes pulled up outside the secretive back entrance to the Eagle 519 hotel, its windows tinted, hubcaps twinkling in the Manhattan sun. Gabriel and I were waiting on the steps.

'Thanks for coming with me,' he said, turning to me. 'I mean it.'

'Oh, I'm just in it for the Mercedes.'

He let out a small laugh, and shook his head. A hotel valet began loading our cases into the boot, and I stepped forward, but Gabriel stopped me.

'Before we get in the car . . .' He lowered his voice. 'I got in touch with the bar owner, in New Jersey. He remembers Little Boy Blue.'

I exhaled slowly. This was actually happening.

'Anyway, it's on the way from here to Newark airport. Well, sort of.'

'Wow.' I raised my eyebrows. 'You actually looked at a map.'

'Yes, I did,' replied Gabriel, a smile tugging at his mouth. 'I'm not just some useless popstar, you know.' He indicated the car's front seats, where two poker-faced security guards were waiting for us. 'I've told Marty we need to stop off there for a little while, and he's cool with

230

it. He likes me, for some reason. But . . .' He looked at me. 'It has to be you. Alone.'

'Why?'

'I can't get out of the car that close to New York. It's too risky. But I spoke to the owner, his name's Nate, and I said one of my co-researchers would be coming by this morning to ask him about Little Boy Blue.' He nodded at me. 'That's you, by the way.'

'I'm a co-researcher now? Check me out.'

We shared smiles, though they soon faded. I'd been keeping the mood light because I didn't want to think about visiting the bar, or digging up the past, but there was no ignoring it now. It was going to happen.

'Are you OK to do this?' asked Gabriel.

I took a deep breath. 'I guess so. I have to be.'

The journey off the island was slow-going, with traffic in the city almost bumper to bumper. While strummy American rock bands played on the radio, I sat in the back, next to Gabriel, texting Melissa.

So you'll stay out of trouble while I'm gone, then?

Aye aye, cap'n. Just as soon as I'm done robbing this bank.

I stared at my phone, fingers poised above the screen.

We're stopping off at the bar in New Jersey, I wrote.

Oh. Wowser. You all right? xxxx

I think so. I shook my head. I'm scared of what I'll find out.

Call me any time, CB. Even if I'm with Leo. I mean, granted, he has just the glossiest hair ever but you are still WAY more important.

It is pretty glossy. But thanks. And I'm glad you two are so loved up.

It's just his face, Charlie. His little face. He's like a puppy, I want to smoosh his cheeks.

I know you do ☺

No, srsly. I want to smoosh them ALL THE TIME. I think I may have some kind of disorder.

Nah, I wrote back. You're just in love.

A pause. Then she sent me four emojis – a mermaid, a fried shrimp, Santa Claus and a sweet potato – and one final message.

232

As we passed through Greenwich Village, I slipped my phone into my pocket and gazed out through the tinted windows, thinking about Melissa's parents. I'd told them that the Fire&Lights management team wanted me to take some solo photographs of Gabriel, and that it meant going away for a few days, and they were actually pretty excited for me. By this point in the tour, they'd got to know the band's security team fairly well, and they trusted them to look out for me. Dad had given his permission too, but when I'd texted him, I'd deliberately not told him which band member I was supposed to be photographing. For obvious reasons, I didn't want him suddenly taking an investigative interest in Gabriel.

I looked at Gabriel, who was staring out of the window himself, deep in thought. Was he just as terrified as I was? Was he worried, like me, that finding out the truth might actually be worse than staying in the dark?

Were we making a huge mistake?

An hour later, we pulled into a mostly deserted parking lot in a small town, just off the highway. A squat, boxy-looking building sat opposite us, its windows murky, its paint job flaky and faded. An unlit neon sign above the door read *Late At Nate's*.

As the car slowed to a halt, I became aware of some discussion from the front seats.

'I'm still not sure about this,' said Amos, clicking off the engine. 'It's not on Barry's itinerary.'

Gabe leaned forward.

'Honestly, Amos, it's cool. I'm staying in the car. This is just a personal thing, for Charlie.'

He gave me a look, and I realised it was my turn.

'Y-yeah, sorry to ask, Amos,' I said, unclipping my seatbelt. 'It's just . . . it's quite important to me.'

'You realise they don't let under twenty-ones in bars around here, right?'

I glanced at Gabriel. This hadn't even occurred to me.

'She cleared it with the owner,' he explained calmly. 'Besides, they're not open yet, so it doesn't matter.'

Amos rubbed his eyebrows with his thumb and forefinger, and sighed. Marty twisted around in the passenger seat.

'It's fine,' he said, giving me a reassuring smile. 'Just . . . try not to take too long in there.'

Stepping out on to the asphalt, I raised a hand to keep the sun from my eyes and closed the car door behind me. As I stared into the building, my stomach twisted. This was the last place Mum's band ever played.

I walked up to the door, hands clenched, and peered in through the grubby glass. There was a man inside, stocking the fridge with beers. I knocked timidly on the window, but he didn't hear. I knocked again, louder, and this time, he stood up, scratching the back of his head.

'Uh, yeah?' he said, a little confused, when he opened the door. He looked like he was in sixties, and had wisps of springy grey hair protruding from his head. He was wearing a Velvet Underground T-shirt under a faded denim shirt.

'I'm . . . a music researcher?' I said, feeling like a total fraud. 'Charlie. I'm looking for Nate. I think Adam's been in touch wi—'

'Ah, the researcher!' interrupted the man, his face opening up into a smile. 'Sure, I'm Nate. Adam mentioned you'd be coming.' He gave me a sideways look. 'Little young for a researcher, aintcha?'

My shoulders tensed. I tugged a strand of hair out of my face.

'I just look young. I'm at univ— college.'

Nate shrugged genially.

'Well, either way, you're underage, so let's gitcha inside 'fore anyone starts snooping.'

Nate led me inside, closing the door behind us. The bar was dusty and deserted, a handful of scruffy-looking booths leading towards a low stage. The back wall of the stage was covered in layers and layers of posters, some colour, some black-and-white, advertising past shows at the venue.

Nate was back behind the bar, stacking beers.

'Sit yourself down, Charlie. Don't mind if I finish this off, do ya?'

I shook my head.

'No . . . no, of course not.'

I perched on one of the tall stools at the bar. 'So . . . Adam mentioned our project, right?'

Nate slid the last two beers into the fridge. 'Uh-huh, yip.'

'We're trying to find out everything we can about this London band, Little Boy Blue. They were kind of obscure, and there's almost nothing on the web, so we're a bit stuck.'

Nate closed the fridge and straightened up. He dusted his hands off.

'Yuh . . . Little Boy Blue.'

'Adam said they played here, back in 2000 . . . ?'

Wandering towards his side of the bar, Nate picked up a cocktail stick from an old ceramic cup and parked it in his mouth.

He leaned his elbows on the counter.

'Uh-huh, s'right.' He chewed thoughtfully on the cocktail stick. 'And lucky for you I remember every last damn rock 'n' roll band who walks through those doors.' He indicated the front entrance with his cocktail stick. 'I'm famous for it. Ask me who headlined here on April twenty-fourth, 1987, and I'll tell ya.'

'Wow. That's impressive.'

Nate grinned.

'Go on, ask me.'

'Oh . . . r-right. Who, um . . . who headlined on April twenty-fourth, 1987?'

He pointed at me.

'God's Personal Robots. Three-piece, from Illinois.'

'Oh. Cool.'

'They were a sack of crap, Charlie, but the place was rammed. There was a big ol' bust-up during the last song, and some jackass threw a bottle of Red Label at the wall. Just there, look. You can still see the dent.'

He gestured at a small hole in the wall, next to the bar, and I nodded, tossing a quick glance out of the window. Amos wouldn't wait for me forever. I needed to get information, and quick.

'So . . . Little Boy Blue.'

Nate touched a hand to his forehead.

'Uh, yeah, sorry, kid. I distract myself sometimes. Whatcha wanna know?'

I shrugged.

'Everything.'

He tilted his head, and chuckled.

'Everything, eh? You don't need to tell me twice.' He dragged over a dog-eared leather stool, plonked himself down on it and drummed his fingers on the counter.

'See, back in the day, Charlie, we didn't get that many British bands out this way. So when some tiny London label sends me a Little Boy Blue CD, hoping for a gig, I thought: why the heck not? They were looking for a place to host the final show of their tour, and when I listened to the album, it blew me away. The songs were good . . . *damn* good. So I booked 'em.

'Then, a week or so before the date, I get a call from the label. They tell me the lead singer, he's run into some trouble and the band are gonna be a three-piece at the show, not a four. I coulda cancelled the gig, but I thought what the hell, I'd let it slide. They'd come all this way, y'know?'

I thought about my mum, sitting at the piano, totally helpless, as Harry walked off the stage, never to return. I thought about her struggling to finish the tour without him, watching her dreams die a little more, every day.

'Anyways, the day after that, this fella stumbles into the bar, and I ain't never seen him before. We mostly get regulars, 'cept on gig nights, so I tend to notice these things. And this cat, he hauls himself up in front of me and stays there all evening, getting wasted. Doesn't talk to me, doesn't say hi to anyone, just drinks. He comes in every single night that week, and every night, it's the same. He sits at the bar, alone, getting tanked.

'Night before the show, he's right there on the stool, where you are now, nursing a whiskey, and the phone rings out the back. I answer, and the voice on the other end says, "I wanna talk to Harry," and I'm, like, "Who's

Harry?" and he tells me it's the guy sitting three metres away from me, drinking a Jim Beam.'

I forced my eyes to the floor. So Harry *hadn't* gone back to England, after all. He'd been here, in New Jersey, the entire time.

'I tell this Harry that he's got a phone call, and he stumbles over to take it, and . . .' Nate leaned forward and, even though we were the only two people in the building, lowered his voice. 'Look, I ain't the kind to pry into someone else's affairs, but something about that voice on the phone, it put me on edge. I mean, the guy knew *exactly* what Harry was drinking, for Chrissakes. So I sneak into my office and pick up the second receiver, and I listen in, and, boy, was that one screwball conversation. Back in the day, if I got a phone call for a customer, nine times outta ten it's his wife telling him to get the hell back home before she leaves his sorry ass, but this call . . . this was different.'

'What . . . what did they say?'

'From what I could tell, the guy on the other end was owed some serious money by this Harry fella. And he wanted it back.'

I sat up straight, the facts clicking into place. This must have been Harry's drug suppliers, chasing up his debts.

A faint dread crept into my bones.

'Problem was,' continued Nate, 'Harry was broke, and he was stuck in America. He was British, see – now that

239

he's stringing more than two words together, I hear the accent — and these people he owed, they were Brits too. And I'm not talking investment bankers. They sounded shady as hell, Charlie. The guy starts threatening to hurt his family, y'know? He tells Harry they can run a car off the road, easy as anything, and make it look like an accident. He says they've done it before.'

I could feel blood thumping in my ears, a clammy heat on my skin. I didn't like where this was going.

'And that's when Harry breaks down. Starts crying, sobbing, and begging them not to hurt his little boy. He's got a son, see. Five years old, or something. "Please, don't touch my boy," he says, and he's desperate. "You can hurt me, or anyone, I don't care. Just leave my son alone."

'So then the other guy, he says: "We've been watching you, Harry, and your son isn't the only person that matters to you, is he?" But Harry doesn't answer. I just hear him, breathing down the phone, all raggedy. There's this long pause, and then the voice on the other end says a single word. A name.'

I waited, my heart in my throat. Nate plucked the cocktail stick from his mouth and flicked it in the sink.

'Katherine.'

19

I felt as if the stool was about to collapse underneath me, and I stumbled off it, my head spinning.

'Jeez,' said Nate, lifting a hatch and rushing out from behind the bar. 'You OK?'

He laid a hand on my shoulder and I closed my eyes tight, willing away the image that was forming in my mind. My mother, hands clasped on the steering wheel, while the headlights from another car sliced through the windows, bleaching everything white. The screech of tyres, the screaming of metal.

'Y-yeah, I am, I'm fine.' I gave him a weak smile. 'I think it's the heat. We don't get this kind of heat in the UK.'

He hurried over to a dial on the wall.

'I'll whack up the AC for ya,' he said, fiddling with it. 'Late July can be a killer round here.'

That word – *killer* – stung my skin, and I grasped the edge of the bar, struggling to breathe. My mother died because Harry West was in debt to his dealers. They sent someone out here to follow him, and when he wouldn't pay up, they ran her off the road.

The things he wrote in his suicide note . . . they were true.

'You want some water, or something?'

Nate was back behind the bar, pulling a glass from a high shelf. I nodded, tight-lipped.

'Makes people crazy too, this kinda heat,' he said, tossing some ice into the glass and holding it under the tap. 'Gotta stay on top of your liquids. Dehydration's a soldier's worst enemy.'

He laughed to himself, a little gruff laugh, and handed me the water. I took it from him gratefully, and noticed my hand was shaking.

'Thank you,' I said, taking a long gulp. Swallowing hard, I set the glass on the counter and lowered myself back on to the stool.

'I went to the cops, you know.'

I whipped my head up. Nate was chewing on a new cocktail stick and polishing a glass.

'You did?'

'After they said the name, the line went dead, and this crazy cat, Harry, he was gone in a shot. It was the last time I saw him. But the whole thing had me spooked, so I buzzed an old acquaintance, a local cop, and told him what I'd heard. He couldn't do a whole lot since I had no idea who anyone was, and the caller had blocked his number, but . . . I thought someone should know.'

Did my father know any of this? If he did, why had he kept it from me? Was he trying to protect me?

'Next night,' continued Nate, inspecting a smudge on his beer glass, 'Little Boy Blue play their show, and, man alive, it weren't too pretty. The crowd in here can be mean at the best of times, and this band, they were struggling without their lead singer. The piano player, she was trying to make up for it, fronting the songs and all, but it didn't do much good.' Nate slid the glass under the bar, shaking his head. 'Second the set's over, the pianist, she runs out, gets into her car and drives off. I don't think much more of it until we're near closing time, and one of my buddies, he's sitting at the bar chewing my ear off, and he mentions a car crash, ten miles south of here, in Breakwater. He'd heard a car had been run off the road, and the driver, some British lady . . . she was dead.'

I pressed a hand to my mouth. *She was dead.* Even after all these years, it still hit me like a punch in the gut.

'As you can imagine,' said Nate, his eyes bulging, 'when I heard she was British, straight up, I thought of Harry. So I rushed into my office and found the Little Boy Blue CD and read through all the information in the sleeve, and when I found the names of the band members, I realised, damn . . . *it was them*. Harry and Katherine, they were the lead singer and piano player in the band. So I called the cops again, and told them what I knew.

Said this crash, it wasn't an accident, it was just made to look like one. I said they needed to find this Harry West fella, and quick.'

I shifted uncomfortably on my stool. My whole body had gone numb.

'But they weren't quick enough, see. Week later, I hear from my buddy that Harry . . . he was dead too. Took his own life.' Nate flipped his polishing cloth over his shoulder. 'Man. You gotta wonder what was going through his mind, eh?'

He knew it was his fault, I thought, anger heating my blood. *That's why he did it.*

'Looking back . . .' Nate was staring into the wall, his lips pinched. 'I dunno, maybe I could've stopped it.'

'You did everything you could,' I said, but my voice sounded hollow.

'Well, maybe, but it was a sad situation, that's for darn sure. I mean, the guy had a son. And who knows if that lady had kids back home, or a husband? Breaks your heart.'

I hunched my shoulders, feeling the threat of tears in my throat.

'Yeah. Yeah . . . it does.'

Nate shrugged.

'That was pretty much the last I heard of it all – like I said, I ain't one to pry – but I never forgot the band. This lead singer, he had one crazy set of pipes, and together, the four of 'em could've gone places. All the way to the top.' He rested a hand on one of the beer taps. 'Y'see, this is what folks who don't play music can never understand. A band is more than the sum of their parts, if you know what I mean? It ain't just about one member, the "star", or whatever. It's about the *chemistry between 'em all*. When the mix is right, you can't just take one cat out, or replace them. In a great band, every member counts. You know?'

I gazed into the scarred wooden surface of the bar, going over Nate's story in my head. Harry's secret phone call, the threats from his dealers.

How was Gabriel going to take this?

'But some bands, I guess,' continued Nate, 'they're destined to crash and burn, and there ain't nothing no one can do about it.'

Thinking about Gabriel reminded me that I'd already spent too long inside, and I stood up, the stool scraping underneath me.

'I have to go,' I said abruptly. Nate looked surprised.

'Oh. Sure. I hope I've helped y'out, anyways.'

'You really have, thank you.'

As I turned to walk away, I heard Nate's voice behind me.

'Oh, Charlie. One more thing.'

I swivelled round.

'For your research,' he said, folding up a cloth, 'I heard that some Little Boy Blue fans, they organised a gravestone for the singer out in some old cemetery, on the way to the airport. Riverside, it's called.'

I nodded, my whole body prickling.

'OK . . . thank you.'

'You take care now,' he called after me, as I stepped back out into the throbbing heat. Ahead of me, through the tinted windows of the car, I could just about make out the shape of Gabriel's face, those dark strands of hair hanging down over his eyes.

I wished, with everything I had, that I didn't have to be the one to tell him.

When I dropped back into the car, I could already feel Gabe staring at me. But I couldn't meet his eye. I didn't want him to know what I knew.

Marty twisted round from the front seat.

'You OK?'

He looked genuinely concerned. I glanced down to find my hands still trembling.

'Uh, y-yeah . . . sure, it's just—'

'It's fine,' said Marty. 'You don't need to tell us.'

Amos began to pull away, checking his watch as he did. Marty was right – I didn't need to tell *them* – but I did need to tell the person sitting next to me, and I had no idea how I was going to do it.

As we pulled back out on to the road, Nate's final words were ringing in my ears. *They organised a gravestone for the*

singer out in some old cemetery, on the way to the airport.
We'd almost certainly pass it on the journey, and no matter
how much it turned my stomach, I had to think of Gabriel.
He would want to see his father's grave, wouldn't he? And
it might be years before he got another chance.

The silence in the car, as we drove ever closer to the
airport, was nerve-shredding. My whole body felt empty,
my bones brittle. I had to act now, or it would be too late.

Taking my phone out, and still avoiding eye contact
with Gabriel, I opened the maps app. I typed in 'Riverside
cemetery', and seconds later, I had a location. We were
only minutes away.

We crossed a rusting wrought-iron bridge, over a
filthy brown river, and up ahead, I saw it. In the distance,
on a hill. An old, neglected-looking cemetery sandwiched
between the road and the riverbank. I leaned forward in
my seat.

'Hey, Amos,' I said. 'I need to make one more stop, if
that's OK?'

He sucked air in through his nose.

'Where this time?'

'Just up ahead. That cemetery, on the hill?'

I could see his expression harden in the rear-view
mirror. Marty leaned over and whispered in his ear. Amos
nodded.

'Sure. Just . . . we can't spend all day here, OK?'

'Uh-huh.'

Amos crossed lanes and pulled into the lay-by in front of the cemetery. With a deep breath, I turned my head to meet Gabriel's eyes. His jaw was locked in anticipation. I chewed my lip, blood thudding through my skull.

Gabriel glanced past me, and I could tell he was reading the sign. *Riverside Cemetery.*

'I need to go too,' he said, his gaze returning to mine. Amos shut off the engine and clamped his hands on the wheel.

'Now, hang on, you heard what I sai—'

'It's fine,' said Marty, looking at his partner, but throwing a glance at me. 'This place is deserted. But you're not to leave the cemetery perimeter, you understand?'

'We won't,' said Gabriel, his hand paused on his seatbelt. He was waiting for me to make the first move. I reached for the door.

Soon, we were both standing outside the cemetery gates, and I thought of all the times I'd visited Mum's grave, back in London. It had never been easy for me, or for Dad, but at least she was buried somewhere beautiful. Not like this place. The grass had grown tall and unruly, and the iron gates had fallen to rust. It felt like no one had visited in years.

As Gabriel and I gazed up the hill, a scattering of headstones peered back at us through the undergrowth, dusty vines snaking around them like dry, bloodless veins. The names of the dead were barely visible.

248

'He's here, isn't he?' said Gabriel.

I nodded, a stone in my throat.

'If you don't want to go in, though, I . . .'

My words died in the arid air as I realised Gabriel was already moving past the open gates. When he replied, his voice was low and threadbare through his back.

'We don't have long.'

The cemetery was rough and uneven underfoot. Over the years, the narrow pathways had been reduced to dust and fractured paving stones, which dug into your feet as you walked. Clusters of tiny flies hung in the air, buzzing, and there was little shelter from the baking heat, just a line of frail, skeletal trees leading up the hill, bent over like old men at a funeral.

My eyes skimmed across the stones as we passed, checking the names and dates. No one had been buried here since around 2005, and none of the graves were laid with fresh flowers. It was a forgotten place. It seemed strange to say it, but this was a dead cemetery.

After a few minutes of searching, I began to wonder whether Nate had been wrong about Harry's gravestone. The whole thing had been hearsay, after all. But then a glimpse of burgundy red in the undergrowth caught my eye, and though I wasn't sure why, I felt a flash of recognition. Hurrying towards it, I found something lying in the grass that was both unexpected and entirely familiar: an album on compact disc, the front cover the

249

colour of red wine. The band name written across it in a spidery white font.

Little Boy Blue.

'Gabe,' I called up the hill to him. 'Down here.'

The memorial at my feet was quite unlike any other in the Riverside Cemetery. Along with the Little Boy Blue album, there were gig tickets, faded photographs of the band onstage and a little pile of plectrums. Everything was dirty and spotted with rain damage, but one thing was undeniable. This overgrown resting place wasn't just a gravestone.

It was a shrine.

Harry West

1969-2000

Music never dies

A rustle in the grass. Gabriel was standing on the far side of the grave, fists clenched at his sides. From where he stood, the name on the stone was hidden from him.

He searched my face and I nodded, the silent answer to a silent question. Brushing through the grass, he navigated around the stone until he was standing at my side. As he read the inscription, I sensed his body tensing and suddenly had the urge to take him by the hand and drag him away.

'Maybe I shouldn't have brought us here,' I said, my mouth dry.

Gabriel shook his head, staring at his father's name on the headstone. His face was contorted in disgust.

'You didn't bring us here, Charlie. He did.'

We stood there, side by side, for a long, hot minute, the air filled with the distant sound of passing traffic. Then Gabe crouched down in the grass, and I felt sweat breaking out along my brow.

'Gabe, I . . .'

He was rifling through the Little Boy Blue paraphernalia and didn't seem to have heard me. I raised my voice.

'Harry's dealers killed my mother.'

He froze, his back hunched.

'What?' His eyes were still on the ground.

'Your father couldn't pay them back,' I began hesitantly, 'so they started making threats. They said they'd hurt his family. He begged them not to touch you, he *begged* them, so . . .'

I stopped myself, barely able to say the words.

'So they killed her instead,' said Gabriel, a horrible realisation in his voice. He rose up stiffly and turned around. 'They killed her . . . instead of me.' He stepped backwards, his hands in his hair. 'Oh, god.'

I moved towards him, unsure whether or not to touch him. He pressed his palms into his skull.

'It should have been me.' His eyes flicked left and right. '*It should have been me.*'

'Come on, you can't think like that. They probably

251

never would've gone near you in the first place. You were just a kid.'

Tears quivered in the corners of his eyes.

'Harry's note . . . he . . . it *was* his fault. He killed her. She died because of him.'

'Please,' I said, reaching for his arm, 'let's just go—'

Spurning my touch, he dropped to his knees in front of the headstone and started rifling through the mementos, flipping the photographs over and tossing the plectrums into the undergrowth.

'He doesn't deserve this,' he said, a panic rising inside him. 'He doesn't deserve any of this.'

'Gabe, stop.'

'He doesn't deserve it.'

'I know, but, please, just leave it all here.'

'*Why?*' he snapped, turning to me. His eyes were desperate. 'No one else on this crappy hill has any souvenirs, do they? But look at this! Where did all this come from?'

I knelt down next to him, collecting scattered keepsakes from the nearby grass.

'The guy at the bar, he said some fans did it.'

'Some fans?' spat Gabriel. 'They didn't know him. They didn't know anything about him.' Searching though the pictures, he found a close-up one of his father, and held it, trembling, in his hand.

They looked so alike, it almost made me sick.

'This is who they thought Harry West was,' he said,

waving the photo at me. 'He was a rockstar to them. They thought he was perfect, but he wasn't. He was a *murderer*.'

I tried to pry the crumpled picture from his hand.

'Gabe, please.'

Pulling away, he rested a hand on Harry's headstone and hauled himself up, bracing to tear the photograph in two. I followed, wresting him towards me, and curled my arms around his. After a second or two, he weakened, and the picture slid from his grip.

It dropped into the grass and lay there, staring up at us.

'Whatever happened,' I said, 'he was still your father.'

Gabriel broke free, his T-shirt askew, hair in his face. He was shaking his head over and over, like a wind-up toy.

'I don't have a father, Charlie,' he said, walking away from me backwards. 'I never did.'

20

We sat in silence for the rest of the car journey. Every now and again, Marty would catch my eye in the rear-view mirror and I'd quickly look away, blood rushing my skin. He knew something was wrong, but he'd never ask about it. His job was to keep us from physical harm: nothing more, nothing less.

When we reached the airport, Gabriel and I drifted, still silent, through the VIP channels, closely guarded by Marty and Amos. We sat beside each other on the plane, staring into space or flicking listlessly through the onboard movies, and spoke only when the stewards asked for our drinks orders. It hurt, acting so distant around each other, but words felt too small for the things we had learned.

It was as if our pasts were trying to bring us together, and tear us apart, at the same time.

'Ladies and gentlemen, please keep your seatbelts fastened until the plane has come to a complete stop. Thank you for flying with us today . . .'

The announcement from cabin crew roused Gabriel from a restless nap, and our eyes met accidentally. For a second, it was as if he'd forgotten it all, because when he saw me, he almost smiled.

Then a strange kind of fear bled into his eyes, and he turned away.

I looked around. We'd been travelling in a virtually empty first-class cabin, and aside from a few excited glances from the onboard staff, we'd been ignored. The handful of corporate types who had shared our journey were either too busy or too old to take any notice of a popstar.

As the plane came to a halt, people began to stand up and click open the overhead lockers. Without saying anything, Gabriel stepped out of the seat and pulled out his bag. As he lifted it on to his shoulder, the flap opened and a stack of sheets fell out, cascading to the floor. I reached over to pick them up for him.

'Hey, you dropped some . . .'

When I saw what was written on the top sheet, I paused.

They looked like lyrics.

'Ah, man.' Gabriel began scooping up the sheets of paper, avoiding my eyes. I pointed at his scribbled handwriting.

'Are those—'

'They're nothing,' he interrupted, shoving them into his bag. He pushed his hair back from his forehead.

'Oh . . . OK.' I unclipped my seatbelt, trying to hide my frown. He'd told me himself that he'd stopped writing songs, and yet the top sheet of lyrics had been dated the twenty-sixth of July. Four days ago.

He looked at me, and I felt my chest burning. We couldn't go on like this much longer.

'Let's get going,' came a voice from behind us. Amos.

Gabriel broke his gaze, and I watched him walk off down the aisle.

Entering Marble Creek, said the large green sign by the side of the road. It was faded from years of scorching sunshine, and one of the corners was bent. At the bottom, an inscription read *Population: 124*.

'Christ,' muttered Amos, under his breath, as we drifted by a rickety old gas station on one side and an abandoned trailer park on the other. 'Talk about middle of nowhere . . .'

After asking around, Barry had decided to send us to an obscure town in a remote part of Georgia, a tiny pinprick on the state map. According to his sources, the locals wouldn't recognise Gabe here 'if he turned up wearing a ruddy Fire&Lights sandwich board'. But as we cruised through the deserted streets, I couldn't help wondering whether a community could genuinely be *that* out-of-touch with the rest of the world. Were we really safe here? Were we really hidden?

Thinking of you, CB.

I picked up my phone to find a message from Melissa. I had told her everything, even though it had felt weird to do it in text form. Her speech bubble was still throbbing.

Are you guys talking yet? she wrote.

Not really.

You'll get through this, I promise xxxx ps. Leo says hi.

Tell him hi back xxxx

I gazed out of the car window, noticing our reflection in the window of a thrift store. Marty and Amos had picked up an average-looking saloon car from the airport, and though it had seemed unusual at the time, it made perfect sense now that we were here. We couldn't afford to draw attention to ourselves, and the luxury vehicles Gabriel normally travelled in would've turned too many heads in a place like this. Not that, right now, there were any heads to turn. Main Street was empty, and the handful of businesses lining the road – a bank, a small grocery store, a seedy-looking bar – all appeared to be closed.

'Here it is, kids,' said Amos sardonically, as we pulled into the parking lot of our motel. 'The Marble Creek International Hilton.'

Across the concrete sat an L-shaped row of sad-looking rooms, their windows covered in a thin film of grey dust, paint peeling like sunburned skin. I instantly thought of the Wildwood Motel in my father's letter, the one I had found in his study the year before. The one he had never posted to Mum, because she had died soon after he wrote it. During the tour, Little Boy Blue must have stayed in endless motels like this. In an odd way, it felt like we were retracing their steps.

'We'll check in separately,' said Amos, shutting off the engine. 'There's no one around, obviously, but we may as well play it safe.' He leaned an arm on the back of his seat. 'And, listen: if anyone here looks at you funny, even for a second, like they know who you are . . . you call us, and we leave. Understood?'

Gabe nodded, tight-lipped.

'Fine,' said Amos, glancing between us. 'You guys go on, we'll follow up in a bit.'

The front desk was unattended when Gabriel and I clicked open the door to the reception area. On a high shelf at the back of the room, a small television was playing a black-and-white cowboy show, the sound turned almost to zero. We stood at the counter, waiting, while distant gunshots popped and pinged above our heads.

'Hello?' called Gabriel, after a while. No response. 'Anyone here?'

Eventually, the shuffling of feet could be heard from the corridor. A man in his seventies appeared in the doorway, a baggy cardigan hanging around his flanks. He looked a little confused.

'Yip?'

Gabriel cleared his throat.

'We should have a couple of rooms booked,' he said, nodding towards the window. 'Under the name King?'

The old man cocked his head to the side, like a bird.

'Two rooms, you say?'

Gabriel nodded. The man shrugged, and waddled towards the desk.

'Lemme check the ledger.'

We waited as he thumbed through an old, tattered logbook. He traced a finger down the page, humming to himself.

'So, what's a nice couple from the city doing all the way out here in Marble Creek?'

Gabe hitched his bag up over his shoulder.

'Oh, we're not . . . together.'

I felt something flicker inside me, faint but warm, like the embers of a campfire. *We're not together*. Would I rather he'd lied, and said we were?

'Y'all should be,' replied the man, crossing off some notes in his logbook. He looked up, and there was a twinkle in his eye. 'This young lady must be about the loveliest thing I ever saw.'

He gave us a wink, and for the first time in hours, we both smiled.

'She is,' said Gabriel, his voice just above a whisper.

Closing the book, the man reached up to the wall and plucked two sets of keys from their hooks.

'Rooms nine and ten,' he said, with a nod. He peered at us more closely. 'Hell, I'll be damned if I know what our sleepy town has to offer a coupla young pups like you, but you enjoy your stay, y'hear?'

I bit back a smile. Amazingly, this was already making me feel better.

'Thanks,' said Gabriel, taking the keys. 'We will.'

Outside reception, we stood beneath the shade of the hotel roof, exchanging awkward glances. Eventually, Gabriel dropped his bag on to the concrete.

'I'm sorry.'

I drew my head back.

'What for?' I asked. He stuffed his hands into his pockets.

'For being unbelievably selfish, back at the cemetery. I made it all about me, like I'm the only one dealing with this. But I'm not. You're going through it as well.' He squinted at me in the dazzling afternoon sun. 'I shouldn't have frozen you out.'

I lifted one shoulder.

'I froze you out too.'

'It's just, this whole thing, it's . . .' His eyebrows slid

together, and he looked into the distance. 'Do you fancy a walk?'

I followed his gaze towards the road.

'See the sights, you mean?'

Gabriel smiled.

'Exactly. All two of them.'

'You're on. See you back here in five.'

After getting settled into our rooms, Gabriel and I wandered out across the parking lot just as Marty and Amos were pulling into one of the many empty spaces. We left them there, unloading their luggage, and strolled into town.

As we emerged on to the corner of Main Street, we were spotted by a wrinkly-faced old lady, sitting in a wooden chair outside the grocery store. She watched every step that we took, her gaze little more than a long, suspicious slit beneath her eyebrows.

We passed her, barely breathing, trying to avoid her eyes. Then, from behind us, she snapped: 'Hey, you.'

We stopped in the street. I could feel Gabriel tensing.

'You,' she said again, and, cautiously, we turned round. She leaned forward in her chair, and it creaked. 'Would you like a peach?'

Gabriel let out a slight laugh.

'A peach?'

She sniffed.

'Uh-huh, a peach.'

Gabe glanced down at me, a smile playing at the corner of his mouth.

'Peach, Charlie Brown?'

'I like peaches,' I said. The lady pointed at a punnet beside her head.

'Fresh as the day is long.' She removed two fruits from the punnet and held them out towards us. Gabriel reached for his wallet.

'Oh, no, no, no,' said the old lady, waving her free hand. 'I ain't sellin', just off'rin'.'

Despite her protest, Gabriel pulled out some cash and took the peaches.

'We're new to this town,' he said, 'and we intend to pay our way.'

The lady kept trying to wave him away, so he balanced the money on a bunch of bananas and tipped an imaginary cap.

'Thanks for the fruit, ma'am. See you later.'

'What is that accent, anyways? Australian?'

Gabriel laughed.

'Yep, Adelaide born and bred,' he said, putting on an Australian accent. The lady looked impressed.

'In that case, while you're here, you need to see the creek, the one we're named for.' She pointed down Main Street. 'Keep walking past the old library, and make a left. You can't miss it.'

We pushed on, with the sun beating down on us, biting into our peaches as we walked. They were sweet, juicy and, just as the lady had said, fresh as the day was long.

'You should stick to pop music,' I said to Gabe, catching a drip as it dribbled down my chin. He paused, the fruit halfway to his mouth.

'Why?'

I smiled into my peach.

'That Aussie accent was terrible.'

Following the lady's instructions, we walked past a boarded-up library building, turned left on to a steep dirt road and headed downhill towards the ragged edge of a forest. A weather-beaten wooden sign read *Marble Creek – keep walking*, and so we did.

Inside the forest, we followed a babbling, crystal-clear stream on a winding journey beneath a rich canopy of trees. Twigs snapped and cracked beneath our feet, and above our heads, sunlight broke through the foliage, illuminating dust motes in the warm air. Eventually, we reached a second wooden sign, fancier than the first, and it was clear that we'd arrived.

Marble Creek, 1797
Birthplace of Jasper Madison, celebrated lieutenant colonel

A small, picturesque bay opened out before us, twinkling in the sunshine, and I immediately regretted not bringing my camera. The stream had widened into a shallow, rocky lake, and on the far side, a rickety wooden bridge looked out over a glittering waterfall. Staring into the lake, I realised straight away where the creek's name came from. Many of the rocks were a mottled white-grey in colour, and beneath the surface of the water, they almost looked like marble.

'I was not expecting this,' I said, lifting a hand to my brow to shade my eyes.

'Purdy,' said Gabriel, with a half-smile. He pointed to the crest of the waterfall. 'Shall we hit the bridge?'

We clambered up the bank and sat down on the creaking bridge, dangling our legs over the edge, the waterfall bubbling and frothing beneath us. For several minutes, we just sat there, saying nothing, enjoying the sun on our cheeks and listening to the sounds of the forest.

'Pretty inspiring,' I said finally, with a satisfied sigh. Gabriel was concentrating on a small stick he'd found.

'Sure is.'

'So this is where you're going to rediscover your "songwriting mojo", then?'

He blew air through his lips.

'God, I don't know. I only told Barry that so he'd let us come.' He pulled a lick of bark off the stick and tossed it into the waterfall. 'I just wanted to get away.'

I thought back to the plane journey, and the sheets of paper I'd seen in Gabriel's bag. I didn't want us to be keeping secrets any more. I wanted everything out in the open.

'What are those songs?' I asked.

He tore off another strip of bark.

'What songs?'

'The ones in your bag. They fell out on the plane.'

'Those aren't songs, they're—'

'I saw them, Gabe. The lyrics, and the dates.'

He lowered the bare stick to his lap and released a reluctant smile.

'You don't miss much, Charlie Brown.'

'I thought you'd stopped writing. That's what you told me.'

'It was true, at the time.' He glanced up at me. 'But you changed that.'

'I did?'

'When I said I couldn't write any more, I wasn't lying. I'd sit in my room, thinking about Harry's letter, how much I hated him, and how much you must hate me for being related to him, and I just couldn't do it. The idea of writing down the thoughts inside my head, it made me sick. But then we talked, backstage at the Garden, and I realised . . . you didn't hate me. Maybe you should, but you don't.' He stared out into the forest, beyond the creek. 'That night, I hardly slept. I just wrote.'

I followed his gaze into the trees, hope stirring inside me. I'd had no idea that my words had got through to him.

'Does Barry know?' I asked.

'Hell, no. Those songs aren't for the band. They're not for anyone, really.'

I crumpled my brow.

'What do you mean?'

'When I was a kid, I never told anyone how I was feeling. I didn't think you were supposed to. And after Harry left me, I had all this . . . *anger*, all this bitterness, inside me, and I never let it out.' He snapped the twig in two. 'The new songs, that's what they're about.'

Of course, I thought, as I gazed out over the bay. He was writing about his childhood.

'I'm really sorry, you know.'

Gabe was looking at me now.

'What for?' I asked.

'I'm sorry that he was a useless drunk, and he quit on your mum, and . . .' He dropped one half of his stick into the waterfall, and it tumbled away beneath the current. 'Let's just say my family has a lot to answer for.'

'You've got to stop taking responsibility for what he did.'

'Someone has to.' He closed his hand, tight, around the remains of the twig, then tossed it in the water. 'How am I supposed to sleep at night, knowing that his dealers were meant to come for me, not her?'

'This had nothing to do with you,' I said firmly. 'You were five years old.'

He watched the fragments of wood being carried away by the current, then closed his eyes.

'I just keep thinking about your dad, waiting at home, getting that phone call. It must have ruined his life.'

I leaned my elbows on the railing in front of me.

'It changed him, definitely. Made him distant. Or, I don't know . . . maybe he was always that way.'

'Maybe,' repeated Gabriel pensively, and a sobering thought struck me. *Distant is better than absent.*

'You know,' I said, 'my dad started dating again this year.'

Gabe looked surprised.

'Only this year?'

'Yeah, I know.' I half smiled. 'I felt a bit weird about it at first, but . . . it's good for him.'

I thought about Christine, my father's new girlfriend, and how meeting her had opened him up, somehow, slowly chipping away at the stone wall he'd built around himself after Mum died.

'He was a different person before the accident,' I continued, as a snatch of bird song drifted down from above our heads. 'I found all these old clippings in his study last year, stuff he'd never even told me about. He had a real talent for mathematics, and he won tons of awards. He was all set to become a respected academic. But when she died, he had to give it up to look after me.'

Gabriel parked a hand in his hair, dark locks tumbling around it.

'He sounds like a good person, your dad.'

'Yeah, he is,' I said quietly. 'The best.'

The waterfall surged in volume, as if trying to join in the conversation, and we both stared out across the creek. The late afternoon sun was turning golden, and it flickered on the surface of the water.

'So when do I get to hear one of these new songs, then?' I said. Gabe shook his head.

'That's not what they're for.'

I shifted round.

'Not what they're for? Isn't all music meant to be shared?'

'Well, it . . . no, the thing is . . .' He shrugged sadly, with one shoulder. 'I just doubt anyone would be interested in hearing them.'

'How can you say that?'

'They're not like my other songs. They're not exactly radio-friendly.'

'Gabe, *I'm* interested.'

His brow creased.

'Really?'

'Really.'

He looked back at me, unconvinced, but I held his gaze. He sighed.

'Fine.' Disentangling his legs from the bridge, he

stood up and held out a hand. 'Come on . . . I've had an idea.'

By the time we reached the top of Main Street, the sun was just starting to dip behind the peaked spire of the local church. The air was still warm, and long, blue-grey shadows stretched across the road. There wasn't a single soul around.

As we retraced our steps from earlier in the day, we passed the empty chair where the old lady had been sitting, handing out peaches, and I found myself wondering whether we'd imagined her entirely. We ambled past the thrift store and the bank, weaving around potholes in the pavement, and soon came to a dive bar named Rudy's. Pinned to the outside wall was a poster of a woman with a beehive haircut, wearing white gloves and a green sequinned dress, and the headline read: *Daisy Clay Sings – Every Sunday Night, half-price Miller Lite!!*

We peered in through the window to find a dingy-looking bar with a pool table, a row of empty booths and a piano on a low stage. An old-fashioned, fifties-style microphone was set up on a stand.

'Shall we?' said Gabriel, indicating the door. I laughed. 'We can't.'

I pointed at a sticker on the doorframe that read, *No persons under the age of 21 allowed.* Gabriel smirked at me.

'You were in a bar *this morning*.'

'That was different. That place wasn't open.'

He glanced up and down the street, and shrugged.

'You see anywhere else in Marble Creek with a piano?'

'Well, no, but—'

'Then get ready to experience the wonder of Rudy's bar.'

He lifted his elbow, like he was inviting me to dance in the eighteenth century, and I shook my head at him, smiling. I looped my arm through his, and we walked inside.

The second the door closed behind us, my smile died. The place wasn't quite as empty as it had first appeared: there was a barman drying a beer glass behind the counter, and in the far corner, bunched around the pool table, was a group of heavy-set men holding cues and looking straight at us. Nobody spoke. The air was silent, and dusty.

I let my arm drop from Gabriel's.

'It's OK,' he said, under his breath. 'Just follow me.'

We walked across the room, still being watched by the pool-playing men, and stopped at the bar.

'Hey,' said Gabe, raising his chin at the barman. The man looked from Gabe to me, and back again.

'Twenty-one yet?' he asked, in a way that suggested he didn't much care about the answer. Gabriel coughed.

'Yep.'

270

The barman made a clicking sound with his tongue, then bent down and slid his empty glass on to a low shelf.

'What can I getcha?'

'Whiskey,' said Gabriel, without hesitation. I nudged his knee with mine. I was definitely not a whiskey drinker.

'JD?' asked the barman, plucking two shot glasses from the back shelf. Gabriel placed a twenty-dollar note on the bar.

'Yup.'

The barman reached above his head and lifted down a bottle of Jack Daniel's. As he poured our drinks, his eyes flicked up at us.

'So what brings you to Marble Creek?'

Gabriel shrugged.

'Just seeing the sights.'

'The sights?' Both shot glasses were now full to the brim. 'You mean Bertha the peach lady?'

Gabriel laughed.

'Yeah, I mean Bertha.'

'You know, it's the darndest thing.' The barman slid the glasses towards us and nodded at the exit. 'We get out-of-towners in this place, oh, I dunno, once in a blue moon, and yet, today, you're the second British guy to waltz on in here.' He crossed his arms. 'Asking a lot of questions, he was.'

271

'Really?'

'Yeah. Asked me if I'd seen two teenagers, one kinda Brazilian-looking, the other' – he glanced at me – 'a brunette, around sixteen years of age.' He leaned his elbows on the counter. 'Y'ain't in some kind of trouble, are you?'

Gabriel straightened.

'No.'

'Well, hell, I dunno if he's coming back or not, so maybe it don't matter.'

I felt a tightness across my chest. A British guy, in this random town, tracking our movements? Could it be Paul Morgan?

I cleared my throat.

'Was he—'

'It's fine,' interrupted Gabriel, lifting our glasses from the bar. He passed one to me. 'Nothing to worry about.'

'Gabe?'

'He's gone now,' he replied, under his breath. 'It's cool.'

I almost protested again, but the look in his eyes stopped me short. It was a look that said he was tired of glancing over his shoulder every five minutes. A look that said he wanted, just for one afternoon, to act like a normal teenager.

'Cheers.'

Clinking my glass, Gabriel knocked back his shot, closing his eyes tight as the whiskey slid down his throat.

When he opened them again, I was still standing there, holding the full glass, whiskey quivering at the brim.

'Hey now, Charlie Brown,' he said, wiping his mouth with his forearm. 'That just isn't fair.'

I sighed, unable to hide my smile.

'Fine. Bottoms up.'

I clinked my drink against his and, after a deep breath, knocked back the whiskey. It burned as it coated my throat, but once it was gone, a warm buzz fizzed through me.

Gabriel set his shot glass on the bar and pointed a thumb over his shoulder.

'Mind if I play your piano?'

The barman coughed, almost choking.

'You wanna play in here? Now?'

Gabriel nodded.

'Are you sure?' He lowered his voice, tugging his head in the direction of the pool table. 'These rednecks can be a tough crowd.'

'I think I can handle it.'

The barman raised his eyebrows, then gestured for my empty glass, pulling the lid back off the whiskey bottle.

'You might want another one of these, in that case.' He refilled our glasses and waited while we saw them off. It tasted horrible, again, but the buzz was relaxing me. 'Mic's on, kid.'

Feeling slightly hazy, I followed Gabriel down the three small steps towards the dance floor. There were a handful of tables scattered about, and I drifted across to one, being careful not to scrape the chair legs as I pulled it towards me.

Meanwhile, onstage, Gabriel nudged the piano stool with his leg, sat down at the keys and lifted the lid. The creaks and moans of the ageing instrument drew the attention of the pool-playing men in the corner, and one or two of them laid down their cues. The biggest of them – a mean-looking guy in a plaid shirt, with a tattooed neck – leaned against the table, watching through narrowed eyes. Onstage, Gabriel had his back to them, and seemed unaware that he had attracted an audience.

Lowering his hands on to the keys, he started to play. The piano sounded old and battered, but strangely comforting, like an antique clock, and the soft, fragmented chords echoed across the room. As Gabriel began to sing, it soothed me, the fuzzy glow from the whiskey still warming me from inside.

I thought that we were a family
I believed I was home
I wanted you to be proud of me
Somewhere deep in your bones

You were tall, blocking out the sun
My hand was reaching for yours
I was small, I was your only son
I watched you walk out the door

The lyrics were curious and haunting, quite unlike anything he had written before. And as he surged into the chorus, and the music opened out, the melodies became more intense and urgent, and his voice almost cracked under the strain.

> 'Cos I was never enough
> Don't you think you owed me more than this?

He was singing about his father. And not just about him, but *to* him. It was as if Gabriel had written down all the things he'd want to say to Harry if he hadn't abandoned him. If he hadn't run away to America, and ended up dead.

> I wasn't worthy of love
> You were supposed to show me what a father is—

'Hey, faggot.'

Gabriel paused, mid-line, the sound of the rickety piano slowly decaying in the gloom. The voice had come from the pool table in the corner, but Gabe didn't turn round. He just waited a few seconds, then started to play again.

'I'm talking to you, you little queer.'

At this, Gabriel stood up and kicked the stool away. He walked towards the front of the stage.

'I'm trying to play a song,' he called across the room. The men around the pool table laughed, and the one who'd been shouting at him passed his cue to a friend and made his way towards us.

One, two, three, he clomped down the steps. Heavy black boots on the creaking wood.

When he reached the stage, he squared up to Gabriel. Gabe was tall, and elevated several centimetres by the wooden platform, but even so, the man was at his eye level.

'We don't listen to fag music in this town,' he said.

Undeterred, Gabriel leaned into his assailant's face and looked him square in the eye.

'Maybe I'm not the problem, then. Maybe it's this crappy town.'

The man's jaw jutted forward and he reached up with a chunky arm, grabbing a fistful of Gabriel's T-shirt. Then I watched, in horror, as he dragged Gabe off the stage and threw him into a wall.

21

I leapt up from my seat as the man pinned Gabriel against the wall, tearing one of the posters off the brickwork. His cheeks had turned crimson, and he had his forearm planted against Gabe's neck.

'Say that again, you little punk.'

Gabriel struggled for breath. The man was choking him.

'I said, maybe it's this crappy tow—'

'Let go of him.'

The words had come out of my mouth before I'd had time to think. The man turned to look at me, keeping Gabriel pinned behind his arm. Gabe caught my eye and shook his head, but I didn't back down.

'Howdy, sweet cheeks.'

'Let go of him,' I repeated. The man scanned me up and down, and whistled.

'Well, ain't you just the cutest—'

'For Chrissakes, Mike, put the kid down.'

The barman's voice. He had stepped out from behind the counter, an empty beer glass in one hand, grubby dishcloth in the other.

'Gimme a break,' said Mike gruffly. 'He's a little punk.'

The barman laughed to himself.

'Whatever, Mike. You're a jackass, but you never hear me complaining.'

Mike huffed a few times, then stepped away from Gabriel, who straightened out his T-shirt and rubbed his shoulder where it had slammed into the wall. Mike gave me another creepy look, nostrils flaring, then pointed a stubby finger at Gabriel.

'Count yourself lucky, prick.'

Gabriel glared back at him.

'What do you listen to, then?' he said.

Mike's face crumpled.

'Huh?'

'If you don't like "faggot music", what *do* you listen to?'

Mike tugged at the collar of his shirt.

'This is a country music town, boy. Always has been.'

'How about some Johnny Cash, then?'

Mike shrugged one shoulder.

'Even better,' continued Gabriel, raising his voice, 'how's about this. If you don't like it, I'll buy you a round of drinks.' He waved a hand towards the pool table. 'All of you.'

Mike scoffed and started clomping back towards his buddies.

'Crazy Brit,' he said, through his back. 'You're on.'

As Gabriel settled down on the piano stool again, the men by the pool table shared a joke and sniggered at each other. Sitting alone at my table, I suddenly felt grateful for the darkness. I swore I could feel their eyes boring into the back of my neck.

'This is called "Hurt",' said Gabriel, into the microphone, and his fingers began to glide across the keys again, playing a rolling, mournful riff. I didn't know much about Johnny Cash, other than the fact that he'd had a hit called 'Ring Of Fire' that drunk students would sing on their way down Reading high street, but this song was different. It was slow, and unbearably sad. It seeped under your skin and into your soul.

As the song unfolded, it told a story. A story of regret and loneliness, of someone who's become convinced that they're a fake, a fraud, only capable of hurting themselves and others. Someone who, sooner or later, is abandoned by every single person they love. And sitting there in the gloom, hearing Gabriel sing those words – hearing him tell a story so close to his own – was almost too much to bear.

I looked around and realised that every last man around the pool table had stopped talking. They were all just standing there, arms folded, eyes glued to the stage. Even Mike.

After the final chord had died out, Gabriel stood up, closed the piano lid and walked off the stage. I joined him as he passed me, and we headed for the bar. All around, silence hung in the stale air.

The barman was shaking his head as we approached.

'You've got balls, kid,' he said, in a low voice. He threw a look at his regulars. 'And I don't think you'll be buying anyone's drinks today.' Pouring two more shots of Jack Daniel's, he pushed them towards us. 'Still, I'd suggest you drop these and get outta here before Big Mike changes his mind.'

Glancing at each other, we tossed back the shots and hurried out of the bar, our brains racing with the whiskey. Pushing open the door, we stumbled out on to the street, laughing, still giddy from the combination of adrenalin and hard liquor.

Gabe's eyes met mine, and they seemed brighter than before. It felt good to laugh with him again.

'You know you could've got us both killed in there, right?' I said, leaning back against the wall, wiping my mouth.

'Maybe,' said Gabe, leaning back beside me, 'but what a place to die.' He glanced up at a poster in the window. 'Look. If you can finish their twenty ounce rib-eye in under five minutes, you get a free hat.'

I shook my head, still laughing, and Gabe ran his hands through his hair. The sun glinted behind him, and I tried my best to recall the lyrics from the song he'd played in the bar. The alcohol wasn't helping, but I could remember snatches, fragments, words here and there. All those pent-up emotions, things he'd been feeling since he was a boy, spilling out through his music.

The street fell quiet around us.

'It's beautiful, you know,' I said.

'What is?'

'Your song. The one about . . .' His eyes dropped, and I trailed off. 'Really, it's stunning.'

'If it weren't for you, I never would've written it.'

'Come on, Gabe—'

'I'm serious.' He turned to face me. 'Do you know what it meant for me when I lost my songwriting? Music is how I've dealt with everything, everything that's ever happened to me . . . and I lost that. But you brought it back.'

We stood there for a while, under the slowly setting sun, just staring at each other. Despite everything that had happened to us in the past few months, despite all the darkness and confusion, I couldn't ignore it. I was falling for him again.

'What's that?' he said, lifting his chin.

'What's what?'

He was listening keenly, though I wasn't sure what for. 'Music.'

I strained to hear it, and he was right. Somewhere in the distance, someone was playing music. Without speaking, as if following the Pied Piper, we drifted together down the road, turning the corner at the end of Main Street, and came to the edge of an abandoned, weed-infested parking lot. About fifty metres away, on the other side of the patch, was an old-fashioned diner, the kind made entirely from sheet metal and red neon. The door was open and, inside, an old man in an apron was wiping the surfaces, his movements stiff and deliberate, like a clockwork exhibit in a museum. Presumably from a jukebox, music was playing – vintage American songs, the kind you heard in old MGM musicals – and it floated across the warm air like dandelion seeds on the breeze.

Gabriel smiled to himself.

'Ella Fitzgerald, if I'm not mistaken.'

I listened again, and he was right. It was 'Dream A Little Dream Of Me'.

Suddenly, Gabriel leapt up on to the bonnet of a nearby car, and the steel structure creaked beneath his feet. The car was entirely rusted out, nothing more than an abandoned shell, and the dying sun was fracturing through its empty windows. Climbing on to the roof, Gabriel steadied himself and, with one arm behind his back, leaned down and offered his hand.

'May I have this dance?'

My brow furrowed.

'Dance?' I cast an eye across the ramshackle vehicle. 'Up there?'

Gabriel gestured around.

'You see another dance floor in the vicinity?'

'Well, no, but that isn't a d—'

'In that case,' he interrupted, stretching his hand out further, 'you really only have one option.'

I side-eyed him dubiously, but he smiled an irresistible smile and waited patiently for my hand. Laughing to myself, I took his hand and let him guide me up on to the bonnet of the car, then on to the roof. We looked around, taking in the panoramic view of Marble Creek, with its crumbling buildings and potholed roads, and my lungs filled with air. The town was far from pretty, but in the fading light, it looked strangely beautiful. The sun was golden, and the sky above us was swirling with vivid oranges, yellows and pinks, as if someone up there was mixing paint.

Gabe slid his fingers through mine and pulled me gently towards him. Then, with me resting my head on his chest, listening to the beating of his heart, we danced. Slowly and softly, while in the distance, Ella Fitzgerald sang a lullaby.

'Do you remember the day we met?' Gabe said, after a while.

'Uh-huh,' I replied, my voice muffled by the fabric of his T-shirt.

'You were shooting photos at the after-party, and I got on that skateboard. Then fell off, like an idiot.'

'I remember that.'

'I did that for you.'

I glanced up.

'What do you mean?'

He looked mildly embarrassed.

'You were meeting everyone that day: Yuki, Aid and Olly, and those guys . . . they're fun. They're fun to be around. And I know it's dumb, but when I saw you with your camera, I thought: *I'm going to act like I'm fun.* I wanted to impress you.'

The corner of my mouth lifted into a smile.

'You *are* fun.'

'Oh, really?'

I gestured at our feet. 'I've never danced on the roof of a car before.'

He dipped his head to the side.

'Good point.'

Ella sang some more, and we danced some more. The rusting metal of the car roof groaned quietly beneath our feet, and the sun fell ever closer towards the horizon.

Then, all of a sudden, Gabe stopped. I felt his hand tighten, just barely, against the small of my back.

'Look, I know everything's totally screwed right now. All this stuff with our parents, it's so messed up I can't even *think* about it, but . . .' He lifted his hand and ran a thumb down my neck, just inside my hairline. 'I'd still

284

rather be here with you, Charlie Brown, than anywhere else in the world.'

I wasn't sure if it was the music, or the sunlight, or the whiskey, but I suddenly wanted him more than I ever had before.

'Me too.'

He leaned into me, and his forehead touched mine.

'You know, my whole life, I've never trusted anyone. Not after Harry left. When I joined the band, I thought the only reason anyone liked me was because of the fame and the money.' He caught my gaze, and his eyes were on fire. 'But not you, Charlie. I trust you completely. And when I look back at the past year, the only times I've been happy . . . they've all been with you.'

He slid his hand behind my neck, across my birthmark – the birthmark that had started this whole thing – and, limb by limb, our bodies fell together. Before I knew it, we were kissing, his hands were in my hair, the fading sun was on my face and it was just us in the world, just us, not a single, solitary person in our way.

I was happy. Happy, in spite of everything. Happy, in his arms.

'I'm leavin' you this time, Bradley, I swear it. I seen you around town with Angel McKenzie, and don't you deny it! Y'all been makin' a fool of me for too long . . .'

Lying on the bed in my motel room, I reached for the remote and switched channels. There had to be something on besides angry Americans berating each other on chat shows. And, sure enough, after sifting through live sports, monster truck rallies and local news, I hit on a channel showing re-runs of *Charlie's Angels*. Perfect.

I settled back against the pillows, my mind still buzzing from the whiskey, skin still tingling from our sunset dance. This was an unusual vacation we were on, but in its own way, it was working. We were actually feeling better.

Gabe knocked at the door, and I clicked off the television. He'd wandered off to find sodas and snacks, but I wasn't holding out much hope. The motel vending machine looked like it hadn't worked since the eighties, and all the shops in town had been closed for hours.

'Now, listen,' I said, in a raised voice, as I walked to the door. 'I seriously hope they had Dr Pepper, because it's a *crazy* hot day and Dr Pepper is—'

'Your favourite,' he said, as I opened the door. But it wasn't Gabriel standing there waiting for me.

It was Olly.

22

'Olly . . . wh— what are you . . .'

Our eyes locked, and I felt the air being sucked from my chest.

'Hey, Charlie.'

It was actually him. Somehow, Olly Samson was here, in Marble Creek, standing outside my motel room. His skin was bronzed from the sun, his gaze very serious. His broad shoulders almost filled the doorway.

'Wh— What are you doing here?' I said shakily. 'How did you find us?'

That little word seemed to hover in the air after I said it. Us.

'It's a long story.' He stole a glance across the parking lot. 'I came here to warn you about something.'

I peered around the doorframe, my heart thumping. I could feel sweat breaking out on my temples.

'Warn me? But . . . listen, Gabe'll be back any minute. I really don't think it's a good idea for you t—'

'Don't worry,' said Olly, floating a calming hand. 'I know you're travelling with him. That's why I'm here.'

I touched a hand to my forehead. It was burning up.

'I don't understand.'

Olly threw another look over his shoulder, and I noticed a black vehicle parked on the roadside, its windows tinted. Security guards sat in the front seats.

'My new manager, he has this contact in the American tabloids. Basically, a guy who gives him a heads-up if one of his acts is about to get hammered in the press. There's not really anything you can do about it, but you can be prepared, at least.'

I crossed my arms.

'What do you mean? Prepared for what?'

'We've been in Atlanta, playing a show, and management got a tip. They said a British pap had been tailing Gabriel around this tiny town across the state, and this afternoon, he got what he wanted. A shot of Gabe in some dive bar, fighting with a local. They showed me, Charlie, and you were in it. I mean, it's dark, and no one else will know it's you . . . but I did.'

I stared back at him, dumbfounded. *Of course*. The 'British guy' that the barman had mentioned, it really had been Paul Morgan, after all. I cursed myself for not being more careful. This was why grown-ups warned you about alcohol: it made you forget. It made you fearless.

'Gabriel's used to this stuff,' continued Olly, 'but I know what these people are like. They're nasty. Pretty soon they'll work out who you are, and things'll get even worse.'

I didn't want to say it in front of Olly, but from our encounter in the StarBright car park earlier in the year, I had a feeling Paul Morgan was already well on his way to working out who I was.

'Charlie?'

Olly was waiting for my response. I pushed Paul to the back of my mind.

'I just . . . why are you here, Olly? You could've texted.'

He sighed.

'I tried, but I couldn't get through. I guess this town has no signal.'

I thought about my phone, lying on the bedside table. Olly was right. The last time I'd had even one bar was on the way into Marble Creek, when Melissa and I were messaging. Since then, all service had disappeared, and I hadn't even kept my phone on me.

'To be honest,' said Olly, 'I figured that since you'd come all the way out here, you'd probably cut yourself off on purpose. It was Gabe's idea, right?'

'How did you know that?'

'He does this now and again, when we're on tour. I mean . . .' He looked sad for a moment. 'When we used to be on tour.'

I felt a tugging in my chest. Sometimes, I forgot how well these boys knew each other.

'Anyway, I knew he wouldn't answer the phone to me, if he even *had* a phone out here, and my security detail said they'd bring me, since our next promo meet is only a few hours' drive away. Plus . . .'

He glanced away.

'What?' I said.

'To be honest . . .' Our eyes met again. 'I wanted to see you.'

'But why?'

'The way things ended between us . . . you didn't deserve that.'

I dragged my hands through my hair. It was clammy from the heat, and it tangled in my fingers.

'It's not about what anyone deserved, Olly. These things happen. We broke up.'

He shook his head, his brow creased.

'But that's just it. I realise now, I wasn't breaking up with you.' His blue eyes focused on mine, and I felt my heart shiver. 'I was breaking up with the band.'

'Charlie Bloom!' came a voice from round the corner. Gabriel's voice. 'Delivery of Dr Pepper for a Miss Char—'

His voice died in his throat. He had seen Olly.

He had seen Olly.

'What the hell?' Gabe again.

Olly pursed his lips and stepped away from the door. I still couldn't see Gabriel, but I could sense him. I could feel the air crackle.

290

'I was just leaving, Gabe.'

'Just leaving? We're in the *middle of nowhere*.'

'Please, just stop it. Both of you.'

I stepped out of the room and found myself standing in between them. I could hear us all breathing. The three of us. Together again.

'What's this about?' said Gabe.

Olly breathed out, through his nose.

'You're being tailed. You've been papped, and the picture'll be online any minute. I thought you should know.'

Gabriel's jaw twitched. His eyes flicked towards me, then returned to Olly.

'Ever heard of a text message, mate?'

Olly sighed.

'Did you even bring a phone?' Gabriel was silent. 'Thought not. And, yeah, I admit, it's weird that I'm here. But I was in Atlanta, Barry wasn't answering his phone and I didn't know how else to get hold of you. I was just . . . trying to do the right thing.' His lip curled. 'Maybe I shouldn't have bothered.'

Gabriel moved forward. There was less than two metres between them now, and I was in that space.

'What are you really doing here?'

Olly frowned.

'What?'

Gabriel shrugged.

'Who drives across the state to help out someone he doesn't even like?'

'It's not like that, Gabe. You know it isn't.'

'And why should I believe you?'

I felt my shoulders tense. Behind Olly, a car door opened, and one of his security guards stepped out. Olly retreated, his eyes on me.

'Just be careful, OK? You can't stay here any more. They know where you are. You both need to leave, tonight.'

He turned around and walked back to the car, and we watched it pull away from the kerb, and head out of town.

I sat on the corner of Gabriel's bed, my knee jiggling, staring at the signal monitor on my phone. I was still getting nothing. The motel didn't have Wi-Fi, and even if anywhere else in town did, it wasn't worth going out there to find out.

Seeing Olly had knocked me sideways. Gabriel and I had made this little bubble for ourselves in Marble Creek, away from the rest of the world, and Olly was the last person I'd expected to come crashing into it.

I was over him, of course. Or, at least, I thought I was. But that didn't mean I was ready to see him again, out of the blue. And what exactly had he meant by saying he wasn't breaking up with me, but with the band?

'Charlie, talk to me.'

Gabriel was perched on the corner of the window sill, his head against the wall. I shoved my phone into my suitcase, and zipped it closed.

'This was a mistake.'

He sat up.

'What do you mean?'

'Thinking we could escape out here, and no one would follow us. This whole thing, it was a mistake.'

He looked at me, for a long time, searching my face. When he spoke, his voice was brittle.

'No time I spend with you is ever a mistake.'

An angry knock at the door.

'Gabe, open up.'

Gabriel peered behind the closed curtain. With a sigh, he walked to the door and opened it up.

'We need to leave,' said Amos, crossing the room to pick up my suitcase. Marty remained in the doorway. 'The paparazzi found us.'

Barely three minutes later, we were sitting in the back of the car while Amos drove us away from Marble Creek. Barry was on speakerphone.

'Jesus H. CHRIST, this is not what I need right now.'

'It's not that big a deal,' said Gabe. 'Just some idiot pap.'

Barry scoffed.

'You let me be the judge of what is and isn't a big deal, pal.'

293

'I've never cared what they think, and neither should y—'

'*Shut up*, Gabe. Just shut up. Let me think.' I could hear him mumbling to himself. 'We can salvage this. You'll be in a new town tonight, new hotel. Throw the scum off the scent. Then tomorrow . . . yep, tomorrow, there're a couple of radio stations up in Charlotte that've been hounding me to have you on. Desperate, they are. I'll send you to one of them. Tomorrow afternoon, before you fly back to New York, you're getting on the radio, and you're telling the world that you've been on a songwriting retreat, finding your ruddy zen or whatever, and that nonsense in the photograph wasn't a fight, it was just . . . friendly banter.'

'You want me to go all the way to Charlotte for some random radio interview?'

'Do you even know where Charlotte is?' No reply from Gabe. 'South Carolina. It's on your way home. And I'll remind you, buddy, if you don't mind, that this whole road trip debacle was your idea in the first place. "This time'll be different, Barry. We'll go some place where no one knows who I am." And yet here I am again, in the middle of another bloody circus. So if I send you to a radio interview in Charlotte, or a TV spot in Chicago, or a pissing *donkey rodeo* in Buttocksville, Tennessee, then you're doing it, no questions asked. Are we speaking the same language?'

Gabriel sank back into his seat.

'Sure, Barry. Whatever you say.'

'And in the meantime, you don't get out of the car, you don't stretch your legs, you don't *sneeze* unless Marty and Amos say you can. Understood?'

I glanced out of the back window, unease creeping across my shoulders. As Amos pulled on to the freeway and pressed the pedal to the floor, I couldn't shake the feeling that we were being hunted.

The sign outside the radio station read: *HIT CYCLE* 98.5 FM >>> *Pop hits all night long!* Above the slogan was a picture of a cartoon man in sunglasses, leaping about, the air around him filled with musical notes.

According to Barry, we only had to be here for forty-five minutes – a quick interview, then on to the airport and back to New York – and this was fine by me. I was missing Melissa and the boys, and I'd barely slept the night before, half-convinced someone was crouching outside my hotel room, taking photographs in the dark.

'Gabriel, *hi there*. Thank you *so much* for coming . . .'

We stood up from our seats. A small blonde lady was tottering towards us on high heels, carrying a clipboard.

'Was your journey OK?'

Gabe nodded, his hands in his back pockets.

'To get you last-minute like this, it's really . . . I mean, for us, we *love* you guys here, Gabe. Can I call you Gabe? We're just *all about* the Fire&Lights at 98.5 . . .'

I walked down the corridor behind Gabriel and the station rep, Marty and Amos flanking us on either side. I was actually pretty grateful to be ignored. The staff at the radio station were exhausting, and they seemed to have a bona fide obsession with Fire&Lights.

As Gabriel settled in the studio, I stood in the adjacent room, watching through the glass, my chest a little tight. I'd never seen Gabriel do an interview alone and, without Yuki there to keep things light, I worried about what might happen. The focus would all be on him.

'Gabriel West, it's an honour and a pleasure to have you here with us on the Hit Cycle 98.5. How're you doing?'

Gabriel smiled genially, and leaned back in his chair.

'I'm good, thanks, Sam. And the pleasure's all mine.'

A wide grin split Sam's face.

'As you've probably figured out, we're huge F&L fans at the station.' He set his hands apart. '*Huge.* But before we talk about the band, can you shed any light on this photograph that hit the web last night?'

Gabriel's eyes dropped to the desk.

'These things happen, Sam. Popstars, paparazzi, that's just how it works.'

'Sad, but true,' said Sam, with a sigh. 'The paps just don't give up, do they?'

'No, they do not.'

Sam leaned forward on his desk.

'I have to say, the guy in the picture, he looked *big*. Like . . . BIG. What actually happened in there?'

Gabriel forced a laugh.

'I don't think he liked my piano playing.'

Sam narrowed his eyes.

'But . . . there *was* a fight of some kind, right?'

Gabriel leaned into his microphone.

'I'm not going to lie to you, Sam, or your listeners. The guy had had a few beers, and he was on edge. And, yeah, he threatened me, but nothing happened. It's not even a story, really.'

As I watched Gabriel talk, my nerves began to settle. Maybe I'd been wrong to worry about him.

'OK, sure. I getcha.' Sam waved a hand, and looked down at his notes 'Let's forget all the gossip for now, and get on to the good stuff. How's the tour going? How are y'all finding America . . . ?'

For the next ten minutes, Gabriel and Sam chatted happily about Fire&Lights, the Empire State Building and pastrami bagels, and the studio was filled with laughter and smiles. I slid my camera from its case and moved around the room, taking pictures through the glass, capturing tiny moments. Gabriel describing a giant subway sandwich, his hands set wide apart; Sam beaming at him from across the desk. It had been a while since I'd felt the weight of a camera in my hands, and it instantly lifted my mood. When I was taking photographs, when I was focusing on the line of someone's cheekbone, or the detail of their eyes, I could forget everything else. I was exactly where I wanted to be.

'So, Gabe, before you go . . . I have to ask you. How are you feeling about Olly?'

Gabe ran his hands down his face.

'Do we really have to talk about this?'

Sam winced sympathetically.

'I know, you're probably sick of it, but this is one of the biggest stories in the world right now. You two, you've been called the greatest rivals in pop, and we all know that things were strained before Olly left the band.'

Gabriel puffed out his cheeks.

'Well, I can't deny that.'

'So,' said Sam, propping his elbows on the desk, 'I guess what I'm really asking is: does Olly miss being in Fire&Lights?'

Gabriel held his hands up.

'I think you'd have to ask him that.'

'Well,' replied Sam brightly, 'you can ask him yourself, because *we have him here today*, folks! That's right, here in the Hit Cycle studios, it's the amazing, the super-talented, Olly Samson!'

The door opposite Gabriel swung open and Olly was led in by a runner, an anxious look on his face. Gabriel glared at him, astonished, but Olly shook his head, as if to say: *I didn't know either.*

The runner sat Olly down beside Gabe and positioned a microphone in front of his face. Sam looked back and forth between them.

'Finally, the moment America has been waiting for! Olly Samson and Gabriel West, reunited. How cool is this?'

Olly managed a smile.

'Hi, Gabe,' he said.

'Hey,' said Gabe quietly.

'I hope you both don't mind,' said Sam perkily, 'but here we were, yesterday, we had Olly booked in for the show, and out of nowhere, Gabe becomes available too! What are the odds?'

I leaned back against the wall, camera in my hands. Had the Fireflights management team known about this? It would be a publicity bonanza for Hit Cycle, and probably for the boys too, but Gabriel would never have agreed to it if they'd told him. Surely Barry understood that a stunt like this couldn't end well?

'So, come on,' said Sam, clapping his hands together. 'You guys have to know, the whole world is *obsessed* with you both. The rivalry, the split, the gossip. But what's the story behind the story? What really happened that night at the Troubadour?'

Olly and Gabe shared a moment of eye contact, and I felt a strange spike of electricity pass through me. The dark chemistry between them, that knife-edge between love and hate . . . that's what had been missing from Fire&Lights.

'Being in a band isn't easy,' said Olly, clearing his throat. 'It's like a family. And, sometimes, families fall apart.'

Sam tilted his head to the side.

'So it wasn't anyone's . . . fault, then? The fight, I mean?'

'It's not about blame,' said Gabe, staring him down. 'It's just life.'

Sam faltered, looking down at his papers. His cheeks were burning.

'OK . . . OK. Olly, on to your solo career.' He took in a slightly shaky breath. 'You didn't write any music in Fire&Lights, and yet here you are, a solo artist, on the verge of releasing a massively hyped, self-penned song. How has that happened?'

'I've actually been writing for quite a while, Sam,' replied Olly. 'Months.'

I thought back to what Olly had told me in the Kingdom Records studio earlier in the year. *When I ask Barry to listen to my stuff, he brushes me off. It's like he thinks only Gabriel can write songs, and I'm just some wannabe. Second best.*

If only Barry hadn't ignored him, maybe Olly would never have left the band.

'It shows, I have to say,' said Sam, pressing both hands into the desk. 'I am *loving* the new song.'

300

Olly smiled.

'I can't take all the credit. I'm pretty new to all this, so my management hooked me up with some incredible writers to bash it into shape. The single would be nothing without them.' He nodded thoughtfully. 'But, yeah, the original idea . . . I guess that came from me.'

Sam glanced at the clock.

'D'you know what, I think it might be time for us to give Olly's debut solo single its first ever play in South Carolina! What does everyone reckon?' He tapped a button on his mixing desk, triggering a round of enthusiastic fake applause. He grinned to himself. 'That's what I thought. Listeners, for the first time in the state, open your ears for the debut single by Olly Samson, this is "She Is The Fire" . . .'

My heart leapt into my throat.

Of course it was that song.

She is the fire in my fingertips
The warm rain that tells me where the thunder is
And I know that somebody has found her heart
But that won't keep us apart

As the song began to play, those familiar lyrics swirling around my head, I turned away from the glass and closed my eyes. I hadn't truly believed it until Melissa pointed it out, but Olly had written 'She Is The Fire' about me. About *us*. And now it was out there, in the world.

> *She keeps a piece of herself inside*
> *But she speaks, and every single star collides*
> *And I know that somebody has found her heart*
> *But that won't keep us apart*

Sitting beside Olly, just centimetres away, Gabriel was rigid, his gaze bolted to the desk. What Olly had told the presenter, it was true. The co-writers had taken his original song, honest and raw, and they'd turned it into a hit single. It sounded incredible. But listening to it was making me want to curl up into a ball and disappear.

'Fantastic stuff, Olly,' said Sam, minutes later, as the song came to an end. 'I just know it's gonna be a huge hit.' He interlinked his fingers. 'So tell me, what inspires your music?'

'That's a pretty broad question,' said Olly, smiling. 'I guess inspiration can come from anywhere.'

Sam poked his tongue into his cheek. 'I suppose what I'm really asking is: who's the girl in the song?'

A veiled panic flashed across Olly's eyes.

'That's a . . . secret, Sam,' he said, glancing at Gabriel. 'Take it to my grave.'

'Maybe *Gabe* knows?' Sam pointed at Gabriel. 'You've spent the last few years living in Olly's pockets, right? If he's been writing about a girl, maybe you know who she is?'

Gabriel's eyes darkened.

'Mystery to me.'

A chilly silence settled in the studio. Sam was about to reply when he touched a hand to his left headphone, as if receiving instructions. He pressed his palms together.

'Well, sadly, that is all we have time for this morning. But Olly and Gabe, thank you *so much* for coming in, you've been great sports. And good luck with the singles releasing tomorrow. May the best man win!'

Barely had Sam faded in the next track when Gabriel stood up from his chair and tossed his headphones on to the desk. Olly extended a hand towards him.

'Gabe, just calm down.'

'Leave it,' said Gabe, walking away. Olly followed him, and I realised, with a jolt, that they were heading for the room I was in.

The door swung open and the handle slammed into the wall.

'Listen,' Olly was saying, his voice strained. 'Will you listen to me? I had no idea they were doing this.'

Gabe wheeled round.

'Oh, really? Is that so?'

Olly parked his hands in his hair, his cheeks turning pink.

'Seriously. You have to believe me.'

'So yesterday,' said Gabriel, 'you somehow figure out – from across the state – that we're being tailed by paparazzi, but today, you don't even know who's turning up to your own radio interview?'

Olly pushed air out through his nostrils.

'*You* didn't know, Gabe, so why would I be any different?'

Gabriel didn't have an answer for this. Olly turned to the wall, pressing his palms against it.

'Why can't they just leave us alone?' he said, almost to himself.

Gabriel's fingers were twitching, and I could sense he was about to say something. He was standing behind Olly.

'Who *is* the girl in the song, then?'

Olly straightened up and turned around.

'You seriously want to do this now?'

'Sure, why not? Who is she?' He threw a hand in my direction. 'Do you see her in this room?'

'Come on, Gabe. Don't bring Charlie into this.'

Gabe's eyes went wide.

'Don't br—? It's your song, Olly, so if she's in it, then I didn't bring her into this. You did.'

'Me? What about you? Every last track on *Songs About Us* was about her, and you know it.'

Heat gathered on my arms and the back of my neck. Two of the biggest popstars on the planet were fighting over me, and maybe I should have been flattered, but I wasn't. Anger was pooling in my stomach. They were talking about me as if I wasn't there.

'You don't know Charlie like I do,' said Gabriel.

'Oh, you think? We were *together*, Gabe. You have no idea what you're talking about.'

'Yeah, you were together, and then you broke up with her. So if you think she's remotely interested in—'

'*That's enough.*'

My words tore a slice through the air, leaving Olly and Gabriel speechless. They stared back at me.

'I've had enough,' I said, trying my best to keep my voice steady. Gabe glared at Olly, then laid a hand on my arm.

'It's fine, Charlie. We'll just go.'

I shook his hand off.

'No, Gabe, *we* won't go anywhere.'

He looked at me quizzically. My fists were balling with anger.

'I'm sick of this. Both of you. I'm sick of you throwing me about like a piece of meat.'

'Charlie,' pleaded Olly, 'we didn't—'

'No, Olly. No. It's too late.' I stuffed my camera back into its case and tugged the zip closed. 'Look, I'm sorry for my part in all this, but I can't take it any more. I'm not some prize for you two to fight over. Do you understand?' My case hanging by my side, I locked eyes with Olly, and then Gabe. A thick silence soured the air. 'I'm not a trophy.'

I could hear my breathing, and theirs. I slung my camera over my shoulder.

'As long as things stay this way, we can't be friends. Until you stop this – until you both stop competing over absolutely everything – I don't want to see *either* of you. Anywhere.'

I pushed between them, heading for the exit. I thought I could hear one of them saying my name, but it was too late. I was already out of the door.

Before I knew where I was, I was sweeping through the station's main entrance and striding down the street. I brushed past people, my camera case swaying at my side, unsure where I was heading. Bus station, maybe? All I knew was that I had to get away from Olly and Gabe.

I'd been so naive. The day before, a day that had started in the worst possible way, had turned into one of the happiest afternoons of my life, and it was all because of Gabriel. The way he'd opened up to me, baring his soul and singing his songs. The way he had looked at me when we were dancing on that car, orange sun sinking behind us. But our time in Marble Creek, our little escape, it hadn't been real. It was like a dream, and the second the outside world came hurtling in, it had turned into a nightmare.

I'd actually started to believe that, after all the false starts, things might finally have worked out between me and Gabriel. I'd convinced myself that he'd changed, but I'd been wrong. We could never be 'normal'. We could never be just us.

We were impossible together.

'Charlie?'

A hand on my shoulder. I assumed it was one of the boys, so I threw it off, upping my pace. Then Marty stepped in front of me, both hands raised in front of him.

'Charlie, please. Stop.'

I slowed to a standstill, my arms crossed.

'What?'

'Where are you going?'

'I'm going to . . . just up . . .' My shoulders slumped. 'I don't know.'

Marty glanced around. He closed the gap between us.

'You realise it's literally my job to look out for you, right? And after yesterday, we can't take any chances.' He nodded towards the station. 'We need to get back.'

I tried to side-step him, but he blocked my way.

'Just let me go. I don't want to see Gabe again. I'll find my own way back to New York.'

I tried to dodge past him, but he held both my shoulders.

'It's fine, I get it,' he said, trying to catch my eye. 'I spoke to Gabriel, and he said the same thing.'

I looked up.

'What?'

'He said you wouldn't want to see him, and I should take you back to New York myself.'

I frowned.

'Oh. Right.'

'Let's just head back to the station, and I'll call a car. Gabriel said he'll go with Amos. It's fine.'

I nodded silently, and Marty pressed a guiding palm against my back, leading me back towards the Hit Cycle studio. Our raised voices had attracted the attention of passing pedestrians, and I could feel eyes on me as we walked.

I suddenly felt very aware, for the first time, of being thousands of miles away from home.

23

'You know Manhattan isn't the *real* New York, don't you?'

Our taxi slowed down at a set of traffic lights, and Melissa swivelled round in her seat, frowning.

'What are you talking about, Mother?'

Rosie was gazing out of the window.

'I mean, sure, it's the part you see in all the movies and postcards, but there's so much more to this place than the Empire State Building. Brooklyn's my favourite part of the city.'

'I totally agree, Mrs Morris. In fact, I was actually born in Brooklyn.'

Rosie turned to Leo, who was sitting next to her in the back row of the minivan. Melissa and I were in the middle row, Brian in the front.

'You see, I knew I liked you,' said Rosie, giving him a wink.

'Ew.' Melissa scrunched up her nose. 'He's *my* boyfriend, Ma. Get your tanks off my lawn.'

'And you're absolutely right,' continued Leo, running a hand through his springy black hair. 'Brooklyn is *way* cooler than Manhattan. The food's better too.'

'Oh my god, *dude*, quit sucking up to my mum.'

Melissa fake-scowled at Leo, and he flashed her his winning smile.

'This is ripping good fun, eh, Brian?' said Rosie, calling to her husband. He looked back over his shoulder.

'What's that?'

'I'd always thought it was basically impossible to embarrass our daughter,' replied Rosie, smiling to herself, 'but it turns out I was wrong . . .'

It was Friday night, and I hadn't seen or spoken to Gabriel since Marty and I had landed in New York the evening before. I had spent the day with the Morrises, behaving like tourists, riding up and down the escalators in Macy's and eating hot dogs on street corners. I'd tried my best to act normal and join in the fun, but Olly and Gabe had been on my mind all day. Tomorrow night was the finale of the tour – the *Make Or Break USA* anniversary show, broadcast live from New York – and, in a gesture of solidarity, Barry had invited Olly to perform his new single before Fire&Lights hit the stage.

Sooner or later, I would have to see them again.

'It looks kinda sketchy around here, Ma,' said Melissa, pressing her nose up against the window. We were passing abandoned warehouses with burned-out windows, and empty parking garages surrounded by barbed wire.

'Hey,' said Leo playfully. 'That's my home town you're talking about.'

'And, actually,' said Rosie, waving a finger, 'Brooklyn is incredibly vibrant and bursting with culture. So, my darling, as you yourself might say . . . sketchy smetchy.'

Melissa rolled her eyes, but she couldn't keep the smile off her face. She was deliriously happy with Leo, and I was happy *for* her. For Leo too. I just wished I didn't have such a dark cloud hanging over me. I'd told Melissa everything, of course, but she was keeping it to herself, and as far as her parents were concerned, I'd simply returned to the city after a few days photographing Gabriel for the Ian site.

'This place looks perfect,' said Rosie, a few minutes later, as we stepped out of the taxi in front of a small Italian restaurant on the corner of Fifth Avenue. 'I hope everyone's ready for a feast!'

'Will you share a pizza with me, CB?' said Mel, on our way inside. 'I want one of those ones that looks like a big Cornish pasty.'

'Calzone.'

'Bless you,' said Melissa, with a snigger.

'You know,' Leo said to me, as he strolled beside us, hands in his pockets, 'I knew from the first second I met your best friend that she was the most extraordinary girl I had ever laid eyes on.' He leaned towards me. 'But, man, some of her jokes are *heinously* bad.'

I laughed, for the first time in a while, and Melissa's mouth dropped open in exaggerated outrage.

311

'How very dare you! We are going to have words later, Leo Zaragoza . . .'

The restaurant smelled of fresh pasta and olive oil, and had a ramshackle, homespun atmosphere. Families of all ages filled the tables, sharing bread baskets and gesticulating and having impassioned conversations in Italian. The whole place was warm, noisy and reassuringly shambolic.

Over the following two hours, Melissa and I shared a 'big-Cornish-pasty-pizza' (she insisted on calling it that all night), Rosie ate a steaming seafood linguine, Leo polished off a huge portion of lasagne and Brian had a little too much red wine and got all gushy about his wife. It was just about the loveliest evening out you could possibly imagine, but it barely lifted my spirits at all.

'What's eating you, my love?'

As the restaurant was emptying, and Melissa, Leo and Brian were at the gelato counter picking ice creams, Rosie nudged her chair closer to mine. I glanced up from my paper napkin, which I'd been tearing into little shreds.

'Huh?'

'You're very quiet tonight.'

I cast aside the tattered napkin and shrugged.

'I'm all right.'

'Was the trip OK?'

I hesitated. I had always wondered exactly how many of my secrets Rosie actually knew. She had this way about her, a sixth sense. She wasn't oblivious, like my dad.

312

'I guess I'm just feeling a bit tired.'

Rosie nodded slowly, her eyes searching mine. Breaking her gaze, I looked over at Melissa, who was cooing into the gelato cooler, and Brian and Leo, who were talking about something that sounded like sports.

'You guys are all so sorted,' I said, flicking the rim of my water glass.

'Who is?' asked Rosie.

'Your whole family. You just . . . *work* together. You always have.'

Rosie's mouth lifted into a half-smile.

'It might seem that way, sweetheart, but things are never that simple. I mean, Melissa was a very difficult baby, and Tom had a bit of a rough time at Caversham High. Plus, before that, Brian and I had troubles of our own. We almost didn't get married, you know.'

I frowned at her.

'What?'

'Oh, yes. He broke off the engagement, just a few months before our wedding. He had what I suppose Melissa might call a "freak-out", and it almost never happened.' She cracked a smile. 'Of course, I whipped him into shape, and the rest is history, but . . . the truth is, no one's perfect. Not me, not Brian, not your dad. We're just doing the best we can, exactly like you.' She dabbed her finger on her plate, picking up a crumb of cheesecake, and popped it in her mouth. 'I know that grown-ups sometimes act as if we know everything, but we really don't. Life is unpredictable, and messy. In fact, learning to accept that is pretty much what makes you an adult in the first place.' She looked at me. 'Does that make sense?'

I gazed out of the window at some passers-by, a heavy weight in my heart. Maybe Rosie was right. Maybe this whole mess – me and Olly and Gabe, Harry West, my mother, Little Boy Blue – maybe all this was just *life*. Maybe I simply had to get used to the chaos.

'Yeah, I s'pose so.'

'Um, hello?' Melissa was standing above us, holding a large ice-cream cone. The gelato was, disturbingly, black. 'Which one of you wants to be first to sample this thing of beauty?'

'That looks hideous,' said Rosie.

'*Liquirizia*,' said Melissa, holding her fingers up like an Italian chef. 'All the more for me, in that case.'

Brian pocketed his wallet.

'Come on, then, ladies and gents. I've paid up, and all that pinot noir is starting to go to my head. I think it's time for us to wander home.'

We left the restaurant and spilled out on to the street, the warmth of the evening settling in our clothes, and on our skin. Leo and Melissa ambled along next to me, whispering to each other and enjoying their ice cream, while up ahead, Rosie and Brian walked hand in hand beneath the Brooklyn street lights.

That night, as I struggled to sleep, a chorus of voices rattled through my brain. Rosie, telling me that life was 'messy and unpredictable', and it would never change. Gabriel, dancing with me on the roof of the rusted-out car, telling me he only felt happy when we were together. Olly, outside my motel room, his blue eyes fixed on mine. *I wasn't breaking up with you, Charlie. I was breaking up with the band.*

I drifted in and out of slumber, head throbbing, skin tacky with sweat, despite the never-ending whir of the air conditioning. Occasionally, Melissa would stir in the bed beside me, or mumble something in her sleep.

Finally, some time after midnight, I fell asleep. But what felt like seconds later, I was woken again by an unfamiliar sound. My mobile phone ringing. I hadn't heard it since we'd left England, and it was coarse and angry in my ear. Melissa was a pretty deep sleeper, but I didn't want to wake her, so I crept into the bathroom, hit the light switch and closed the door.

The number on my phone screen said 'HOME'.

'Dad, wh— It's three o'clock in the morning.'

'Charlie, are you safe?'

I squinted at myself in the mirror. The whiteness of the lights was hurting my eyes.

'Safe? What do you mea—'

'Are you somewhere safe? Please, just tell me.'

I shook my head, confused.

'Yes, of course. We're in our hotel. It's the middle of the night.'

As I said it, I realised that it wasn't the middle of the night where he was. It was eight a.m.

'It's . . . god, Charlie . . . I don't know how to say this. They're here. They're outside the house.'

My heart juddered in my chest. The tone in Dad's voice, I'd never heard it before. It was like fear, but worse.

'Who's outside the house? Dad, you're not making sense.'

'Reporters. Hundreds of reporters.'

I leaned my forehead on my hand. My brain was still foggy from sleep.

'But why would th—'

'I know.'

There was a pause. I drew in a breath.

'You know . . . what?'

I could hear my father's shaky breathing, and the phone trembling in his hand. My stomach dropped.

'Charlie, I know who Gabriel West is. I know the real reason you're in America.'

24

'Gabriel? But . . . no, Dad, I'm just here for Melissa . . .'

Even as I heard the words coming out of my mouth, I knew it was useless. But I couldn't stop myself lying. I'd been doing it for so long.

'This boy, Gabriel, from the band. He's Harry's son. He's Harry West's son.' Emotion was rupturing Dad's voice. He was choking as he tried to speak. 'That's who you've been with all this time.'

As my body woke up, and the reality of the situation began to sink in, I felt tears building inside my chest.

'Dad, I'm sorry. I'm sorry I lied . . .' I was starting to sob. 'Please, it wasn't meant to turn out this way . . .'

Tears crawled down my cheeks, leaving tracks on my skin, and a darker thought dawned on me. Something must have happened to give me away.

'How did you find out?'

I heard Dad sniff, then swallow, trying to compose himself.

'It's in the papers, Charlie. It's on the front page of *The Record*. I saw it on the television.'

317

Sickness rose up inside me, and I pressed a hand to my mouth.

It was finally happening.

'It's the biggest news story in the country,' continued Dad, his breathing heavy in my ear. 'How Gabriel lied about his parents, how Harry was a drug dealer . . . it mentions the band, and Katherine, and . . . that's why they're here. The reporters. I can't leave the house. There are too many of them.'

'Maybe you should call the police, or . . .' I was babbling. I didn't know what to do. I didn't know what to tell him.

'I'm coming to America.'

I gripped the phone tighter.

'What?'

'I'm coming to America, to get you.'

I dragged a shaking hand through my hair.

'But, Dad . . . aren't you mad at me?'

'Charlie, I . . .' I could hear his voice tearing up. He pushed out the words. 'All I care about is making you safe. The news will reach New York in a few hours' time, if it hasn't already, and the whole country will be knocking on your door. So I'm coming out there. I'm bringing you home.'

Tears were streaming down my face now.

'Wh— Really?'

'Don't leave your hotel, don't go anywhere. As soon as

I can get past these damn reporters, I'm going straight to Heathrow.' He took a deep breath. 'I'm not going to let anything happen to you, OK? I'm not going to let *anything* happen to you.'

We both fell quiet, and I realised I could hear the faint sound of people shouting, outside our front door, back at home.

'I'll be there as soon as I can.'

And he hung up the phone.

Next thing I knew, I was out in the corridor, leaning against the wall, my phone hot and clammy in my hand.

I had to read that article. I didn't want to, but I had to. I had to know what they'd written about me, about Gabriel. About my family.

Sliding down the dark, plush wallpaper, I crumpled in a ball on the floor and unlocked my screen. It only took me seconds to find the story.

<><><><><><>

EXCLUSIVE: THE WORLD'S BIGGEST POPSTAR IS LYING TO YOU

Today, only in The Record, *undercover reporter Paul Morgan reveals the sordid secrets of Gabriel West's hidden past, from drug deals and foster care to petty crime and suicide.*

Is this the most sensational exposé in
the history of pop music?

The writer credit made my skin crawl. Paul Morgan. It had played out exactly as he threatened it would. He'd followed us to Devon, he'd set Gabriel up outside the StarBright Arena. He'd stalked me from a car, in my home town. He'd leaked the Thunderland story, probably the prison video as well, and then he'd followed us to Marble Creek and photographed us in the bar. Maybe he'd even listened in on our conversations. And the whole time, he was building up to this moment. The defining story of his career.

Wiping my cheek with the back of my hand, I carried on.

Remember when Gabriel West, mysterious star member of record-breaking boy band Fire&Lights, told you his parents were living in the South of France to avoid press attention? Remember when he told you they couldn't make the band's recent show at Madison Square Garden because of a "family emergency"?

He was lying.

Because his parents have been dead for nearly fifteen years.

And when you hear what kind of man his father was, you'll understand what has turned Gabriel West from untouchable pop prince into a violent, angry thug . . .

*Sources close to this newspaper can now reveal that Gabriel's parents were the British-born Harold Thomas West (1969-2000) and Rafaela Sofia Domínguez (1970-2000), an **illegal immigrant** from Salvador, Brazil. In the late nineties, Harry West was a **part-time drug dealer**, living in squalor in Wembley, North London, with his undocumented partner – who could **barely speak a word of English** – and his young son, future superstar Gabriel Tiago West.*

When he wasn't pushing drugs on the streets of London, Harry was the lead singer of struggling indie-rock band Little Boy Blue, who were often seen performing at the Troubadour Coffee House in Earl's Court—

I clamped a hand to my mouth. They'd printed the photograph. The one of the band outside the Troubadour, holding their instruments, with a handful of fans in the foreground. The drummer and bass player were standing at the back with their instruments, next to Harry, whose face had been circled in red. But his face wasn't the only one the newspaper had singled out.

They'd circled my mother's face too.

This photograph shows the band outside the Troubadour club, circa 1998. Harry West is highlighted at the back, and in the foreground, the band's piano player, Katherine Bloom, can be seen wearing a Little Boy Blue T-shirt.

*In early 2000, Rafaela Domínguez tragically died of a **drug overdose**, leaving Harry as Gabriel's sole guardian. But Harry was not cut out for fatherhood, and he abandoned Gabriel in a children's home, **funded by the British taxpayer**, while he swanned off to America with his band.*

*But Little Boy Blue's American adventure proved a disaster. Harry, by this time a **reckless alcoholic**, quit the band before the tour was complete, leaving his bandmates to struggle on without him. A week later, Little Boy Blue pianist Katherine was **killed in a car accident** on the way back from a gig, and the following day – racked by guilt, perhaps? – Harry **committed suicide**, leaving his son to fend for himself back in London.*

I paused, thinking about the secrets I'd learned at Nate's bar. I was grateful that Paul had either failed, or not bothered, to dig up the truth about Mum's death. The thought of it splashed across the front pages turned my stomach.

*The young Gabriel went from bad to worse. As a teenager he was involved in **gang violence** and anti-social behaviour,* *stealing from supermarkets and vandalising property. But against the odds, he was **saved from a life of crime** by music industry mogul Barry King, who plucked him from obscurity on the TV talent show* Make Or Break *and made Gabriel his fortune as a member of wildly popular boy band Fire&Lights.*

Amazingly, last year, fate conspired to have Gabriel cross paths with boy band groupie Charlie Bloom – the sixteen-year-old daughter of Little Boy Blue pianist Kathe—

Bile flooded my throat, and I bent over on the carpet, trying not to be sick. *I was in the article.* I knew I would be, but actually seeing my name in print, it made it all real. I struggled, hard, to hold back the tears, rocking on my knees with my eyes closed tight.

Eventually, chest heaving, I dropped back against the wall. I had to get to the end of this article.

*. . . Katherine Bloom. **It is now believed that Gabriel and Charlie are engaged in a romantic relationship**, a fact which he has deliberately kept secret from the fans. Until now.*

Another photograph. The infamous selfie of Gabriel and me, standing on the empty stage in Brighton.

My face, in a national newspaper.

*But, then, lying comes naturally to Gabriel West. Instead of telling the truth about his sordid upbringing, he lied to the world. **He lied to the fans**, the very people who put him where he is today. And as time goes on, the world watches as the ghost of Harry West pulls his son's strings, making him more **violent and unpredictable** with every passing day. In April, he even started the fight that **forced Olly Samson to quit the band**, causing heartbreak for fans all across the globe.*

*So can a troubled teen – the son of a **drug-dealing coward** and a **junkie immigrant** – ever escape what's in his blood?*

Only Gabriel knows the answer to that question.

Story by Paul Morgan. Troubadour photograph provided by an anonymous source.

I couldn't breathe. I needed some fresh air.

I knew I wasn't supposed to leave the hotel on my own, but I had to get outside, just for a few minutes. Panic was crawling up my shoulders, and I felt like there was a creature on my back, whispering in my ear. I jabbed impatiently at the call button for the lift, my mind racing. It was still the middle of the night, and I had a few hours before America would wake up and read the story. I had time. I still, just about, had time.

When the lift doors opened into the lobby, I walked straight out across the tiled floor, keeping my eyes down. I was in my pyjamas, but I didn't care.

As I emerged into the Manhattan air, it hit me, like it always did. The intense heat, the stuffiness. It was always hot in New York. The summer was claustrophobic and never-ending.

I turned in a random direction and walked down the street, unsure of where I was heading or why. I just needed the air on my face, the lights in my eyes and the hum of car engines in my ears. After a few minutes, I unlocked my phone and stared at Gabriel's name in my message inbox, thumb trembling above the screen. I had to say something. I had to reach out.

Paul Morgan published his story. I don't know if you've heard. I hope you're OK xx

When the message had sent, I looked up and found I was standing outside an all-night diner. Trance-like, I wandered inside and slid into a window booth.

Peering out through the glass, I tried to compose myself. For the middle of the night, there were still quite a few people on the pavements, and taxis on the road. I guessed this was why they called it The City That Never Sleeps.

'You good, darlin'?'

I looked up. A waitress with kind eyes, and her hair in a bun, was standing above me, holding a notepad.

'Um . . . yeah, sure.'

I dragged a hand across my sticky cheeks. She glanced out through the window.

'Seem awful young to be on your own this time of night. Are your parents nearby?'

I sniffed.

'It's . . . fine. They're in a hotel, just down the road. I had a nightmare, I couldn't sleep.'

She pressed her lips together.

'Oh, darl, that's sucky. How's about I fix you a drink?'

'Americano, please, white,' I said, without thinking. I figured I wasn't going back to sleep anyway, so I may as well do what New Yorkers do.

'Comin' right up.'

She left the table and headed over to the coffee pots on the counter. I looked around the almost-empty diner, feeling my heart turn in my chest.

This was it. This was the last time I would walk down a city street, into a diner, a shop or a train station, and not be That Girl from the article. Not be Charlie Bloom, the 'boy-band groupie'. Would this follow me around forever? Would I ever shake it off?

'No more nightmares, OK?'

The waitress had returned, holding a steaming cup of

coffee. I watched her set it down on the table, and attempted a smile.

'No more nightmares,' I said, in a small voice.

'Just holler if you need anything else,' she replied, before pocketing her notepad and drifting away to wipe tables.

I stared into the hot coffee, stirring it vacantly with a spoon. In just a few hours, America would wake up and read the news. And life as I knew it would never be the same again.

25

Melissa and I were sitting cross-legged on the bed, just like we'd always done at home. But we weren't at home any more, we were in New York City. Sitting on satin sheets in a luxury Manhattan hotel, fourteen floors above the ground, with a thick-necked bouncer standing guard outside our door.

'This is so weird,' said Melissa, shaking her head. 'I wish I could help you.'

'You are. Just having you with me always helps.'

My phone pinged on the duvet. I reached for it, but Melissa grabbed my hand.

'Don't look at it,' she said. 'It'll just be more hate.'

The year before, when the photograph of me and Gabriel had first appeared on the web, Aimee Watts had leaked my phone number on Melissa's fan site. Melissa had deleted it straight away, but it must have found its way on to some F&L forums because, afterwards, my phone had buzzed for hours with abusive messages.

In the end, the messages stopped. But some random fan must have dug up the number again, because since the article had broken, the floodgates had opened.

hey CHARLIE BLOOM stay away from fire&lights

you poisoned gabriel you dumb slut

i'm gunna hunt u down bitch

'Seriously.' Melissa leaned over and slid my phone out of reach. 'Why don't you turn it off?'

'I can't. I need to keep it on, for Dad.'

'He'll be in the air for hours, CB. You have to give yourself a break.'

I side-eyed my phone, lying among the folds of the duvet. Melissa was right, but there was still a dark part of me that wanted to read every word.

'So, listen.' Melissa made a pained face. 'Mum and Dad asked me to go with them to Ground Zero today, but I can stay here with you, if you need me. We can order disgusting amounts of room service and watch wildlife programmes about naked mole rats.'

'It's OK,' I said, tucking a matted clump of hair behind my ear. 'You should go.'

'You're still coming to the filming tonight, though, right?'

'I . . . I'm not sure. I don't really know what I'd say to Gabe, or Olly.'

Melissa's shoulders dropped, and I gazed up at the ceiling, thinking about how we'd left things in South Carolina. The boys fighting over who knew me the best;

329

me giving them an ultimatum and storming out. It was such a mess.

Since the day had begun, I'd had messages from both of them.

I just wish he'd left you out of it, Gabriel had written. You shouldn't have to deal with any of this, Charlie. I'm sorry x

It had made me ache, reading his words. I knew that, however bad this was for me, it was a thousand times worse for him.

Meanwhile, Olly had messaged me on Facebook.

I doubt you want to hear from me right now, but I wanted you to know I'm thinking of you. And I understand now. All the secrecy between you and Gabe – I shouldn't have made it about me. Hope to see you at the show tonight. O xxx

I felt like I was losing control of everything, and everyone. As if our friendships were falling apart, right in front of my eyes.

Melissa squeezed my fingers.

'Think about it, OK? I know everything's screwed up right now, but it'll still be an amazing night. And, hey, if things get super awkward, we could always just hang out with Yuki and Aid, eating M&M's.'

I managed a weak smile. Yuki and Aiden had sent me messages too: Aiden's was sweet and thoughtful; Yuki's was boisterous and surreal and included a short video of a pony riding a skateboard.

'So what do you reckon?' Melissa pinched the fabric of my pyjama bottoms and gave them a little tug. 'The show's going to be huge, and you and me can still have a fun time, whatever's happening with—'

A knock at the door. We both sat up, like meerkats, and Melissa threw me a glance. I shrugged, and she slid off the bed and walked to the door.

'Oh. Hello, Mr King.'

'Hi, Melissa. Is Charlie in?'

Melissa opened the door a bit wider and Barry stepped into the room. There was a strange little silence.

'I have to go and see Mum and Dad,' said Melissa hurriedly. 'Make some plans for the day. Message me, Charlie, OK?'

I nodded, and Melissa ducked out of the room. Barry took another few steps inside, and sat down on the corner of the bed. He looked unusually bashful.

'So . . . how are you doing?'

I cleared my throat. It felt scratchy and tired.

'I've been better, if I'm honest.'

'These tabloids, they're the absolute worst.' He fiddled with one of his gold rings. 'But we rely on them to hype our acts, so they're kind of a necessary evil.'

I bit the inside of my cheek, hard.

'I don't rely on them for anything.'

Barry sighed, and smoothed out the duvet.

'No, Charlie. You don't. And it's not fair on you. I feel like I should have done more to protect you from this.'

I hung my head.

'Paul was going to publish the article anyway, no matter what happened. He's been building up to it for ages.'

Barry shuffled closer.

'Truth is, Bloom, I care about you. A lot. You're kind of like a, I don't know . . . niece or something. And you don't deserve this.'

'Thanks,' I said, feeling emotion surge in my chest. I swallowed it down.

My phone dinged again, and it happened to be closer to Barry than me. His eyes dropped to the screen and nearly doubled in size.

'Jesus, Bloom. How long has that been going on?'

'Oh.' I sniffed. 'Pretty much since the article came out.'

'Bloody Nora, these people are in-breds.' He tapped my phone with a stubby finger. 'We can change your number for you, if you like. In an instant. You just say the word.' He checked his Rolex. 'Ah, cripes, I have to dash. I was supposed to spend today celebrating five years of running the most popular TV show in America, and instead I'm fending off the biggest media crapstorm I've ever seen.' He waved the thought away. 'But, listen. You need anything at all, and I do mean *anything*, you just call me. Understand?'

I nodded.

'Sure.'

Barry stood up and jerked his head towards the door.

'We've laid on extra security for you today, tomorrow, for as long you need it. For your old man too, when he arrives. Trust me, if any of those bastards tries to get within a hundred metres of you, we'll string 'em up by the balls. No mercy.'

I laughed, despite myself.

'Thanks.'

'I'll see you in a bit, all right?'

'All right,' I said, watching as he left the room and closed the door behind him.

Dropping back against the big, squishy pillows, I picked up my phone and slid my finger over the power button. Like Melissa said, Dad would be in the air right now, and I had nothing to gain by leaving it on. The message on the lock screen – *GROUPIE SLAG* – made that very clear.

Just as I was about to power it down, though, an email notification appeared.

1m ago

Charlie my dear, I dunno if you're checking emails, but I wanted to say, I'm in N . . .

It was from Carrie Shakes.

Sitting up, I unlocked the screen and opened the message.

Charlie my dear, I dunno if you're checking emails, but I wanted to say, I'm in New York if you need someone to hang out with. That slimeball at *The Record* has a whole lot to answer for.

I got your message earlier in the summer, and like a major airhead, forgot to reply (you mighta twigged – I suck with emails!!!). Anyways, I figure you might be in town for the big MoB show tonight, and after what's happened, Mr King probably has you locked down in a hotel somewhere.

But, listen, from one photographer to another, I kinda get what you're going through, and if you need a pal, I'm at The Marshall hotel in the East Village. I'll be here until 5. Holler if you need me.

Carrie xoxxox

I peered through the gap in the curtains. I was beginning to experience cabin fever, holed up in that room, and while it was maybe a weird time to meet Carrie, this might be my only opportunity.

Slipping my feet into my shoes, I opened up my contacts and dialled Barry's number.

'You know what you need? Lapsang souchong.'

Carrie picked up a brightly patterned teapot and ducked the spout at me.

'Pardon?' I said.

'Man, I love you Brits. "Pardon". Like you're Oscar Wilde.' She started to pour the tea. 'It's black tea, from China. Winston Churchill used to drink it.'

I shrugged.

'Well, if it's good enough for Winston . . .'

Carrie set down the teapot and gave me a sympathetic smile. She was small, not much taller than me, and dressed in ripped jeans and a Bikini Kill T-shirt. Her hair was shaved on one side and bouffant on top: a dark, sweeping quiff like a wave about to hit the shore.

'So how you doing? Not great, I'm gonna bet?'

I felt myself turning red.

'Yeah. Pretty crappy, actually.'

Although at first Barry had been against me leaving the hotel, when I'd told him I wanted to go and see Carrie, he'd let me go, albeit with four security guards in

335

tow. We had snuck out of the back entrance of Eagle 519 (built for these precise situations, apparently) and they'd driven me across town to The Marshall, which was just about the coolest hotel I'd ever been in. All matte grey paintwork and brushed steel.

Now, Carrie and I were sitting in a private dining area, afternoon tea on the table, while my security guards stood just a metre or so away behind Japanese-style partitions. I could barely cough without one of them rushing to my rescue.

'If there's one kinda creature I've grown to hate,' said Carrie, settling back into her chair with a fresh cup of tea, 'it's those scumbag reporters you have over there in the UK. They're ruthless. And they don't care who they hurt, neither . . . they only care about the story.'

'He'd been following us for ages. It was bound to come out eventually.'

Carrie inhaled the steam from her tea.

'So you going to the show tonight?' she asked.

'I was supposed to, but . . . now, I don't know. I'm not ready to see either of them.'

Carrie's eyes narrowed.

'I assume you're talking about our very own Luke Skywalker and Han Solo, right?'

I let out a hollow laugh, resting my cheek on my palm.

'Yeah, something like that.'

She set her tea down and leaned forward.

'You know, I knew straight away, the second I met the boys, that those two had something *deep* going on. I'd run around, shooting the band, and trying to get a picture of Olly and Gabe together was . . . I don't know . . .'

'Impossible?'

She clicked her fingers at me.

'Exactly. You found that?'

I chewed my lip.

'Uh-huh. Not like Yuki and Aid . . . those guys are like puppies.'

'Dammit, I love those two. I have a *billion* photos of 'em.'

'Me too.' Something broke the surface of my memory. It was a secret, but my gut told me Carrie already knew. 'Did you . . . did you know that Gabe gets stage fright?'

She lifted a shoulder.

'It had crossed my mind, sure. He was always so quiet before shows.'

'He's got a lot of . . . stuff going on in his life.'

'Yeah. Yeah.' She paused. I was pretty sure we were both thinking about Paul's article. 'He's got a wounded soul, that one. The things he's been through. And then you have Olly, and he's just the sweetest, most open guy on the planet, and you can kind of understand why they're at each other's throats all the time, but . . .' Her eyes lit up. 'But, then, if you're patient, if you wait and you watch them, and that perfect moment comes and you *do* get that picture, then . . . wow.'

337

I thought of Carrie's photograph of Olly and Gabriel that I'd seen in the Slash Gallery in Reading, earlier in the year. The two of them standing onstage, in an open-air arena, just staring at each other. The moon behind them, throbbing in the sky, stage lights burning all around. Everything Carrie had described was, in a way, visible in that photo. The rivalry, the friendship, the bad blood.

'Your live shot,' I said, 'the one from São Paulo . . . it's amazing.'

She smiled at me.

'You're too kind, Charlie Bloom.' Her smile faded, and her voice softened. 'They need each other, you know. There's no doubt about that. They're too young to understand it right now, and maybe they had to break away from one another just to let off some steam . . . but it might not always be that way.'

I picked up my cup and wrapped my fingers around it.

'You really think so?'

'Sometimes people break up not because they're meant to be apart, but because they're meant to be together. And they just have to be alone for a while so they can figure that out. Does that make sense?'

I stared into the blackness of my tea.

'I guess so.'

Carrie dunked a spoon into the sugar bowl and added a mound to her tea. Her spoon clinked against the teacup.

'I think you should go tonight, Charlie.'

I winced.

'I don't know.' I glanced at the Japanese partition. It depicted an ancient temple, with people flooding the steps, praying on their knees. 'It's, like, as long as I stay inside one of these fancy hotels, I'll be fine. I'm hidden. But if I go out there, people will be looking at me, and judging me, just like in the article.'

Carrie propped her elbows on her knees and pointed at me with both hands.

'Ah, no. See, this is what you have to understand, sister. *You've done nothing wrong.* But if you stay at home, then, I dunno . . . that's kinda like admitting defeat.'

'They called me a groupie.'

'Yeah, that sucks. But you know what? During the first five years of my career, I got called a groupie every . . . single . . . day. And not just by men. People see a strong, talented woman in this industry, they see us hanging out backstage, making friends with the bands, and they don't like it. They *want* all the girls to be groupies, 'cos it makes more sense to them, right? It fits into their blinkered worldview.

'Man, I can't even *tell* you the number of rockstars who've tried it on with me after the shoot. They see the camera, and they think, "oh, hey, this chick, she's carrying around an expensive piece of kit so she can get her rocks off with the lead singer," and it's just so in*sult*ing. Things have changed a bit since I started out, but the music business is still sexist as hell. That said, I tell you what.' She smiled, and pointed at me. 'It's women like *you*, Charlie Bloom, who are gonna change that. You're the future, dude.'

I sunk into my chair, feeling strangely self-conscious. Nobody had ever called me a 'woman' before. Was that how Carrie saw me?

'And in a few years' time, you'll sit back in your warehouse studio up in, I dunno, Brooklyn Heights or whatever, and you'll look back on all this crap, and you'll see it for what it is. Hot air. Maybe there'll always be some sexist pigs treating you like a groupie, 'cos they're too damn ignorant to see you any other way, but trust me: anyone with half a brain could tell in a second that's not who you are. It's obvious to me, for a start.'

I smiled at her.

'Thanks, Carrie.'

'Hey, no thanks needed. I've seen your photos. I've pored over them, and I can tell that you *get* it. You get that it's not about technology, or framing, or focusing, or the stuff you can learn on the internet. It's about energy. It's about the things no one can teach you. Energy, passion and imagination. And, chica, you got those *in spades*.'

Carrie glanced at her phone, face down on the table, and flicked it over.

'Ah, crap. It's later than I thought. I need to make a move.' She tossed the phone into her handbag. 'But, listen, anything I can do to help, any time, you let me know, OK? This better not be the last time we hang out.'

A distant light glowed inside me. It felt something like hope.

'It won't be,' I said.

She stood up, and paused.

'Actually, what about tonight? You wanna ride with me to *Make Or Break*?' She slid on a pair of gold-rimmed shades. 'I have a pretty cool car.'

I stood up too.

'You're on,' I said. 'I'll have to face the world sooner or later.'

Carrie gave me a salute.

'Ha, that's my girl. She's back in the room . . .'

As I looked out over the *Make Or Break* arena, I felt my insides turn to water. Gabriel would be standing in the bowels of the building at that very moment, waiting to come onstage, like a slave about to be thrown to the lions. He would have to look out into that auditorium, lights in his eyes, knowing that every last person in the crowd knew his secrets.

That might be enough to break him for good.

My father, meanwhile, had landed at JFK airport, and would soon be on his way to the studios. When I tried to imagine what I'd say when I saw him, all I felt was shame. Shame for lying all this time, for digging up family secrets behind his back.

'I know today's been a pretty weird day for you,' said Melissa, standing next to me, 'but this has been kind of cool, right? Seeing how the show gets filmed?'

I gripped the balcony rails, listening to the distant rumble of the crowd below. Millions of people across the world would have given their left arm to watch *Make Or Break* being filmed from a VIP box, but the excitement had passed me by. For the anniversary show, Barry had invited back all of his most successful acts to perform on the programme that launched their careers, and for Melissa, it had been a celebrity-spotting fiesta. But Olly Samson and Fire&Lights had been saved for the final half-hour, and I'd spent the entire time crippled with nerves.

'You're right.' I tucked my hair behind my ears. 'Sorry, Mel. I've been rubbish company tonight.'

She looped her arm through mine.

'You could be on a sponsored silence and have a bag over your head, and you'd still be my favourite person to hang out with.'

I allowed myself a tiny smile.

'Even over Leo?'

Melissa wrinkled her nose.

'Even over Leo.'

'Ladies . . . and . . . gentlemen!'

A massive cheer from the auditorium. Onstage, *Make Or Break USA* presenter Eric Leroy was introducing the closing segment of the show. The big finale.

'This is the moment you've all been waiting for: the return of the biggest stars to ever make it out of *Make Or Break* boot camp. These guys came out of our UK show, but they're touring Stateside right now and they're just as huge here as they are back home. So let's give an incredible welcome, first of all, to the amazing, the newly solo . . . Olly Samson!'

Olly's face appeared on the big screens, his world-famous smile spreading wide across his face. The opening bars of 'She Is The Fire' kicked in, and the whole building erupted.

At first, you could barely hear the music over the shouting and screaming of the crowd. Olly ran down to the edge of the stage, past his backing musicians, and the fans on the front row lifted their arms, reaching out for him. Then he pressed his microphone to his mouth and began to sing.

> *She is the fire in my fingertips*
> *The warm rain that tells me where the thunder is*
> *And I know that somebody has found her heart*
> *But that won't keep us apart*

'This is so cool!' shouted Melissa, above the music. 'So proud of my boy.'

Olly was hitting every note perfectly, his pure, powerful voice soaring high above the driving beat. He had the whole crowd singing along, and to the casual observer, he was doing everything right. He was at the top of his game.

But something was missing.

I'd known Olly for a long time. We'd barely spoken in months, of course, but that didn't change how close we'd been before he left the band, and I felt like I understood him. Whenever I'd watched him onstage with Fire&Lights, it was as if I could *feel* the energy pouring off him. His eyes were always bright, his shoulders square. But tonight, up there on his own, he looked smaller, almost. His smile seemed shallow.

And as the song went on, and I watched him moving across the stage, alone, all I could see was the space around him where his three best friends should have been.

'People, make some noise for Olly Samson!'

When the track ended, more maniacal cheering shook the walls of the auditorium, and Olly waved to the crowd, retreating to the side of the stage. His face filled the big screens again, and I studied his eyes, trying to read his expression. Was it just me, or did he look a bit lost?

'We'll be catching up with Olly later on, but first, our climactic performance of the evening. That's right, it's the biggest boy band on the face of the planet, the incredible . . . Fire&Lights!'

The four boys appeared at the back of the stage, and it felt like cement was hardening inside me. My fingers tightened around the balcony rails as a strobe flickered across the arena and the catchy synth riff that opened 'This American Girl' began to play. Meanwhile, lasers fired left and right, slicing through dry ice.

Jake stepped forward to sing the opening lines, and the fans greeted him with enthusiastic cheers. He smiled, lapping it up. Yuki sang next, and then Aiden, and soon the entire auditorium was clapping along. But as the chorus neared, and Gabriel took the lead, something horrible happened.

People started to boo.

It wasn't obvious at first – just a few pockets here and there – but by the end of the chorus, it was impossible to ignore. They were booing Gabriel. And as the song went on, every time he took the microphone, the noise started up again. When he appeared on the screen, it was written all over his face. It was destroying him. And every second he was up there, my heart broke a little more.

As for the rest of the band, they couldn't ignore it. They were losing their swagger, and the stage began to look too big for them. They weren't united, not in the way they used to be. They weren't a *band*.

I tore my eyes away, unable to watch, and found myself staring down at Olly, who was looking on from the wings.

The band needed him, and he needed the band. It was exactly like Nate had described it, back in New Jersey, just before I walked out of his bar ... *A band is more than the sum of their parts, if you know what I mean? It ain't just about one member, the 'star', or whatever. It's about the chemistry between 'em all. When the mix is right, you can't just take one cat out, or replace them. In a great band, every member counts* ...

At the time, I'd been so caught up with the revelation about my mother that I hadn't given it any thought, but looking back, he might as well have been talking about Fire&Lights. It wasn't as if they *couldn't* perform without Olly. Jake was exceptionally talented, and on paper, they were still the same band. But underneath, where it counted, they weren't. Because without Olly, they weren't Fire&Lights, and they never would be.

They would never be the same unless he came back.

'Let's hear it again for Fire&Lights!'

The presenter led the crowd in another round of applause, but when Gabriel's face flashed up on the screen, it was soured by a ripple of booing. Gabriel clenched his jaw, genuine fear in his eyes. He looked like he was about to come apart.

It was just so unfair.

'Come on over here, then, guys. Olly, you too.'

The boys gathered around Eric Leroy, Olly on one side, Fire&Lights on the other.

'Great show, Olly. Great show. But tell me . . . what's it like seeing your old bandmates again?'

'What's it like?' repeated Olly. A smile warmed his face. 'Amazing. I've missed them, you know?' He locked eyes with Aiden, who gave him a quiet nod.

'What about you guys?' Eric turned to Fire&Lights. 'It's been a crazy summer for you four, rocking the States with a brand-new line-up. What's next for the band?'

'Personally,' said Yuki, 'I plan to invest all my money in a Suffolk cheese farm, cultivate a gigantic beard and grow old playing Scrabble with my cats.'

Eric laughed.

'Can cats play Scrabble?'

'Mine can,' said Yuki matter-of-factly. 'They all have PhDs.'

Delighted whooping from the audience.

'And what about the rest of you?' continued Eric. 'Gabe, how's it been for you since Olly left?'

I waited, my fists clenched, for the audience to start booing. A few jeers vaulted over from a distant corner.

'It's been tough,' said Gabriel, his eyes steely. 'But Jake really brings something new to the band.'

'Sure,' said Eric, 'I can see that. You guys killed it up there.' He took a pause, and moistened his lips. 'So let's cut to the chase: your new single is out today, and so is Olly's. Next week, when the chart's released, we'll find out who's won. We'll find out who those people out there –' he pointed across the arena – 'want to see in their number one slot. So while you've got their attention, Gabe . . . while the eyes of the world are on *you* . . . I have just one question.' Eric tilted his head. 'Why should they buy your single instead of Olly's?'

I felt my throat closing. The crowd had already turned against Gabriel, already judged him. So what could he possibly say now to make things better?

I heard my own words echoing back through my mind. *Until you stop this – until you both stop competing over absolutely everything – I don't want to see either of you . . .*

'Oh, god,' said Melissa, next to me. 'I can't watch.'

'They're waiting, Gabe,' said Eric, holding the microphone under Gabriel's face. 'Why should the fans support your record, instead of Mr Samson's?'

The lights shifted subtly, from blue to red, and the crowd fell quiet. Gabriel leaned forward into the mic, and it felt like my heart stopped in my chest.

'Don't buy our single,' he said into the silence. 'Buy Olly's.'

26

The crowd gasped, and Eric let out a baffled laugh.

'You can't be serious.'

Confused chatter bubbled up from the audience. Olly's face was frozen in amazement.

'I am serious,' said Gabriel, over the hubbub. 'I'm not saying our record isn't any good, but . . .' He gestured towards Olly. 'Olly's song, it's actually *about* something. It's got heart.'

Melissa and I turned to each other, our mouths open in shock. Had that really just happened on live television?

'Wow.' Eric dragged a hand across his forehead. 'I gotta say, I was not expecting that! Gabe, you're honestly for real here?'

'Olly deserves it. He's the most talented guy I know.'

Eric laughed to himself, shaking his head.

'Well, I've never seen anything like this before, but, folks, you heard it here first. Gabriel West's hot tip for Tuesday's number one.' He planted a hand on Gabe's shoulder. 'I have to ask you, though . . . what about Fire&Lights? What does all this mean for the band?'

Gabe looked between Yuki, Aiden and Jake, and his brow furrowed.

'Honestly? I don't think there is a band any more.'

Before Eric could quiz him further, Gabriel turned and walked off the stage, to a rising commotion in the audience. There was confusion and panic onstage, techs running across the back, people standing up in the crowd, shouting and pointing. Nobody knew what would happen next.

But I knew one thing. I had to find him before anyone else did.

Within minutes, I was dashing down the corridor that led to the dressing rooms, ducking past people, shoulders brushing against the walls. If I was lucky, Gabriel would go straight there, and we could talk. If I wasn't, he might just leave the arena altogether.

'Everything OK, Charlie?'

Marty was standing outside Gabriel's dressing room, hands clasped across his belt. I was out of breath.

'Is Gabe in there?'

Marty stuck out his bottom lip.

'I heard that he just left the stage, but—'

'Gabe!'

At that moment, Gabriel appeared at the end of the corridor, pushing through the double doors. A handful of people followed him through.

His face was flushed, his hair tangled. He was untucking his shirt from his jeans and wiping his forehead with a rag.

I rushed towards him.

'Oh my god, Gabe. Are you OK?'

His forehead creased.

'What are you doing here?'

'I ha—' I looked up, suddenly aware of all the people watching us. 'Can we talk in your dressing room?'

Gabe nodded, and raked a hand through his hair. Together, we walked towards Marty, who opened the door, keeping his head low. He closed it gently behind us.

It was comfortingly quiet inside the room, the buzz from outside little more than a murmur through the walls. Baskets of champagne lay untouched in every corner.

'This is all such a mess,' said Gabe, rolling up his sleeves. 'Are you all right?'

Thoughts were crowding my brain. I was still overcome by what he'd done onstage.

'I can't believe you did that for Olly.'

Gabriel stared back at me, flexing his fingers.

'It was the truth.'

'What happens now?'

His breath hitched in his throat, and his shoulders dropped.

'I think I'm finished.'

A sharp knock at the door. And again.

'What is it?' snapped Gabe. The door opened cautiously, and Marty set one foot inside the room.

'You have a visitor.'

Gabe shook his head.

'I don't want to see anyone right now. Is it Barry?'

'No, but . . . I think you should let them in.'

'I told you, Marty, I don't want to see anyone.'

Marty stepped further into the room, and spoke in a hushed tone.

'He says he's your father.'

27

'What?'

All the blood drained from Gabriel's face. I touched my hands to my temples. What was Marty talking about?

'Your father's here.'

'That's not possible, Marty. Whoever it is—'

Before Gabe could finish his sentence, a man passed through the door and stopped beside Marty. Somewhere in his mid-forties, he was tall and handsome, his gaze dark and intense. His face was horrifyingly familiar.

It was Harry West.

'No . . .'

The single word fell from Gabriel's mouth, desperate and small. Then he said it again.

'No.'

And again.

'No . . . no. No, don't you—'

'Gabriel,' interrupted Harry, walking towards his son. 'Please, just let me expl—'

'You're dead,' said Gabriel, backing away, shaking his head. 'You're supposed to be dead . . .'

Gabriel kept going until he was pressed against the wall, and for a moment, I thought his legs were going to buckle underneath him. Harry reached for him, then thought better of it. He pressed a fist to his mouth.

'That was all a mistake, Gabe. It was a mistake. It wasn't meant to turn out this way.'

Gabe didn't reply; he just kept shaking his head, his eyes wild. Letting out a sigh, Harry turned away and his gaze fell on mine.

I felt like the room was going to burst into flames.

'You must be Charlie.'

Rage throbbed inside me, filling my ribcage, burning my skin. A smile threatened to grow across Harry's face.

'You look just like her.'

'Don't you *dare*,' said Gabriel, pushing away from the wall and grabbing a fistful of his father's shirt. He shoved him away. 'Don't you dare even *talk* to her.'

I stared at Harry, my body stiffening. I wanted to hurt him. I wanted to run at him, choke him, pull him to the ground. But my feet stayed rooted to the spot.

'OK, OK,' said Harry, backing away, his palms up. He came to a stop against the counter. 'Will you at least let me explain?'

Gabriel turned on Marty.

'Why did you let him in here? We should just throw him out on the street.'

Marty waved a calming hand.

'He was cleared by security.'

'Why?'

Marty softened his voice.

'Gabe, his face is in all the papers. We recognised him the second we saw him.' His clasped his hands over his belt again. 'Look, you guys have a lot to talk about. I'll be outside if you need me.' He aimed his gaze at Harry, his jaw rigid. 'I'll be listening.'

Marty left the room, closing the door behind him. Gabriel clenched his trembling fists.

'What's all this supposed to mean, then, huh? What are you saying? You faked your own death?'

Harry frowned.

'It's not like that, Gabriel. You've got it all wrong.'

'Got it all wrong?' Gabriel's neck was turning red. '*I stood on your grave.*'

Harry's face crumpled. 'What?'

'We've been to the cemetery, Harry, so just save it.'

'I had no idea,' said Harry, his eyes searching the floor. He pressed a palm into his forehead. 'Honestly. I mean, if someone put a gravestone up, then it must have been . . . I don't know—'

'The fans,' I said. Harry looked at me, his eyes widening.

'Oh my god. The fans did it? I can't believe . . .'

His face was pale with astonishment. Gabriel and I shared a glance, our brows creasing. He really didn't know.

Harry pushed a hand through the air, his fingers splayed.

'But, look, Gabe, none of that really matters. I came here to talk. Will you let me talk?'

Gabriel thrust his hands into his pockets and took two steps backwards. His mouth was twisted in disgust.

'I can't stop you.'

Harry pulled up a chair and sat down. He rested his elbows on his knees and swallowed thickly.

'After I heard about the crash, I was a total mess. The guilt, the shame, it kept me up all night. I hated myself. So I hitchhiked to the highest bridge in the county, drank a bottle of vodka and jumped off. I wanted to die.' He dragged a shaking hand through his hair. 'I must have been knocked out, because I woke up hours later, downstream. And I just thought . . . maybe I was being given a second chance. A chance to start over. Without Kit, there was nothing left for me in New Jersey, and there was nothing left for me at ho—'

He cut himself off, and Gabriel raised his head. *There was nothing left for me at home.*

'I knew I'd be no use to you back in England,' he continued, avoiding Gabriel's stare, 'and the staff at your children's home, they were good people. They were better parents than I could ever be.'

'Your dealers,' said Gabriel, his voice fraying at the edges. 'They could have come after me. They went after

Katherine, and she ended up dead . . . so what made you think I was safe?'

Harry looked at me, as if I could help, then back at Gabriel.

'I thought . . . I don't know . . . I thought that, if I was dead—'

'It wouldn't be your problem any more.'

Harry shook his head desperately.

'No, it's not like that. I didn't mean that. I begged them, Gabe. I begged them not to hurt you. I . . .'

Gabriel pressed his lips together. He was thumping a fist, backwards, against the wall.

'Anyway, I . . .' Harry smoothed his hair down with a trembling hand, and cleared his throat. 'I jumped on the first long-distance bus I could find, and ended up in the South. Nobody knew me there, so I could start again.' He looked up. 'Back in those days, there was hardly any internet, and America's such a massive place, you could just change your name and . . . disappear. I didn't know that anyone had found my suicide note, so I just figured that, eventually, everyone in England had forgotten about me. I've been in Alabama ever since.'

Gabriel's head was tilted. His fist was still bumping softly against the wall.

'I don't . . . I don't underst—'

He began to choke on his words, his breathing strangled. I thought about the song he'd played in the bar in Marble

357

Creek – the song about the things he'd say to his father now, if only he could see him again – and the irony chilled my blood. His father had actually returned, as if from the dead, and Gabriel could barely get the words out.

'I know this must be hard to process, Gabe, but—'

'Why now?' Gabe was yelling, the veins on his neck standing out. Tears quivered in his eyes. 'You left me to rot in that foster home when I was five years old, and *now* you come back. Why?'

Harry pressed both hands into the back of his head.

'I saw the article in the paper, OK? I saw what the press were doing to you, and I realised I had to do something. I had no idea there was anyone left who knew or cared about Little Boy Blue, or knew anything about me and Kit, but this article . . . it changed everything. It was like my old life was calling to me.' He stood up from the chair and took a step towards Gabriel. 'I've always followed your career, since the beginning. I've watched you from a distance. I'm proud of you, son.'

Gabriel straightened, and seemed to grow, as if his anger was expanding inside him.

'You don't get to call me that. You don't get to say you're proud of me, *ever*.'

Harry pressed the heel of his hands into his forehead.

'Please, both of you.' He turned to me, his shoulders heaving. 'You *need* to understand. I was messed up back then . . . and Charlie, your mother, she was my only friend, and I was . . . I was more devastated than anyone when she died.'

I stared back at him, sorrow prickling my skin.

'I doubt that.'

'We were *partners*. We depended on each other. The music we made together, it was beautiful, but I was useless without her. I haven't written a single song since the day she died.'

'I've heard enough,' said Gabriel, pacing across the room. 'I want you out of here. I want you gone.'

My phone burred in my pocket. I slid it out, on auto-pilot, but when I saw the message on the screen, my heart froze.

Just came through security at the venue. They're bringing me to you. Dad x

'Oh, god . . . no. *No* . . .'

My blood surged with panic as I realised what was about to happen. Pushing past Harry, I ran to the door and shoved it open, desperately searching the corridor. My whole body turned cold as I saw him, my father, hurrying down the corridor, flanked by management.

'Charlie . . .'

Dad picked up his pace, almost jogging towards me, and pulled me into a hug. I tried to choke the words out.

'Dad, please. Let's not stay here, let's just lea—'

'My god.'

Our embrace turned to stone and Dad slipped away from me, his gaze settling on the dressing room doorway, over my shoulder. His head began to shake.

'It's not you . . . it can't . . . be *you* . . .'

I spun round, chest thudding. Harry was ashen.

'Ralph?'

Dad looked down at me.

'Why is he . . . how . . .' As the words fell out of his mouth, his shocked expression began to harden, and turn. His eyes darkened. 'Get away from my daughter.'

'Ralph, please,' said Harry, stumbling backwards, 'it's not what you think.'

Dad swept past me into the dressing room, advancing towards Harry. I followed him in, closing the door behind us, grabbing at Dad's shirt to hold him back.

'Dad, don't.'

'It's not what I think, Harry? Why aren't you *dead?*'

Harry held up his palms, the whites of his eyes huge beneath the lights.

'I tried to kill myself, after the crash. I tried.'

Dad's breathing was ragged. He clamped his hands on top of his head.

'But . . . they said the fans, they made a grave . . . I don't . . .'

'It didn't work,' said Harry, hugging his arms to his chest. 'I don't know why. I didn't drown, so instead I . . .

360

I just ran.' He sucked in a deep breath. 'I've been living in Alabama since it happened. No one down there knows who I am, and I was supposed to stay hidden. But then this article came out, and . . .'

Dad dropped against the wall, pulling at his shirt collar. For the first time, his eyes fell on Gabriel.

'I think I need to sit down. I need to . . . sit down . . .'

He sank into a chair, and a delicate silence hovered in the air. Thin, ready to crack, like an eggshell.

Suddenly, Gabriel turned on his father.

'How does it feel, eh?'

Harry looked back at him, forlorn.

'How does what feel?'

'Mama died because of you. You know that, right? If you hadn't left us on our own in that flat, she'd still be alive. She didn't know how . . .' A sob threatened to burst from his chest. He forced it down. 'Mama couldn't read the prescription bottles, and you knew it. She was sick, and *you knew it*. You left your family, you split up the band, and Katherine . . .' He glanced at me. 'She died because of you too. Everything you touch, it burns.'

Harry moved towards his son, his hands pressed together, his face stricken.

'I know, Gabe. I know it was all my fault. And with Kit, I . . . I owed them so much money, but I was broke. I couldn't stop them.' He turned towards Dad. 'Ralph, it should've been me. I should've died, not her. I'm so sorry.'

361

'Sorry?' spat Gabriel, his arms wide. 'No one cares that you're sorry. *You killed her—*'

'What are you talking about?'

My father's voice. He was looking at Gabe, his face warped with confusion. He pointed at Harry.

'What do you mean, he killed her?'

Gabriel caught my eye, for a fleeting moment.

'The crash . . . they made it happen.'

'Who did?' said Dad, baffled. I moved closer to him.

'Dad, *we know.*' My voice was hushed, heat colouring my cheeks. 'We know that Harry owed money for drugs, and that the other car in the crash . . . it was them. The dealers. They sent someone to run her off the road.'

A strange sound burst out of Dad. It was almost a laugh.

I recoiled, my head swimming.

'Look,' he said, leaning towards me, 'I know this is confusing, and upsetting, and I know I told you when you were little that it was the other driver's fault . . . but it wasn't. It was an accident.'

I wrung my hands, exasperated.

'That's the whole point, Dad. It was made to *look* like an accident. The other driver was sent there to make it happen.'

'The other driver was an elderly man,' said Dad, addressing us all. 'His wife was sick, and he was taking her to hospital. He had his grandkids in the back.'

'What?' Gabriel's voice was whisper-thin.

Dad pursed his lips.

'For years, I wanted someone else to blame. Trust me. The police said the old guy arrived just after the crash happened – they even had an eye-witness – but I refused to believe them. I told them Katherine was a good driver, and it couldn't have been her fault. He must have been driving too fast, I said. He was in his eighties, and his vision was probably going.

'As far as they were concerned, though, it was an open-and-shut case. And I was angry for a long time. I felt paralysed. Nobody believed me, and we lived thousands of miles away from where it happened, so what could I do?' He cradled one hand inside the other, rubbing a thumb against his palm. 'Eventually, years later, I heard from the county sheriff, out of the blue. He said that a local business had been archiving their old security footage and discovered the crash on tape. I guess no one thought to check it at the time, because they didn't need to, but the video proved it.' He closed his eyes, and I felt a sudden urge to put my arms around him. He was reliving the footage in his head. 'Katherine swerved to avoid an animal in the road – a coyote, it looked like, or a fox – and she hit a tree. The other car arrived a few seconds later, and stopped across the street. The driver called the police himself.'

Nobody spoke. I felt something shift inside me, like debris turning on the ocean floor. My father's voice softened.

'This story you're all telling me, I don't know where it comes from, but it's a fantasy. Katherine's death was an accident.'

I forced the breath in and out of my body, eyes fixed on the floor. I didn't know whether to feel joy, sadness, or regret. We'd got it wrong. Nate had got it wrong. Gabe's father had got it wrong, and he . . .

I looked up, and my eyes met Harry's. Relief was bleeding into his face; fifteen years of guilt, suddenly ebbing away.

'You thought it was your fault,' said Dad, staring at him. 'You thought you'd killed her, and that's why you . . .'

I dug my hands into my hair, pressing them into my skull. What Nate had told me in his bar, it had been an honest mistake. But it was a mistake that had torn my heart in two.

'None of this makes any difference, you know.'

Gabriel was pacing the room again.

'What?' said Harry.

'So the crash wasn't your fault? Who cares? That doesn't change the fact that you ruined everything.'

'I was young, Gabe. I was stupid. I really thought the band could make it, that if we could just break America, we'd have everything. Enough money to look after all of you.' He tried to smile, but it looked weak, diluted. 'We had something, me and Kit. If you could have seen us, kids, honestly . . . Ralph, you saw Little Boy Blue at the Troubadour. You *know* we had something special.'

Dad went quiet for a while, deep in thought. When he spoke, his eyes were fixed on Harry.

'You were in love with her, weren't you?'

Harry grimaced, and ran his hands down his face.

'It . . . it was complicated, Ralph. We made music together, and I was nothing without her. I knew she would never leave you, I knew she never saw me as anything more than a friend, but the way she made me feel . . . it . . .'

'You wanted to break the family up.' My father's voice was growing firmer. 'I was just an obstacle to you. Charlie too.'

Harry swallowed.

'I know it sounds bad, but families, they get in the way of bands. If you want a band to succeed, it *has* to be number one for everyone, and I could tell . . .' He looked at me. 'I could tell there were things in the world more important to Kit than Little Boy Blue, so . . . I hid her letters.'

Dad straightened. I thought, suddenly, of the unmailed letter I had found in his study, the year before. *Katherine, I've hardly heard from you in weeks, just a few late night phone calls, and barely a single email. No letters . . .*

'You did what?' said Dad.

Harry hung his head. 'I told her I was posting them to you, along with my own letters to Gabriel, but I never did. I never even wrote to you, Gabe. I was trying to cut everyone off.'

There was a pause. Then something rose up inside my father.

'I knew it,' he said, standing up. He took a step towards Harry, tears brimming in his eyes. 'How *could* you? I thought she'd forgotten about us.'

I drifted to my father's side, closing both my hands around one of his. Above us, the skylight began to pitter-patter with summer rain, mixing with the dying evening light. The raindrop reflections dappled our faces like tears.

Gabriel walked up behind Harry, and spoke into the back of his neck.

'This won't bring her back, you know.'

Harry jumped, and wheeled round. He held up his hands.

'I know, Gabe. I'm not trying to bring her back, I just—'

'You've made your confession. Now I think it's time you went.'

Harry tried to smile.

'You have to understand, Gabe . . .' He twisted around and pointed at me. 'Charlie . . . there were so many good times. Bombing around London, playing gigs, hanging out at the Troubadour. We were *happy*. We used to open up our guitar cases for soundcheck and find these secret mix-tapes in there, tapes that Kit had recorded for us. Aretha Franklin, Ella Fitzgerald. She was obsessed with mix-tapes.' He laughed to himself, lost in the memory. Then his face dropped. 'But I ruined it. God, how did it go so wrong?'

'I have some ideas,' said Dad coldly.

'I know it was my fault. I said some terrible things to Kit when I quit the tour. I couldn't hack the pressure, and I was wanted half the time, so I just decided I was going to leave. She said they were still a band, that they'd go on without me, and I just laughed and told her: "I *am* the band".'

My head snapped towards Gabriel. He was staring at his father, white as a ghost, and I knew he was thinking of the exact same memory I was. Something he had said last year, to Olly, on the roof of the Rochester Hotel, beneath the lashing winter rain. *What are you gonna do, Samson, huh? You gonna fire me? You gonna throw me out of the band? . . .* I am *the band*.

Gabriel stumbled backwards, steadying himself with a hand on the counter edge.

'Get out of here,' he said.

Harry looked up. 'What? Son, please—'

'Don't call me that.' Gabriel coughed, spluttered. 'Get out of here, I can't look at you any more.'

Harry walked towards him.

'I know this seems bad, Gabe, but think about it. Something good came out of all this. Everything you've done, this empire you've built . . . you finished what we started—'

'No. Don't say it. Don't even think it.'

Something had turned in Gabriel. His sadness had withered, consumed by his anger.

'Gabriel, calm dow—'

'Don't you *dare* try and take credit for this, for anything I've done. I did this without you, I did it on my own. Do you have any idea how many nights I cried myself to sleep, until my throat was bleeding, until *I couldn't speak*, because I thought you didn't want me? So don't come in here saying that I finished what you started. Don't you dare say that.'

Harry reached for his son's hand, but Gabriel brushed him away.

'I've heard your songs, though,' protested Harry. 'You used our lyrics.'

A look of wretched realisation passed over Gabriel's face.

'So *that's* why you're here? You want money? Fine.' Gabriel started circling the room, turning things over, scattering papers. He reached into a nearby bag and pulled out a wad of cash. 'How much do you need, Harry? How much so that I *never have to see your face again?*'

Instinctively, my father drew me into his chest. My hands tightened around his.

'No, Gabe . . . no. I don't want money. God, most of those lyrics were Kit's anyway. I just . . . I want you to understand that the man who left you, the man who dealt drugs and wrecked the band, that's not who I am any more. I've changed. Over the years . . . I've changed.'

'What, and all this time, you never thought to say hi? You never thought, I don't know, that I might want to know I wasn't alone?'

'I thought about it, I really did. Every second of every day. But look at you. You're everything I ever wished I could be, and all I saw in you were my own failures. I thought . . . I thought if I came home, I'd ruin you.'

Gabriel glared at his father, his eyes smouldering with hate.

'Well, that's funny, isn't it? Because here I am now, and I'm ruined anyway.'

Harry grabbed his arm.

'You're not. We can be together again, Gabe. Whatever you think of me, however much you hate me, we're still family. I'm still your father.'

Gabriel threw his arm off.

'You have *never been* my father.' Harry started to reply, but Gabriel shouted him down. 'You were never here! You were *never* here for me, not once. You're supposed to be dead.'

'But I'm here now, aren't I?' pleaded Harry. 'I'm alive, and I'm here now.'

Gabriel paused, his chest rising and falling. He leaned forward and spoke in a flat, chilling tone.

'You'll always be dead to me.'

Then he turned and strode out of the room, slamming the door behind him.

On instinct, I ran after Gabriel. It meant leaving my father behind, alone with Harry, but I didn't have a choice. Wherever Gabriel was headed, he needed somebody with him.

'Gabe, slow down . . .'

I trailed him along the main hallway and watched as he turned off down a smaller side corridor. It looked like it led to an exit, and probably should have been guarded, but for some reason, it wasn't. Then I discovered why: at the far end of the hallway, two security guards were chatting to each other, laughing, comparing something on their phones. While I had my chance, I ducked round the corner and found a heavy-looking fire exit door, standing wide open, but slowly closing on itself.

Standing outside in the rainy twilight, his back to the building, was Gabriel. He had his arms wrapped around his chest, and his T-shirt was beginning to soak through.

I stepped outside, the smell of fresh rain on hot tarmac

flooding my nostrils. The rainfall was picking up, and it began to dot my cheeks.

'Gabe. Are you OK?'

He said nothing. I raised my voice.

'For what it's worth, it seems like he's sorry.'

Still no reply. He was barely moving. I glanced back over my shoulder, just as the door clicked shut.

'Look, we probably shouldn't even be out here. The audience will be leaving soo—'

'What if I'm turning into him?'

'Gabe, no.'

He turned around. His face was ravaged with tears.

'You heard what he said. "I am the band". It's like I *learned that from him.*'

I moved towards him, splashing through the gathering puddles.

'But you're not that person any more. Whoever you were on that roof, when we first met, you've changed. I've seen it happen.'

Gabriel shook his head insistently. He was staring at his hands, which were slick with rain.

'He's in my blood. I can *feel* him. I have to . . . scrub him out.'

'Listen to me. Your father was – I mean, god, your father *is* – jealous and petty, and small. But what you did for Olly tonight, that was selfless. Harry would never have done that. You know that's true.'

He looked up at me, and his body seemed to crumple, like burning newspaper. I closed the gap between us and clasped his hands in mine.

'Something's wrong with me, Charlie.'

'Don't say that.'

Fresh tears filled his eyes. He blinked through them.

'All he had to do was love me, but he couldn't even do that. Something must be wrong with me.'

I pulled him into a hug and he buried his face in my neck. He began to sob against me, smothering his words.

'Something must be wrong with me . . .'

'Nothing's wrong with you,' said a female voice, behind him.

I straightened up, confused.

'You're perfect.'

I side-stepped away from Gabriel, and he swivelled around, stumbling a little. A girl with long, dark hair was standing in front of us, carrying a notebook with pictures of Gabriel sellotaped to the front.

An icy feeling trickled down my spine.

'Um . . . you shouldn't be back here,' I said, trying to sound authoritative. 'This isn't for fans.'

'I'm not a fan,' she replied calmly. As she looked at me, I felt a sudden rush of recognition, like I'd seen her before. But I couldn't place it.

She took a step towards Gabriel.

'I knew we'd meet,' she said, the faintest smile growing on her face. 'I'm Delfina.'

Delfina: I *knew* there was something familiar about her. But the girl I'd photographed at the theme park had shocking white hair. It was the most distinctive thing about her.

'I'm sorry, Delfina,' I said, trying to smile at her, 'but Gabe and I need to go insi—'

'I haven't finished,' she interrupted, her voice starting to strain. She gripped tight to her notebook. 'Charlie.'

I stiffened.

'What do you want?'

'Look at this,' she said, pulling a folded-up piece of paper from her notebook. She let it drop open. It was a print-out of Paul Morgan's exposé in *The Record*. She pointed to the photograph of me and Gabriel together, and I watched it blot with rainwater, a lump rising in my throat. 'I've been waiting for you to notice me, Gabriel, but you never did. Then I saw the picture, and, look . . . you don't like fair hair, do you? You like brown hair.' She ran her fingers through her long, chocolate-brown locks, and that's when I noticed. Her roots were still white.

'Now I have what Charlie has,' she said, her eyes wide, 'we can be together.'

I lunged for the door, finding it locked. I pulled at it hard, and it clattered, but didn't open. We were locked out.

'Gabe, we need to go. Call someone.'

'I don't have my pho—'

'Don't go,' said Delfina, reaching for Gabriel's face. He flinched.

'You have to leave, OK? You can't be here.'

'Leave?' she said, reaching inside her coat. 'Why?'

'Because—'

Gabriel's words died in his mouth when he saw what Delfina had pulled from her coat pocket.

It was a long kitchen knife. Gleaming in the rain.

'Whoa . . . OK . . . Delfina.' Gabe stepped backwards, both his palms in the air. 'Put that down.'

'Down?' she said curiously. I tried the door again, then banged on it with the flat of my palm. No response. Gabriel took a deep breath.

'Listen to me, Delfina.' He tried to catch her eye. 'Listen to me . . . you don't want to do this.' There was a tremble in his voice.

'I do,' she said.

'You don't. Do you hear me?' He softened his tone. 'You're not going to use that knife on me, are you?'

She lowered the knife, shaking her head, and Gabriel's shoulders relaxed. Then she looked at me.

'I'm going to use it on her.'

28

Before I knew what was happening, Delfina was lurching towards me, the knife protruding from her hand.

It was too late for me to dodge. I had nowhere to go.

As she fell towards me, Gabriel threw his weight against her, sending them both crashing to the ground, rainwater splashing as they fell. There was a moment of confused silence, and then the clang of the knife hitting the tarmac. Delfina stumbled up, walking backwards, dazed, but Gabriel stayed down, his back hunched, his palms pressed against the ground. He was trying to push himself up, but he was hurt.

And that's when I saw it. The blood.

Soaking outwards from a tear in his T-shirt, blossoming through the material. He tried to press a hand against it, but he was too weak. Somehow, as they fell, the knife had gone into him.

'Oh my god . . . Gabriel . . . no . . .'

I rushed to his side and knelt down, struggling to hold him up. I kept shouting his name, but he was drowsy, and barely responding. Reaching over, I desperately banged my palm against the iron door.

'Help! Please, somebody . . . !'

Delfina was gazing, moon-eyed, at Gabriel. I yelled at her.

'You need to find somebody, Delfina. You need to get help.'

She stared at me momentarily, like a confused animal in car headlights. She went totally still for a passing second, and then ran away across the tarmac, her feet splashing through puddles.

Someone needed to stop her, but now wasn't the time. Gabriel was losing consciousness.

I slammed a hand against the door again. Rain was pouring down my face.

'Please! Somebody . . . someone help us . . .'

There was a loud thud, and the door swung open, the missing security guard tumbling through. The second he saw us, his face opened up, and he spoke into the walkie-talkie on his shoulder.

'We need a medic to exit nineteen. I repeat: we need a medic here, *now*.'

I looked up at him, still cradling Gabriel in my arms.

'Don't let him die,' I said, my voice cracking. 'Please don't let him die.'

'It's OK,' he said, although the look in his eyes said otherwise.

I touched my bloodied hand to Gabriel's face.

'Gabe, it's me . . . it's Charlie . . . please, don't go. Don't go. Please . . . don't go . . .'

Inside, I could hear panicked footsteps, and shouting. The sounds began to blur and decay inside my head, as if I was somehow losing consciousness with him. All I could do was sit there, holding him, my eyes swimming with tears, his blood staining my fingers, as my heart shattered into a thousand tiny pieces.

The paramedics slammed through the hospital doors, pushing Gabriel on a stretcher. I was behind them, trying to keep up, peering between the bodies of the medics. All I could see were a few locks of Gabriel's hair.

Barry was with us, and Tara, and a few other members of the Fire&Lights management team. There were cops too, talking to each other in urgent tones, and nurses clearing the way up front.

I was trying my hardest not to think the worst.

That he might not get through this.

That he might—

'Are any of you next of kin?'

A member of the hospital staff was talking to Barry, Tara and me. She had stopped us in our tracks, and the stretcher began to drift away from us.

Barry shook his head, frustrated.

'Sort of, yeah.'

'Are you blood relatives?' she asked impatiently. Barry sighed.

'No, we're not.'

'Does he have family with him?'

Barry and I glanced at each other. Did he know about Harry? He must do, by now. Barry ran a hand around the back of his neck.

'N-no, he doesn't. Look, is this really necessary? That's my . . .' He stopped himself, emotion turning his neck red. 'That's my boy down there. I need to know he's going to be OK.'

'We're doing everything we can,' said the woman. 'He's going straight to surgery. You'll have to wait here until they're done. I'm sorry.'

Barry worked his jaw, his eyes starting to glisten. He nodded.

'OK . . . OK. But you look after him, do you hear?'

'We will.'

He pressed his lips together, watching the stretcher disappear down the hallway.

'That's my boy down there,' he said, his voice ragged round the edges. 'That's my boy.'

The waiting room was eerily silent. The only sounds were the metallic hum of the air conditioning and the occasional squeak of a wheelchair from the corridor outside. Barry was fussing on his phone, and Tara was standing at the window, staring out into the night.

I was curled up on a low chair, knees hugged to my chest. Gabriel's words were playing on a loop inside my mind.

All he had to do was love me, but he couldn't even do that. Something must be wrong with me . . .

'Charlie? Charlie!'

I looked up. It was my father.

He rushed towards me and I stumbled off the chair, falling into his arms.

'Thank god you're OK,' he said into my hair. 'My Charlie, thank god . .'

'Dad, he's in surgery.' I looked up, feeling the tears returning. 'The knife, it was so big, I—'

'It's all right,' said Dad, stroking my hair, as I began to cry. 'It's over now. It's over.'

I wiped my face with my arm.

'But what if . . . if . . .' I choked through my tears. 'I'm scared I'm going to lose him.'

'You won't,' said Barry, standing up. 'He's a strong kid, strongest I know. You take my word for it, Bloom. He's not going anywhere.'

'You're all here for Gabriel West?'

Our heads turned in unison towards the doorway, where a doctor had appeared, carrying a clipboard. She looked very serious.

'We have some news.'

29

I pressed my hands to my chest. It felt like my lungs might collapse inside me.

'Gabriel's out of surgery,' she said, in a measured tone, 'and he's stable. He's going to be OK.'

I almost fell over with relief, my father curling an arm round me, and pulling me into his body.

'Can we see him?' said Barry.

'You can,' said the doctor warily, 'but, please, one at a time. And don't expect much yet; he's still sleeping. But he's going to be fine.'

For the next half an hour or so, I sat with my father, snoozing on his shoulder, waiting for Barry and Tara to have their time with Gabe. Dad stroked my hair and drank coffee from a styrofoam cup.

I awoke suddenly, with a jolt, a memory surfacing in my mind.

'Where's Harry?' I said, my head foggy. Dad stared into his drink.

'Uh . . . he left.'

'He left?'

Dad set his coffee down.

'Before the . . . before it happened. He wanted to talk to me more about Katherine, but I asked him to leave. I suspect he won't give up trying to see Gabriel, but that's none of *my* business, so—'

'Charlie?'

Tara was standing in the doorway.

'You can go in and see him now. He's not awake yet, but you can sit with him, if you like.'

Leaving my dad in the waiting area, I walked down the corridor to Gabriel's room. He was lying in the bed, hooked up to various tubes, a machine beeping in the corner. I sat on the chair beside him, gazing up and down his sleeping form. He was motionless, aside from the slow rise and fall of his chest.

As the sight of him began to sink in, I felt my face fold in on itself.

'You scared the hell out of me tonight,' I said, wiping my eyes. I knew he couldn't hear me, but I kept going anyway. 'I thought I was going to lose you.'

Beep. Beep. Beep.

I glanced out of the window. The rain had stopped, but droplets of water were still clinging to the glass.

'Olly was right, you know.' I laid my hand on his, and stroked his skin. 'What he said to me, after the Troubadour gig, he was right. I've fallen in love with you. You drive me crazy, and you're stubborn, and difficult, and you're basically not normal . . .' Amazingly, I found myself laughing. 'But I don't care. I love you.'

Beep. Beep. Beep.

I closed my hand over his, squeezing gently.

'It's just, the thing is . . . I don't know if we can be together right now. Things have been so intense between us, and I don't know how we'd function as a couple. How we'd ever be normal. One day, maybe, in the future, when all of this is behind us—'

The door opened, cutting me off. It was my father.

'Sorry to interrupt, kiddo, but . . . can we talk?'

'Sure,' I said, with a weak smile. 'One second.'

Dad stepped backwards into the corridor, and I let go of Gabriel's hand.

'See you when you wake up.'

I walked out of the room, listening to that lonely beep, and nudged the door closed behind me.

'Hey.'

Dad was standing in the corridor, his hands in his pockets.

'Hey.'

A nurse walked past us, and offered a small smile. When he'd gone, Dad and I sat down on the plasticky sofa opposite Gabriel's room.

I buried my hands in my lap.

'I'm so sorry for everything, Dad. I'm not really sure where to start—'

'I'm sorry too.'

I frowned at him.

'Why?'

'For not telling you about Little Boy Blue, and your mother's music career, and . . . well, for not telling you about Harry.'

I was suddenly six years old again, asking my dad why I didn't have a mum, like all the other kids at school. Or lying on my bed at home, staring at the ceiling, having pretend conversations with her.

'Why *didn't* you tell me about Harry?' I asked.

Dad went quiet, his eyes on the floor. Through the wall, Gabriel's machine beeped like a robotic clock.

'I was trying to protect you.' His mouth almost curled into a smile. 'You're so like your mother, Charlie. You have her artistic flair, something I've never had. But half of you is me too, and believe it or not, in some ways, you do take after me. You're analytical, and somewhere in there, there's a mathematician. You want answers and explanations, and you want things to line up. I'd spent so many years trying to blame the crash on somebody, and I worried that if I told you about Harry – how he quit on your mum, in a foreign country, and left her carrying the band on her own – you'd blame him for it. You'd draw a line from his betrayal to her death, and it would consume you. You'd feel hateful and angry and bitter, maybe for the rest of your life. And it might have been wrong of me, but I wanted to save you from that.' He touched a hand to my shoulder. 'You're my little girl, Charlie, and the last thing I wanted was for you to repeat my mistakes. I guess I just didn't bank on you randomly bumping into Harry's son, the world-famous popstar. I mean, what are the odds?'

I let out a dry laugh. The odds were astronomical, or at least appeared to be. Which is why I knew that, somewhere, there was a missing piece in this puzzle that explained the coincidence. But now wasn't the time for that.

'I guess that makes sense,' I said, with a shrug. I couldn't exactly be angry at my father for keeping things from me when I'd just spent the best part of a year lying to him every day. 'And, hey, since we're getting things out in the open . . . I'm sorry for all the lies. For everything I've been hiding from you, and the sneaking around.'

He breathed in through his nose, his mouth pursed.

'It hasn't been easy for me, I'll give you that.'

'I hated keeping secrets from you, Dad. I just didn't know how to tell you. They were small lies at first, but they just started getting bigger, and out of control. And when I found out about Little Boy Blue, I knew I couldn't open up to you unless you opened up first.' Shame blossomed on my cheeks. 'I'm so sorry.'

Dad cleared his throat.

'Well, you're right to be sorry . . . but I had a part to play in it too. If I'd been honest with you from the beginning, maybe you wouldn't have had to keep all this to yourself.' He sighed loudly, and brushed a hand through his hair. 'Which brings me on to something else.'

'Something . . . else?'

He shook his head sadly.

'I can't very well be angry with you about keeping secrets when I've been keeping one of my own. Something big.'

I shifted in my seat.

'We're in trouble,' he said, his eyebrows crimping. 'Money trouble.'

'Money tr—? What do you mean?'

'When Rosie and Brian told me about this American trip, part of me really wanted to come along. But I couldn't afford it, because . . .' His gaze dropped. 'I've lost my job.'

'What? How?'

'My own stupid fault, really. I've been stressed out this summer, I've been worried about you, feeling as if you were slipping away from me, and I think it must have got to me. I started getting sloppy at work, and losing my concentration, and one day my supervisor asked me into the office and said they were making redundancies . . . and I was one of them.'

'Why didn't you tell me?'

'I didn't want to worry you, kiddo, especially around exam time. So I kept it a secret. And . . . well, that's not all.' He sank back into the sofa, and the plastic creaked under his weight. 'You know me, I'm pretty sensible with money, but running a house on one income hasn't always been easy. We have savings, but they're disappearing quicker than I expected, and . . . I've been getting behind on the mortgage.' He balled his hand into a fist, and tapped it against his thigh. 'Truth is, we could end up losing the house. Not straight away, but it could happen. And after everything we've been through, I wanted you to know. I didn't want to hide it from you any more.'

I felt a wobble in my stomach, but willed it away. Right now, Dad didn't need any more grief in his life.

I leaned against his shoulder.

'It's OK, Dad. We'll just . . . move to a smaller house, or sell all our stuff. I don't care where we live. Just as long as we get to be a family.'

I felt him looking down at me, and glanced up.

'Are you sure?' he said.

'Positive.'

A doctor nodded at us as she passed, and disappeared into Gabriel's room. Dad and I sat next to each other in silence for a while, listening to the distant blips and clinks of the hospital ward. After a few minutes, the door opened and the doctor walked out.

'He's awake,' she said, with a smile. 'D'you wanna go and say hi?'

That night, we stayed in a hotel around the corner from the hospital. I'd wanted to sit with Gabriel all night, but it wasn't allowed, and in any case, I needed the sleep. I drifted off the second I hit the pillow, sleeping deep and unbroken for nearly ten hours.

We were accompanied by the Fire&Lights security team everywhere we went. Paparazzi and media vans were camped out in the hospital grounds, yelling at us and clicking their cameras whenever we stepped in or out of our blacked-out cars. It was like living in an alternate reality. Meanwhile, word was spreading among the fans, and the walls either side of the building's main entrance were a barricade of flowers and handwritten tributes.

In the morning, I returned to the hospital to see Gabe. We sat together in his room, flicking through random TV channels.

'Man, this is the last time I opt in for a near-death experience,' said Gabe, tossing the remote away. 'The TV in hospital *sucks*.'

'You're just giving up too easily.' I set down my coffee, picked up the remote and flicked to a random channel. 'Something interesting might be ... just around the corner.'

My voice deflated as I realised what I'd switched to. It was a music entertainment report.

'. . . The *sensational* news in the entertainment world today,' the newsreader was saying, 'is that Gabriel West is recovering in hospital after being stabbed by a deranged fan, who was later apprehended by law enforcement.'

'West is reported to be in a fragile but stable state,' added her co-reporter, 'and lucky to be alive. Incredibly, all of this comes hot on the heels of his chart-topping boy band Fire&Lights apparently splitting up on *Make Or Break*, the very show where they started, after performing on the same bill as former bandmate, Olly Samson.'

'It makes them, then it breaks them,' said the first newsreader wryly. 'The headlines write themselves . . .'

I pointed the remote at the screen.

'We don't have to watch this, you know.'

Gabe reached out and lowered my hand.

'It's fine,' he said. 'I want to see it.'

'In an extraordinary turn of events, the troubled superstar told a live audience of millions last night *not* to buy the latest Fire&Lights record, but to instead buy Olly Samson's debut solo single.' A photograph of Olly flashed up on the screen. 'As a direct result, Olly's single "She Is The Fire" has now become the most downloaded track of the year so far, with pundits calling it an almost dead-cert to hit the Billboard number one spot on Tuesday.'

The picture of Olly was replaced by a shot of him and Gabriel onstage, facing off against each other.

'Samson and West have undergone a very public rivalry in recent months, with many fans blaming Gabriel for his bandmate's departure. However, thanks to West's act of selflessness last night, the hashtag "thankyougabe" has become the number one trending search term in the world. It would appear, perhaps, that the media got Gabriel West all wrong—'

Click. Gabriel turned off the television.

'Hey,' I said jokingly. 'I was enjoying that.'

'No one enjoys that kind of rubbish,' he said, with a smile. 'Didn't I tell you not to believe everything they tell you in the press?'

'Something like that, yeah.' I let out a contented sigh. 'Hashtag "thankyougabe", eh? That's pretty cheesy.'

Gabriel laughed, then winced and held his side.

'You can't make me laugh,' he protested. 'You're only allowed to say incredibly dull things to me for at least three months.'

'I'll see what I can do.'

Gabriel sat up against the pillows. His expression tightened.

'I'm sorry I put you through all this, Charlie. You could've been hurt, and—'

'But I wasn't,' I said firmly. '*You* were. Without you, I might've been . . .'

Our eyes locked, and the words caught in my throat. Breaking his gaze, I picked up my coffee and took a slow sip.

'So ... Tara booked us some flights home. The Morrises, and my dad. We're flying back on Tuesday. In fact –' I checked the clock on the wall – 'I'm meeting them any minute. We're heading out of the city for a couple of days to ward off the press.'

Gabe glanced towards the window. The blinds were down, and for good reason. The world was desperate for a shot of Gabriel West in his hospital bed.

'Smart move,' he said, shifting beneath the covers. 'You leave the press to me. Just as soon as they let me out of this room, I intend to whoop every one of their sorry asses.'

I eyeballed him.

'No ass-whooping for you, pal. Anything more strenuous than a game of Boggle is absolutely out of the question.'

He threw me a salute.

'Orders received.'

Gabriel's phone buzzed beside him. He picked it up cautiously, and read the message. He almost smiled, but his eyes were foggy.

'Everything OK?'

He passed me the phone. 'It's from Yuki.'

STOP LYING AROUND IN BED YOU GIANT SACK OF
POTATOES xxxx p.s. Love ya, bud. See you tonight.

'They're coming round later, then?' I asked, returning the phone. He dropped it on the duvet and let out a small sigh.

'Yeah.'

I pulled at a loose thread on my jeans.

'So, the band . . . is it . . . ?'

'I guess it's all over.' He stared into the blank TV screen. 'I saw to that last night.'

My body felt empty. The idea that Fire&Lights were finished: I couldn't get my head around it.

'None of it seems real,' I said, trying to imagine how Yuki and Aiden – and Jake, too – must have been feeling at that very moment. Even Barry would find this one hard to get over.

'Maybe we're all dreaming,' said Gabe, with a dry smile. I laughed to myself, my gaze drifting back to the clock.

'It's half-past. I really have to get going. Do you need anything before I leave?'

Gabriel shook his head, and I slid off the bed. Finishing my coffee, I dropped the foam cup in the bin and picked up my bag.

'Look after yourself, Gabe.'

'I will.'

He looked back at me, unblinking. I was supposed to be leaving, but my feet stayed rooted to the spot. All I could think about were the things I'd told him, the day before, when he was asleep. Should I have been saying them again now, to his face? Was it possible that he felt the same way I did?

Then, as if he'd been reading my thoughts, he said:

'I'll miss you.'

But what if he *didn't* feel the same? There was so much between us now, so much history and baggage, that it was hard to know what was real and what wasn't any more.

'Me too.'

Leaning down, I pressed my cheek against his, my heart stuttering as our skin lightly brushed. He reached up and sunk his fingers into my hair, and we paused there, unmoving, like stone statues in a country garden. For a split-second, the words were almost on my lips, but his hand dropped away and we broke apart.

Taking a deep breath, I walked to the door and curled my fingers around the handle.

'I guess I'll see you around, then?' he said, from his bed. I clicked the door open, and nodded.

'I guess you will.'

30

Staring out of the plane window, I watched Melissa in the departure lounge, holding Leo so tight it looked like she'd never let go. When eventually they pulled apart, her face was a mess of tears. He was crying too and, in the end, it took a hand on Melissa's shoulder from one of the airline staff to keep her from missing the plane.

She walked sadly across the boarding bridge, pulling her little case behind her.

A few minutes later, she was standing in the aisle beside me, tugging her sleeves down over her wrists.

'Hey there, buster,' I said. 'Y'all right?'

Melissa chewed hard on her lip, and nodded slowly. Then her face crumpled and the nod turned into a shake.

'Nooo,' she managed to choke out, as she started to sob. 'What if I never see him again?'

She sank down into the seat next to me and lay her head on my shoulder, sniffling. I tapped a finger on her thigh.

'You will,' I said, glancing out of the window again. Leo was still there, standing at the departure gate window, watching us taxi away. 'I'm sure of it.'

As the pilot guided the plane towards the runway, I noticed Rosie, Brian and Dad looking over at us, their faces creased with concern. 'She OK?' mouthed Rosie at me. I gave her a half-shrug, half-nod.

'I feel blue,' said Melissa into my shoulder, once we were in the air. 'Our American tour is over, Fire&Lights are gone forever . . . and I finally found a boy who actually likes me and he lives halfway across the world.'

I was leaning on the armrest, watching America shrink and disappear below us. The seat belt sign pinged off, and Melissa sat up, rubbing her eyes.

'Will you tell me something happy? I need some happy.'

'As it happens,' I said, turning to face her, 'I do have something that might cheer you up.'

She frowned.

'Really?'

I reached into the seat pocket in front of me, pulled out a packet of sweets and opened it up.

'Gummy bear?'

'Huh?'

I shook the bag of sweets at her.

'Take a bear,' I said, giving her a knowing smile. 'You're going to need it.'

She pulled a gummy bear from the packet, not taking her eyes off me for a second.

'CB, you're kinda freaking me out here.'

I plucked out one of the sweets and popped it in my mouth.

'I have a story to tell you.'

Melissa chewed at me suspiciously.

'What are you talking about?'

'OK.' I placed my hands on my lap. 'You already know this, but Friday night was the scariest night of my life. I just kept thinking about what could've happened, about how one of us could've died, and how Gabe's dad has wasted all these years pretending he doesn't exist. And I realised that none of us really appreciate what we have until it's not there any more.

'Like the band. The boys, they have – they *had* – this amazing bond, and they let it slip away. I know everything's super complicated with them, but I couldn't help thinking that if they could just *remember* what was so amazing about Fire&Lights, maybe they'd change their minds.'

Melissa sat forward, intrigued.

'Have you done something, Charlie?'

I wrinkled my mouth.

'I may have done.'

For the first time since she'd stepped on the plane, a smile crept on to Melissa's face. She clapped her hands.

'Oh my GOSH, tell me more.'

I shrugged.

'I don't know, it probably won't work. But I had to *try*, you know?'

Melissa's eyebrows climbed her forehead like they were being pulled by wires.

'Jeez, go ahead and *tell* me already, sister.'

'OK. Sorry. So here's the deal . . .'

With the plane's engines roaring around us, and a blanket of cloud settling outside the window, I sank back into my seat and told Melissa my story.

Around about now, Gabriel, Aiden, Yuki and Olly would be arriving, in separate cars, at a warehouse on the outskirts of the city. They would all have been told by management that they were there for a photo shoot, but when they arrived, they wouldn't find a photographer, or any cameras. They'd just find each other.

At this stage, they'd be confused, maybe a little angry, but on the main entrance to the warehouse, they'd find a sign inviting them to come inside. They'd walk into the building, and on a table in front of them, they'd find a letter.

Yuki, Aiden, Olly & Gabriel

You're all here for a reason.

You're here because I want you to see what I see. What I saw on that very first day, back in November last year, through my camera lens. I didn't know it at the time, but the four of you were about to change my life forever. Because what you have when you're together is extraordinary. Magical. If you ask me, it's worth hanging on to.

And if you don't believe me . . . look up.

They would look up, all four of them, and above their heads, they'd find hundreds of polaroids, hanging down from the ceiling like stars. Tiny lights would be tangled around them, illuminating the images: all the pictures that I'd taken of them, backstage and on their various travels, from the very first, to the very last. Every emotion imaginable, from excitement to joy to despair; all the adventures, the memories, the heartache and the happiness that we'd shared together. A miniature universe of moments, right there in front of them, real enough to touch.

The rest of the note would read:

This is all part of your story. It's an incredible story, and maybe right now you can't see that yourselves, but trust me – millions of others see it, every single day.

I can't force you to do anything you don't want to do, and I wouldn't want to. For now, just stand back and look at these pictures, and try to remember why you all started this in the first place.

Thanks for the songs, the stories and the laughter.

Your photographer, Charlie B x

'And that's pretty much it,' I said to Melissa, as the tea and coffee trolley wheeled past her. She stared at me, open-mouthed.

'Charlie . . . you're a GENIUS.'

'Hardly,' I said, shaking my head. 'But who knows? Maybe it'll make a difference.'

'How did you even come up with this?'

During the week before Gabriel and I had travelled to Marble Creek, I'd archived all the photographs I'd taken of Fire&Lights, and I'd seen a story emerging. A story of four friends, brought together and then pulled apart by their incredible talent. A story that needed to be told.

But it wasn't just that.

'Something Carrie said to me,' I explained, thinking back to our time together, drinking fancy tea in her hotel. 'She told me that, sometimes, people break up not because they're meant to be apart, but because they're meant to be together. And sometimes they need to spend time away from each other to figure that out.'

Melissa let out a quiet whistle.

'She is one smart cookie.'

'And then . . . well, then I was standing in that *Make or Break* VIP box, watching the boys perform without Olly, and it was so obvious . . . they'd never be the same unless he came back.'

Melissa scratched the side of her head.

'But this whole warehouse caper . . . how the heck did you pull it off?'

'Barry helped me out,' I said, smiling at the thought. 'He thinks I'm a bit bonkers, I reckon, but he was willing to give it a shot. He really loves them, you know.'

Melissa sighed

'Me too,' she said, her face turning a little sad. 'Me too.'

Coming home was a very strange feeling. 33 Tower Close wasn't the same place it had been when I left, and I wasn't the same person.

'You all right, kiddo?'

I realised I'd been standing stock-still in the hallway for several minutes. Dad was holding a pile of post and standing in the kitchen doorway.

'Uh . . . yeah. I think so.'

He lowered the envelopes.

'Weird to be home, eh?'

I looked up the stairs, to the bedroom I had slept in since I was a toddler, and then back outside, where a bouncer was standing guard at our front door and a car with blacked-out windows was blocking the driveway.

'*So* weird,' I said, letting go of my suitcase. Dad jerked his head towards the kitchen.

'Come on through, I'll make you a cup of tea.'

While I sat at the table, trying to process my thoughts, Dad boiled the kettle and sifted through post. When he reached the third or fourth letter, his face turned pale.

'What's the matter?' I asked. Dad's eyes didn't move from the envelope.

'It's from the mortgage people.'

My stomach dropped. I'd told Dad that I didn't care if we lost the house, but that wasn't really true. I did care. We didn't have much to hold on to as a family, and our little house meant everything to me.

'Maybe . . . don't open it just yet?' I suggested feebly. 'Wait until the morning?'

'I can't,' said Dad, running a finger along the seam. 'I won't sleep until I've read it.'

He slid the letter out and unfolded it. I watched impatiently as he read.

'What are they saying, Dad? Are we going to lose the house?'

He looked up, steadying himself on the kitchen worktop.

'You're not going to believe this.'

'Believe what? Dad, tell me.'

'Our mortgage,' he said breathily. 'It's been paid off.'

I leaned forward on the table.

'What?'

'It's been paid off. In full.'

'But . . . how?'

'It doesn't say,' said Dad, scanning the letter again. His eyes darted from left to right. 'It just says that my account is settled, and no further charges will be incurred.' He stared at the wall. 'This is unbelievable . . .'

He drifted out of the kitchen, into the hallway, and towards his study. I followed him.

'Where are you going?'

'I have to, uh . . . I have to check my accounts,' he said distantly, as he passed into the study. He dropped into his chair and hit the power button on his computer, muttering to himself as it booted up.

I stood in the doorway, my fingers tingling with an odd mixture of excitement and confusion. I was incredibly relieved, but, even so, something about this whole situation was making me feel uneasy.

'What's going on?' I said, as Dad navigated to the banking page on his browser. He shrugged.

'I have no idea,' he said, with his back to me, as he logged into his online account. 'I mean, don't get me wrong, it's a huge weight off my mind, but . . . no. What? *No.*'

I stepped into the room, my head spinning. Dad was holding his computer screen in both hands.

'This isn't *possible* . . .' he said, shaking his head. I was beginning to lose patience.

'What, Dad? What are you talking about?'

He spun round on his chair, and dragged a hand through his hair.

'There's a quarter of a million pounds in our account.'

31

I was standing on the doorstep of the Fire&Lights mansion, my hand poised on the elaborate brass knocker, a hundred questions rushing through my mind.

I couldn't be entirely certain why Yuki had invited me, or what I'd find when I went inside. Would all the boys be there? Were they even still living in the house, given that they'd been unofficially split up now for over a week? Fire&Lights HQ had said almost nothing to the press, and fans around the world were in turmoil over the radio silence. Olly had successfully landed his first solo number one a few days before, and the gossip sites were desperate for a reaction from his former bandmates, but they were having no luck. As for me, I hadn't heard anything, not even from Barry, about the secret warehouse reunion, which I had decided could only mean one thing.

It hadn't made any difference.

'Umm, *wait a minute*?' A tinny voice was emanating from a speaker in the brickwork. 'Is that C-to-the-HARLIE BLOOM on my doorstep?'

I looked around, confused. I hadn't even knocked on the door.

'How did you do that?'

'Magic! Also, I can see you on the monitor.'

I stuck out my bottom lip.

'Oh . . . right.'

'Don't go anywhere, I'll be with you in two seconds.'

Moments later, the door opened to reveal Yuki standing on the doormat, grinning.

'How the devil are you?' he said, gesturing for me to walk inside.

'I'm . . . OK,' I said, joining him in the hallway. I glanced around. The house was strangely quiet, and there was no sign of the others. 'You?'

'Oh, you know. The doctor says my gout is getting worse, and, lord, if this summer's bean harvest continues to be meagre, then little Christabella will have to go without shoes for another yea—'

'Yuki,' I said, suppressing a smile.

'Yip?'

'What exactly am I doing here?'

He recoiled.

'What? I can't just have my good friend Charlie round to shoot the breeze and chat about the bean harvest now, is that it?'

I arched an eyebrow at him. He smiled.

'OK, you got me. Come upstairs.'

Yuki led me up the stairs to the first floor, then along the corridor, past Olly's old bedroom. He turned right, into one of the communal rooms – the one where we'd watched Desi's prison video earlier in the year – and I followed him through the doorway. The room was just as I remembered it, scattered with beanbags and pinball machines, a jukebox standing against one wall and a large plasma screen bolted to the other.

Aiden and Gabriel were standing in the corner.

'Hey,' I said, giving them a small wave. They both smiled at me.

Silence fell.

'Look,' I said, 'I'm still not entirely sure what I'm do—'

'We wanted to thank you,' said Gabriel, sliding his hands into his pockets. 'For what you did for us last week, in that warehouse. It was amazing.'

'*The best*,' added Aiden.

'Oh . . . thanks.'

I folded my arms. Had it worked, then? They'd brought me all the way out here, so—

'Hopefully you know this already,' said Yuki, 'but we really appreciate everything you've done for us. Seeing all those photos, it just brought it all back. How important the band was to all of us. How tight we were.'

My heart began to expand.

'But . . .' began Yuki, and I stepped forward, shaking my head.

'No, come on . . . there's no "but". Is there?'

His shoulders dropped.

'The truth is, Charlie B, that we're broken. Without Olly, we don't think we can ever put this band back together again. I'm sorry.'

An emptiness scraped through me. I shouldn't have believed it – I knew I shouldn't – but a part of me had really believed it might work.

I looked at the three boys, in turn, my chest aching. They were giving up. *Why were they giving up?*

And then I noticed something. The hint of a smile tugging at the corner of Yuki's mouth.

'Yuk?'

He bit down, hard, a grin threatening to light up his face. Aiden dug him in the ribs, but it only made his smile grow larger. Soon, all three of them were beaming, their eyes darting past my shoulder, towards the doorway.

'Aren't you going to say hello?' came a familiar voice, from behind me. I spun round, and almost gasped when I saw him standing in the doorway.

Olly.

'Oh my gosh . . .'

Olly walked towards me, that warm, wonderful smile lifting his cheeks, and opened his arms. I ran to him, hugging him, and before I knew it, someone was crashing into me from behind.

'Group hug!' laughed Yuki, as Aiden and Gabriel piled in too. Soon, we were all laughing, and very nearly toppling over into the pile of beanbags. When the hug broke apart, I stumbled backwards, straightening my messed-up hair.

'So, does this mean . . . ? Are you . . . ?'

Olly shrugged.

'We decided it was about time we gave it another crack,' he said breezily. 'Turns out photographers can be pretty persuasive.'

I touched my hands to my mouth, unsure whether to laugh or cry.

'This is . . . this is just *the best news*.'

Yuki buffed his nails against his T-shirt.

'I had no idea you were such a fangirl, Charlie B. That's kind of embarrassing . . .'

I hit him playfully, and pointed in between his eyes.

'I can't believe you punked me, Yuki Harrison! I will kick your ass so hard for that later.'

'Anywhere but the face,' said Yuki, with a wink. I turned back to the others.

'And you're all onboard with this?' I said.

'We sure are,' replied Gabriel, looking happier than I'd seen him in months. 'One hundred per cent.'

'What about Jake?'

'Barry's taking him on as a solo artist,' said Olly. 'He's over the moon.'

I shook my head.

'Wow. Melissa is going to *freak* . . .'

Yuki held up a finger.

'Ah! Speaking of which, our good man Jeeves, in the kitchen, is just about to whip up freakshakes and pizzas for us, if that floats your boat. You staying for food?'

'You asking?'

Yuki wrinkled his nose.

'Might be.'

'Then I think I could be persuaded.'

'BOO-YAH! Last one downstairs has to start their own solo project . . .'

Yuki bounded out of the room, slinging his arm around Aiden's shoulders on the way. Gabriel followed their lead, briefly meeting my eyes as he walked past. Suddenly, it was just Olly and me in the room.

'So this is pretty weird, right?' he said, smiling.

'It is, yeah.'

We looked at each other, unsure how to act. I glanced out of the doorway.

'Your chef isn't really called Jeeves, is he?'

Olly laughed.

'Not last time I checked.' He thought for a second, then pointed at the terrace doors. 'Fancy some fresh air?'

The balcony was only small, but it was high enough up that you could see out over Maida Vale, through the leafy trees and across tall, chimneyed rooftops towards the canal.

Olly leaned his elbows on the metal railing.

'That really was an amazing thing you did for us, Charlie.'

I shrugged.

'I don't know. I just wanted to do *something*.'

'No, seriously. Being in a band like this, you're surrounded by people who think they know you. Who think they know what's best for you, and what you want. But most of them are only guessing because, to them, you're just a popstar. You're a celebrity.' His eyes narrowed slightly. 'But not you. You actually *know* us . . . all of us. I'm not sure we'd have believed it coming from anyone else, but standing there, underneath your photos, I think we all got it, for the first time. We're not just one of those bands who got put together on a TV show . . . we're four friends, who share a dream. You saw that in us, even when we couldn't.'

I focused on my fingers, tightening around the railing.

'I'm sorry things didn't work out between you and me,' Olly said. I looked up.

'Yeah.' I nodded. 'Yeah, me too.'

'When I came to find you in that motel, I'll admit . . . I was kind of hoping the spark might still've been there.' His cheeks turned a pale pink. 'You're a difficult person to get over, and I guess I was confusing our friendship for something more.' He breathed in the fresh summer air, and exhaled. 'But now I think we're on the same page. And I'm just grateful you're in my life.'

I smiled.

'Let's keep it that way, shall we?'

We locked eyes, and for a moment, I thought about telling him how much I'd learned from our fleeting relationship. He had taught me what a gentleman was; he'd taught me what it was like to be treated right by another person. And I was pretty sure that, if any boy ever messed me around, he'd have something to say about it.

But standing on that balcony, the sun on our faces, I realised I didn't need to. Because, in a way, I think he already knew.

'Yo, dudes!' Yuki's voice, from downstairs. 'Pizza's up!'

Olly and I grinned at each other.

'Hey, whoa!' Yuki again. 'Which one of you barbarians ordered ham and pineapple?!"

'Aiden,' said Olly, laughing, but there was a second voice mixed in there as well.

Gabriel was standing in the corridor, leaning against the doorframe. I could still see the shape of his bandages underneath his clothes.

I felt my body tighten.

'Um . . . Gabe, wh—'

'Someone needs to teach Aid a lesson about anti-social snacking etiquette,' suggested Olly, walking through the terrace doors and back into the chill-out room. Gabe laughed.

'Couldn't agree more.'

I followed Olly inside and looked back and forth between them, barely able to believe my eyes. Olly gestured out the doorway.

'You guys coming for food?'

'We'll be down in a sec,' said Gabe, catching my eye. I tried to speak, but couldn't find the words.

'OK, cool.' Olly headed for the door, and as he left the room, said: 'I'll make sure Aid saves you some fruity pizza . . .'

Once Gabriel and I were alone, I pointed after Olly.

'You're not . . . I mean . . . are you two—'

'Friends?' said Gabe, giving me a funny look. 'Don't expect me to let the guy win at *Mario Kart* or anything, but . . . yeah. I guess we are.'

I gazed through the open door, astonished. Gabe cocked his head.

'So how are you?'

I was listening to the soft *whump* of Olly's sneakers as he walked down the stairs. My mind was addled. The impossible had actually happened.

'Charlie . . . ?'

Twisting round, I found Gabriel staring at me, amused, and it all came rushing back. The letter from the mortgage lenders, our debt being paid off, the unexpected money in my father's bank account. The random name on the transaction – *HOLDINGS* – had given nothing away, and that left only one explanation.

'Why did you do it?' I said. Gabe frowned.

'Do what?'

'Don't, Gabe. I just want to know why.' He didn't reply, but his eyes were giving him away. 'I mean, seriously. Dad and I come home to find that the mortgage is paid off and someone's randomly sent us two hundred and fifty thousand pounds?'

He pushed a hand through his hair.

'Charlie, I don't know anything abou—'

'Stop, please. How many millionaires do you think we know?'

He stubbed his socked foot against the carpet.

'We don't have to make a big deal out of this.'

'Wh— A big deal? Are you kidding me? Have you any idea how long it would take my dad to make that much money?'

'That doesn't matter.'

'It does to *us*, Gabe.' I lowered my voice. 'This whole time, I've never once asked for your charity. Why would I want it now?'

'Because this isn't charity.'

I glared at him.

'Yes, it is.'

He scratched his temple, and blinked a few times.

'You remember when the nurse came out of my hospital room and told you I was awake?' I nodded. 'Well, I'd been awake for a while. About ten minutes, in

412

fact. I couldn't move, or open my eyes, but I could hear the things going on around me.'

'So you heard—'

'I heard everything your dad told you. About his job, and his savings, and the fact that you guys might lose the house. It's not fair, Charlie.'

I flicked at my thumbnail.

'Well . . . you're right. But none of that's *your* fault, is it?'

'This money that I've sent you, it's not charity, because it was never mine to begin with. Your mother *earned* this money, with her songwriting. Most of those lyrics that Harry claimed were his . . . they were written by her, and she never got credit for that.

'When I used those Little Boy Blue lyrics for Fire&Lights, I thought I was borrowing from him, but I wasn't. I was borrowing from her. Those hits we had, they might never have happened without Katherine. It's hard to say exactly how much your family are owed for that, but I figure what I sent last week is a pretty good start.'

I touched a hand to my chest, overwhelmed.

'Gabe . . . that's just . . . that's incredibly generous, but it's *so* much money—'

'I know you, Charlie. I knew you'd refuse to take the money if I asked you, and I know you feel weird about it now. So if you really won't keep it, then send it to charity.

413

Something your mum would've supported.' He slid his hands into his pockets. 'Or . . . I do have another idea.'

I inclined my head.

'What's that?'

'Do you remember when we walked down to the creek, in Georgia, and we sat together on that bridge, and you told me how your dad had to give up his academic career to raise you? I thought about it, and I figured that, if it hadn't been for Harry, and the American tour, that never would've happened.' He fixed his amber eyes on mine. 'I can't change any of that, I can't erase the past; but I can pay back the debt. With this money, I don't know . . . maybe your dad could go back to his studies.'

I gazed out through the open terrace doors, letting the idea sink in. My father could be happy, again. Actually *happy*.

'I can't believe . . . I can't believe you would do this for us.'

Gabe lifted one shoulder.

'I got to live my dream, Charlie. Your dad deserves the same chance.'

I was suddenly overcome by a tide of emotion, powering up through my body, and I flung my arms around Gabriel, burying my face in his neck.

'Thank you,' I said, my voice smothered. 'Thank you, thank you, thank you.'

We stood there, locked in an embrace, and it was so warm, I didn't want to break away. Then Gabriel spoke in my ear.

'There is . . . *one* other thing.'

I pulled back slightly.

'That conversation wasn't the only thing I overheard in the hospital.'

I squinted at him, confused. Then it hit me. *You drive me crazy, and you're stubborn, and difficult, and you're basically not normal . . . But I don't care. I love you. It's just . . . I don't know if we can be together right now . . . One day, maybe, in the future, when all of this is behind us—*

'O-oh my god,' I stammered, panic pulsing through me. 'I didn't know you could hear me. I thought you were sleeping. I didn't mean to freak you out—'

'I feel the same way.'

I looked up at him, and a smile bloomed across his face. 'You do?'

He leaned forward until our faces were almost touching, and curled a lock of hair behind my ear.

'*Exactly* the same way.'

'Um, seriously, CHABRIEL! Chow time.' Yuki's voice, vaulting up the stairs again.

We pulled apart.

'Chabriel?' I said, with a grimace. 'I do *not* like that.'

'Me neither, but I think we can both agree it's better than Garlie.'

'Good point.'

'Shall we?' he said, gesturing out of the door. I nodded cheerfully, and we walked out on to the landing, heading for the stairs. 'Pineapple pizza, man. That guy needs locking up . . .'

32

In the past, visiting Mum's grave had always been difficult.

When I was little, I was just confused. Why had she been taken away from us? When would she be coming back? As I grew older, and began to realise she was gone forever, it became almost too painful to look at her gravestone. Then, in the last few years, as I had begun to question all the mysteries surrounding her life, standing by her grave had felt like standing in front of a stranger. But not any more.

'Do you want to go ahead first, kiddo?'

After I'd left the Fire&Lights mansion, I'd taken a bus to the cemetery in West London, where I'd met Dad and Melissa. It was a stunning day, the August sun hot and high in the sky, and for the first time ever, I actually felt uplifted being there. I was holding a bunch of sunflowers in my hands.

'Thanks, Dad,' I said, with a smile. 'I only need a few minutes.'

I walked slowly along the gravel pathways, passing

tombstones that I recognised from years gone by. Fathers, sons, grandparents.

Soon, I came to my mother's.

Katherine Charlotte Bloom

1972–2000

Beloved wife, mother and daughter

Back in November, after Dad had grounded me for lying about the writers' retreat to Devon, he had postponed our visit to the cemetery because of an unexpected business trip, and after that, we'd never made it along. So it had been nearly two years since I had stood in this spot.

I knelt down in the soft grass and ran a finger along the engraving of Mum's name.

'Hey, Mum. Sorry I haven't been here in ages. It's been . . .' I let out a small laugh. 'It's been a pretty crazy year.' I lay the sunflowers in front of her stone. 'But I wanted you to know that I figured everything out. I know who you were now, I know all about the band, and it makes me so, so proud. The best thing is, all those lyrics you wrote, they found a way into the world. You wouldn't believe it, but millions of people have heard them. *Millions.*' I smiled. 'You've had quite a few hits, actually. And the money from those songs, it might be just what we need to get Dad back into mathematics.' I glanced over at my father, who was ambling along the gravel towards us. 'Don't tell him yet, though. It's a surprise.'

As Dad arrived, I stood up and he pulled me into his side, wrapping an arm around me.

'Hey there, my love,' he said, to the gravestone. 'What about our daughter, eh? Rock photographer extraordinaire.'

'God, Dad,' I said, nuzzling into him. 'You're so embarrassing.'

He laughed, squeezing me closer to him. Birds chattered and sang in the trees above us

'You know what the worst thing was about losing her?' he said.

I shook my head.

'There were so many things that I never got to say. I never got to tell her how proud I was, of everything she achieved. She was so passionate about music, and she didn't let that go, not for one second.' He inhaled slowly. 'And I never got to tell her, one last time, how much we loved her.'

I could feel the tears building in his chest, and mine.

'I think she knew, Dad.'

He reached behind his glasses with a single finger, and wiped his eyes. Then he looked out across the cemetery, jingling the keys in his pockets.

'Melissa's all on her own over there. Why don't you call her over?'

419

My best friend was sitting on top of a pillar by the cemetery entrance, staring into space. I beckoned her over, and she shook her head. I insisted, waving harder, and she hopped on to the grass and walked over to join us.

'Whaddup, Blooms,' she said, giving us a funny little smile.

She moved closer to Dad, and he pulled her in to his other side.

'If you're ever afraid I'm stuck on my own, Katherine,' Dad said, 'don't be. These two are always looking out for me.'

Melissa sniffled, her eyes edging with tears.

'I hope it's not out of line for me to say that I think Katherine Charlotte Bloom may have been the COOLEST human being in the history of all humans.'

Dad nodded.

'She was something else, Melissa. I'll tell you that.'

I stared at my mother's name on the gravestone, and my lungs filled with air.

You really were something else, Mum. I'll love you forever. Charlie xxxx

On the way home, I sat in the front passenger seat of the car, beside Dad, watching the scenery go by.

For the first time in months, I felt a strange kind of calm.

As we left the motorway, I glanced over my shoulder and through the rear window. This was the journey my father would have made, for the first time all those years ago, with a three-year-old me sitting in the back of the car. The two of us, facing the world alone, moving out of the big city for a quieter life on the outskirts of Reading. Without Mum.

Destined for a new house, our little home, just round the corner from a certain Olly Samson.

Something must have brought us here.

'Dad,' I said, turning the volume down on the radio.

Dad changed gear as we approached a roundabout.

'Uh-huh.'

'Why did we move to Reading?'

He tutted at a nearby driver, who was failing to indicate.

'Why did we . . . ? Where did that question come from?'

'I've been wondering, that's all.'

'Well . . .' He edged forward cautiously, his eyes on the road. 'The simple truth is, we couldn't afford to live in London any more. My PhD had been cancelled, and your mother was gone, and there was nothing keeping us in the city. I was at a bit of a loss for where to go, to be honest, but then I remembered something. This couple we knew from the Troubadour – artist friends of your mother's – who'd been talking about packing in the bohemian life and moving out of the city. I forget their names, but, uh, she was an actress, I recall, and wasn't getting anywhere in the theatre world, and they'd basically had enough of the whole thing. I asked for their advice, and they told me they'd bought a house just outside Reading, in this sort of suburban village called Caversham. Good schools, safe and friendly, that kind of thing. So I suppose, in a way, I followed them out here.' He thought for a moment, staring at the road ahead. 'Haven't seen them since, of course. I guess you fall out of touch with people, don't you? Oh, damn. What were their names?'

'Alan and Jenna.'

Dad's eyebrows shot up, and he glanced at Melissa in his rear-view mirror.

'What did you say, Melissa?'

I twisted round in my seat. Melissa was sitting dead still in the back, her eyes enormous.

'Their names were Alan and Jenna,' she repeated. Dad returned his gaze to the road, shaking his head.

'Do you know, I believe you're right! That's incredible.'

'Alan and Jenna . . . *Samson.*'

Dad patted the steering wheel.

'Good grief, yes! You've got it. Alan and Jenna Samson. I haven't thought about them for years . . .'

I dropped back in my seat, utterly stunned. *That* was

how the three of us – Gabriel, Olly and me – were originally connected. We all came out of the same gang of musicians, artists and actors who used to hang around at the Troubadour club before we were born, and in some distant past, our parents knew each other. We all came from the same place. A messy, confusing place, but the same place nonetheless.

All it ever would have taken was a few gentle twists of fate to bring us back together.

'Wait,' said Dad, touching a hand to my leg. 'That Olly boy, from the band   isn't he a Samson?'

'Yip,' said Melissa proudly. 'Olly is a Samson. Alan and Jenna are his parents.'

Dad laughed, delighted.

'It's a small world indeed. How on earth do you know all that, Melissa?'

'*Everyone* knows that Olly's mum trained as an actress, Mr Bloom. That's fandom 101.'

'Is it now?' said Dad, amused. 'Sounds like I need to up my game.'

I also knew, as it happened, but only because Olly had told me himself, on a windy beach in Devon, the year before.

'I wouldn't try and compete with my best friend,' I said, beaming at Melissa. 'She's a Fire&Lights encyclopaedia.'

Melissa smiled back, but her face soon dropped.

'Fat lot of good that'll do me now they've split up,' she said grumpily, and I gasped. In all the excitement, I had entirely forgotten to tell her.

'Holy cow,' I said, grabbing her knee. 'Melissa Morris, I have got some *amazing* news for you . . .'

33

Walking through the school gates, I took in the familiar grey buildings, the blue double-doors with the paint peeling off and the Caversham High sign with its illicit smiley face, scrawled in black marker. It felt like a very different place, today. Calmer, quieter. Smaller, even.

'Man, people are *tripping out*,' said Melissa, between her teeth, as we walked across the tarmac in the sunshine. Our security guards were still standing by their car, just outside the gates, and it was causing a ripple of excitement among our classmates. The guards had been very keen to drive us here, to keep our profile low, but we'd declined. We wanted to do the walk to school – *our* walk, the reason we'd become friends in the first place – one last time.

'Let 'em stare,' I said, with a smile. 'They'll forget about us when the results come out.'

I was right. We were being pointed and stared at from almost every angle, but the moment Mr Crouch and Mr Swift arrived with boxes full of brown envelopes, all attention swung their way.

'OK. OK.'

We were standing in a quiet corner of the car park, holding brown envelopes in our hot hands, eyes fixed on the sealed flaps. Melissa was rocking back and forth slightly.

'OK,' she said again. 'Shall we do this?'

I stared at my name on the envelope and gritted my teeth.

'Now or never.' I looked up. 'But we have to open them at the same time.'

'Ready?'

Melissa braced her hands, ready to rip. I nodded.

'Now.'

We tore through the paper and pulled out the contents. My heart was slamming against my ribcage.

'Oh my god. Oh my god. Oh my god.'

Melissa was staring, agog, at her results. I jiggled on the spot.

'What did you get?' I said.

She gawped back at me.

'Ten A-stars.'

My mouth fell open and I grabbed her, pulling her towards me and squeezing her tight.

'So, so, *so* proud of you,' I said, my face flushing with pride. She made squeaking sounds into my hair.

'Oh, Melissa!'

We broke apart to find Miss Woods hurrying over to us, waving. She stopped next to Melissa and, out of breath, laid a hand on her shoulder.

'You've scored the best results in the whole *county*,

Melissa,' she was saying gleefully, as I unfolded my results. 'The papers want to talk to you!'

'Oh . . . oh, crikey.'

I read my results, one by one, and gradually, my shoulders relaxed. Somehow, I'd got through it. And I'd actually done OK.

'Well?'

Melissa was grinning at me.

'Well, what?' I said coyly.

'Pass me your results, you dingbat,' she said, grabbing the paper off me. I smiled as she read through them.

'All As and Bs! And an A-star in photography. Charlie, you *nailed* it.'

I shrugged.

'I can't complain.'

'We have news for you too, Charlie,' said Miss Woods, clapping her hands at me. She lowered her voice. 'Highest photography grade this school has ever seen! Quite extraordinary.'

'Thanks, Miss Woods.'

She clicked her fingers at us.

'Don't go anywhere, either of you. I'll be back in five with a journalist or three . . .'

Miss Woods hurried off towards the school, and Melissa turned to me.

'I can't flipping believe it,' she said, shaking her head. 'Everything's going to be all right. Neither of us will have to live out our days, like, scrubbing the toilets in Burger King and sitting alone in front of *Geordie Shore* eating Doritos from a sock.'

'Well, that is a relief.'

'Seriously, though,' she said, pinching my sleeve. 'I am ruddy bloody proud of you, CB.'

'Right back atcha.'

'Hey . . .' Melissa frowned, tapping a finger against her lips. 'Didn't you say the announcement was today?'

I felt my eyes widen.

'Oh, yes. You're right.' I whipped out my phone and checked the time. 'It's probably online by now. Here.'

I passed her my phone and she opened the browser, thumbs wiggling in anticipation.

'You did it, Charlie,' she said, typing into the search box. 'You actually did it. You saved the biggest band in the world. You're the new Jesus.'

'Nah,' I said, wrinkling my nose. 'I could never pull off the beard.'

Melissa bit her lip as she waited for the results to load. Seconds later, she lifted my phone screen and showed it to me, her whole face lighting up.

'Best. Day. Ever.'

I smiled back at her, perfectly content. On my screen, the headline read:

FIRE&LIGHTS TO REUNITE

ONE YEAR LATER

34

'*Il tuo caffè, signora.*'

The waiter placed the small, white espresso cup down in front of me. I smiled at him from behind my sunglasses.

'*Grazie.*'

He walked inside and I settled back into my chair, breathing in the warm air and the scent of fresh bread wafting out of the café. The piazza was getting busier as people began to arrive for lunch, meeting friends, shaking hands, snacking on olives.

My phone buzzed with a message.

EMERGENCY, CHARLIE BLOOM. I'm going to my first rodeo on Saturday and I do not own a cowboy hat.

A pause.

Or . . . wait, should that be cowGIRL hat? No, screw the patriarchy. I wanna be a cowboy.

I laughed, and typed back a reply.

Leo never struck me as a rodeo kind of guy.

He isn't, but his family are.

I smiled, impressed.

You're meeting his family already??

Oooooh, yeah. I only hope I don't accidentally swear or burp or say something angry about Republicans.

They'll love you, Mel. Just don't get carried away and get shotgun-married in Vegas.

I make no promises xxxxx

I took a sip of coffee and closed my eyes. I liked Italy. Everyone was so laid-back here that it began to seep into you, forcing you to slow down, to appreciate your surroundings. From where I was sitting, I could see the eight-hundred-year-old church that I'd spent the morning wandering around, a large monument with a statue of a soldier on top of it and, in the distance, one of the most beautiful bridges in Florence, leading away across the winding Arno river. I found myself thinking of my mother's letter, the one she'd written to me before she died, and one line kept repeating in my head. *You can be anything, Charlie. You can be anyone. I want the world for you.*

A lump formed in my throat, as I realised that the world was exactly what she'd given me.

'Excuse me, aren't you . . . Charlie Bloom?'

I glanced up, and my pulse tripped.

'That depends who's asking,' I replied, trying to sound nonchalant.

'Oh, I don't know,' said Gabriel, removing his sunglasses. 'Just a popstar who's down on his luck.'

'Down on his luck? Aren't you in that band that just won six MTV awards . . . ?'

Gabe laughed to himself, hooking his shades on to the collar of his T-shirt. On the far side of the square, I noticed Marty standing beside the entrance to the church, hands clasped at his belt. He gave me a nod.

'Been recognised yet?' I said, standing up.

Gabe took a quick glance around. 'Not yet; I'm sticking to the backstreets. Plus . . .' He produced a black fedora from behind his back, and wiggled it. 'It's amazing what dark glasses and a well-placed hat can do.'

For a few seconds, we stood opposite each other, not saying a word. I caught his scent on the air, that curious mix of smoke and leather and blackcurrant that I remembered so clearly from the first few times we'd met, and then he stepped forward and pulled me into an embrace. I felt his strong hands on my back, and his

433

cheek moving slightly against mine. When his lips brushed my skin, something smouldered inside me.

Ding. My phone buzzed on the table. Gabriel pulled away.

'I see you're in demand, as usual,' he said, a smile tugging at his mouth.

'Oh, not really.' I dropped back into my chair and slipped my phone into my bag. I could feel myself blushing, but I liked it. 'That's just Melissa. She's doing a summer abroad in the States. AKA, chasing after a boy.'

Gabriel sat down opposite me and laid his hat on the table. Our smiles grew in tandem.

'So this is one heck of a first date, Charlie Brown.'

'Thanks,' I said, gazing out across the piazza. The river was twinkling in the sunshine. 'I figure, when you wait as long as we have, you may as well do it right.'

Gabriel nodded thoughtfully.

'I'm glad we waited.'

'Me too.'

Just as Barry had predicted, it had taken months for the gossip mill to stop turning. The press were hungry for more romance, more scandal, but we'd refused to feed the machine. Time passed, the rumours faded to grey, and while I settled into sixth-form college, Gabriel travelled far and wide with Fire&Lights, visiting every corner of the planet, barely returning to England for more than a few days. Throughout it all, though, we never fell out of touch. We'd even taken to writing each other letters, like wartime sweethearts, and now, we were finally in the same city, at the same time.

Secretly, my heart was pounding.

'Of course, you're not an easy girl to pin down these days. Berlin one week, Florence the next. Carrie's working you hard.'

I took another sip of coffee.

'It's *meant* to be hard work, being an apprentice. I love it, though.'

'Yeah, well ... from what she's told me, you're absolutely killing it. A mini Carrie Shakes in the making.'

I laughed, and finished off my drink.

'It's good to see you,' I said.

'I'm glad,' he replied, his amber eyes settling on mine. 'This would be kind of awkward otherwise.'

Suddenly, I was back on the roof of that rusted-out car in Georgia, music playing in the distance, our foreheads gently touching as the sun melted into the horizon.

Today was going to be a very good day.

'So ... how did it go last week?' I said. 'Seeing your dad again, I mean?'

Gabe pitched his head from side to side.

'Better than could be expected. He's actually getting his life together.'

'What about you, though?'

'What about me?'

435

'Do you think you two could ever . . . be a family again?'

'Never say never, I suppose.' He shrugged. 'This time last year, I couldn't stand to be in the same room as the guy, so I guess we're making progress.'

'I guess you are.'

He toyed, thoughtfully, with his sunglasses. I started gathering my things.

'Shall we find somewhere for lunch?' I said, rising from the table.

'Uh, yeah. But first . . .' Gabriel stood up and reached into his back pocket. 'I have a present for you.'

'I didn't know we were doing presents!'

He passed me a small package.

'Well, in a way, this was originally your present to me, so . . .'

Confused, I unwrapped the package to find a cassette tape inside. I grinned.

'Hey, it's a mix-tape.'

'Not . . . quite.' He leaned forward. 'Here's the thing. After my dad told us that Katherine was really into cassette tapes, I thought, I don't know . . . like mother, like daughter, maybe? And this is something I've been meaning to finish for a while.'

I flipped the tape over and found a handwritten message on the back.

I thought about it, and you're right.
Music is meant to be shared.

Thanks for changing my world, Charlie Brown.

G x

Rotating the case back round, I found a title written on the front.

SONGS ABOUT A BOY
An album by Gabriel West

My heart expanded, and I pulled him towards me.

'Thank you,' I said, meaning it, and before the words had disappeared in the warm air, we were kissing.

Kissing, like it was the first time. Like the moment finally belonged to us, and nobody else; like we had fought through every hour, every second of the heartache and insanity to get here. But I wasn't kissing Gabriel West, the popstar, any more. I was kissing the boy only I knew; the sweet, caring boy with the serious gaze; the piano player with music in his soul; the songwriter with a big, beating heart; the boy who, I was certain, would do anything for me.

His hands were on my cheeks, soft and strong, and I felt safe, like we could be anywhere in the world, and nobody could touch us.

We slowed, still breathing against each other.

'So far,' he murmured against my mouth, 'greatest . . . first date . . . ever.'

We smiled together, our lips brushing, and I reached upwards, sinking my fingers into his hair.

'Technically, it hasn't started yet.'

Turning his face a little, he looked across the plaza and held out an open palm.

'In that case, Charlie Brown . . . you lead the way.'

Picking up my bag, I pulled out some cash and left it on the table for the waiter. Then I took Gabriel's hand and we walked across the square together, the sunshine on our faces, the endless hours of the afternoon stretching out before us.

CREDITS

In chapter nine of this book, Kirsty – the pilot of Fire&Lights' private jet – is named after Kirsty Connor, who won the Songs About a Boy lot at CLIC Sargent's annual 'Get In Character' auction. CLIC Sargent is the UK's leading young person's cancer charity; find out more at www.clicsargent.org.uk.

Huge thanks to Sean Fang for lending me his formidable medical brain for the hospital scenes.

WORTHY
Gabriel West

I thought that we were a family
I believed I was home
I wanted you to be proud of me
Somewhere deep in your bones

You were tall, blocking out the sun
My hand was reaching for yours
I was small, I was your only son
I watched you walk out the door

'Cos I was never enough
Don't you think you owed me more than this?
I wasn't worthy of love
You were supposed to show me what a father is

XXX

Summer days in a graffitied room
I knew something was wrong
But I was fine, I never needed you
I never cared you were gone

Why was I never enough?
Don't you think you owed me more than this?
I wasn't worthy of love
You were supposed to show me what a father is
You said 'Ah son, I'll be home soon,
I can't wait to see how much you've grown'
But I'm still waiting here for you
And I'm waiting alone

You were tall, blocking out the sun
My hand was reaching for yours